To: Lisa Derrick,
my beloved niece,
and her family.

Louise Murphy Guerin

June 17, 2007

Separate Paths

Louise Murphy Gearin

ISBN 0-7414-4016-4

Published by:

INFI∞ITY
PUBLISHING.COM

1094 New DeHaven Street, Suite 100
West Conshohocken, PA 19428-2713
Info@buybooksontheweb.com
www.buybooksontheweb.com
Toll-free (877) BUY BOOK
Local Phone (610) 941-9999
Fax (610) 941-9959

Printed in the United States of America

Printed on Recycled Paper

Published May 2007

Dedication

This novel is dedicated in appreciation to my writer's critique group

Pat Smith
Michael Dennington
Beecher Smith
Nina Sally Hepburn
Pat Crocker
Ann Carolyn Cates
Sarah Hull Gurley
Terry Thompson

Separate Paths

Donegal, County Kilcar, Ireland
December 20, 1849

Chapter One

Frank saw the young thugs and darted back into the nearly empty store. He rushed toward the back, hoping to escape.

"Let me out the back way," he said tugging the arm of a white-haired old man wearing shabby brown clothes.

"What did you steal?" the old man asked.

"Nothing. Nothing. I bought a little food but the ruffians want to take it away from me."

"They're ever'where now. The back won't help you," the old man said.

"You work here?" Frank asked. "Sell me a few stale cookies."

"None to sell. I have some moldy cakes I was giving my pigs. Here take a handful." He reached to the bottom of a small barrel on the counter.

"I'll be thanking you," Frank said. "A toss away from me and maybe...."

"I hope you make it. They robbed me, they did. Yesternight."

Frank clutched the cakes in his hand and opened the back door. He saw no one at first. But then a few steps and he saw the five of them approaching. He threw the cakes into the air and as far away from them as he could. They were not fooled. They rushed toward him. He barely made it back inside the store.

"They want more than food," the old man said. "Ye'll need to wait 'til it's dark and hope they've made their way elsewhere."

"It'll be dark soon," Frank said, "and it's snowing again."

"Ah well, what can be the answer? Even if ye slept here, there's the morrow."

"I'll go soon. My wife and little girl will worry."

Screams from outside the store alerted Frank and the

1

old man. "It's ye chance," the old man said. "They got another just now."

Frank slipped out the door and ran into the darkness. He ran until he felt he could run no more, his breath cold and searing his lungs. Surely he had outrun them—lost them. But no! He heard their coarse young voices and their laughter. He sought wildly for a place to hide. There was none. He knew the area well. Only the hull of a cottage where a peasant family once lived—before the landlord ripped away the roof and drove the starving skeleton of a woman and her frail child out—as if they could have saved the rotting crops. No time for his anger now. The footsteps crushing the snow and ice came nearer. He heard the laughter. Again he ran but what about the treasures in his coat pockets. Surely they would rob him. In one desperate move he shucked his coat and threw it hard beside the broken cottage. Then he ran faster, harder into the darkness until he fell.

***

The clean, new snow sparkled in the early morning sun and the pungent smell of burning peat drifted across the green hill where thatched roof cottages stood. Below, at the edge of a shallow valley, a rippling tide caressed the coastline and nearby metallic blue lakes glittered in the sunlight.

Sally McKelvy stood at her cottage gate with her arm around her small daughter. She stared down the narrow rutted road and swallowed. Where was Frank? He should have been back yesterday. She struggled against the panic rising in her.

Emily's small face felt warm against her arm and she heard her cry, "Ma, Ma, I'm hungry."

"I know me darling, but Da will bring us food soon." Would he? What if something had happened to Frank? People desperate for food wandered about robbing those who had anything. What chance would he have if the robbers were in gangs? Dear God! Dear God, please spare him.

2

What ever could they do unless help for Ireland came soon? She wished for the lovely white blooming of the pratie patches and the gathering, but that was no more. Few if any even had the seed potatoes to plant if the blight ever vanished. Now the gardens brought forth only the stench of death. She ran her hand gently over the small mound of her belly. Surely there had never been a worse time to bring another child into the world.

"Ma...."

"Soon now. Da will come."

Gulls calling and dipping into the ocean beyond McGuffey's field barely reached her attention. Nearby elderly neighbors, the Wallace sisters and their brother, dressed in thin rags, clawed in the muck for a possible overlooked pratie. Sally shivered. She thought their old bones must ache in the chilly dampness as they crawl around on hands and knees. Sally drew her shawl around her shoulders and wished she had spare warm clothing to offer them. Soon, judging from their squeals of delight, they made a find. But it could only be a half-rotten pratie. Even if part of it was yet white it was sick throughout and unsafe to eat. Sally placed her hand against her throat. The notion of their eating the gritty, unwashed thing turned her stomach. She felt queasy enough already with her pregnancy. She turned away from the miserable, arguing threesome and the noisy gulls. But before her slippers crossed the last flat stone in the pathway, sounds of their gagging up their rotten food drew cold chills and she shivered.

Back inside the cottage Sally stirred the fire in the stone fireplace. When the silent gray coals moved aside to reveal red crackling ones, a faint smile crossed her face. At least there was warmth to appreciate. She pulled her ma's old rocker closer to the hearth and reached for Emily, who whimpered and climbed on her lap.

Sally pressed her child's head against her shoulder and gently stroked her hair and cheek to comfort her.

She gazed at the empty cabinet that once held her grandma's Guinness Fruit Cake and Gingerbread for

3

Christmas. The spices and the sweet scents of the fruit lingered in her memory, but now even a wee mouse would find nothing—not even the smallest crumb of anything.

A step on the doorway and a cough made her realize Frank had arrived.

"Da's here," Sally said, lifting Emily from her lap.

Emily ran to the door and grabbed it open. "Da! Da!". Then seeing the blood on his face and hands she withdrew. "Oh, oh," she said.

Sally moaned. "You're hurt," she cried.

"Yes, some," he said, "but the scoundrels didn't find my coat. I was ahead in the chase and threw it beside the hull of the old Kelly house. All they got was some coins in my pocket."

Sally dipped a cloth in a basin of water. "Here," Sally said, "gently dabbing the blood on his cheek with the damp cloth.

"They beat me up, knocked me out, but when I came to I made the walk home as you see. I'm thankful they didn't find my coat. A blessing that is for sure."

"Da's hurt," Emily said, "poor Da."

Frank lifted Emily up in his arms. "There's Da's girl. I'm alright now I'm here with you." He reached in his pocket with his free hand. "For you, baby," he said placing a turnip in her hand and letting her back down to run to the table.

"I was worried." Sally said, "Was the food harder to come by this time?"

He shook the dampness from his cap leaving a dewy mist still on the edges of his dark curls.

"This is all I could get." He held one small and three medium-sized turnips in his hands. Seeing that he hesitated, she braced herself for bad news. She recognized the downcast glance as one he wore when he was about to reveal something she would not like.

"I took the extra walk and time to collect from the landlord what he promised for our belongings.," he said. "We must leave Ireland now."

"Oh, no, Frank," Sally cried her eyes wide and her

voice full of resentment. "Why now? Why for God's sake?"

"We must leave, Sally. Ireland means death." He spoke with patient resignation. "We have no choice. We've lasted far longer than most, but our time has come."

"Surely, the wealthy Irish, the British—surely some will rescue us soon." She protested.

"They have known for years and what have they done? Precious little. We've been more fortunate than many because we had some funds, but we've come to near broke now ourselves. What I could get together is for our leaving."

She grasped his arm. "We can't leave. Frank, you know this has been my home since the day I was born. Please, go back to McHerry and tell him you that you've changed your mind—that we won't sell."

Frank shook his head. "Sally, you've shut your eyes even to what is close around us. Did not the McGuffey family tarry too long? At least we, now with the selling to McHenry, have funds enough to pay passage on one of the smaller, sturdier ships going to America."

"No, No, Frank! We'd have to leave everything we own but what little we could carry."

She saw his stance and the determined look on his face. What could she do or say to change his mind? Her chest ached and her breath came short with the mere thought of it. All around her she'd seen how patiently people suffered, but at least they weren't leaving home. There was always hope and comfort with home, wasn't there? And a voyage on one of the dangerous old ships to a strange new land—Oh dear God!

Frank laid the turnips on the table and took her in his arms. "People are eating anything and feeding their children grass. Do you not remember the two-year-old child who was fed seaweed and died?"

Sally laid her head on his chest and felt his arms tight around her. Her tears blended with the damp wool of his coat. The faint musty smell filled her nostrils but she was more aware of his comforting embrace. She wanted to agree with him—to please him, but her heart ached so!

5

Frank spoke softly. "I wish it could be different, but we must think of Emily. She's only six years and thin for her age."

"I know. I know," Sally said.

"Remember the gun my father gave to me. It's no longer mine."

Sally raised her head. "Oh, no! That gun meant so much to you." She lifted the hem of her skirt and dried her eyes. "I hate this! Surely, if we but wait a little longer. You could get your gun back then, Frank."

He stroked her auburn hair and kissed her lightly freckled face. "It's too late, Sally. If we stay, my father's gun, our family furnishings—well, we'd be leaving them behind anyways as we went to our graves."

Three turnips lay on the table after Emily reached for the smaller one. "Here," Frank said, handing two to Sally. How like him to sacrifice for her and their child. A rush of love for him filled to her heart.

"No, you take two," Sally said. "A man needs more. One will be fine for me."

"Two for you," Frank said. "You and the babe in the nest."

Sally smiled. She reached for a knife and cut the larger turnip in half. "We'll share as we always have," she said.

When they had eaten the turnips, Frank said, "One more thing. I booked passage for us to leave tomorrow. We must get up in the dark and make our way to the ship by dawn."

"So soon!" Sally cried, "so soon. It's like our lives are on a spinning wheel." She dropped in a chair and sobbed covering her face with her hands.

"Sweetheart," Frank knelt beside her and whispered. "I'm sorry."

She lifted her head then, saw his stricken face, and touched his cheek. Her breath came short and the tears would not stop, but she hesitated only a moment before walking to the far side of the room where she picked up a large battered suitcase of black leather. "Thank God, your grandfather bought this portmanteau in London." She said sniffing still from her crying, but drying her tears with the sleeve of her dress. "It's at least one family item we must keep. Thank God for it. So many have only the cardboard cases."

"Ah, yes," Frank said, "and we'll have music." Sally caught her breath. He meant to take his instruments and space in the portmanteau was at a premium. She stood with fingers to her lips to prevent the protest she wished to make.

Frank pulled his violin case from under the bed. The cheap gray case was wrapped and tied with rope, but he handled it tenderly while laying it in the portmanteau. Then he stepped to a wooden chest at the end of the bed. There he lifted his flute from a tray and placed it also in the suitcase but not before carefully wrapping it in a faded red shirt.

"You bought that violin with your first savings as a boy," she said trying to see the matter from his view. At least the instruments were two more things besides the portmanteau they could take that reflected their lives at home.

Frank smiled. "I thought you might complain of the space, but a good wife you are. You'll be glad we have the music. You'll see."

She nodded and turned aside to collect other items—necessary items, not elective ones. She would not take the vase her grandmother gave her on her sixteenth birthday although she had hoped to pass it on to Emily one day. She removed the pale green vase from the shelf, studied it lovingly, held it against her heart with her eyes closed before replacing it on the mantel above the fireplace. She glanced quickly at Frank and was grateful that he seemed not to witness her farewell to Gran's vase.

Emily sat beside the fireplace, holding a rag doll Sally had made for her. She hummed a child's song in a high-pitched voice and rocked her doll in her arms.

Frank said, "It's getting colder. I'd hoped the awful winter was gone." He stirred the fire in the fireplace and added a thick, matted clump of straw, which crackled and flamed lighting the shadowed room. A faint sweet smell from the burning straw filled the room.

Sally cracked the door and shivered as the cold air reached her. "It's snowing. Falling thick. How will we get to the ship? By morning who knows how deep it will be?" Now it was not only the dreaded voyage, but the deep cold in getting to the dock. If only help had come in time! A rush of anger filled her in thinking of the English and rich Irish. Surely, they could have done more.

"We must get to the ship," Frank said. "The passage is paid. We have no choice. Besides, others are going to the ships. Some in wagons. I doubt we'll have to walk the whole way."

"This snow! If only it will stop."

"Don't worry, me darling. It may not be so bad," Frank said. "We'll wear most of our clothes. The layers will keep us warm and unlike some we do have shoes. If we are wet when we arrive, we can dry out. Think of the good. Why in America, we'll start anew—like newly weds. Who knows, one day we may even be rich. Think about that.'"

"Oh, Frank. You're such a dreamer. A darling ye are, but a skyful dreamer," she said giving him a playful shove. She turned again to packing the portmanteau, adding and then removing items as she considered what was most important. She sighed. No need to fight about it anymore. No need, but her heart ached. Who would wind up with dear things of their parents and grandparents? What meant so much to her and her children would be lost forever. And the graves—no more visits there for quiet moments and placing of flowers.

She glanced across the room at Frank who sat looking around the room. He had lit a candle and set it on the mantel then drew up a chair near the fireplace. She watched as he looked about the room, his glance lingering on every familiar object. His eyes rested thoughtfully on the carving of a fishing boat complete with a man and a boy on high water— surely representing himself and his da. She remembered the day his father had nailed the carving there years before. Ah, fish! If only they had fish, but the bitter winter had made fishing impossible even before the boats and tackle were pawned to buy food.

She stopped packing and went to cuddle his head against her body, saying nothing. He did not protest, but relaxed against her. She knew at Mullin's Pub he played his fiddle, would drink the pints and fight like any man, but with her he was different. She was grateful for moments like this when he allowed her to comfort him. At least the dark trip and the strange new world would be less frightening with him beside her.

Emily left the fireside and climbed on her cot clutching her doll in her arms. Within moments she was asleep.

A strong wind whipped around the cottage reminding Sally of the cold outside. She prayed the snow would cease.

Frank kept the fire going rising from time to time during the night but still the room was cold. Sally knew he must feel stressed when the ancient grandfather clock grated a rusty sound and then struck four times. "Come back to bed for a few more minutes," she said and held her arms out to welcome him. "For the last time here," she said.

He slipped back between the covers and embraced her. He kissed her tenderly and then with passion. "For the last time in this house," he said, "but not the last time, you wild woman."

Afterward she cuddled to him for a long moment before arising. She smiled. At least she had a husband any woman with a speck of passion in her would want.

Sally dressed herself and then awoke the drowsy Emily and pulled her clothes on her thin body. She felt a moment of sorrow for her child. If only America would be a place of wonderful food for her little girl.

When they were fully dressed and ready to go, Frank took three biscuits from his coat pocket. "I saved these for our breakfast," he said passing them out then eating one himself.

"You played a trick on us, Frank McKelvy, but thank goodness," Sally said.

"Any jam, Da?" Emily asked.

"No jam, Baby, but just you wait until we get to America. There'll be jam everywhere. It's going to be a wonderful place, you'll see."

"Time to go," Frank said opening the door. He picked up the heavy leather bag with one hand and hoisted Emily on his opposite hip. Sally took a basket stuffed with some bedding and small items for the voyage and passed through the open doorway. She glanced back at the cottage in which she had been born and married and in which Emily had been born. She fought tears as she realized this dear scene would never be hers, ever again. She looked back trying to fix in her mind the smallest detail of the house and surrounding area.

"Look," Frank said, "there are wagon tracks in the snow. Someone has passed this way."

"But will anyone else?" Sally asked. She still looked back at her home again and again, sometimes to stumble, to almost fall into the snow. It looked so dear with the white all around. Used to they would have laughed and played in it, then huddled around the fireplace warming themselves.

Frank was saying, "At least it's not quite as cold as I'd feared and we'll see some daylight before long."

Sally saw that he smiled and somehow it lifted her spirit. "Frank Mckelvy you are always the hopeful one. Why did you marry a pest like me?"

"Because you have a bonny little butt that swings when you walk."

"Is that all?"

"Well, maybe by the time we get to America I can think of another reason." She saw that he was struggling under the weight he carried.

Sally said, "Emily show Da you can walk just fine and keep up with him."

"For a bit," Frank said lifting Emily from his hip and changing hands for the portmanteau.

"It's making my feet cold," Emily said.

"Well, walk faster then," Sally said.

Emily ran a small distance and returned. Then ran again laughing as she kicked the snow in a little dance step of kick, stamp, kick, stamp.

In the distance a black carriage appeared coming over the hill down Kilcar Road. Frank shouted. "That's old Doc McAfee! He'll give us a ride for sure."

"If it's not filled up already," Sally said.

Within minutes the carriage drew to a stop. A black curtain snapped open and a grizzly head poked out. Sally smiled. There was hope—maybe. Despite all the clothing her face felt frozen and she worried that Emily might be sick from the freezing dampness.

"Get in," Doc said, "I reckon' you're going to the quay at Donegal."

"We are," Frank said, "and bless you for the ride."

"'Tis a chilly morn," Doc said, "still a bit warmer inside."

"We're grateful," Sally said. Once seated she pulled Emily close in her arms so that they might share in each other's warmth.

Frank who now sat beside Doc McAfee asked, "And are you sailing as well?"

"No. I'm going to see a Mrs. Campbell. Word came that she's in great distress with this birthing."

A shiver ran through Sally. She remembered the birthing pains. And a baby at this cruel time. Without knowing Mrs. Campbell she felt sorry for her. At least, her own would not come for months."

The doctor slapped the reins gently and the horse picked up his pace. "It should be daylight when we arrive," he said. "What time is your leaving?"

"I was told to be there by dawn, although I think that's to line up for the boats going out to the ship."

"Probably," Dr. McAfee said, "The wharf is small. Pretty wild land around there with the cliffs and so much taken up with the beaches."

Sally thought of the combination fear and excitement she'd felt on a stormy day at the wharf. "I like seeing the tide high in the roaring winds.and floods of water rushing ashore to wash the beaches, and I like seeing powerful waves crashing and spraying against the cliffs," she said, then laughed. "It's the girleen still in me I suppose, but I hope and pray for calm today."

Dr. McAfee glanced over his shoulder momentarily at Sally. "Though not stormy today, my dear, but still rolling, I imagine."

"I wish we didn't have to go," Sally said. She thought how different it was observing the turbulent sea from a safe distance than being on it in an old wooden ship that could break apart. The tiny bits of spray above the crashing storm waters now seemed like tears and therefore no longer lovely. "I so hate to leave our home for a strange land," she said.

"Would pain me as well, to leave all the grand loveliness of Ireland—the glens and lakes, the grand costal places," the doctor said, "Still, what good is it if the body is starved? My wife and I may yet leave for England or Australia."

"Oh," Frank said, "'tis hard to leave the home place, but I hear America offers so much good. I have my thoughts now tuned to it."

"I hope you find it so," Dr. McAfee said.

Within minutes the daylight revealed the wharf and a cluster of people huddled there. A heavy mist was rising from the sea. Sally saw The Naomi O'Hare rocking in the turbulent waters and two other gray ships just beyond it.

"The O'Hare's smaller than I had expected," Frank said obvious disappointment in his voice, "but I trust she'll make the voyage."

Dr. McAfee drew the carriage to a stop and the small family stepped down. Frank shook the doctor's hand. "I do thank you, Doctor," Frank said, "You saved us much chill and weariness."

"God go with you," Dr. McAfee said.

"And with you," Sally and Frank said in unison.

"And God be with the poor mother and babe," Sally added. She laid her hand on the as yet small mound of her belly thinking if, by God's, grace they reached America, surely the birthing would be better for herself and her

12

newborn.

Within minutes the black carriage disappeared around a curve. Sally watched the new tracks being pressed in the snow. She pulled her shawl closer to her cheek to ward off the icy damp air and took Emily's hand to walk toward the huddled group on the wharf.

A tiny building stood on the left edge of the wharf. Nearby a swaying lantern hung from a post its light now being dimmed with the opening of the morning sky. Seagulls sailed and cried over the bay area and somewhere nearby foghorns moaned. A lone gull winged in gracefully and landed on a dark post near the crowd of waiting passengers.

"Look!" Emily cried. "He likes us."

"Probably hopes we'll feed him," Sally said. "Some might more likely eat him."

"Ah, Sally," Frank said, "Don't talk such to Emily. In America we'll feast every day."

A balding young man dressed in a ratty gray coat appeared from inside the tiny building. "Let's get in line now, people." He spoke kindly. "Over there. The Naomi first, please. 'Tis time to leave dear old Ireland—at least for now."

Not just for now, Sally thought, *forever*. Why come back with nothing to return to except the silent graves of loved ones?

The passengers struggled with baggage as they lined up. Hardly anyone spoke and Sally saw there were those who looked back at the land with tears in their eyes. She rubbed her own wet eyes with the back of her hand.

Chapter Two

Deck hands rushed the passengers getting out of the access boat onto the ship. Although they weren't gentle, Sally was glad for the speed in getting out of the swaying boat since nausea had welled up in her.

Immediately aboard ship a stocky, pock-faced young man shouted, "Aw right git a move on. Hi! Hi!! Git movin'." The wind blew his cheek-length black hair across his face. He drew his fingers in the thick strands and slapped a cap from his coat pocket down on his head. "Awright, get movin'. Step lively. No shufflin' around No shufflin' around." He shoved many as they tried to make their way below into the dim quarters. One child stumbled and fell. Sally heard her crying to her mother.

The deck hand placed a heavy hand on Sally's shoulder. "Git below. Git movin'," he said.

"Take your fecking hands off my wife," Frank said. He shoved the deck hand off balance causing him to fall on the deck. "Learn some manners, swab, or ye may get worse."

The sailor quickly picked himself up and continued guiding the passengers into steerage, but not before he pointed a stubby finger at Frank. "I'll be rememberin' the likes o' you," he snarled.

"And I you," Frank said.

Sally saw the earlier fearful faces of some passengers now as they suppressed smiles, but she felt deep concern. Fighting in the pubs was one thing, but fighting with a man in charge made her anxious for Frank's safety. Besides, the sailor was younger and appeared stronger.

As they descended into the quarters below others were moving about in the dim light complaining, squabbling over spaces. Dirty sawdust covered the floor and the stench of urine met them like a blow in the face. The only light came from a swing lantern hanging from the wooden ceiling, but bloody stains and filth could be seen on the bedding. Sally

14

covered her nose with one hand. A sense of great helplessness swept over her. "I can't do anything," she said under her breath. "God help us that we don't die of filth."

She saw the crestfallen expression on Frank's face. "My God," he said, "What have I done? What's this hell hole with the foul air of a workhouse? And I paid good money for it."

"Ye paid?" an old hag asked propping her head up from a dirty blue striped pillow. She laughed. "We're free ones that landlords kicked out."

Frank flushed. Sally knew he had been tricked and that he was humiliated. Surely they were doomed to make the terrible voyage without protest. She put an arm about his waist.

"Da," Emily asked, "why is it stinky?"

"Because," he said, fighting tears of anger and frustration, "we're poor and some don't care for us." Sally saw, however, that he quickly recovered. "Never you mind, Baby. In America it will be grand and everything will be shining clean. This old ship is only for a little while."

Sally moved from one boxed wooden bunk to another looking for the cleanest, best choice. There was none. She took the bedding from her straw basket and spread it over a stinking, blood-stained mattress of straw.

The loading ship rocked, laboring against the anchor. Sally fought the resurgence of nausea but she could not contain the vomit. Having eaten so little the amount was small, but she continued to gag.

"Sit down, me darling," Frank said, giving her a hand to steady her. Quickly then he swung open a coarse jute curtain and disappeared. Within minutes he returned with a damp cloth.

"Here, Sweetheart," he said gently wiping Sally's face, folding the cloth and placing it on her forehead. "Maybe you should lie down."

Emily climbed in the box-like space with her mother and sat with her back against the bulkhead looking around at the ragged people, many of whom were thin, pale figures lying with their eyes closed while making moaning sounds. A bald, red-faced man snored with open toothless mouth. From time to time he snorted and gasped for breath before resuming his sleep.

"What's wrong with them?" Emily asked. Her face crinkled in concern, her fingers pressed to her lower lip.

"They don't feel well," Frank said.

"Sick?"

"Many are sick, I'm afraid. Some very sick," Frank said.

"Will they die?"

"Some may, Honey. We don't know."

"Will we get dead?"

"Oh, no. I don't think so. We'll be strong. Don't you worry. A few weeks and we'll be in America...America where the fields are green and lush with the growing of wonderful food. No rotten praties there, and we'll have plenty of jam for my girl. You'll see." He scooped her up in his arms and kissed both cheeks that left her giggling. Sally smiled while thinking of her own father and how great a gift a good father is for a child.

Other passengers continued to crowd in and complain, but eventually each settled down in resignation. Young women with crying babies and toddlers, sallow-faced young men, shaggy old men and crones all breathed the rancid air with discomfort, but they stayed. Some spoke of how they looked forward to the great new world they'd heard about. Others wept quietly at being forced to leave their homeland. One young mother of a toddler rocked him gently and said to no one in particular, "I will hold forever in my deepest heart the green sweeps of my homeland from vale to hill to lake, the last words of my dear ones." She wiped tears from her cheeks, but continued her soft speech in an inaudible tone while her child looked at her with a questioning expression. Sally wanted to put her arms about the woman and comfort her but her nausea made her hesitate to arise from her bunk. Later, she would speak with her.

The last passenger, a little man wearing leather laced

boots, brown knickers, a red shirt and a red tam-o'-shanter, bounced down the steps. He readjusted the sack he carried over his shoulder, threw out an arm and cried, "Ye lucky ones, ye now have Trimble Tramble, a poet and an actor to entertain ye."

"Aw, shut yer lip," the hag near the door said. Others groaned or merely looked at him.

"Now, now," he said, "ye have here a descendant of Robbie Burns hisself. Here's jest one short line of me talent. 'Let the mourning folk become morning folk. Let 'em rise and shine. Shine as the planets trine....'"

"Trine? What's trine?" the crone asked, frowning.

He widened his large pale blue eyes and shuffled his feet in a little dance before responding. " 'Trine, oh a very favorable sign. In some far off place there's trine that has that word in their speech. Now what their 'trine' means I cannot say. They knows what it means. We don't—can't know everything lovely lady. Life is a great mystery with languages all about. Why almost any sound is language somewhere in this great world. Hinkle, spinkle, how the rain does sprinkle."

"Shut yer trap, yer no poet," she said waving him away.

"A doubting Tomascina ye are," he said doing a little foot shuffle before seeking a place to settle down. "In America I'll be famous, just you wait and see. Then ye'll be happy to claim, 'Oh, yes, a friend of mine. I knew him well.' I'll let ye claim it though ye turns me the cold face now."

The hag stuck her tongue out and blew a breath of spittle.

He saluted her then looked at the only space left—a filthy, narrow bunk, small even for his frame. He surveyed it for a long moment. "Ah," he said, "all true artists must suffer, but soon t'will be over." He spoke in deep tones as if delivering a sermon before he fluffed the flat pillow and folded the blanket stiffened in spots with filth. Then he smiled, shuffled his feet in his little dance, stretched his arms up and wide and lifted his voice in a musical chant. "America see, Trimble Tramble, shine for thee. Shine for thee. 'Tis me from across the shining sea, pining for thee, shining for thee."

Although Sally thought him silly, she was pleased to see that Emily and some other children laughed. Some little ones clapped their hands and Tramble bowed to them in a series of exaggerated bobbing bows. A few adult passengers smiled and shook their heads while others moaned and turned their faces to the wall of their bunks.

Up on the deck a chorus of men's voices arose. A shouting of orders and the rattling of chains as the anchor was coming up made clear the time of departure had arrived. Soon the ship began to move out of the harbor and into the restless, pounding sea.

Sometime later when the old craft was well under way, moldy, strongly yeasty smelling biscuits were passed out. No one complained. The starving group eagerly consumed them.

During the night Sally heard the snapping and rattling of the ship's rigging as winds came up. She visualized the sails strutting and flapping like desperate white bodies struggling to hold on while the ship fought helplessly against the heavy surging of the sea. Nausea came to her once again and she swallowed against it. Would the old ship fall apart and spray their poor bodies among the creaking old gray boards out into the sea?

Sally realized she was not alone in her fear. Others cried out and some prayed. She was grateful that Frank and Emily slept unaware. She knew no good could come from awakening them. If the worst happened—she shuddered with the thought, they would know all too soon.

Hours later the wind lay and she relaxed. She drew close to Frank and cuddled to his back feeling comforted.

In the semi-darkness the next morning after exhausted sleep in their tight quarters, Frank whispered to Sally. "Let's go up on deck and watch the sun rise."

They arose and left the sleeping Emily and the other passengers still in their bunks to quietly make their way to the deck. A light wind caressed their clothing. The wind, however, was surprisingly mild; not as cold as Sally had

18

expected it to be. She took a deep breath inhaling the salty freshness. "I love it," she said and spread her arms up and out letting the breezes touch her body. "You had a great idea, Frank."

"'Tis nice, isn't it?" He took her hand and led her to a big wooden box where they seated themselves. "Now you see, it's not all bad."

"No. It's nice up here."

"Look," Frank said. He pointed toward the sky. "There's light on the horizon. Soon the sun will rise. And Sally, me darling, our own personal sun will rise and bring us joy in the new world. Think of it Sally. We'll be happy there."

"I hope so, Frank, but I will always miss Ireland."

"Maybe not forever. Some day we may return—at least for a visit."

She wanted to say that even so it would not be the same, but she smiled and kissed his cheek. "Always the hopeful one," she said. As the sun began to rise she felt she must try not to think back so much. Yes, she must try hard to think of the future for Frank's sake. Anyway, it could be so much happier a place for them.

"Perhaps, we should go back now," Sally said, "Emily may be awake and wondering where we are."

"Soon, hopefully, we'll have some more of those great biscuits," Frank said.

Sally laughed and gave him a little shove. She wrinkled her nose. "Wonderful biscuits," she said. "Perhaps, we can do some cooking today of our rations. Shouldn't the brick pit be fired on a day like this?"

"What and have fresh, warm food instead of the great biscuits?"

"I hope the day comes when I never have to eat one of those clammy, stinky things again."

"In America...." he said.

"I know. Lush, green America and jam for Emily's bread—fresh bread," She said and followed him back down into the miserable air of the hole.

19

Later than expected, the sun-bronzed older sailor who had dispensed biscuits the night before returned. This time he passed out not only the biscuits, but small pieces of cheese as well. "A treat for ye," the man said. "A wealthy one sent it to us just before we sailed. Maybe generous. Maybe guilty. Can't say. Anyways, we have it."

"When can we go up on deck?" A young mother asked.

"I'll call ye when," the sailor said. Frank and Sally glanced at each other and smiled.

Frank reached for her hand and gently squeezed it.

***

Twelve days into the voyage a two-year-old boy who had come aboard starving clung weakly to his mother all day before dying. When the sun was sinking low on the horizon, a sailor claimed the toddler for burial at sea. The child's pale mother wept and begged to keep her dead child, "just one more day," but her pleading went unheeded.

The sailor wrapped the small body in a dingy white cloth and carried it up on deck. He spoke a few muffled words as some passengers watched. Then as near darkness covered the area he dropped the small body into the rippling seawater.

"Couldn't ye at least let him go in the morning light?" The grieving young mother cried out in anguish. "He was afraid of monsters at night."

Sally went to her and embraced her. "The Lord lifted him up. His little soul is surrounded by light and love this very moment. Only what he lived in while on earth is in the water, no longer really him at all."

"If only that's true!" The young mother said sobbing. "If only that's true." She seemed momentarily comforted, but Sally knew her broken heart would ache for her child for years to come.

Fear arose in Sally as the days passed and other bodies were cast into the tumbling waters of the cold sea. More passengers were deeply ill with the fever. Would they take on the fever next?

The wife of an ancient bearded man moaned for days untreated and uncomforted except by her old husband who stroked her hair saying, "There, there, Maudie, ye'll be well soon." When her body was dropped in the deep, dark waters at nightfall, the old man threw himself overboard and was swept away with her.

Frank tried to hide as much of the sorrow and the burials from Emily as possible. Sally and Emily especially looked forward to the times on deck when the weather was clear and sunny. Although all of them were hungry most of the time, Frank relaxed in seeing them enjoy at least this part of the voyage. He continued to speak in glowing terms of the future. "When we get to that grand new land—ah, then we'll soon forget this miserable voyage. We'll take on a fine new life of fresh air and sunshine. Oh yes, and there'll be lovely green fields in the summer, dancing red and gold leaves in the autumn. Even the snow will be white as Ireland's snow. Ah, yes, think on it. It will be grand."

One clear, sunny day when they were on deck, Emily said, "Da, play the fiddle. I want to dance in the sunshine."

"For sure," Frank said, ruffling her hair. He went below to bring up the instrument.

As soon as Frank struck up a merry tune, people began to laugh and clap their hands. Emily danced happily all around, stamping her feet, holding her arms by her side. Her reddish brown curls bounced on her thin shoulders.

"Aye! She dances fine for a wee one," a toothless old man said. He clapped his hands and tapped his foot. Soon other passengers joined in until the deck of the small ship was full of the sound of tapping meet and joyful music. Wiping sleep from his eyes, Trimble Tramble appeared and with a shout, flipped his body over landing solidly on his feet and began dancing kicking his toes merrily in the air as he pranced about.

The rough, passenger-loading sailor stomped up on deck. It was the first time that deck hand had reappeared and Sally wondered about his absence. She had asked other passengers about him. Some said he was the top hand that his name was Ezra Dollard—the one in charge, and other sailors did most of the work while he lounged about and barked orders.

The sailor took a solid stance, hand on hips and shouted, "Are ye out 'o ye minds? Stop it! Ye'll rock the ship into the sea." He took a step closer to Frank. "I might 'o known it was the likes 'o you." Dollard stood as tall as his short boxy body would allow before shouting in Frank's face. His spittle hit Frank's cheek and his left eye. "Ye are to ask, not jest do. Ye got that?"

Sally grabbed Frank's arm, "No, Frank," she whispered. "Let it go. Let it go." But Frank jumped to his feet dropping his fiddle in Sally's lap. He swung hard at Dollard punching him repeatedly in rapid succession in the face and stomach. A cut opened in Dollard's left eyebrow. Blood streamed down into his eye. He wiped at it with his sleeve spreading a red streak onto his cheek and ear.

The passengers cheered. "Yeah! Yeah! Yeah!"

The sailor flushed and staggered back, but recovered quickly. He landed a punch to Frank's solar plexuses then punched Frank hard in the face. With one swift move Dollard bent low, grabbed Frank's fiddle from Sally and threw it far out into the sea.

Frank bellowed as his fiddle fell into the churning waters to disappear forever. Sally saw his sudden tears, red face and his clinched fists. Emily buried her face in her mother's heavy woolen skirt.

Sally screamed, "No, Frank. No! Let it go! Let it go! You still have the flute."

Frank lunged with all his strength at Dollard and pounded him while passengers cheered him on yelling and clapping their hands.

Frank staggered, breathing hard, still he landed a solid blow to Dollard's left cheek. Sally watched in horror as the sailor pulled a cudgel from his belt.

"Frank!" She cried. "Let it go. Move away! Let him go!" She knew Frank was weaker than the well-fed sailor.

Oh, Lord, for once let him forget his Irish pride!

Frank seemed to muster strength and stepped forward, but Dollard struck him rapidly with his cudgel alternately landing blows to each side of Frank's head. Blood flowed freely from gashes on his cheekbones and forehead. Still Frank would not give up. He pushed Dollard hard and the sailor landed against a passenger. He quickly regained his stance and repeatedly beat Frank hard across the head and face until he fell to the ship deck.

"Da! Da!" Emily cried.

Sally rushed to Frank and lifted his head to her lap. Blood oozed through his dark curls down his cheek and onto her skirt. "Oh God," she whispered seeing the red stream move across his unseeing eyes, "Oh, my God. My God." She gently brushed the blood aside, feeling the warmth of his flesh, and prayed he would live but knew that he would not. "Oh, Frank, Frank, me darling," she sobbed.

At first Sally did not realize Emily sat beside her holding her father's hand. They continued to hold him until his body was taken away and slipped into the churning ocean waters without ceremony other than Sally's soft prayer and Emily's calling after him, "Da, don't go!."

Sally sobbed and bowed her head low, "Frank, Frank, Frank," she cried--his blood wet on her hands and her clothes. A painful thought accused her. Why hadn't she stood in between them? Maybe she could have saved him! Oh, if only this were a nightmare! Oh, God, oh God! Let this be a dream. Let me wake and find his dear self still whole and well, but she knew the reality. How could she live with it?

Emily touched her mother's arm and shook it. She asked in whispered voice, "Was it my fault?" Tears ran down her cheeks. She fought them with her small fists.

Sally took her in her arms. She must think of her child. "No, no. Never think that, me darling. It was the bad man who hurt Da. Some people are not good, Emily."

"He didn't like Da's music?"

"It wasn't the music. It made him angry that we could

have a little joy."

"I asked Da to play. Was it my asking?"

"No, Sweetheart, it surely was not your fault and your Da would tell you so if he could. Evil men do horrible things."

For a long moment Emily looked at her mother with wonderment.

"Why?"

"We don't always know why."

"I want Da.," Emily cried burying her face against her mother's shoulder.

"I know, baby. I know. We both want him."

Sally wanted to scream with all her breath to rid the pain from her soul, but she held it not wanting to frighten Emily. Later, when Emily was asleep Sally slipped up on deck and looked out on the dark rolling waters. Frank's body was out there somewhere deep. If only she could take some comfort from some imagined closeness, but she could not. Her heart ached knowing never again would she hear the lilt in his voice or to see his jaunty step--never again would she know his kisses and the warmth of his body. She cried out his name again and again in the darkness. Who would hear her except God in Heaven?

She felt as vulnerable as a child and found herself longing for the comforting arms of her mother, but she knew she could not allow herself to be weak. Frank would want her to be strong and bear up for Emily and for the sake of their unborn child.

***

In the days that followed Frank's death, Sally sobbed softly into her pillow at night and worried about what they would do if they survived to reach the new world. She held back her tears for the most part until Emily was asleep although at times they wept together. At least she still had money pinned to her underclothing in a small packet. But would it be enough to last them until she could find work?

Or what if they were not permitted to leave the ship? Some were not let into America. What if she became ill and died leaving Emily alone? It was too much to even consider. Oh, if only Frank were here with his glowing view of the future!

Some days later, Sally realized that one man about Frank's height seemed to have only the clothes he wore. She noticed that his bony shoulders poked against his thin shirt and that he sat much of the time bent over reading a book. Occasionally he ran his wrinkled fingers through his matted white hair or twisted one lone strand over his forehead. Although the days were long and boring she wondered what book he could read every day. Initially, she thought it was a Bible, but when she finally could see the cover she realized it was not. When the old man's shirt caught on a nail and ripped apart she decided to offer him Frank's few clothes— all except his Greek fisherman's cap which she wanted to keep forever. In her thoughts she could still see Frank wearing that cap cocked at an angle over his thick, black curls.

She gathered Frank's clothing and approached the shaggy-haired old man.

"Would you like these, sir?" she asked. "You know my husband...."

"Yes, ma'am I know, dear lady. I'm sorry for your loss. Lost me own mate," he said. He reached for the garments. "I thank ye from my heart."

"You are most welcome," Sally said. "May I ask what book you read every day?"

He laughed revealing tiny teeth like bits of yellow corn. "Ye noticed?"

"I did."

"It's a book with all the words in it. A dictionary. I find there's much here to read and maybe to memorize. Helps to take up the time. Ye see?"

"Oh."

"Would ye like to read it, ma'am?"

Sally smiled. "No, thank you, Sir. I have me own wee Bible and I should read it more." With that she turned to go.

"From my heart I thank ye and let me pay ye something," the old man said. "Could I ask your name?"

"Sally McKelvy and ye owe me nothing."

"I'm Michael Finn. If I may help you in any way, do let me know."

"Thank you, Mr. Finn," Sally said and returned to her bunk where Emily sat playing with her tattered rag doll."

Sally began to fear the voyage would never end even if the old ship continued to weather the restless sea. The cries and moans of the suffering passengers in the hold troubled her, but worse was the treatment they often received from the sailor, Ezra Dollard. She felt the depth of her hatred of him for killing Frank and now witnessing his cruelty toward her poor fellow voyagers she knew she must try to find a way to defeat him. But how? She lay awake trying to devise a plan.

The best times were the hours on deck. Even when misting rain fell, Sally and Emily stayed above letting the light spray cool their faces. Rain and salty air was so much more to be desired over the stench below in steerage—particularly now that more of the passengers were ill and dying. Sally knew seven had died within the last week. She prayed every day that she and Emily would not fall ill. What would happen to Emily if she...she—oh, she couldn't bear the thought of that, nor of losing her dear child. A little one near Emily's age, a six-year-old girl had died a month after Frank was gone. Only a few infants remained and one of them had been flushed and crying for two days.

One evening, just after the pale oil lamp was lit near the ceiling in the hold, a dark storm blew up. Sleet, icy rain and snow beat against the old ship. Murky water leaked in, ran along the rafters and dripped down on the passengers. Strong winds caused such squeaking and moaning of the old wood that Sally feared the ship would fall apart for sure this time. She saw an elderly woman weakly lifting her arms, trying to cover her face, and went to assist her. The caulking of the boards on the floor became slack and the gaps between the planks opened and closed with the movement of the ship. Sally's skirt caught between the boards. She knew that sometimes passengers were held in place like this for hours and fought against the panic arising in her with the storm becoming more fierce.

"Get in the bunk, Ma," Emily cried, "Hurry!"

"I can't. I have to wait."

Within minutes the planks opened with the ship sifting in the wind on to a new course releasing her. Sally gasped, fell into her bunk and wept briefly in gratitude.

Still, the ship swayed dangerously in the storm causing many to become seasick. Sally held on to Emily in an effort to steady them against the heaving waves and hoped her queasiness would settle. Some passengers fell from their bunks to the floor. Sally could barely see the figures now as almost total darkness engulfed them. Some wept and others pleaded for help, but it was if each poor sole were alone. No help came for them and none would come.

Sally heard the crashing of thunder along with the creaking of the ship and the cries of the sailors on deck dealing with the sails. She imagined Ezra Dollard sent the others, but how safe was he? How safe were any of them. Sally prayed softly for the storm to cease. Yet somehow she did not have the same fear arise in her that she would have earlier. If they were spilled into the sea, at least they would be the same as Frank. She knew this was an unreasonable comfort, but it allowed her to be more relaxed with Emily.

Eventually, in what seemed hours to Sally, the winds settled and the ship moved in a normal manner. She awoke to a clear, sunny day and was grateful. As was usual now a few of the passengers were allowed on deck to wash themselves, their clothing and to cook whatever rations were still edible. Sally knew that of the sixty original passengers, only half now survived, but the remaining ones appeared to be reasonably well although thin and underfed.

Soon the smell of porridge and raisins cooking made the morning seem pleasant. Sally breathed in the scent, felt a gentle ocean breeze and her mood turned more hopeful.

Sally left the deck and went below to check on Emily who was still sleeping. She would cook some porridge with raisins for their breakfast also. As soon as she stepped down into the hold she heard a slap and an agonized cry. She saw an elderly man fall back into his bunk and heard Ezra Dollard say, "No! It's not for me to tend to ye. God damn ye old fool! I should beat yer ass and pitch ye to the sharks. Learn some respect for ye betters." He shoved the old man back in his bunk. "Don't ye ever ask me to tend ye again, do ye hear, old bastard?"

"Oh, God, I pray ye have mercy! I only want—I beg ye let me have a breath of fresh air. If ye'd just let me hold on to steady myself I think I could make it up there. I'm dying in this stench-ridden hold. My lungs are choked with it."

"Didn't ye hear?" Dollard jerked him up by the collar of his shirt and spat in his face. "Ye damned old fool! Old Ass, I said 'NO'! I have my position on this ship and it's not to be the servant of scum."

Sally felt anger arise in her like burning blood. She went quickly to the side of the elderly man. "I'll help you," she said. "Hold onto my arm."

Dollard shoved her aside. "Keep yer place, woman," he said.

Sally looked for a weapon, but finding none, she took off her shoe and began beating Dollard wildly on his arm and managed one lick on his jaw.

He caught her arm and jerked her around putting her wrist in a painful position, making her cry out.

"Stop it, Slut" he snarled. "Don't think ye can do me in and don't spill another brat out here making a mess."

Sally shouted at him. "You killed Frank! You treat all of us like pests. I don't know how, Ezra Dollard, but somehow I'll make you pay."

He laughed. "Sure. I see ye have the power of a peasant. Oh, such great influence. I am shaking." He trembled his whole body and widened his eyes in mockery.

"You don't know what influence I have in America," she shot back.

"And with that great influence ye're sailing in high class at this very moment. I know what kind of influence ye have, so shut the mouth and mind the manners around ye betters on board this ship."

From the corner of her eye Sally saw Trimble Tramble. He seemed to appear from nowhere and flew into Ezra Dollard with movements so quick and precise the burly sailor was stunned. When Dollard could steady himself he said, in a still breathless voice, "Ye weakling! Ye didn't hurt me. Ye're like a buzzing fly—a pesky little thing to be done away with and I'll kill ye now!"

The big sailor lunged at him but Tramble moved quickly aside. With a splat Dollard fell to the filthy floor. In a rage, he bounded to his feet and grabbed for Tramble, but again his attempt failed. Sally watched in wonderment as every effort Dollard made was fruitless. Finally, the sailor, breathing heavily pointed a finger at Tramble declaring, "I'll get ye yet and when ye least expect it."

"He didn't hurt you," Sally cried. "Leave him alone." When he turned to walk away, Sally shouted after him. "You evil man. You devil! One day you'll pay."

As quickly as he had appeared, Trimble Tramble was gone. Sally glanced around for him and saw that he had returned to his bunk, head propped up on a pillow, reading a small volume that he held in one hand.

The old man who begged for fresh air now lay still with tears running down his cheeks. Sally went to him.

"Let's go," she said, offering her arm. "Take hold and we'll go up."

"No. I can't put ye in danger," he said.

"We let him win if we do nothing. Take my arm," she said.

He brushed aside his tears and reached up with frail, shaking arms to accept her offer. Then slowly they made their way across the floor. Sally noticed another elderly man arise from his bunk. "Here let me help ye manage the steps," he said. He walked uprightly in quick short steps, his arms palming the air as he walked. A mass of white hair lay on his shoulders against a gray shirt.

"What if he sees you, sir?" the unsteady old man asked.

I should have stayed in my bunk rather than have ye two hurt."

"It's past time we stand up to this bully," Sally said. "We need to work out a plan; stop being afraid and letting him have his way." She heard noises of movement and saw that other passengers were rising from their bunks.

"Tell us what we can do," a fragile old woman with bony arms said. She held a wooden hairbrush in her hand.

"We must make a plan," Sally's helper repeated. She noticed that he seemed somehow energized and younger with a straighter stance and determination in his voice.

Sally watched in amazement as many continued to stand out from their bunks. But she soon realized that all were not in agreement.

A small woman holding her little girl on her lap spoke. "Ah, yes," she said, "ye talk, but when he comes swinging his shillelah—then what? I say we stay quiet, make no move at all to set off his rage."

A tall, stooped man with balding, scraggly black hair stood. He backed the young mother's suggestion. "We can't fight. We're too old and frail. You know that Harold O'Conner."

"But, Carson," protested Sally's helper, now having been identified as Harold O'Conner, "we have the numbers. He is only one."

Feeling the old man on her arm about to fall, Sally led him to a bunk. "Sit here, sir, and rest until we are ready to go up on deck."

"Dollard is one with a big advantage," Carson was saying as Sally returned. She saw he nervously shook his head of shaggy black hair and his lips twitched.

"Considering 'only one', sir" Sally countered. "Did you not see what Trimble Tramble did?" Sally asked.

"I did. He is young and wiry, but we can't take on his fight. We are too weak," Carson said. His tic had grown worse. He stretched his small, blue eyes wide and then blinked rapidly. "God have mercy on us," he whispered and crossed himself.

Sally looked toward Trimble Tramble. She saw that he was observing them and motioned for him to come.

He pointed to his chest. Sally nodded and beckoned again.

Before Tramble crossed the floor the woman holding her child on her lap said, "Do ye not realize he could hurt our little ones? As a mother think about it."

Sally drew a deep breath. How could she have not thought of that? She found her resolve diminishing. Still, if Dollard were left free...who knew what cruelty might fascinate him next? His next victims could be the children. Had he not already been callous in handling the sick and dead children? All the more reason they must stand against him.

Sally, momentarily preoccupied in her thoughts, was unaware that Trimble Tramble had arrived and stood facing her. "You wish to speak with me?" he asked. He did his little dance and bowed.

"Yes," she said. "We are greatly troubled by...."

"I know who," Tramble said.

"Is he the captain?" several asked in unison.

"No," Tramble said. "His older brother, Quarry, is the captain—a crazy one, but owner of the ship. Ezra is often in charge which allows him to carry on as he pleases."

"Why do we never see the captain?" Sally asked.

"Because he is a drunkard."

"How did you know this?" O'Conner asked.

"Ah, I have traveled much and know many of the ship people. Had my funds not been so low, I would not have chosen this ship and that's no lie. With so little money now, I must get to America to make my fortune."

"He has threatened to kill you," Sally said. "Are you not afraid?"

"I know him to be an evil, frustrated man. Yes, I'm afraid that he may murder me if I am asleep, but my travels to the Orient have taught me many skills in self defense— and even how to kill a man if I should choose." He danced around making several moves with both arms and legs. I can perform a dance of death if I choose—though you see entertainment is my real goal. Oh yes, I will become famous in America."

Sally watched him and was fascinated. She would have dismissed his claim as foolishness except that she had witnessed how well he handled himself with Dollard. "We must by all means protect you," Sally said. "When you are asleep certain ones of us will be awake and alert. I'll take my turn."

Voices arose in unison supporting Sally's statement. "Count me in."

"Give me my turn," sounded in a chorus of voices.

"Dear God," the young woman with the child on her lap cried. "We will all be killed! What a stupid—foolish thing you propose! He will beat us and kill us all."

Harold O'Conner, ignored her plea. "Yes, we must plan watches and prepare ourselves with whatever weapons we may have."

Sally looked across the dim area at the thin, ragged group standing, offering help, and tears blinded her. She wished to embrace each one, but instead she spoke. "I had no idea I traveled with such brave ones as you are. We will survive. We will." To the frightened young mother and the balding man, she said, "Remain still and quiet if you must, but think of how Dollard has already treated many. His cursing and beating of the sick and innocent—we should have stood against him before now."

Chapter Three

After a greater struggle than Sally had expected, she and Harold O'Conner were able to get the frail man up on deck. Sally was appalled to see how ashen and moist the man's face was—like a pearly slice of fish. Poor fellow he was almost dead.

"Let's seat him on that wooden box," she said nodding toward the box where she and Frank sat the morning before his murder.

O'Conner nodded. "There you are, Sir. And what is your name?" he asked.

"Joshua Perkins," he whispered breathlessly.

"Are you all right, Sir?" Sally asked.

The old man inhaled deeply, then coughed. "I am," he said. "'Tis joy to me heart now that I see the sun. And lovely it 'tis to hear the music of the waves against the ship."

"Good," Sally said. "The air is balmy. You chose a good day to come to the deck. I'll prepare some porridge with raisins and you'll have some. I trust you like porridge."

"I do indeed and 'tis good that I do with me teeth most gone."

He smiled revealing three widely spaced upper teeth to the right side and two long ones on the bottom right. Sally felt warmed by his obvious pleasure.

"It's on the voyage we've been for weeks," Perkins said, "Let's pray America will soon be in sight."

"I fear we have yet some time to go," O'Conner said. "We best pray our food and water will last the voyage. The water ration has already begun."

Sally wished O'Conner had not spoken of the water ration. She saw the look of distress on Perkins' face. Even though he spoke the truth she did not want the old man's happiness on deck to be shadowed with anxiety.

" 'Tis sorry I am more for others than for myself," Perkins said, "me havin' had four score and ten plus."

"I trust we'll make it," Sally said placing her hand on the old man's bony shoulder.

He reached up to touch her hand and she wondered if the mere touch of her hand meant so much for she saw tears on his lashes.

Not long after midnight Sally saw the looming figure of Ezra Dollard desending the steps into the hold. She slipped quickly to Tramble's bunk and shook him, but he slept soundly. In the far corner she saw Harold O'Conner rise from his bunk. Whispering caught her attention. Soon others stood.

Sally saw Dollard, swinging his cudgel in a circular motion as he walked briskly toward Trimble Tramble's bunk. A thin young woman was in his path.

"Ye know better," he said and swung his cudgel catching her hard on her shoulder. She screamed in pain. Sally cried out in sympathy, fearing that the fragile woman's shoulder could be broken. The young woman's small boy began to cry.

"Shut 'em up," Dollard said and swung his cudgel hard at the child barely missing his head.

In a movement so sudden Sally was unprepared for it a pair of long scissors flashed briefly in the dim light before plunging in Dollard's neck. A forceful jet of blood spurted from the anguished man. He grabbed his neck and tried to run, but crashed to the floor instead near the stairs. Sally knew, as surely the others did as well, that he would die. None went near him but stood apart watching him.

"Me soul may flounder in hell," the bearer of the scissors said, "but I did it for me child and the handful of babes still with us. Had his blow connected to that little lad's head one more of our babes would have been cast into the sea. Who was to say me own little daughter would not be next."

Sally saw in amazement the young mother who had protested their standing against Dollard fearing his reprisal. She understood her protective fury, and felt she owed the young woman a debt of gratitude. Dollard had not attacked Emily, but clearly he had no regard for the children or the adults.

O'Conner approached Sally. "How has Tramble slept through this?"

"I don't know. Let's see if we can awaken him now," she said.

They went to his bunk and called to him, O'Conner shook him gently then more vigorously. Tramble slept on.

"Surely, he has been drugged," Sally said. "Someone, possibly Dollard must have put something in his water ration."

O'Conner raised his eyebrows. "Yes, that could be. Yes, to be sure he could kill him without Tramble being able to defend himself. But, Ma'am we have now another problem."

"We have many problems," Sally said.

"I mean—the drunk, crazy captain. Who now will take the helm?"

Sally swallowed hard. Dollard had at least kept the ship on course.

"I have never seen the captain," She said.

"Neither have I." O'Conner said, "but we need to see him now."

"Somebody has to give him the news...."

"I'll do it," O'Conner said, but first I'll need help with that heavy body." He smiled at Sally. "I'm not suggesting you help."

"Wait. We'd best get the body overboard," Sally said. "We don't want the captain to be looking for his brother's killer. Maybe...."

"We could suggest he lost his balance and...."

"Yes. He did lose his mental balance. Let's keep it as close to the truth as possible. I don't like lying," Sally said.

O'Conner shook his shaggy head. "You're one for the books," he said, smiling. He turned to the others and called out. "You men, such as ye are able, come help me toss the body overboard. Keep in ye mind, he lost his balance—his mind's balance, I'm told."

Sally shrugged. "We'll do what we can down here to

35

clean up the blood, and when you return, I'll go with you to see the captain," She said.

"Would that be proper for a young lady?" O'Conner asked.

"And why not? It's not as if I never saw the likes of a drunk Irishman before."

"Och! Ye have a point there, Ma'am. Very well. A woman's touch may be needed for the captain. After all, 'twas his brother."

Before they were to deliver the news to the captain, Trimble Tramble woke. He blinked his eyes, shook his head and looked around him in the pale light of early morning seeping through the cracks in the ceiling.

Sally saw him sit up rub his eyes and yawn. She approached him. "Are you all right?"

"Strange. I feel a bit strange, but I think I'm getting at myself now."

"We think Ezra Dollard drugged you, but he is no longer with us."

"He's not?"

She told him what had happened and their concern that the ship could be without a navigator."

"Some say he can do it drunk," Trimble said, "but I think not. Very experienced he is, but drunk? No. Besides, he gets out of his head completely at times. Sees the snakes and such."

"Can you do it?" Sally asked.

"No, not well. Maybe one of the other sailors can, although I think most of them are not too apt."

"Then I say we sober the captain, toss his pints overboard and guard him," Sally said.

"Aye, well, we may try, but he's a big one with a set mind," Trimble did his little dance. "Aye, we can try, but fate will be what fate will be."

"It's no joke," Sally said and turned to go.

"Wait, Ma'am. I may be able to help. There are things I learned in my voyages. I'll do what I can."

"And what would that be?"

36

"The water gives messages in the shape and direction of the waves as does the temperature and humidity of the wind, and then there are the birds—certain migratory birds and certain fish. I know some of this. I hope it's enough. Still someone must turn the wheel and if the captain or whoever steers won't listen...but don't worry. We'll be safe. My fame and fortune in America is a promise."

"A promise? Promise from whom? Not God, I think."

He did his little dance, clapped his hands above his head and said, "I know it. I know it. I know it."

"I don't know it," Sally said. "I am going to pray very hard. God alone will decide if we live or die." She looked about her in the gray light. "Pray with me, please, all of you—pray that God will save us out on this vast ocean. Pray that this old ship will hold together. Pray for yourselves, your children, for all of us," she cried.

A chorus of "God have mercy on us," arose with frail hands crossing bony breasts.

As if in protest of prayer, a sudden storm arose with rain beating down in torrents. Powerful winds rose blew the ship in reckless angles. Sally held Emily close in her arms and prayed silently for forgiveness for the murder and for mercy. She felt water spraying from the leaking ceiling in the torrential rain, and shuddered as the waves drove hard against the timbers of the creaking old ship.

For what seemed hours the wild, cold winds battered the ship about. Many passengers cried. Some screamed when it appeared the ship would surely break apart, but finally the winds and waves abated and the sun came out. Sally whispered a prayer of thanks, but she wondered how far off course they might be and if they might yet starve or die of thirst before they reached America.

In less than an hour a shout rang out from the deck, "America! America! God has answered our prayers."

An old hag said, "God or maybe dumb luck."

Later, as the ship was guided safely into New York harbor, a sailor brought the bleary-eyed captain forth. Sally saw what a giant of a man he was and marveled that the smaller young sailor could manage to support the big man's unsteady steps.

"Did you guide the ship during the storm?" Sally asked the young sailor.

"I couldn't. No one did, but the captain guided us into port, of course."

"Does the captain know his brother...?"

"He knows he went overboard in the storm."

"Ezra had no sense," the captain said, "Served him right."

Sally felt initially shocked at his words, then saddened. She knew not every family was blessed with love but it troubled her.

The ship shuddered briefly as it made a final stop. She realized she had arrived in the new world and felt afraid without Frank. Indeed without any family but her child.

Chapter Four

At dawn sixty-nine days from the time the Naomi O'Hare had left the small quay at Donegal, she arrived at a wharf in New York. Sally heard the rattling of chains and the thumping sounds of boxes being moved and tossed. A deep voiced sailor was yelling orders. Through cracks around the doorway she could see a gray daylight. A ripple of water from rain drifted along a rafter.

Soon the crewmember that dispensed the food arrived with stale biscuits. Then he called off a list. "Ye'll see the doctor and we'll see if ye stay or ye go back. Up on deck, all ye that can walk."

Trimble Tramble danced up to be first in line although Sally noticed he looked thinner and less able than before. The elderly Michael Finn made it in second place. He was wearing Frank's clothes. Sally swallowed and fought tears. For a moment, from his back, except for the white hair, he looked like Frank standing there.

"Come Emily," she said, "we must get in line." They took a middle position, allowing some of the seemingly weaker passengers to go ahead of them.

On deck a brilliant sun shone after a rain. Sally blinked against the brightness, but it soon faded into a cloudy overcast. A wet sail flapped in a sudden wind and the air felt chilly. Sally hoped the rain would hold until they could cross the gangplank onto land for the examination. The cobblestones in front of the brick building were wet and likely slippery already. She worried about the feeble people crossing over and prayed all the survivors of the voyage would pass the doctor's standard for entry into the new world. Sally shivered against the damp chill and forced away the rising fear of failing the entry exam. Shrill cries of sea gulls distracted her, and she shaded her eyes to look at the swarm of them. "See, Emily," she said, hoping to remove some of the tension, "America has sea gulls like in Ireland."

"I like them," Emily said, "I wish they'd come down and visit us like that one at Donegal quay." She clung to her mother's hand and rested her head against her mother's waist.

While they still waited in line, Trimble Tramble and Michael Finn finished their visits with the doctor. Tramble cried, "I'm here! I'm almost famous!" Joyfully he shook his red tam-o'-shanter above his head and danced his happy dance, clicking his heels together in a way Sally had imagined might be too difficult for him in his thinner state. Surely some special energy came from a happy spirit. She wondered and worried about Harold O'Conner. He had seemed unwell the past day or two. Glancing back she saw him near the end of the line. Although pale, he appeared to stand without difficulty. Hopefully, he was better.

Michael Finn smiled at Sally and Emily--indeed at all in line. "I made it," he said. "I made it! This old piece of humanity made it." He raised his hand toward the sky. "I thank Thee, Lord, I thank Thee."

Inside, the stuffy reception building smelled of dust and tobacco smoke. Sally and Emily moved along in a line and were quickly examined by a bearded young doctor. He passed them on to receive their clearance papers. Sally, smiling broadly now, took Emily's hand again and led her back to the ship. "Soon, baby," she said, "soon we'll leave the Naomi O'Hare for good. Maybe a better ship will one day take us back home to dear old Ireland. Would be my greatest wish, but if God doesn't grant that, we are here at last in Da's America.

"Da said America is right next to Heaven."

"Oh, I know, me darling. It's just that however wonderful America may be, Ireland is home."

Later, when they disembarked, Sally was amazed at the mob of people waiting to greet have been living when she became the first woman in America to graduate from medical school the passengers. She felt lonely and frightened. There was no one to meet them--no one to embrace and welcome them in this strange place.

A man flashing a wide smile, rushed up to Sally offering to find her lodging for a fee. She was uncertain what she should do. She had heard there were evil men and women who cheated new arrivals. She held off. In the near distance she saw Michael Finn being greeted by a large, frowzy-haired young woman. She took Emily's hand and urged her along to approach him and the woman who was embracing him.

"Mr. Finn--."

"Oh, yes, Mrs. McKelvy. This is my dear sister's child, Mary Frances Bray."

"Mrs. Bray, I wonder if you could guide me to some living quarters. I know no one here."

"Well, me own quarters are not for braggin'. Are ye lookin' for somethin' special?"

Sally shook her head. "No, only something livable for my child and myself. I have little money."

"Then I'll show ye our place in the Five Points where we lives."

With a glance at Mr. Finn, Sally smiled and said, "I thank you from my heart. Truly I do."

When they arrived in the slum district the stench of open sewers, and the filth of rotting garbage assailed Sally. She cupped her hand over her nose.

A group of tough-looking young boys in dirty clothes swaggered down the muddy street. They wrestled with each other, laughed and shouted.

"Jest, ye never mind them," Mary Frances said. "Jest keep yer distance and yer eye on what's about ye. We has the gangs what steals and fights the bloody fights, but them ye see there, well, they the young upstarts. The older ones what's called 'the dead rabbits,' well, them and others like 'the Bowery Boys' is the ones what's bad. But killing--well, mostly they kills each other."

Sally's chest tightened. "Mostly?"

"Sometimes it's others what gets in the way, but never ye mind. Jest, keep yer distance and watch what ye own."

Sally pulled Emily to her side but continued to follow

Mary Frances and Michael past ramshackled gray buildings, noisy groups of women and children, and peddlers selling bread, fruits and vegetables. A few sheets of dingy paper blew along the street past piles of refuse. The smell of latrines and garbage seemed worse even than the fetid air of the ship's hold. Her hand over her nose did no good. Why on earth had Frank believed so in this terrible place?

Mary Frances said, "'Tis bad on the breathing, but a little farther on where we live, it's some better. But dearie, Five Points is not known for being like the fresh green of dear old Ireland."

"I imagine we'll get used to it," Sally said.

"Oh, ye will. Ye'll hardly notice it after a time except, of course, when the heat of summer gets to it. Then ye'll weep for the old country for sure."

Emily said, "Ma, could we leave now and go to Da's America?"

Mary Frances laughed. "Oh, ye was 'specting something sweet and pretty, wee lass? Well, 'tis not here. Maybe somewhere out in the country--somewhere away from this crumbling, stinking place."

"For now we must be here," Sally said.

"Ye looks thin, 'cept for—are ye early in a family way?"

"I am. I'll be needing a mid-wife later. Do you know of one?"

"There's a little woman who's rented herself rooms at a red brick house not too far from here. Shingle hanging outside, they say reads 'Elizabeth Blackwell. MD' Now least ways she calls herself a doctor and some says she's kind. She does babies as well as a mid-wife, though mostly only the poorest see her for anything else. You know when they has no money at all."

"If you'll direct me...."

"I'll do better. I'll take ye there tomorrow."

"I'll be most grateful," Sally said.

"Later, I suppose ye'll be looking fer work. Well, that ain't so easy. Signs in windows say 'No Irish Need Apply.'

'Bout the only work for the likes of us is home sewin' and the pay is pitiful—jest pitiful."

Sally felt her face tingle with fear. What would happen if no one would hire her? If she could do home sewing would it be enough? Oh, if only Frank were here!

Mr. Finn spoke up. "How would they know she wouldn't be a good worker, just because she's Irish?"

"They wouldn't but that's the way it 'tis," Mary Frances said. "Fortunately, me man owns the tenement and we gets by."

"I hate this," Mr. Finn said, " 'No Irish Need Apply.' Why I've always been willing to tote the skillet level with any man...yes, a fair man I am and a good worker."

"Well, Uncle Mike ye won't have to work. What bit we have we'll share with ye. I well know how ye helped out me dear mother when she needed ye back in Ireland."

In the near distance a two-story tenement slightly leaning with age came in view. "That's it," Mary Frances said. " 'Tis our own and there's a small flat in it fer you there if ye likes it. Has the bare necessities in it, too."

Sally swallowed. It looked to be such a dismal place although unlike other buildings they'd passed, little debris was piled out front. "I thank you," Sally said, "what would I have done with out you, my new friends?"

"Well, ye know we Irish, at least the good 'uns among us, look out for each other. Since ye ain't a child, Mrs. McKelvy, ye know there's the bad 'uns, too."

"Please, do call me 'Sally.'"

"I will if ye'll call me Mary Frances."

"Now," Mr. Finn said, "since you have no family, you could call me Uncle Mike, if you would want to claim such a one as you see here." He made a funny face with an exaggerated smile showing his stubby little teeth.

Sally laughed. "Thank you. I'm happy to claim you both. It's comforting to me. I thank you from my heart." Despite the dingy slum, she breathed a sigh of relief.

Mary Frances soon showed her the small, nearly bare apartment. At least, as had been described, a bed, two wooden chairs and a rocker made one room livable. In the kitchen Sally saw a few faded dishes on a shelf. A frying pan and a medium-sized pot sat on a coal stove. In the middle of the floor a small, unpainted wooden table was covered with a faded red-checkered cloth.

"Ma," Emily asked. "Could we go tomorrow to the America Da liked?"

"Quiet, honey," Sally said.

"In the corner there's a pail for water and a little pan for the washing of dishes." Mary Frances said. "For now I'll have me husband, Henry, to fetch ye some water. And I'll send over a bit of soap by him. Tonight ye'll join us for a bowl of soup if ye wish."

"You are most kind," Sally said. "I accept and thank you. Tomorrow I'll need to shop for food."

Very soon after Mary Frances left, her husband, Henry, appeared. Sally was surprised to see a handsome well-built, red-haired man.

"Henry, here," he said extending his hand and when Sally took it, he laughingly, briefly pulled her to him in an embrace. "Just let me know anything ye want, me dear," he said. "I take care of me lady tenants. Of course, for now that's the hauling of water. Later--well, whatever ye needs."

Sally felt momentarily stunned. She swallowed, then spoke awkwardly. "Your good wife," she said, "and Mr. Finn are lovely people."

She sighed and looked down at her hands. What else did she have to face now? She ran her hand gently over her swollen belly. What kind of man was this who would approach a woman in her obvious condition? It was true she missed the pleasure and excitement of a man, but not one— though handsome he was—like Henry Bray. She'd never understood why anyone would want a person who was everybody's man or woman. Sudden tears filled her eyes. How she longed for Frank! If only he could have lived. Well, there was his baby to consider now. Soon she would let Mary Frances go with her to see the doctor—a woman doctor? Well, as good as a midwife, Mary Frances said.

Chapter Five

Dr. Elizabeth Blackwell sat in a chair by the window and looked out on the street through lace curtains. Since setting up her private practice of medicine, she had hoped for more patients. She knew so many needed her services, but they seemed to prefer illness and even death to being treated by a woman doctor. When she walked the streets people yelled at her calling her "abortionist," "mesmerist" "clairvoyant" or even, "harlot." The rejection and hostility was often like that she experienced when she was applying for medical school.

She remembered hearing it was impossible for girls to learn difficult subjects. Women's brains, they said, were simply too small to learn the difficult studies.

"Nonesense!" her father had exclaimed. She could hear him in that argument almost as clearly as if she were hearing his voice now. Well, thanks to dear father, she had been tutored the same as her brothers. He was a man apart from others—even his own father, who thought girls need not be educated—in fact, that they *should* not be, as it was "folderol." The boys, Grandfather had declared must be educated as they must earn money. But dear Father saw far beyond that. How she wished that he could. How proud he would have been! The thought lifted her spirits, but she wished with all her heart he could have lived to witness it. They seemed to be of the same spirit and she knew she was his favorite child.

The rejections she had received in the community seemed only worse now that she was a qualified physician. Elizabeth knew her landlady was ashamed to have her there and might at any time ask her to leave. She would move if she must, but she would not give up her hard won battle to practice medicine.

She thought of the long, jarring carriage ride to Ash-ville, North Carolina, to work as a music teacher to earn money to study medicine. How weary she had been! But that night she'd known the turning point. From her bedroom window she had looked out at the dark mountains feeling discouraged and questioning her course. She remembered how frightened and desperate she had felt that night crying out loud in desperation, "Christ Jesus, help me!"

Never would she forget the great peace that flooded her then. A deep conviction came over her as to the rightness of her course and never since had it changed. Whatever happened, she knew from that moment on that she would never give up.

Well, today there had not been a single patient to darken her door. She was about to leave her chair and prepare herself a small lunch when Mary Frances and Sally knocked on her door. She greeted them with a smile. "Do come in," she said.

"I brung you a patient," Mary Frances announced.

"I see. Please, sit down." She gestured toward a couch near the chair where she had been sitting. She took her chair again. "How may I help you?"

Sally sat on the end of a couch close to the doctor. "I'm expecting a baby in months...July or August, I believe. I would like you to deliver it. That is, if I can afford your charges."

"Don't worry about the charges," Dr. Blackwell said. "If you can afford to pay, that will be fine. If not, I still will be happy to care for you."

"You are most kind," Sally said, "but I can afford to pay a small fee."

"Very well. Let me examine you."

When the examination was finished, Dr. Blackwell laid a gentle hand on Sally's shoulder. "Eat as well as you can, get your rest and as much fresh air as you can for your sake and the sake of your unborn child. I realize that may not be easy, but do what you can and come back to see me in a month."

Sally saw such gentleness in the doctor's face that she felt immediately comforted.

When they left the office, Sally said, "I like her very much."

"It don't bother ye none then that she's a woman callin' herself a doctor?" Mary Frances asked. "Not big and strong like a man neither. See how little she is? Not more'n five feet, I'd wager."

"I don't mind that she's small. She is a doctor. Didn't you see her diploma on the wall?"

"Oh, well that was jest a piece of paper with writin' on it," Mary Frances said, "Don't make her a real doctor like a man. Still, I reckon' she's as good as a mid-wife."

Sally looked at Mary Frances and frowned, realizing now that her friend probably couldn't read. She was sorry about that. Sally felt fortunate that she could read and had indeed read many books provided for her by her father out of his old bookcase--all of which she had to leave behind in Ireland. The thought of it saddened her anew. Even if she could get back to Ireland some day, how could she ever find that great old bookcase or any of the books her father once held in his dear hands?

***

Next day Sally found her way to the sewing factories, but each time the boss heard her Irish accent, she was turned away. Some took a look at her auburn hair and her lightly freckled face and turned her away before they heard her voice. Had they decided she was Irish before she spoke? She knew plenty Irish women had white skin and black hair. Well, maybe it was because she was so thin they could see she was pregnant.

At the first factory, an obese boss man with a cigar stuffed in the corner of his mouth, said, "Get yer sewing cloth and make the shirts. We don't fool with no Irish."

Mary Frances had told her about sewing the shirts, but that it was hard work and paid very little. She fought tears. It was so unfair!

A small black haired woman whispered to Sally as she

47

was leaving the sewing floor at one of the factories, "Some rich women hires Irish maids. You'd live in a fine house day and night."

"Thank you," Sally said. She smiled at the woman.

"No talking!" The boss man hollered. "No talking!"

Sally passed a place where she could apply as a maid, but decided against it. How could she live day and night away from Emily? And then when the baby came—no, she couldn't do that. She'd buy the cloth and make the shirts at least for now. Maybe if she worked really hard there would be enough money to survive.

Before she left the work district, she entered a dingy building to apply to sew at home. A thin elderly man with watery, squinting eyes studied her but he observed her kindly.

"I need to work. I want to sew at home. Could I--?"

"Ye pays a dollar for checked cloth, but that sewing can be hard on yer eyes. Two dollars buys the solid colors."

"I have two dollars," Sally said, "and thank you for telling me."

"Now here's how ye makes the shirts," the old man said showing her the pattern. "Bring 'em back in when ye finishes and I'll pay the going rate." He took her money with an unsteady hand, reached inside the counter and brought out a package of green cloth.

Chapter Six

Henry Bray reappeared daily to bring Sally and Emily water. While he did not embrace Sally again, he made many remarks about liking tall, slender women with auburn hair. "Like ye," he'd say. Once he reached to cover Sally's hand with his, but she quickly withdrew it and turned aside to attend to the small chore of folding a cloth.

"Aye," he said, "ye're a shy one. I like shy ladies. They're the best when ye do git their notice."

Sally felt like crying. Why wouldn't he leave her alone? She knew she would so hate to lose the friendship and companionship of Mary Frances and Michael Finn, but after the baby was born, she needed to seek another place to live? But how? The very thought of it upset her. Where could she go with so little money? What would other neighbors be like? Many seemed so coarse and there was always much drinking of the pints.

The months passed somehow. The heat and oppressive smells of late June made it difficult for Sally to keep up her strength by eating enough. She wished for the birth of her child, but not before time. She'd seen the tiny ones who didn't live.

The months passed and late summer came at last. On August 19th the pains began. She took Emily by hand and went to Mary France's flat. She tried to walk without showing the pains in an effort not to upset Emily, but twice she had to lean against a wall and hold her stomach until the pains eased away.

The moment Sally appeared Mary Frances said, "Oh, I see ye needs me, Sally. Uncle Mike can take care of the child while I fetch the doctor fer ye."

Emily looked at her mother questioningly. "Ma are you sick?"

"No, honey, not sick, but well—you'll understand later. For now stay with Uncle Mike for a while."

"We'll play some games and she'll likely beat this old man." He smiled at her, tousled her hair lightly, then reached for a scarred board bearing red and green playing pieces. "Here," he said, "let me get us set up."

Out in the hallway Mary Frances said, "Do ye think ye can make it? Ye looks awful pale?"

***

As soon as Dr. Blackwell arrived she directed Mary Frances to be careful about cleanliness. "Please, madam," the doctor said. "do wash your hands with soap and water and then bring me some clean cloths."

"I will for sure, Ma'am," Mary Frances said. "Sally told me jest where she laid them. A neat, clean one she is. Fussy I'd say but maybe better fussy than some ye see about. All 'round here knows your preachin' on it, ma'am. Some laughs about it. I reckon ye know that."

Dr. Blackwell glanced at her, but made no reply.

Sally wanted to say, "Don't say that to the doctor," but she held her tongue. She thought Mary Frances is not a mean spirited person. She just doesn't understand. I know she laughs at me sometimes.

Dr. Blackwell smiled and laid her hand on Sally's. "We are right," she said.

Due to Sally's undernourished condition the birth was difficult. The doctor stayed in constant attendance, patiently comforting her. Hours later in the small dingy apartment a tiny baby girl was born. "I'll name her Elizabeth after you, doctor," Sally said. "She's a wee one like you and beautiful as you are."

"I'm honored Mrs. McKelvy, but I've never been beautiful—a colorless blonde as you can see, but your child has soft, dark ringlets and a perfect face. She truly is beautiful."

"Those curls. She looks much like her father. I'm so grateful. But I see beauty in you, Dr. Blackwell. I hope my Elizabeth will be like you."

"My dear lady, perhaps you should not wish her life to

be as mine has been thus far," Dr. Blackwell said, and quickly changed the subject. "You have another daughter, I understand," she said. "An Emily. I have a younger sister named Emily, but we call her 'Milly.'"

"Is she a doctor, too?"

"Not yet, but I hope she will be and then join me in my practice. I come from a large family and I feel lonely when I'm apart from them for very long," Dr. Blackwell said.

"I also had a good family, Doctor, only most are dead now. I have only some distant cousins back in Ireland if indeed they are still alive," Sally said.

"I hope they are, my dear. A good family is such a blessing. I have a little daughter—a child I adopted from the orphanage," she said. "And now you have two daughters. I trust they'll be a blessing to you."

Dr. Blackwell collected her black bag and prepared to leave. "Get some rest now. I will check on you later, and in a few days I'll send a friendly visitor to check on you."

When the doctor was gone, Mary Frances, who had remained quiet except to assist Dr. Blackwell as needed with hot water and towels, said, "She's a friendly one. Not a bit stand-offish."

"She's a good woman," Sally said. "A very good woman."

Within a few hours, Dr. Blackwell unexpectedly returned. "You're going to be all right," she said, "but I want you to eat more to regain your strength. I brought you some soup made with chicken and potatoes."

Mary Frances' eyes widened. "I heard she took food sometimes to folks, but now I seen it with me own eyes."

Later, when Emily first saw her baby sister, she said, "She's too little! I want a sister who can play with me."

Mary Frances laughed. "She'll grow into a little girleen. Probably be big as you one day."

***

Two days later, the friendly visitor, appeared as promised. She said her name was Nancy Evans and that she had recently come to New York from England. She looked around and commented, "I see I don't need to talk with you about cleanliness, except perhaps I should mention the boiling of water. A gentleman in England, named John Snow, believes that diseases like cholera may be the result of contaminated water and we are seeing cholera increasing here once again."

"I didn't know that," Sally said, "I mean about the water, but I've been boiling it because I hated the smell of it. I drop a little vinegar in it as well to help the taste."

Nancy Evans smiled. "Not a bad idea. She paused then added, "Diseases like cholera are to be avoided. People who contract it may seem well, but then begin terrible vomiting and gushing diarrhea many even dying within hours. Do keep boiling the water. It could save you and your girls."

"I boil the water I wash our clothes in--well, for the same reason. I don't like our clothes to smell dirty."

"Your neighbors must think that odd."

"Some do. They call me 'fancy woman,' but I don't think they mean to be unkind."

Some days later, when Sally was well enough to be up and around, she resumed her at-home sewing of shirts. Month after month Sally carefully put away a few coins. She hoped within four years to have savings enough to seek better housing, but unexpected expenses occurred. Sometimes the girls would become ill, or she herself. Always, they visited Dr. Blackwell and Sally insisting upon paying a just fee, which although small, diminished her savings. She raised her goal to move to a better area in five years.

Chapter Seven

While Sally had many reasons to desire other living quarters one reason was to avoid Henry Bray. Although, Henry made some cautious advances, she always found a way to avoid him until one day when he suggested she could keep the rent money if "We might nap a bit together. I could visit after the girls are asleep and we could—could cuddle a bit."

Sally flushed with anger at his crude approach. Forgetting her intention to remain calm and in control, she shouted at him. "Leave me alone, Henry Bray! I'll tell Mary Frances of your crude attempts to seduce me if you try it just once more. You miserable man! I can't stand the sight of you any longer!"

"No need for the tellin'," Henry said taking a few steps backward. "I jest thought ye might be a bit lonely for the lovin' of a man."

"I'm not, but if I were, it wouldn't be with another woman's husband."

Henry's visits after that were brief. He stood barely inside the door to collect the rent money and was gone. She sighed. Now she realized that when she had said little, he had believed his manly charms were enough to eventually win her over. She felt angry with herself for not standing up to him earlier.

Sally believed the problem of Bray's advances was solved. If only her finances would improve! She so wanted to bring some security and happiness into her children's lives.

On a walk some distance from her neighborhood, Sally met up with a gentle elderly woman who was herself taking a stroll. She immediately liked the dumpy, little Irish woman whose smile was wide and whose middle shook when she laughed.

"Mary O'Sullivan I am," the woman said. "I was a

teacher but now I'm past that, left with my memories. Good memories mostly, yet—well, we all have our problems. We do."

"Yes," Sally said. "Sometimes we forget to consider blessings. I have two beautiful little girls."

"Aye, I've always loved children. Would you care to visit and tell me about them? Don't live far from here and we could have some tea and cakes."

***

At Mrs. O'Sullivans' neat house Sally relaxed. "This is so nice. I wish I could afford to move to this neighborhood, but I can't—not just yet anyway."

While telling the kindly lady of Emily and Elizabeth, the retired teacher offered to lend Sally books. She assisted her in choosing for Emily's education as well as for her pleasure, and then selected picture books for Elizabeth.

In studying the shelves of books Sally felt a rush of joy. "Books my father had back in Ireland! Well, not his, but ones he used to read to me."

"Then," Mrs. O'Sullivan said, "Take and enjoy the reading."

"I thank you," Sally said. "I will certainly return them in good condition."

***

Back in her tiny apartment, Sally opened the borrowed book of old Irish tales her father had read to her. She could almost hear her father's voice. She remembered his salt-and-pepper beard, his full head of white hair and his bright blue eyes. He had laughed at some old tales she barely understood when she was a wee one, but she was glad that he re-read them when she was older and could laugh with him.

"Aye," he would say, "laugh, little one. Laugh. It's like a fine tonic, it 'tis."

***

On the first day of October Mary Frances and Michael came to Sally's apartment. Both were smiling.

Mary Frances said, "We have a little surprise for ye, Sally. We rented a small wagon and a horse to take us out of the city for a day in the fresh air of the country."

"We want you and the girls to go with us," Michael said. "No cost. We'll be treatin' ye."

"Oh," Sally said. "How generous of you! Fresh air and the country! Why Elizabeth has never even seen a rural area and she's four years old."

"Ye needs the rest, Sally," Mary Frances said, "and we can all use the lovely countryside."

"But won't that cost too much?" Sally asked.

"Not so much. We do have a bit of savings from the rent and we want ye to do this," Mary Frances said.

Sally crossed her chest with both hands. "Oh, it would be heavenly, but I need to work every hour I can."

"Oh, Sally," Mary Frances cried, "think of the girls if not of yourself. But if it will make you feel better take a little sewing with ye that ye can do sitting by the lake on the green. A bench was there and likely still is."

Sally embraced Mary Frances. "Bless you, dear friend," she said, "and you too, Uncle Mike," she added glancing in his direction. "We'll go. We'll go!"

***

Uncle Mike drove the rig up just after dawn for their trip to the countryside. Although it was barely daylight, Sally heard the raucous laughter of prostitutes and drunken men in the streets. Grunting pigs scurried about and dogs barked and howled. The stench of rotting garbage made Sally thankful to be leaving the Five Points if only for a day and what a blessing for her children! If she could find better housing she would move but she would sorely miss Uncle Mike and Mary Frances.

Emily and Elizabeth promptly went to sleep to finish out their night's nap in the wagon bed on an old quilt Sally had brought. Neither appeared disturbed by sounds around them as Uncle Mike drove the wagon down the street.

"I've only been to the countryside once before," Mary Frances said, "and that was of a springtime. Never seen the fall colors so I'm a lookin' forward to them now that its October."

"I'm wantin' the harvest fruits—yellow pears for sure. Aye, will be a good day," Michael said.

"A little gray wooden store is there what sells 'em and other things—some bread and cheese for our picnic by the lake."

"Is it like Ireland?" Sally asked eagerly.

"No, but it's a lovely place with trees and flowers—yes, and butterflies and birds. Ye'll love it." Mary Frances said, "And oh the glorious fresh air! The fresh, clean air. Ye'll want to breathe and breathe it in with joy."

**

When the morning sun rose bright and warm and a cool breeze ruffled their clothing, Emily and Elizabeth woke, sat up rubbing their eyes of sleep and looked all around. Sally smiled at them. "See girls, the city is vanishing back of us. We're on our way to the country for our picnic. You can play in the fields where there probably are flowers to gather and maybe see butterflies and hear birds singing."

"Is it Da's America?" Emily asked.

"What's Da's America?" Elizabeth asked.

"A wonderful place where there's everything and lots of jam."

Mary Frances laughed. "Well, I'm not sure about the jam."

"It's part of what Frank told Emily we'd find in America," Sally explained.

They grew silent. Sally thought each adult must be remembering their lovely homeland, and remembering how

56

they'd found America. Maybe somewhere a Da's America flourished. Perhaps, someday her children would find it even if she never could.

***

Later during their picnic by the lake, Sally watched her laughing children running about trying to catch little yellow butterflies. Yes, this was what Frank would have loved. This part was at least a little Da's America! Emily ran through red and gold leaves, scattering them and laughing for joy. Sally watched her and delighted in her pleasure.

As if she'd read Sally's thoughts, Emily cried, "Ma, we've found Da's America! Oh, Ma can we move here?"

"I wish so my darling, but I must work and there's no jobs for me here."

"I'll help you. I've watched you sew. I'm twelve now. I can help."

Sally smiled. "I'm afraid we still could not make it, not yet anyway."

"Do show me, Ma. I want to sew with you."

"Very well, but I can't promise we could live here. We'll see. We'll see what we can do."

Chapter Eight

Autumn and winter passed and early spring came with occasional warming days taking the chill from the area. The prosperous areas of the city began to show colorful shrubs and flowers, and an occasional brave jonquil dared to poke its self through grassy areas of the slum. But the rain...there had been too much rain.

***

An early morning rain in Five Points washed down the rickety settlement, but it was a hopeless cleaning, like the whisking of dust from a grimy coat. The lanes and alleyways had been worsened by the gurgling water. Deep oozing mud made walking from one building to another almost impossible.

Elizabeth sat alone on the stoop of the decaying tenement waiting for Ma and Emily. Soft dark curls framed her pretty face and topped the collar of her faded blue dress. Her black high-top shoes were cracked and turned up at the toes, too big yet for her feet. She wrinkled her nose against the stench of seeping sewers and privies, now made worse by heat of the early afternoon sun. Small ponds of black water clung to the curbs of the street in front of her. When a horse-drawn cart clacked by, wary pedestrians quickly jumped back to avoid being splashed. Elizabeth laughed.

"Elizabeth," Sally said, coming near her, adjusting the flimsy cord basket on her arm, "we're ready to go now."

"Yes, Ma," Elizabeth said, but she didn't move. She knew there was still waiting to be done. Emily had not appeared.

"I declare," Ma said, "it's almost like a disease—being thirteen."

Elizabeth had seen Emily gazing at her reflection in their small, dim mirror, turning this way and that, smiling and fingering her long auburn hair, until Ma would grow impatient and call out, "Emily McKelvy, do come on!" Today they would take a wagon to the Italian street market to buy fresh vegetables and fish, too if they could afford it. There was some money. Sally and Emily had turned in the sewing.

Sally had quickly learned to keep back two dollars for a deposit on solid-colored flannel. Once when she had no money for a deposit, she had to sew the checked material and found the eyestrain and lower pay such punishment she vowed never to let it happen again.

In one of her many little lessons to Emily, Mama said, "Remember, if we can't buy the solid material to make the shirts, we have to sew the checked cloth. Less money and harder. Now, Emily do remember that, honey."

"Yes, Ma. I will."

Lately, Sally worried more about preparing Emily in case something should happen to her. Not that she was ill but she knew many were and some were speaking of the growing spread of cholera.

Sally thought of Frank. How she missed him even after more than seven years. If only he were here! She would feel so much more secure. She cherished the memory of his saying he loved her rosy face and gray-blue eyes "glorious with your bonny orange curls." She'd protested her hair was not orange, but blond struck with fire and he'd best watch out! Him and his teasing, and that full-of-fun laughter that was so much a part of his personality! At night she longed for the warmth of his body next to hers and their joyful love making which would never be again. Sometimes she dreamed of him so clearly that her disappointment was overwhelming when she awoke.

Just before Sally meant to call Emily again she appeared in the doorway...a tall girl, and sturdy for her age. Still with her wide dark eyes and turned-up nose she somehow appeared younger than her years. "Do I look suitable, Ma?"

"Yes, of course. We're not going to church, only to the

market." Sally said, but then realized that Emily wanted to hear something else. "You look pretty, Emily. You're a very pretty girl and a good girl. I'm proud of you," she said and reached out to give her a hug.

Sally said. "I see the wagon coming. Come on let's get down to the curb."

When the wagon arrived, it was crowded with other Irish passengers going to various places on the driver's route as usual.

Sally and Emily sat in the last vacant seat, and squeezed the petite Elizabeth in between them. Again the corpulent Mrs. Peake covered most of the seat in front of them. Sally had hoped to avoid her on this trip, but there she was, arms folded and pompadored head held high. Apparently, her feelings for Sally indicated dislike as well."Hummp!" she grunted when she saw Sally.

"Good morning," Sally said and several passengers responded to her friendly greeting. "I see you're still riding with us, Mrs. Peake," Sally said.

"My last time," Mrs. Peake said. "I'm getting my carriage any day now."

Another passenger, a thin lady who sat besides Mrs. Peake said, "Well deserved I'd say. Mrs. Peake does such Christian work gathering up the starving children and sending them on the train to loving families."

"Yes, I do what I can and I must say I've learned to be good at it. I can within minutes know a good young'un from the urchin."

"But," Sally said, "perhaps the more spirited child needs a chance as well...if indeed sending them out west to strangers is a worthy plan."

"If? If?," the thin lady asked. "Haven't you seen the ragged ones who eat of the garbage?"

"We all have," Sally said, "but I wish for much better planning than I understand is done. Who knows what a child may face at the hands of strangers? I've heard unfortunate ones are used to toil long hours in fields and beaten. Others are used in unspeakable ways. Some boys have even struggled back to The Points to tell of such cruelty."

"Oh," Mrs. Peake said, "You know so little about it, Sally McKelvy, better you should keep your opinions to yourself. The few who have drifted back from the west telling stories were no doubt troublemakers who were of criminal minds. Now they steal and rob honest people at every chance."

The thin lady defendant said, "Most anything can be better than eating garbage and sleeping huddled in doorways with other little ragged ones. Yes, 'tis a fine, Christian work she does. And so many are taken into loving homes where they are treated like birth children."

"For those I am glad," Sally said. "If only more could be known about the strangers."

"We do know of some of them," Mrs. Peake said, "but everything can't be done your way. I know what I'm doing and I don't require any advice from the likes of you, Sally McKelvy, who only knows how to handle a needle and sew shirts."

A number of voices arose in protest from the other women who sewed for a living.

Mrs. Peake said, "I grant you, what you do is honest work, but as I said earlier, I'll soon be leaving you to each other's company. I'll ride in my carriage."

One angry woman near the front started for Mrs. Peake but was restrained by the driver. "No more, me ladies, no more," he said.

***

Near dark, when their shopping was done, they picked up the sewing for their next work and joined the other wagon passengers. Not far into their trip several passengers cried out. In the near disctance, too close for comfort, they saw smoke drifting toward the skyline and creeping fires covering a whole block. Sally pulled her daughters close to her side. Oh again, the angry Irish and the freed Negro slaves were fighting with clubs, with thrown objects, with any weapon at hand. They fought over jobs lost and jobs taken. The driver drew the wagon aside on an adjoining street, but still they heard the cries of the angry men and saw struggling silhouettes as shop and store one after another was ignited into a rush of flames. They could see the reeling carts, drays and lone figures staggering, pushing wheelbarrows piled high with loot. The fighting and the bloodshed sickened Sally. *If only they could find a way to share; to care about each other!*

"Emily, dear," Sally whispered,"keep as far away as possible from the fighting."

"Me, too, Ma?" Elizabeth asked.

"Oh, yes, darling, you too," Sally said pulling her close and kissing the top of her head.

Chapter Nine

Three days after Sally's trip to the market, Henry Bray came to Sally's apartment saying that Mary Frances was very sick.

"She pours the foul vomit and stink water from her intestiments. Like a storm—oh, I can't tell ye how bad it 'tis." His face was flushed and she saw tears standing in his eyes. "Could ye help?" he asked.

Sally paled. Cholera! She remembered the nurse visitor had said the vomit and diarrhea was like water gushing from a gutter. "She needs a doctor," Sally said. "Get Dr. Blackwell."

His face grew red in anger. "That woman who says she's a doctor? I wouldn't think ye being a friend of Mary's would say such a thing."

"She delivered Elizabeth. I trust her completely," Sally said. "Do go to her. It may be your dear wife's only chance. Please--."

"A mannish woman, I'd bet ye. No, I'll ask about for some decent lady," he said and stomped out.

Sally felt dismayed knowing he was refusing the best possible help for Mary Frances. Also, she was puzzled. With all his flirting, he really loved Mary Frances. Well, men could be so hard to understand in their ways with women. She put aside her sewing and went to see about her friend.

In the hallway near Mary Frances' flat, the stench of vomit and excrement assailed her. She cupped her hand over her nose and gasped. "Oh, God!" she whispered, "This is terrible. Poor Mary Frances!"

Michael Finn met her at the door. "Don't come in, Sally. Ye might come down, too, me dear. I'm sure she has the cholera. It's raging the neighborhood again."

Sally stood in the doorway. She wanted to comfort Mary Frances and to help her but she was afraid to risk her health. What would happen to Emily and Elizabeth? She backed away but she would help. She would prepare and bring food every day--an expense that would leave little for her and her girls, but enough so they would not go hungry.

The next day, no one answered her knocking. Sally opened the door to look inside. She saw now that both Mary Frances and Michael Finn were bedfast. She called to them softly at first and then louder. Mary Frances made no response, but Michael whispered, "She's gone, Sally. Soon I shall be, too. Don't come in ye might—."

"Are you saying she's dead?" Sally felt prickles of fear and pain on her face. How could this be? Only yesterday she had seen Mary Frances alive—sick but alive.

"I can't be sure, and yet I am," Michael said, "She hasn't moved all day and she was greatly miserable last night."

"I'm so sorry! I can't tell you how sorry I am. She was my best friend," Sally cried. She saw he wept and focused her attention on him. "Who is caring for you, Uncle Mike?"

"Henry comes and goes and he brought an old woman to tidy up."

"Are you hungry? I brought some soup."

"No. I have no appetite. Well, I'm an old man so it's expected if I go, but Mary Frances...." He choked on his tears.

Two days later Mary Frances' body was removed and a week later, Michael Finn's. Once more Sally grieved. Once more she felt alone and now concerned about the spreading cholera. She kept herself, Emily and Elizabeth inside as much as possible. She prayed they would not contract the horrible disease. If they did would they, like some very few people, manage to survive.

The day she expected Henry to come for the rent another man came. He said he was a cousin, "James William," he said. He bore some resemblance to Henry having the red hair and manly build, but with his long jaw line he was not as handsome.

"Henry has the sickness," he said, "so I'll be taking over."

"The cholera?" Sally asked.

"Yes. Ye know it's all around in the Points. Mary Frances...."

"Yes," Sally said, "I know. She was a wonderful friend. I miss her very much."

"Henry, he's a tough one, but I don't know...."

"Some few overcome it, but only a few," Sally said. She wished he would leave. The talk was disturbing. She felt increasing fear in thinking what could happen to Emily and Elizabeth and herself.

"Down the way from here on Orange Street it's the worst," James William continued. "Aye, the worst of all. I've seen 'em bent with the leg cramps. They says they is freezin' cold and they starts turnin' blue and they skin falls against they bones as they cry. 'Tis a pitiful sight. On my way, I saw two small boys lyin' dead in the road—not more'n five or six years old, I would say." He shook his head. "Some say it's because they is bad people, but the little boys? No, I don't think so."

"Neither do I," Sally said. "It's the terrible lack of everything--of good food and clean water and there's so much filth."

"Aye, 'tis true. They eats the spoiled pig's meat—eats anything and drinks what water they can come by even if the color ain't right."

Sally thought *now in America we see the city leaders and the wealthy hold back giving but little help—sometimes none at all—like in Ireland.* She thought of Mary Frances and Michael Finn who might still be alive had the city done more in the Five Points. Tears collected on her eyelashes.

When she spoke no more, the man tipped his cap and went on his way.

The deaths continued...bodies being collected from the pathetic basement rooms with dirt floors, in the street, on stairs—anywhere. The sudden death came to both young and old. As usual, pigs and dogs ran in the whole district, and now hundreds of rats as well. But some of it was fortunate. After the scows unloaded bodies in the city cemetery on

Randal's Island the dead were laid in a wide trench, one body on top of another only a foot or two below the surface. Thousands of rats swarmed each day to devour the bodies before the odor of their putrefaction could infect the city.

Eventually, the tide of cholera subsided although other chronic diseases troubled and destroyed many of the residents of Five Points. Sally felt safer staying in much of the time and besides her days were filled with the sewing. Still, she felt lonely having lost Mary Frances and Michael. Even neighbors she knew only casually had lost their lives in the terrible epidemic. The tenement now was filled almost totally with new residents. She wanted friends, but she needed to work hard, long hours to survive and to put pennies aside for savings. Only now and then did she feel she could spare a moment to chat with anyone, and none did she find as warm and caring as Mary Frances and Michael.

Weeks and months passed. Sally's world was a small circle that included Emily, Elizabeth and her sewing. She made time to read to Elizabeth and study with Emily.

"You are a fast learner," Sally said as she happily watched Emily study on her own many times during each day.

"Now let me sew more, Ma." Emily said, "I know I can do it. Then we can make more money and move to Da's America."

***

Six years from the time she arrived in Five Points passed, and still Sally found no way to move from the slum. She was, however, at least grateful they had escaped the cholera.

Happily, now and then because Sally carefully saved for it, they revisited the rural area Emily called "Da's America."

"When can we move here?" Emily asked.

"Oh, honey, I don't know that we ever can move here, but we'll visit as often as possible. Your sewing has made it possible a bit more often." Sally kissed Emily's cheek. "You're a good girl, Emily. I'm very proud of you."

"Are you, Ma?"

"Oh, yes, my darling. Very proud."

"Me too?" Elizabeth asked.

"You, too," Sally said picking Elizabeth up and kissing her cheek as well.

They breathed in the fresh country air of springtime and never wanted to leave. Emily and Elizabeth gathered wild flowers and again chased small yellow butterflies. Sally watched them and delighted in their pleasures. At a nearby small café they sipped cool lemonade.

Back in the dismal slums they still talked of their trips. Bright flowers decorated the table after each visit. The collections were kept as long as possible as a delightful reminder.

***

Something occurred that Sally never expected to happen again. The last visit at the Italian market she saw a man—a handsome man with curly chestnut hair and dark eyes. A man like frank but different, too--darker with high cheekbones. She thought she must speak to him to at least hear his voice. Her heart was pounding as she approached him.

"Yes, young lady, could I help you?" No familiar accent. Of course he was not Irish. Of course he was not Frank. 'Young lady,' he had said. Sally smiled. She had not felt young. Was thirty young to him or did she look younger? She thought she was being foolish, but her feelings reminded her of the first time she saw Frank. Love at first sight some said but, she'd been only sixteen then. Surely she was being ridiculous, but somehow it was good to feel this way. She'd forgotten how exciting it was to be in love.

"Maybe some pasta?" he asked.

"Oh, yes. A little," she said.

He smiled at her. "A little? This much?" he asked

67

gathering a small bunch of it.

"Yes. Yes, that will be fine."

Nothing more happened, but she thought of him all week. Was there any possibility he would feel attracted to her? She would try to get his attention in some gentle way. At the thought he could turn a cold face to her she moaned. Oh, no! *Sally, Sally* she whispered *you are as taken as you were at sixteen!* Well, she remembered Ma speaking of a sixty-year old woman behaving like a young girl 'floating on a cloud' when she fell in love again. Maybe then it was not so unusual at thirty. Still, it was her secret. Who could she tell anyway now that Mary Frances was gone? Then, belately, she wondered if he were married. Why hadn't she considered that possibility? All her dreams would suddenly crash. She thought she probably would be unable to put him out of her mind. It was a troubling thought and dashed her lighthearted moment.

***

Today they would go back to the markets. Sally washed her hair and was pleased to see her red curls fall softly in place around her face. For the first time she was glad for the sprinkling of a few freckles across her nose and cheeks. She hoped it made up for the otherwise lack of color in her face.

A few minutes later, she picked up her shopping basket and prepared to leave. Observing that Emily was dressing, she waited a moment and then walked from the room. From her window in the kitchen she could see Elizabeth sitting on the stoop below. Sally smiled. She knew Elizabeth hoped for something interesting to see while she waited. Such a curious child, always alert and trying to be independent beyond her years. "I'll do it myself!" she'd exclaim when Sally attempted to help tie her shoes or button her dress. So persistent. Sometimes she had to make many attempts to solve a problem but she often was eventually successful. When she failed she would stamp her feet and break into tears but she would try again. Sally found that behavior distressing and frustrating but at the same time she admired her child's persistence.

Emily had not been so determined to do for herself, but she was an eager learner all the same. Sally felt blessed and proud of her daughters.

While she waited Sally thought of the man at the Italian market. She didn't even know his name. Maybe if she could find out without being too obvious, she might learn if he had a wife. Such a handsome man with that warm smile... certainly other women were attracted. She sighed heavily. There was probably no way she could win him even if he were single, but thoughts of him lifted her spirits and make her feel more alive.

Sally called to Emily, "Hurry, little girleen. The market wagon will soon be coming."

"Ma, I'm not little," Emily responded. "I'm thirteen now."

"Barely," Sally said, "You are little. You just don't know it yet. Wait until you're an old woman of thirty."

"I'm coming," Emily said but still she tarried.

"Do hurry Emily. You look just fine."

Sally felt a touch of guilt for speaking in an impatient tone, now that she again found herself primping more for the trip to the market. In thinking of Emily's growing maturity, Sally wondered for the first time about her daughter's future romances. Who in this miserable Five Points would be suitable? She must somehow manage to move into a better place, and soon, but how? How with so little means? In her preoccupation, she barely heard the wagon approaching.

"Ma, the wagon," Emily cried as she ran to join them.

The creaking old wagon was crowded with other Irish passengers going to various places on the driver's route.

Sally would have preferred to avoid seeing Mrs. Peake, but there she was again sitting on the same seat in the wagon. Apparently she had not yet been able to buy her carriage. She turned and nodded her head. "I see you're dragging your girls off to that terrible market again." she said. "Sally McKelvy, you know very well the Italians don't like us."

69

"Ah, well," Sally said, "each little village is so distrusting of the other. 'Tis a shame."

Mrs. Peake lifted her chin. "The Dutch, the Germans we may understand, but the Italians! Not a serious bone in their bodies. All that shouting and arm waving. And celebrating! They celebrate when better they should be weeping."

"A little joy may not be so bad, Mrs. Peake. We have sadness and death enough for all of us."

"Hummph!" Mrs. Peake folded her fat arms and turned around in her seat.

An elegant black carriage crossed the road as they neared the markets.

A skinny woman in a gray dress ripped in the shoulder said, "I thought you wuz buying yerself a carriage."

"I am, indeed," Mrs. Peake said and lifted her chin in a superior gesture. "Very soon now."

Emily whispered to her mother. "She takes up boys and girls for that Orphans' Train West."

"I know," Sally said.

"Ma, not just the doorway sleepers, but others, too. They say she makes more if she gets contacts out west to pay her for 'hand picked' servant girls."

Sally felt a chill. She didn't trust the woman. Some people thought her spending time with poor young girls was dear of her, and generous when she brought gifts, but Sally believed it was in some way self-serving. Some of the girls had disappeared. No one knew if they ran away, were encouraged to leave or were kidnapped. Sally heard that some of the parents were distressed, but others seemed relieved to be free of supporting an older child. It was hard to understand. Sally knew she would be overwhelmed with grief at the loss of her own, and she'd never give up searching for a child of hers. Still, she realized she didn't have the depth of problems many had. She had come to America with some funds and had found a job that at least kept them fed and a roof over their heads, such as it was.

When they arrived at the markets, Sally tried to put

aside her worries. She smoothed her face with her hands and lifted her hair to fluff her curls. Within minutes she was inside the Italian market. In a quick glance around she did not see the handsome man anywhere, and felt a pang of disappointment.

A large, older Italian man called out, "Tony, be-a quick. Your babe is-a here." So Tony was his name! She saw him then stand up from where he had been unpacking cabbage.

"All right. Be there soon as I finish this."

Sally saw a slender, dark-eyed girl holding a little boy of possibly two years of age. Her heart sank. Of course, he was married. Or was he? He certainly was much older than this young woman. Could it be his sister? No, the man said 'your babe.' The little boy? She had to know.

"Is this pretty girl his wife?" she asked the obese older Italian.

"His? Who 'his' ?"

"The one you called Tony," she said.

"No, is-a his daughter. You like-a Tony?" He asked and spread his arms, "All-a the ladies like-a Tony." Then to Sally's complete embarrassment, he called out, "Hey, Tony—another one." He laughed. His big body shook and he nodded his head, "Another one."

"I--I," Sally stammered.

"Yeah, you like-a him. Pretty fellow." He slapped both hands on his round belly. "A good fellow like-a me, you don't-a want. All you see-a is the outside." He stooped and whispered, "Good-a on the inside. I'm-a good on the inside."

Sally saw some other shoppers who had been on the wagon were listening. What could she do? She said the first thing that came to mind although it was not true, "I didn't come to see him. I came to tell—tell him the pasta was not what I expected. I want a replacement."

"Tony!" he called, "your babe is here."

"I know. I'm coming, Ramon."

"You not capture a hundred percent-a, brother. This lady only wants-a-pasta—not-a you." Ramon laughed, nodding his head. "Maybe she's-a smarter."

71

"Papa," the pretty dark-haired girl called, "never mind. I'll see you at home."

"All right, Babe," Tony said.

Sally walked quickly to the back of the market where Tony was finishing unloading the cabbages.

"I'm sorry," she said. "I...well, I was not truthful about the pasta. I...."

He smiled. "Sorry, my brother embarrassed you. Ramon likes to tease."

"Thank you," Sally said. "I'm surprised you are brothers. You seem nothing alike."

"He was raised in the old country but I was born here." He said. "My mother was American so I do speak differently."

"I see." Sally dropped her gaze and studied her fingers. "Well, I must be going. My children are waiting."

"And your husband?" he asked.

"My husband was murdered on the ship coming to America," she said and added, "That was almost eight years ago."

"Murdered?" He laid a gentle hand on her shoulder. "I'm sorry."

Tears blurred her vision.

"I understand the loss," he said. "My wife, Carolina, died in childbirth with our second child. I will never marry again. Never." Sally thought there was both sorrow and determination in his voice. She rubbed the tears from her eyes with the back of her hands and turned quickly away.

***

One of the wheels came loose from the old wagon necessitating a repair job and a delay for the driver in returning his passengers home. Some passengers went into stores to shop, but Sally simply waited with Emily and Elizabeth on a bench outside the market. She hoped Tony would come to say something more; to offer her some kind of clue that he might change his mind about marriage. She saw him gather his coat and place a cap on his head—a Greek fisherman's cap similar to Frank's and then he left through a back door.

***

Near dark another wheel on the old wagon began to wobble, but when this happened they were near home.

"Unload," the wagon driver ordered. "I don't want to take a chance with crashing and ye fallin' out."

Sally climbed down and held her hands for Emily and Elizabeth to dismount. "We'll be home soon now," she said, but knew they still had three blocks to walk in muddy streets. She feared the rats especially in the dark, but kept quiet about it. In one arm she held her small purchases and guided Elizabeth with her other hand.

Emily complained, "I hate this! I hate this! I want to go to Da's America."

Chapter Ten

The middle-aged Irish woman in Dr.Elizabeth Black-well's office talked incessantly as she was examined. "My cousin is dead and for what?" she said, "The riots, that's what. The fighting and killing over businesses and jobs is a sin. Yes, he hired a freed Negro to work in his carriage business. He hired him because the man was sober and worked hard. He hired him over a fellow Irishman, 'tis true. And we Irish are known to stick together; known as clannish. But is not business, business? I speak frankly. The Irishman was a drunk. How can you get the work done if drunk? The freed man was sober. Well, my cousin was killed— murdered, him and his Negro worker. The burning, the stabbing and beatings, I tell you, it is a war within itself and no end in sight."

"It is sad, Mrs. Coogan," Dr. Blackwell said. "You may sit up now. I'll give you some laudanum and you should feel better soon. I'm sorry about your cousin; about all the cruelty people carry out against each other."

"My cousin. He was only trying to make a living—to support his family. Now there's the funeral rentals to pay for if he's to have the decent putting away. I tell you, the world gets worse year by year."

When the patient was finally gone, Dr. Blackwell looked about her empty office and sighed deeply. Not only did her office barely pay for itself, but once again she had been denied the right to practice in a hospital because she was a woman. She walked about the empty room with her hand pressed to her forehead in thought. She had endured endless insults, but she remained determined to make her practice of medicine useful to people, and especially to women. But how? What could she do?

Aloud, she said, "The young need to learn what I can convey to them for the sake of their health." She stopped pacing and sat at her small desk. Perhaps, if she wrote down information for them that would help. She picked up her pen but put it down. Surely the intimate information she needed to write would bring more insults. She shook her head. So be it, it would be nothing new and her heart was in the effort. She picked up her pen again and began to write.

Since so few patients came, she wrote the book more quickly than she might have otherwise have been able. The Laws of Life with Special Reference to the Physical Education of Girls poured forth in detail what she wished to convey.

But now that the writing was done, how could the message reach those who needed to be informed? The writing of the book was not enough. She steeled her determination as she often had done many times in her life. In this case, she knew she would have to stand against her shy nature and set up a lecture on her subject. Her fear now was that no one would come but she knew she had to make the effort.

On the day of the lecture, the hall began to fill. She was amazed, but still feared women would walk out when she began to speak in intimate details about a girl's physical development and the means needed to promote healthy living—facts contrary to some old wives' whispers and customs of the day. In her need for income, but also because she felt her lecture worthy, she charged two dollars per person.

When she began to speak her anxiety was high but her determination higher still. Soon she was surprised and pleased to see many intelligent women from the Society of Friends responding to her lecture. In feeling their warm personalities, she was able to relax and speak freely although she knew her subject was shocking to many.

"The present age," she told them, "has lost sight of the truth ancient societies like the Greeks had considered elementary—namely that life to be complete must be a unity of body and spirit." She urged her listeners to tear swaddling clothes off their babies and to encourage their daughters to engage in free play in childhood—to actively use their bodies in exercise and to refrain from strangling corsets. In all sincerity she encouraged mothers to give their daughters worthwhile goals in life and to avoid too early marriages.

After a series of lectures, Dr. Blackwell happily realized that her decision to write and speak had been the right thing to do. Prominent women from the Society of Friends became her patients and her practice grew. She began to look toward a day when she might have her own clinic, perhaps even a hospital and eventually a medical school. Those who denied her practice because of her womanhood could not prevent her building on her own initiative. Still, much more support and money would be needed. Somehow she would find it; would make it work. Had she not believed that God was with her since that night in the North Carolina mountains? There would be a way in God's own time. She felt sure of it.

***

Sally was deeply troubled by the number of criminals, prostitutes and other low life characters who were flowing into her neighborhood. Not that there hadn't been enough of such degenerates there already, but these were the worst of the worst. They had been turned out from The Old Brewery where the overcrowding had become unlivable even for those who reportedly were near stacked upon each other and lived in debauchery and filth. She believed her safety and the safety of her children were at stake, and became more desperate to come by some means to find other housing.

She remembered Mary O'Sullivan and decided to walk again to visit the elderly schoolteacher. A plan had come to mind she wanted to present to the pleasant old lady. She wondered why she had not thought of it before and maybe it wouldn't work, but if it did...if it did...well, she would have to see. Considering it now, Sally walked faster in her eagerness.

Sally thought it must have taken her an hour to reach the small O'Sullivan house and now she prayed the lady would be at home. She knocked gently on the door and listened, but heard nothing. A louder knock brought no results. Sally sighed and shook her head. Now she had wasted time she could have been sewing, all for a failed attempt to see Mary O'Sullivan. She turned to go when she saw her new friend walking toward her.

"I see you went for a walk again," Sally said.

"Oh, it's you, Mrs. McKelvy. Yes, I made a little trip down to a small market this time for a bit of dried fruit. It was useless, but oh well, small ones can't stock everything. Sometimes I have better luck buying from the street vendors."

"So do I, and when taking a wagon to the bigger markets," Sally said.

"Oh, yes, on occasion." The elderly woman walked to her front door and unlocked it, turning then to look at Sally. "How are you, and your dear little girls?"

"Well, thank you," Sally said, "and yourself? How have you been?"

"Not too well. I've had a bit of a cold, but I may wear it out soon. Won't you come in?" she asked, holding the door open.

"Thank you, I will." Sally walked in the small front room. Although, the parlor was sparsely furnished it was smaller than she had remembered which brought her pause. She'd hoped the room and the whole house was larger.

"Do be seated," Mrs. O'Sullivan said. "I'll get us some cold tea. That is, if you'd care for some?"

"I would. So nice of you. May I be of help?"

"No. It will only take a minute."

The minute seemed longer to Sally, but she tried to relax and consider how she would approach Mrs. O'Sullivan with her request.

When they were both sipping the tea, Sally said, "I have something I want to talk with you about. You know my daughters and I live in the miserable Five Points district. I am concerned about them growing up there and desperately need to find a better place for us to live."

"Yes," Mrs. O'Sullivan said. "I understand that, my dear. Where did you plan to move? I know your Emily prefers the country."

"Oh, you have no idea how much we would all love that, but with the tiny income we have, there's no way."

"Well," Mrs. O'Sullivan said, "and the sewing work may not even be available in the country."

"Right." Sally set down her glass of tea and looked directly at Mrs. O'Sullivan. "Oh," she said, "this is so hard for me to ask, but I was wondering...I was wondering if we could move in with you. I would do everything to help you and I could pay something, too." She felt her heart racing as she watched the startled expression on Mrs. O'Sullivan's face.

"My dear! How could that be?" the elderly woman asked. "You see my place is so small. Only two bedrooms, this room and a kitchen. I'm so sorry. I wish...."

"We could manage in one bedroom and share the kitchen. I know it's asking too much of you, but I am truly desperate. Please, at least let us try. I'll do all that I can to help you and I am a clean person with well-behaved daughters."

Mrs. O'Sullivan studied her wrinkled, freckled hands. "It's the landlord, too, my dear. I don't own the house and he's a picky fellow. My niece, Arlene, who lives in New Jersey, found this place for me, and Arlene can get along with anybody, but finds him a difficult fellow. I don't think he would allow it."

"If he would, would you? If I could convince him, pay him a little more," Sally said.

"Ah, now that might get his attention. More pay. It might indeed. Truth is I would like your company. 'Tis a rather lonely life I live much of the time as the neighbors are younger, and as you can see they all have the bigger, finer houses. I have felt at times they'd like this small house to disappear. Sally smiled and learned forward. "Where can I find him—the landlord?"

"He lives in the best house; the brick one at the end of

this street, but I don't encourage you, my dear. You see this house is very small. I'm up and about much of the night, a restless sleeper and when I do sleep I snore."

"I—we will adjust to your ways. I must move. I must." Sally stood and reached out to touch Mrs. O'Sullivan's hand. "I thank you from the bottom of my heart that you're willing. Yes, I do, even if the landlord says I cannot--."

"You will let me know. His name, I forgot to say, is Preston. George Halpin Preston I'm told. Halpin is a family name he's proud of so takes it as his first name. I don't know anything of a Halpin family. I didn't like the man so I never asked."

"I'm going now straightway to see him," Sally said. She had not expected the tears that filled her eyes and she turned quickly away to hide them.

"Don't build your hope too much, my dear. I'm sorry if he denies you."

***

Sally reached the large brick house within a short time. Before she knocked on the door, she took a moment to try to calm herself. She meant to be as persuasive as possible but hopefully without in any way offending a difficult man. Or was it possible that Mrs. O'Sullivan misjudged him? She knew that sometimes people disliked even strangers simply because they were reminders of offensive people they had known earlier in their lives. She had once had that experience—a sudden unreasonable dislike of a child simply because his voice reminded her of a mean teacher. At first she hadn't understood it, but later while almost asleep that night, the meaning had come to her. Well, she would soon know if Halpin Preston was truly disagreeable. She heard footsteps within the house.

A lady in an ankle-length brown dress with white lace collar appeared at the door. Sally saw that she was elderly and appeared quite sophisticated with her white hair coiled neatly around her head. Her small brown eyes were near covered by gold-rimmed spectacles.

"Hello, Ma'am," Sally said, "I'd like to speak with Mr. Halpin Preston."

"He's not here."

"May I ask when you expect him to return?" Sally asked. With some discomfort she saw the old lady was staring at her, lifting her chin and turning her head. Why? Was her vision that poor or could she be a strange one?

Without answering her question, the woman asked, "Would you be that little red haired girl of the O'Neill family in Donegal? Forgive me for asking, but you look so like the mother."

Sally exclaimed, "Yes! You knew my mother! How was it that you...?"

"Come in," the lady said. "I'm Mrs. Kilsheelin, Mr. Preston's mother-in-law. If you have time, I want to talk with you about home. I get dreadfully homesick here and now I see—oh, I'm so pleased to see someone from Donegal! Halpin is out collecting the rents on his many properties."

Sally entered the fine house and was impressed with the beauty and elegance of the parlor--chairs covered in red velvet, polished tables with lovely figurines and vases of flowers. On the floor was a fine carpet and the walls were decorated with mirrors and large paintings. In contrast to the room and Mrs. Kilsheelin, Sally felt she must look like a ragamuffin in her faded blue dress.

When they were seated, Mrs. Kilsheelin said, "Do tell me when last you were in Donegal and about yourself. Does your dear mother still live? And your father? I believe you were an only child. Is that correct? Tell me about the neighbors and the church and if the praties have begun blooming again."

When Sally had told her story and why she wished to speak with Mr. Preston, Mrs. Kilsheelin said, "Oh, he would not agree, but I tell you to go ahead and move. He has numerous properties and many of them filled to over capacity with people so it's unlikely he'll notice. My advice is to move and say nothing. Pay your rent to Mrs. O'Sullivan alone since she's willing to share her home, and do tell her I said to say nothing about changes to him."

"But if he should notice, what would I do?"

"Tell him I gave you permission. He would not like it, but that's all. He would not want to upset my daughter who loves me very much." She smiled. "Fortunately, she is a beautiful girl and a feisty one. So go ahead and move, and my best wishes to you and your daughters."

Sally thanked her profusely and left in a happier mood than she had felt in a long time. Some success at last! Of course, there would be an adjustment and the space was small, but being able to at last leave Five Points was such a relief.

When she reached Mrs. O'Sullivan's house, she eagerly knocked on the door. The elderly woman called to ask who was there and in learning it was Sally, let her in. She was dressed for bed in a long gown and with a cap on her head although it was still daylight.

"I'm not feeling well," Mrs. O'Sullivan said. "this cold has me feverish."

"I'm sorry," Sally said. "What can I do to help you?"

"Not anything, my dear. Well, I suppose he turned you down." She coughed and took a sip from a glass of water.

Sally then eagerly explained what had transpired.

"I can hold my tongue," Mrs. O'Sullivan said, "but I can't lie if I'm questioned."

"Neither will I," Sally said. She hesitated then added. "Since you don't need to be bothered just now, I'll wait a few days before moving in. Will that be agreeable?"

"Yes. I'll look for you in three or four days, and, my dear girl, I'm glad I'll be having your company."

***

Sally walked so rapidly she became breathless on the long walk home. She could hardly wait to tell Emily and Elizabeth. Although she had missed time from her sewing and money was low, she stopped at a small grocer and bought an orange to take home and share in celebration. It seemed to her she was being especially blessed on this day as the grocer let her choose the largest orange for the same price as for smaller ones.

As she continued on her way she was giddy with success and happiness. Now if only she could somehow touch Tony's heart! If only she could! He reminded her so much of Frank it would almost be like having Frank back in her life, back with the laughter and the comfort and joy of love. She could imagine his kisses and embrace, and the final falling peacefully asleep at night, believing together they could face whatever troubles the world might bring their way.

Sally's elevated mood was dashed as she approached the Old Brewery. The shouts and cries of the gangs fighting frightened her. She knew from what she heard the Bowery Boys and The Dead Rabbits were shedding each other's blood again. How she hated their vicious animal behavior! She took an out of the way street to avoid them, but passed crumbling brothels and swaying drunks in the back street. A filthy man grabbed at her shawl, but he was unsteady on his feet and she was able to shove him aside. She ran then, taking the best route she could through the brawling mob and finally emerged a block from home.

Once inside her apartment she embraced Elizabeth and Emily, telling them the good news. "We are moving, my darlings. Outside Five Points. Not far, but outside this miserable place."

"Oh, Ma," Emily cried. "are we going to the country? To Da's America?"

"Unfortunately, not that far, but blocks away from here. Remember that Mrs. O'Sullivan with the books? We'll be living with her."

"Will she read to me?" Elizabeth asked.

"She may, but right now she isn't well so we must wait a bit."

"Oh, Ma!"

"I know, but it won't be long and we'll be in a better

place. I must take you for a visit since you haven't met Mrs. O'Sullivan, but I'm sure we'll all get along just fine. Oh, I'm so thankful for it," Sally said. Already she was thinking also of how she would perhaps look better to Tony living in the O'Sullivan house. She laughed. He didn't know where she lived. She was being silly. She realized her giddiness had returned the joy she'd lost in seeing the gangs fighting. Mrs. O'Sullivan's hopefully was far enough away that they'd not be bothered by the criminals, or if they were surely not as bad or as often.

The next day Sally dressed carefully and returned to the Italian Market. She left Emily and Elizabeth alone in the apartment, but reminded them as usual. "Don't go out and don't answer the door to anyone."

"We know, Ma," Emily said. "We know. Besides I'm almost fourteen now."

"Of course, you are, dear," Sally said and kissed the top of Emily's head, brushed her daughter's auburn hair from her forehead and kissed her forehead."

Emily laughed. "You feel happy don't you Ma?"

"I do," Sally said.

"Can I get a kiss?" Elizabeth asked.

"You can." She lifted her small daughter and kissed both cheeks.

Moments later Sally stood on the wooden walkway and waited for the horse drawn wagon that would take her once again to the Italian Market.

While she waited Sally tried to think of how she would approach Tony. What could she possibly say or do to catch his eye? She thought her dress, though a faded sky blue, was becoming. She was pleased, too, that her hair turned curls attractively against her cheeks. But looking pretty probably was not good enough to turn Tony's head--set as he was against romance. She sighed. She would have to take opportunities as they might arise. It could take more time than pleased her, but she considered it would be worth the wait. What if he never...no, she wouldn't allow that thought! There must be a way. Surely it must be that destiny had led her this way. How else would she have met someone so like Frank a world away from Ireland?

When the wagon stopped the horse snorted and shook his head. It seemed like a forewarning to Sally. She saw more strangers on the wagon this time and heard more vulgar voices than usual. She comforted herself in the thought that she would be moving away from this area at last! On the ride she tried to shut the noises out and concentrate on the fresh morning. The sun was shining. It was an especially pleasant day for late March.

At the market Sally looked around through the crowd of shoppers for Tony. She saw him at the back, arranging bread. She took a deep breath and walked past other customers to reach his side.

"Good morning," she said.

He turned his head and smiled. "Good morning," he said. "Need some bread?"

"Uh, well, yes."

"This is a nice fresh loaf," he said handing it to her.

She felt foolish. Nothing came to her mind to say, but she continued to stand holding the loaf of bread cradled like an infant against her chest. Barely thinking, she asked, "Do you remember who I am?"

Children racing down the isle bumped into her throwing her awkwardly against a wooden shelf causing her to drop the bread and fall to her knees. Tony picked her up. "Are you all right?"

She knew she was not hurt, but she leaned against him pretending to feel dizzy. She loved the warmth of his closeness and the scent of the yeast breads on his shirt.

"Are you hurt?" he asked. She heard the concern in his voice.

Reluctantly, she stood apart from him. "I think I'm all right now."

"I'll give you another bread," he said. "no charge."

"Do you remember me?" she asked. "We talked about...."

"Yes, I remember now. You're the lady who lost your

84

husband on the ship over."

"And you lost your wife," Sally said. She kept back the words 'in childbirth' considering the pain that might still cause him.

"Yes." He looked beyond her toward the front of the market. "I see my daughter coming in now."

Sally turned to look. "Yes, I saw her once before. A beautiful dark haired girl. She was holding a little boy about two years old."

"Yes, Babe—Angelica—takes care of him sometimes when she's not in school. A neighbor's child," he added.

"Oh, then she's a student," Sally said.

"Yes," he said and turned back to arranging the bread. Sally felt he was dismissing her but she waited standing only a short distance away until his daughter arrived.

"Papa," the girl cried, "I need the money today for my dress."

"Angelica," he said. "You have dresses."

"But Papa, not a white one. I need a white one for graduation."

Sally stepped closer. "I couldn't help but hear," she said. "I can sew her a graduation dress."

Angelica's eyes widened. "Oh, would you? Papa, please!"

"Too much fuss is made over the color," Tony said. "I don't think it's necessary."

Without considering the fact that she was behaving too personally, Sally used his given name and expressed her opinion. "Tony," she said, "it's hard for a man to understand a girl's need for this kind of thing. I'm sure if her mother were alive she'd want Angelica to have the dress. Do buy the cloth and I will sew it for her without charge."

Angelica pleaded. "Oh! Please, Papa. Please!"

"When do you need the dress?" Sally asked.

"In a month. I knew it would take time and Papa, dear as he is, has to be begged on things like this."

Tony shook his head. "Well, go ahead but don't try to outshine every other girl at graduation. Sister Rose should

85

supervise it."

"She does. We know just what to...."

"I'll go with her to see Sister Rose and we can work from there," Sally said.

"Oh, thank you!" Angelica cried. She gave Sally a quick embrace.

"When should we go?" Sally asked.

"Tomorrow would be fine or even next Tuesday," Angelica said.

"Next Tuesday would be better for me," Sally said. "I'll meet you here, Lord willing, at noon. Will that be satisfactory?"

"Yes, ma'am, and thank you so much Miss...."

"Mrs. Sally McKelvy. I have two daughters myself."

Tony looked at her then. She couldn't interpret his look, but it seemed to her one of interest. He reached for a loaf of bread and handed it to her. "No charge for this," he said, "and let me know the cost of sewing the dress. I could pay you or we could trade in food from the market."

"It won't be a problem," Sally said taking the bread. She smiled at him. "Thanks for picking me up when I fell."

"Sorry it happened, but glad you weren't injured," he said, turning back to his work. He felt a sense of gratitude toward the pretty Irish woman. Carolina always said he was such a sensitive man, so easily touched by the needs of others, but he'd not been sensitive to Angelica and that bothered him now.

On the way back home Sally retraced every memory of the contact.

She at least now had a legitimate way stay in touch with Tony and she genuinely liked Angelica.

That final glance from Tony played in her mind. She couldn't decide exactly what it meant, but she felt certain he would not forget her.

Preoccupied with thoughts of the morning's events, Sally was suddenly jolted by a woman shoving past her. It took a moment for her to understand why others in the wagon were restlessly moving about in their seats and interrupting each other with alarming talk. Then she heard it—the roar of rioting in the distance ahead.

The driver announced, "We'll have to make a drive around. Looks like there's a barricade on Bayard Street."

A thin boy passenger sat forward peering around a man in front of him.and said in an excited voice, "It's them gangs--them Dead Rabbits. I know. It's them for sure."

When the wagon drew nearer they saw not only fierce fighting in the streets but a hail of flying objects from windows and roof tops.

"Women and young'uns is throwin' them bricks and bottles," a white-haired woman said. "It ain't just the gangs now."

The driver said, "Women are fighting for the Roche Guard. They hates the Dead Rabbits. Look at that rain of rocks and bricks! Well, I can't drive through there. I'll have to put you off and let you walk or run your way home."

Sally whispered, "Oh, no! I'll have to get past them somehow."

Minutes later the driver stopped. "This is as close as I can take you needing to get to the Baxter street section."

Sally stepped down and tried to think of her best route around the fighting mob. She was eager to get home to Emily and Elizabeth and hated having to take a long walk out of the way. Perhaps if she could skirt around the outer edges of the fighting she would be safe. She hurried in that direction but stumbled and fell hurting her arm on a castaway piece of wagon wheel iron. "Oh, oh, oh!" she cried rubbing her arm, but she got up and resumed her hurried pace.

On the outer edge of the screaming, bloody mob, she ran trying to make a quick get away. She felt a great bump to the side of her head and a hard blow to her lower rib cage. She collapsed to the ground in silence. A dirty, bearded young man stumbled over her, cursed and kicked her in her side before picking her up and casting her in some weeds.

Chapter Eleven

Later, when the riot ended, the dead and wounded lay bleeding in the streets. The police gathered up and piled the dead bodies on a rugged, bloodstained wagon and loaded the wounded in an ambulance.

A tiny, exceptionally wrinkled woman passed near Sally. Realizing she knew her, she went to check Sally's breathing and called out to the police. "This one ain't dead. I know her." She stroked Sally's hair back from her face. "Can you hear me, Dearie?" she asked. "This here is Kate Maudeen. You know I'm a neighbor."

Sally moaned. "Home," she breathed in a barely audible voice.

After the police had taken her to her apartment, Emily bathed the blood from her face and arms. "Ma," she said, "you need Dr. Blackwell. I'm going for her."

"Elizabeth, Stay right by Ma. Get her anything she needs while I'm gone."

***

The New York Infirmary for Women and Children at Second Avenue was within walking distance from Five Points. Emily ran most of the way, stopping only once to catch her breath. Would Dr. Blackwell come? She knew the good doctor had gone out into the neighborhood, visiting her patients or having them seen by nurses she called Sanitary Visitors.

Surely she would come! Hadn't Ma admired her so much that she'd named Elizabeth after her? Ma and Elizabeth were special, weren't they? When other women put the doctor down saying, "Ahhh she's tryin' to be a man," Ma would say, "She's not! See how womanly and modest she is? Why shouldn't a woman be a doctor? Who better knows another woman's pain?"

Yes, surely Dr. Blackwell would come.

***

The hallway of the infirmary was filled with disheveled women and noisy children. Emily pushed through the smelly crowd to a nurse.

"My Ma is hurt real bad. I need Dr. Blackwell to...."

"Girl, don't you see this?" The nurse waved her hand toward the waiting patients.

"Yes, but...."

"Bring your mother here. Perhaps, she can be seen later."

Emily's eyes filled with tears. "You don't understand! She is hurt real, real bad."

The nurse sighed and shook her head. "What can we do? There is no way."

Emily took a deep breath and pushed past the nurse to the examining room. There she was!

"Dr. Blackwell! Dr. Blackwell!" Emily cried running to her.

The tiny woman in white turned from her patient--a small, screaming boy trying to withdraw his bloody hand from examination.

"It's Ma," Emily cried. "She's...."

Breathlessly, the nurse rushed into the room. "I'm sorry, doctor. I'll get her out right away."

Dr. Blackwell shook her head. "Leave her." To the small, screaming boy, the doctor said, "Just a little cleaning and fixing, Jimmy. It won't hurt that much. Hey, you're a big boy now."

Emily choked out her message.

Dr. Blackwell's face was soft, troubled. Gently, she touched Emily's shoulder. "I can't come now. I have a baby to deliver right away, but I'll send a nurse. She glanced across the room. "Georgette, have Mary take a carriage and go with this child."

Nurse Mary, a young woman with soot black hair piled

in a loose mop on top of her head appeared carrying a small case. Emily thought Mary was pretty with her large black eyes and brown skin. The slight accent with which she spoke was pleasant, but most of all Emily was glad that she moved quickly. "Let's go," she said taking Emily's arm briefly as they passed through the crowded waiting room.

***

Nurse Mary spoke gently to Sally. "Can you hear me?" the nurse asked.

Sally opened her eyes and spoke with obvious effort, "Yes."

"I see the injury to your head," the nurse said, "and that you're in pain."

Sally moaned as she slowly moved her hand to her side.

The nurse said, "Yes, oh yes, the blood is there, too. Mmmmm, you have been hurt for sure, ma'am. I'll give you some Laudanum for the pain and Dr. Blackwell will visit you later." The nurse opened her small case and found the medication.

"What can I do?" Emily asked.

"Me, too." Elizabeth said.

Nurse Mary smiled down at Elizabeth. "How old are you?"

"She's small for her age," Emily said, "but she's five."

Elizabeth frowned. She stood feet apart, arms akimbo. "I know how old I am. I could have said."

The nurse spoke to Emily. "Bring me a glass of water with sugar stirred in. That way the medicine will taste better."

Elizabeth rushed past Emily to get a glass and reached for water. Emily spooned sugar into the water and spun the glass around mixing it as the nurse poured in a small amount of Laudanum.

Sally moaned as Nurse Mary gently lifted her shoulders to take the drink. "There now," she said, "soon you'll feel better."

"Girls," the nurse said, "just let her rest and sit beside her in case she needs something, but she'll probably go to sleep soon."

"When will Dr. Blackwell come?" Emily asked.

"A little later, but she'll be here so don't worry." The nurse picked up her case and walked to the door. She glanced back at Emily and Elizabeth, hesitated, but then opened the door and left.

***

Dr. Blackwell frowned as she examined Sally. "She needs to be in the hospital."

Sally teared and shook her head.

"I know you don't want to leave your girls," Dr. Blackwell said, "but surely Emily is old enough now to manage for a while."

"Yes, ma'am," Emily said. "I know not to open the door to strangers and much more that Ma has taught me. I sew and I know to save back two dollars so I can get the solid colors to make the shirts—not the checked as that hurts the eyes to sew."

"I see you're a bright girl, Emily, and your mother has taught you well."

"Me too," Elizabeth said. "I help. I pick up scraps and pins and bring things to Ma."

"Smart girl there, too." Dr. Blackwell said. She turned back to Sally, "The Friendly Visitors will keep check on your daughters, but you must be where we can take good care of you. You are badly hurt and I want to give you every possible chance to recover. Are you willing to let me try to help you?"

Sally looked at Emily and Elizabeth.

"We'll be fine, Ma," Emily said, "we want you to get well."

Tears again flooded Sally's eyes, but she whispered, "Yes. I...must."

Less than an hour after Dr. Blackwell left the apartment

the horse drawn ambulance arrived to transport Sally to Dr. Blackwell's Infirmary. She was ashen and breathing quietly through parted lips, sleeping now after another dose of Laudanum.

Emily and Elizabeth followed the ambulance workers carrying their mother on a stretcher to the wagon. A dusty wind blew trash along the roadway and flipped papers in the hand of one of the attendants. Curious neighbors watched the process but they stood apart talking among themselves. The tiny wrinkled woman was among them explaining how she had found Sally. "At the gang fights," she said, "but 'twas thrown things that got her. One jagged brick with blood and a big rock, still there beside her.

"Gracious, Mrs. Maudeen, must have been somebody strong what threw 'em to hurt her that bad," a chubby girl with pigtails said.

"And for sure it was," Mrs. Maudeen said shaking her head. The loose black scarf she wore fell from her gray curls to her shoulders in the drafty wind.

"Yeah," a woman with her hand on the girl's shoulder said, "Well, them folks was really mad, and really mad sometimes gives a person power."

"I'm sorry she got hit,' the chubby girl said. Tears brightened her gray eyes.

"Laurie is sensitive," the woman with her hand on the girl's shoulder said. "We are sorry, but so many are hurt every day, we can't cry for everybody."

Emily and Elizabeth heard their neighbor's remarks, but said nothing. Emily held Elizabeth's hand as they stood and watched. Soon the ambulance moved away. The wheels rumbled over the flagstone street making little clacking sounds, for the first time separating them overnight, and for an indefinite time, from their mother.

Only when the horse drawn ambulance was out of sight did Emily and Elizabeth go back inside the apartment. Although she had not admitted it earlier, Emily felt afraid. Yes, she knew how to sew but she'd never gone without Ma to buy the fabric. Would they sell it to her? What would she tell them if they asked about Ma?

Elizabeth said, "Will we move now to Mrs. O'Sullivan's house?"

"Oh," Emily said, "we can't until Ma gets well. I don't even know where Mrs. O'Sullivan lives." She pressed her fingers to her lips and sudden tears blinded her.

***

Sally became aware of the smell of coffee mingled with acrid scents of medications. Was she dreaming? She looked around trying to understand where she was then she tried to sit up but pain and weakness overwhelmed her.

"Good morning, Mrs. McKelvy," Nurse Mary said. "How do you feel?"

"Where...?"

"You're in the New York Infirmary. Dr. Blackwell is..."

"My children!" Again Sally tried to sit up and lay back in pain.

"Your daughters are here. I'll bring them to you. Do you feel like some breakfast?"

"No...Oh...."

Before nurse Mary could call to them Emily and Elizabeth came from a waiting area. "Ma!" Emily cried bending over her. "Are you all right?"

"Ma!" Elizabeth ran to Sally's bedside and threw her head against Sally's arm.

"Darlings," Sally whispered.

Nurse Mary said, "Girls, be careful. Don't tire her."

Sally touched each of her daughters. "Are you...?"

"Yes, Ma," Emily said, "we're fine. That nice little lady who found you brought us soup last night."

In her weakened state Sally fell asleep and nurse Mary ushered Emily and Elizabeth away. "You can see her again later," she promised.

***

Dr. Blackwell walked through the wards checking on and comforting her patients. Some had improved and it pleased her that she had been able to help them, but she worried about others--those who had been brought to her too late or were suffering from incurable diseases. Nurse Mary walked beside her making notes as the doctor commented or gave orders.

When she reached Sally she examined her gently and sighed. She hated all the rioting and hurting of innocent people. "I fear people will never learn to live in peace," Dr. Blackwell said.

"Her injuries are very serious aren't they, Doctor?" the nurse asked.

"Yes, but she's a woman of strong will and we'll do all we can." Dr. Blackwell said, "She's so warm. Bathe her down a bit with some cool water."

"You know she has two daughters...."

"Oh, yes. I delivered the younger one before you ever left Mexico. The mother has encouraged patients to come to me—not a woman prejudiced as some are."

"She's a pretty woman though frail," Nurse Mary said.

"Undernourished and works too hard," Dr. Blackwell said. She touched Sally's head gently then turned aside to leave.

Later, when Emily and Elizabeth again visited her bedside, Sally spoke with effort against the pain, "Emily... Italian market...Tony...go tell about me."

Emily asked, "Why, Ma?"

"A dress...I was...." Sally said, "Oh."

"I'll tell him," Emily said. "Don't talk, Ma. Rest." Emily bent and kissed Sally on her cheek. "I love you, Ma."

"I..."

"I know, Ma. You love us."

Sally smiled weakly and closed her eyes.

***

In the early afternoon Emily returned from the Italian

market and went immediately to her mother.

"I know about it now, Ma," she said, "you were going to sew a dress for Tony's daughter. He said tell you to get well and not to worry. He'll get the dress sewed. Then, Ma, he gave me a basket with cheese, apples and bread. He just gave it to me!"

Sally whispered, "Good." She relaxed and fell asleep.

Chapter Twelve

The customers at the Italian market shopped early before the August heat descended. The store was quiet and empty. Shoppers were at home to prepare a noon meal for their families. Ramon Pellegrini sighed and pulled up a stool near the cash register. Tony stood nearby, hands on hips, looking out on the roadway as Emily left with the basket of food.

"I saw you give-a the girl...."

"Yes," Tony said, "her mother is hurt and the girls are alone. I wanted to help them."

"Good-a, good-a, no problem. The mother, I think she-a sweet on you. She get-a you yet," Ramon said laughing.

"You know how I feel about another marriage." Tony's voice trembled.

"All the women they-a crazy for you. One make you papa again."

"No, never. Ramon, you don't understand! Maria gave you babies so easy. Carolina couldn't. "

"Tony, Tony! I tell-a you hundred times—not your fault."

"It was my fault!" Tony said. "I knew she was fragile. I knew but...."

"She-a beautiful woman. You a man, Tony-boy. A man." Ramon threw his hands in the air. "How long it been now? Angelica was-a—was-a...."

"She was nine when I caused her...."

"You didn't cause her to lose-a her mama. I know what-a you always say."

"Carolina would be thirty-one today." Tony said.

"So that's why you're so touchy. You-a thinking about Carolina on her birthday. I'm sorry, but little brother, you-a sad too long now. You-a alive. Act like it"

Tony turned on his heel and walked to the back of the market.

He was thinking now of more than Carolina's birthday. He was thinking of the cold November day she died. He remembered how there on Mama's old poster bed she had clung to his hand in her suffering trying to birth their son. She had birthed Angelica nine years before. God, why couldn't it happen? She couldn't make it happen.

The doctor said, "The baby is too big. Too big!"

Her face—so pale, her beautiful dark eyes wet with tears, and her cries, her screams! And he was helpless. "Darling, Sweetheart," he'd whispered to her.

"Don't leave me, Tony," she cried, "Tony, don't leave me!"

But he had left—slipped his hand from her cold, damp grip when he could no longer bear it. "In a minute, Sweetheart," he'd said, "I'll be back." Outside the room, he ran to the front door and into the falling snow. Still, he could hear her tortured cries. Oh, God, he could hear her. The sound tore through him. He hardly knew how far he'd gone when he finally turned back.

He hit his chest accusing himself bitterly. How could I have left her? I protected my rotten self! I was still brushing snow from clothes when I reached the bedrrom door. The silence struck me. God, how still and quiet she was lying under the quilt.

"The baby died," the doctor said. He pointed to a small lump under a blood spotted sheet. "No," he cried, "No, Tony, don't look!" but I did look. Our child dismembered.

"It had to be," the doctor said. "He was dead. He felt nothing."

"Tony!" Ramon called from the front of the store, "Do we need-a order more pasta?"

***

The next day Emily returned to the Italian Market. She looked through the crowd of shoppers until she spotted Tony. Then making her way to him quickly she extended a folded piece of paper.

"Here, Mr. Pellegrini, is a note. Ma told me what to write."

"Oh?"

"Yes, she wanted to thank you for your kindness—for giving the basket to Elizabeth and me," Emily said. She smiled at him and started to turn away.

"Wait," Tony said. "How is your mother? How is she...?"

"Dr. Blackwell says her injuries are serious and Nurse Mary always looks worried when she checks Ma." Then in a whisper Emily confessed, "I'm scared."

Tony frowned. "I'm sorry, little girl," he said.

"My name is Emily."

"Emily, yes. Your mother. She's at the New York Infirmary for Women and Children? Is that right?"

"Yes, sir."

"Do you suppose—she might have a visitor?" He asked then shook his head, "No, she's too ill. I shouldn't...."

"She would want to see you," Emily said without hesitation.

"Are you sure?" He felt uncomfortable at the thought of the visit but he seemed drawn to going.

"Yes. I know she likes you. I could see that when we came here. Besides, your brother said so."

"My brother talks too much sometimes."

"Well, he's right, though," Emily said. "Maybe it would help her. Ma says 'It's Christian to cheer up sad and sick folks.' "

Tony gripped his hands and then relaxed them. "I'll come a little later today. Just for a short time." He felt something leading him he didn't understand, but he reasoned at least it wouldn't hurt to be kind.

***

At the Infirmary a nurse brought Tony a chair and placed it beside Sally's bed. Sally was asleep and her breathing was erratic.

Tony felt sad in a way he hadn't expected. He reached for Sally's hand and held it gently. What was he doing? He barely knew the lady. He withdrew his hand and started to leave when Sally opened her eyes. She studied him for a long moment. Her breathing became more regular and she smiled. In a whisper she said, "I must be dreaming."

"No," Tony said. "I came for a visit. I'm sorry I woke you."

Sally spoke slowly and barely above a whisper. "I'm happy you came."

"Is there anything I can do for you, Mrs. McKelvy?"

"Sally."

"Sally, then."

"Stay awhile. Tell me about Angelica's dress."

He laughed then. How could he describe a dress like a woman would? "I don't know how to tell you, except it's white with little fluffy things at the neck and wrists."

Sally laughed softly while holding her hand against her side. "That's good. I can see it."

"Thanks to you," he said, "she'll have a happy graduation."

"I'm glad," Sally said. "I know she'll look lovely. She's such a beautiful girl. Her eyes so dark and unforgettable."

Tony swallowed. "Like her mother," he said. "Carolina had those eyes."

"My Frank had such wonderful hair, curly and dark much like yours, Tony."

"We miss them, don't we?" He said.

"Oh, yes. Life can never be the same again, but thank God we had them for a while. That was the blessing." Her eyes closed briefly and it appeared she was fighting sleep.

"I'm staying too long," he said and stood. "I mustn't tire you."

"I'm sorry--so little energy," she said weakly, "but I'm happy you came."

"I hope you feel better soon," he said.

"Tony," she whispered.

"Yes?"

"Please, come back again."

He hadn't planned to do so, but he found himself saying, "I will."

***

Nurse Mary and Dr. Blackwell stood by a window looking out on the street where some ragged children played with sticks and rocks. It was a blistering hot August day but the children merely wiped their sweaty faces with their arms and kept shouting, laughing and playing.

"It's wonderful they can have that much joy," Dr. Blackwell said. "I imagine they've hardly eaten today."

"At least they are still innocent," Nurse Mary said and sighed. "Later, they may join one of the roving gangs of thieves."

Without suggestion she might change the subject Dr. Blackwell said, "I'm concerned about Sally McKelvy. Her internal injuries are more serious than I'd first believed."

"Do you think she'll die, doctor?"

"I hope not but she's in poor condition. I've done all I can for her so it's up to time and the hand of God."

Mary looked away from the window and picked up a tray. "I should get back to work with the medications. By the way, do you know Mrs. McKelvy has a daily visitor other than her children?"

"Yes, I've seen him. A handsome Italian man," Dr. Blackwell said. "It seems to lift her spirits, but unfortunately, it may not make her well."

***

Emily and Elizabeth came early mornings for visits. They sat quietly by Sally's bed trying to avoid waking her. Sometimes the wait was more than an hour. Today it was longer—almost until lunch time.

When Sally awoke and saw Emily and Elizabeth she whispered, as had become her custom, "Darlings!" She made her usual effort to raise her arms to embrace them but was barely able to do so. Emily saw the change and felt alarmed. Did this mean Ma was getting weaker?

"How are you feeling?" Emily asked.

"Not so strong, but I think all this time in bed is why," Sally said.

"Ma," Elizabeth asked, "when are you coming home? I want you home."

Emily said, "She can't. Not yet, Elizabeth. We still have to wait but we can see her here every morning."

"I miss you, Ma," Elizabeth said. "Come home soon. Verrrrrry soon!" She bent to kiss her lips.

Sally smiled weakly. "Soon as I can, darling."

Emily said, "Ma, I'm sewing in the afternoons and at night. I'm faster, too, now. Maybe we can move to Da's America."

Tears wet Sally's eyes. "Oh, my baby. It's too hard for you. I need to be there helping you."

"No, Ma. Really, I'm doing quite well," Emily said. "You would be pleased seeing my work now."

"I help," Elizabeth said. "I hand her things and get her water to drink."

Sally swallowed. "I see you're pushing yourself, Emily. Surely you could stop for a drink of water."

"I could," Emily said, "but why when Elizabeth can get it for me. Please, Ma, stop worrying."

"Are you sleeping enough? You mustn't overtire yourself," Sally said. Her breathing was quick and shallow.

"Ma! I'm fine. I've packed up some things so when you get home we'll be ready to move to Mrs. O'Sullivan's. I would take them there now, but I don't know where she lives."

"You can't Emily," Sally said. "It's a long walk and not safe for a young girl. We'll move when I get home. If we both sew, well, yes, one day we might even move to the lovely green countryside."

***

Ramon Pellegrini saw Tony preparing to leave again in the late afternoon.

"You-a going back to see her? I think you love that Irish woman, Tony. But she probably die. You-a wanta go through that again?"

"She's a fine woman and beautiful even as she is, but she's not Carolina."

"You don't say you don't love-a her," Ramon said.

"I care about her," Tony said. "We've spent hours, a little at a time, getting to know each other these twelve days. Had I met her before Carolina would I have married her? I might have."

"Yes, see you do love her," Ramon said, "but why her when-a there's all the others who want you?"

Tony looked thoughtful. "There's a kind of innocence about her that—I don't know, she touches me in a way somehow that draws me to her."

Ramon threw up his arms. "Foolish. Foolishness. You could take-a your choice of beautiful, healthy ones. You take on a dying Irish woman and...."

"Her name is Sally."

"So her name is Sally. Think about what-a you doing, Tony."

Tony grabbed up his horsewhip without a word. He walked out the door and down the street to where his brown mare and carriage waited under a shade tree.

***

Before he arrived at the Infirmary a summer storm flashed lightning across the sky and drops of rain began pelting his carriage. Well, no matter, he would find a shelter nearby and make it to the Infirmary with his rubber poncho and his Greek cap sheltering him.

When Sally saw him she whispered, "Frank. Oh, Frank. Did you bring more turnips?"

Tony felt his chest tighten. Oh, God, she was worse! She thought he was Frank. Should he let her think that?

Should he say, "No, it's Tony."

"I see your cap, Frank. Your favorite. So handsome on your dark curls."

Tony removed his cap and his poncho. He drew up a chair close to her bed and sat near her.

Her eyes began to close and her breathing sounded irregular. Oh, God, don't let her die. He stood abruptly moving the chair causing it to scrape against the floor.

Sally opened her eyes. "Tony?"

"Yes, but I don't want to tire you," Tony said.

"Don't go," Sally breathed. "Don't go."

"I'll come again," he said, but he sat back down when he saw her tears.

He took her hand then. "I'm sorry," he said.

She seemed so weak and fragile. Like Carolina. He sat holding her hand knowing he must not leave this time. He heard her make small gasping sounds. His heart beat hard and fast. He wanted to leave, to run out the door. No! Not again. He would not leave her. He must not!

Nurse Mary appeared as Sally's breath seemed to cease. The nurse checked her quickly. "I think she's gone. Yes, surely she is, but I'll call Dr. Blackwell."

***

Tony stood for a moment in silence before he replaced his cap and poncho. He walked out of the Infirmary without a word to nurse Mary. How could he explain the tears washing down his cheeks? What could he say? At the same time he wept he felt somehow elated. It would take time to sort out his feelings, but at least he'd stayed this time. It was not Carolina, but Sally had needed him, too. He walked to his carriage thinking he would go to church on Sunday and light a candle for Sally and for the unusual blessing she had brought into his life.

Chapter Thirteen

Nurse Mary stood in thought for a long moment before covering Sally's face with the sheet. Yes, she would wait until morning to tell Emily and Elizabeth their mother had died. It was a task she dreaded, but she would arise early and go to their apartment.

When she knocked at the door, a sleepy-eyed Emily answered. Her auburn hair was tangled and she still wore her nightclothes. Elizabeth was curled up asleep on her cot.

"Emily," Nurse Mary said, "I'm sorry to bear bad news. Honey, your mother has passed away—died."

For a long moment Emily looked at the nurse and then burst into tears. Nurse Mary embraced her and whispered over and over again, "I'm sorry. I'm so sorry."

Elizabeth awoke then and was told. "But she'll get well and come home later," Elizabeth said.

"No, Elizabeth," Emily said. "She can't."

"She can! I want her home." Elizabeth stamped her foot. "She can!"

Emily still sobbing, took Elizabeth on her lap. "No, Elizabeth she can't. She's gone to Heaven. She's with Da."

"But she'll come back," Elizabeth said.

Emily dried her eyes with the sleeve of her gown. "Elizabeth, remember Mary Frances and Uncle Mike? It's like that."

"No, no, no!" Elizabeth cried. "She'll be back."

Nurse Mary, who did not consider herself religious, found herself saying, "Elizabeth, one day you can go to her, but just not now."

Elizabeth buried her face in Emily's shoulder and wiped her tears on Emily's gown.

"Don't cry," Emily said, "we'll make it."

A sudden thought occurred to Emily. "They won't take us away, will they?" Emily asked nurse Mary. "We don't need the poor house. Ma and me took in shirt sewing and I know how. I know about saving for the solid flannel deposit and everything."

The nurse sighed. "I doubt you'll be bothered. The orphan asylums are full. Surely, you know children are in the streets picking rags, sleeping where they can in doorways, in boxes, against walls...."

"I know," Emily said, "but they're mostly boys."

"Well, then...."

"Mrs. Peake. They say she takes orphans and sends them on that train far away. You won't let her take us, will you?"

"Mrs. Peake? Who is Mrs. Peake?"

"This big lady. She gets a fee. She sends orphans off to farms out west."

"Oh, well, fresh air out of this dismal city might not be so bad for you."

The nurse turned to go. Emily tugged at her sleeve demanding more attention. "One boy ran away from there and came back here," Emily said. "His seven-year-old brother had to work without shoes in a frozen corn field and...."

"Oh, my dear," the nurse said soothingly, "probably just a tall story."

"No! It was Sammy Dougan. His feet turned rotten. They had to cut them off! Please, don't let them take us away. Ma taught me. I can make it for Elizabeth and me. I can!"

"Well, don't worry, dear," Nurse Mary said. "I'll see what I can do." She embraced Emily and Elizabeth. "I'll send the ladies from The Christian Service to help you." She picked up her satchel and was gone.

The ladies from The Christian Service? What would they do? Emily put her hands over her face. Ma had always said she would need to be strong. That life wasn't easy. She didn't feel strong. She felt scared and vulnerable. Tears dimmed her vision, but she quickly wiped them away. It depended upon her alone to take care of herself and Elizabeth. She needed to draw comfort and courage from somewhere. Maybe if she sat in Ma's chair and touched the rough fabric where Ma's hands often rested.

***

There would be no wake--no wine and food for merry-making to combine with the mourning. Father Wallace would arrange a pauper's funeral as Mama had requested if anything should happen to her. Emily knew that. She heard her tell him when Mary Frances died.

Emily noticed the neighbor's disapproving faces as they whispered behind their hands to each other in her presence. She overheard one woman, not too quiet in her whispers, said, "Well, class will tell at the time of a funeral. Surely, Sally knew. We all know to save for the funeral rental."

Emily shrugged it off. Of course Ma had seen the company signs reading, "For rent: Everything needed for a successful funeral," but she had considered living more important than dying. Would they have made the trips to 'Da's America,' sometimes had oranges to eat, and would they have been to a musical once if Ma had saved for a proper funeral? Emily had no doubts. Ma had always been clear in her wishes and expectations. More than once Ma had said, "Watch over our little savings, Emily. The burial doesn't matter. What counts is Heaven. Besides, I want my girls to have the money."

***

On the morning of Sally's funeral roving dark clouds threatened a summer storm. Winds rippled scraggy weeds near the battered old church and dust from a dry week flew in gusts along the roadway.

Inside the quiet church candles cast flickering shadows on the walls; a strong odor of burning incense permeated the sanctuary. Elderly Father Wallace, dressed in vestments, instructed three young altar boys regarding the upcoming service. The boys wore black cassocks and white surplices, but the small, blond boy, Joseph, required a considerably smaller size than he had donned. Father Wallace smiled in seeing the innocent face of the small figure comically dressed in such overflowing garments. He opened a case, searched and came up with a better fit for the thin child. "There," he said and patted the boy's blond head. He glanced with satisfaction at the two other boys noting their sturdy young frames were suitably fitted.

Within the hour the morgue wagon transporting the single pine coffin stopped at the door of the church. Winds ruffled the mane of the black horse and fluttered the covering on the coffin. The wagon driver sat with hunched frame on his board seat and waited under a black rubber cape for the sudden rain shower to stop. When the rain did not stop, he jumped from the wagon and ran to the church to stand briefly on the small porch before pressing through the door. He would wait to shift the coffin onto the dolly. He knew he was early and the pallbearers would not arrive for another half-hour.

***

Despite the absence of a wake and celebration with food and drink, Sally's funeral in the battered old church was attended by five Irish women from her neighborhood, including Kate Maudeen. Kate whispered to the others, "I didn't know when I found her it would come to this. 'Tis a pity she didn't plan ahead, but late it 'tis now, too late." She made a little sucking sound between her teeth. "Too bad, I'd say. No wake, no celebration makes for low class. If only she'd planned ahead."

The elderly woman who sat beside Kate said, "She was at least a quiet and peaceful neighbor, she was." She dried her eyes but more tears came.

"Cellene McLane, why are ye weeping?" Kate asked. "Ye barely knew her."

"I weep for all of us who left dear old Ireland to die in this miserable place. I know with the age upon me like it 'tis, I'll be dying here meself."Cellene said.

"Have you prepared for the proper funeral?" Kate asked. She sat up rigidly and looked directly at Cellene with raised eyebrows.

"I have, but it's no comfort to me. No comfort a'tall. Oh, here comes Father."

Beside Cellene, a stout woman with a black lace covering on her head, said, "I fancied the Father as younger. Why he's all white-haired and stooped."

"Aye," Cellene said, "but look at his face. I'd say he has the countenance of an angel, and might be what with the lovin' struggle he makes to serve the evil ones in the Points."

Father Wallace stopped to speak with Emily and Elizabeth who sat with Nurse Mary and Tony. "Dear little girls your mother would not have left you if she could have stayed. You must remember that, but know that she is in a wonderful place where you both will join her one day."

"Can we go now?" Elizabeth asked, "I miss Ma."

"Not now," Father Wallace said. "We all must wait our turn. For now, you and Emily try to do as your mother would want you to do."

"We will, Father," Emily said, swallowing and wiping her tears with the sleeve of her dress.

It was ten o'clock and time for the funeral. The smallest altar boy walked slowly down the aisle bearing the Crucifix followed in the processional by two pallbearers who moved the coffin along on a dolly. Shadows in the pews of the church became illuminated as the two larger altar boys followed the coffin with lighted candles. Father Wallace, in flowing robes, his white head slightly downcast, followed the procession. All was quiet except for the tapping of a gentle rain on the roof.

Once he stood beside Sally's coffin, Father Wallace paused for a moment to look out at the small group before he began the mass. In a deep, rich voice sounding almost musical, he recited in Latin, "In nominee patris et filli et spiritus sancti. Amen."

Tony held Elizabeth's hand and was conscious of how small her warm little hand was. He told himself it was for her sake that he struggled to maintain his composure. He had been brought up in the church, and remembered the funeral was a time of sadness but also as a Christian, a time to rejoice. Perhaps later he could think of Sally in Heaven and rejoice, but not now. He mourned in silence, swallowed his hurt and held back his tears.

The priest was saying, "Our Lord has won the victory over death and made it possible for Sally McKelvy--for all of us as Christians--to pass over to a new and eternal life."

When he looked at Sally's rough coffin, Tony felt a weight in his chest. He wished it weren't necessary for Sally to be buried in Potter's Field. However, under the circumstances it would have been awkward for him to make other arrangements. He barely heard Father Wallace read the familiar scriptures, "A time to be born, a time to die...Eye has not seen nor ear heard...In my Father's house are many mansions..." Instead, he was aware Elizabeth had fallen asleep against his arm. He cuddled her head gently. Father Wallace spoke in a final tone, "...the word of the Lord."

Voices responded, "Thanks be to God."

When the brief mass was over, Tony lifted the dozing Elizabeth to his chest and she woke. "Where's Ma?" she asked struggling to look around the church.

Momentarily, he thought of Sally wrapped in shroud paper and sealed in that pine coffin, but he said, "In Heaven, baby." He lifted her from his chest and let her stand.

Elizabeth frowned. "Where is Emily?"

"I'm here," Emily said and Elizabeth went to her.

"How will you girls live now? Do you have someone to care for you?" Tony asked.

"The Ladies Christian Service will help them," Nurse Mary said.

"I don't need service," Emily said. "I sew the shirts and I know about the plain flannel. Ma taught me. We can make it just fine."

"I help. I know how," Elizabeth said.

Tony smiled. "Sure, you do," he said. He turned to Emily, "Do let me know if I can do anything for you,"

Chapter Fourteen

Six days after the funeral the landlord came for the rent. He was a big, red-bearded man who wore suspenders holding up wrinkled tan trousers over a bright green shirt.

"But Mr. Preston," Emily protested. "It's a week 'til the first."

The stubby, bearded man patted his round belly. "Like as not ye won't have it anyways. Besides, I've a new family what needs the place. Just off the boat today, they are."

"But...."

"Move tonight and ye owe nothing now."

"No. Ma paid the rent for the whole month."

"Oh, well, I was allowin' fer that. See I've other places. A little basement room--be jest right for ye."

"Basements are dark and smelly. I won't take it."

"Ye'll take it all right or be on the street."

"No. I'll get Dr. Blackwell to help me."

"A doctor? Now how would the likes of ye be friends with a doctor?"

"Come Elizabeth. We'll get Dr. Blackwell."

"Now wait. I guess I could give ye--let's see, an upstairs room. Yes, a ways from here. Down by the river."

"I'll have to see it first."

"Now I admit it's small, but ye don't need this much room. Looks out to the river. Folks like that. What do ye say?"

"I'll see it first."

"Tomorrow then. I'll be back."

When the man was gone, Emily sat on her cot and took Elizabeth on her lap. "It might be good to move," she said. "I'd feel better if Mrs. Peake didn't know where we live." Tears flooded Emily's eyes. She sobbed as she held Elizabeth close.

"What's the matter?" Elizabeth asked.

"I miss Ma, that's all."

"Don't cry, Emily. Nurse Mary said we'll see Ma again." With her small fingers she wiped away Emily's tears and placed a wet kiss on her cheek.

***

The building was a ramshackle brick with faded green shutters half-falling from the walls. Gray wooden steps with rickety railings clung to the outside of the structure. Debris covered most of the front yard. Still it was no worse than where they lived. In some ways it was better because the breeze from the river seemed to dispel some of the odors.

They walked up three flights of steps attached to the outside of the building. With a flourish Mr. Preston pushed open a marred wooden door that scraped against the floor. "There," he said as if revealing a prize.

"This is hardly bigger than a closet," Emily said. Her brow furrowed. "You must have cut it off an apartment."

"Oh, well, we must make room for so many," Mr. Preston said. "The rent will not be more, and ye have a view. See the boats on the river?"

"The boats won't make room for us. No. We won't take it."

Mr. Preston frowned. "This is all going to be so temporary for ye anyways. How ye going to make it without yer ma? Perhaps, another plan. Now there's a lady who...."

"Have you no other room? I can pay. I sew."

"Well, up one flight is a much bigger room, but the roof leaks a bit."

"We'll see. We might take it, but only if you repair the roof by the end of the week."

***

At dusk, Mr. Preston and a man so much like him they might have been twins, moved Emily and Elizabeth's small trunk of possessions to the fourth floor room facing the East River.

111

As the men were leaving, Emily said, "Remember the roof? I won't pay the rent next week if it hasn't been fixed. Understood?"

"Understood. Ah, ye are a battler, ye are. I see yer ma taught ye well." He smiled.

When the men were gone, Emily said, "I think he came to like us a bit, Elizabeth."

"I know. He gave me this." Elizabeth held a small paper-wrapped article to her chest.

"What?

"Candy."

"Oh, good! Give me some."

"No!"

"Elizabeth a witch will get you if you don't share."

"I'll give her some."

"You rascal!" Emily said, laughing. She grabbed her little sister, threw her on the cot and tickled her ribs. Elizabeth squealed and giggled. It was the first time they'd laughed since Ma died.

***

Two days later Emily heard slow, weighted steps on the staircase. Glancing out the window she saw the wide figure of Mrs. Peake.

Emily looked closely. Was there a sharp-faced, wiry man with her? Emily had heard a Mr. Wimple did the actual capture and carry work of the older more resistant orphans. Emily's heart raced. She checked the latch on the door. Moving silently and holding her breath, she checked at the window again. She saw only Mrs. Peake--a red-faced, puffing bloat holding two packages in her arms as she struggled up the steps. Packages? What could that be?

Emily slipped back behind the curtain. Mrs. Peake knocked on the door and waited. Then she knocked again louder and waited.

"Elizabeth," Emily whispered with pointed finger, "remember you don't ever open the door just because

112

someone knocks. Remember?"

"I know. Ma said that."

The knocking continued. Emily glanced out the window once more and saw only Mrs. Peake. "I'm going to open it this time, but don't you ever open that door to anybody when I'm not here."

"Why?"

"Because you're too little to--never mind, just do as I say."

"I open it if I want to," Elizabeth said, arms saucily akimbo.

"Elizabeth!"

"You're not Ma."

"I am now, and I'll spank you if you don't mind me."

Elizabeth pouted and stamped her foot. "You're mean!" she yelled, tears filling her eyes.

The knocking ceased. Mrs. Peake called out, "Girls, I know you're in there. Please, open the door. I brought gifts for your birthdays."

Emily opened the door and held it aside, but she said nothing.

Mrs. Peake bustled inside and took the only chair in the room. "My!" she puffed, "such a long way up here. But then I guess you girls climb better than I do."

"Yes ma'am," Emily said.

"Well, I just happened to think of your birthdays. When exactly are they, Emily?"

"I'll be fourteen very soon. March 21st. Elizabeth will be six on July 19th."

"Oh, then I'm not on either date, but I just wanted to do something--something in memory of dear, dear Sally and what better than to give her girls presents?" She extended a small package to Elizabeth and a bulkier one toward Emily.

"Thank you, Mrs. Peake," Emily said, "but we don't need anything. I'm taking care of us quite well."

A flush covered Mrs. Peake's puffy face. After a moment of silence she appeared to recover. "Oh, it's not a matter of need, my dear. Just a trifle, a wishing you well on your birthdays, that's all. As I said, I didn't know when they were—the birthdays I mean, but this is a year you'll be without your Ma so I thought...."

"Thank you for remembering, but we don't want to be owing to anyone."

"Emily, my dear child! You are in no way obligated. Can't an old neighbor simply give you girls a little gift? No strings. No obligation."

"Well...."

"Good. Here is something for you, Elizabeth, and this is for you Emily," she said once again extending the packages.

Elizabeth tore the paper open to reveal a small rag doll in green-checked dress with pink shoes and yellow strands of wool for hair. Giggling in delight, she held the doll to her chest.

"What will you name her?" Mrs. Peake asked.

Elizabeth frowned, then smiled. "Miss Pink Shoe."

"Miss Pink shoe? Really?" Mrs. Peake looked unsettled. "How about Nancy or Polly?"

"No!"

"Very well."

Emily, having waited, now slowly unwrapped her package to find a ruffled brown blouse.

"The color of your nice brown eyes," Mrs. Peake said.

"It's pretty. Thank you," Emily said quietly.

"Well." Mrs. Peake stood up. "I must go. Can I do anything for you dear, dear girls?"

"No, thank you. Ma told me everything I need to know. We'll be fine." Emily's voice was firm. She stood with her feet slightly apart, planted solidly, arms folded over her chest.

Mrs. Peake's forehead wrinkled and her eyes went flinty for a moment. "I see you have a lot of your Ma in you, Emily." She patted Elizabeth on the head and left.

When she was gone, Emily said, "She thinks she's going to sweeten us up and then capture us unaware." Her eyes grew large and she swallowed. She whispered, "Just like Ma told me, that woman can turn from sugar mouth to mean and back again. Watch out, Elizabeth. Stay as far away from her as possible."

Elizabeth giggled. "See Miss Pink-Shoe! I'll never let anybody take her away."

"Oh, Lord help me! You're such a baby, Elizabeth. It's not Miss Pink Shoe she wants. Remember never let anyone in if I'm not here--especially don't let Mrs. Peake in. Do you hear me?"

"I hear," Elizabeth said, swaying gently and humming, cuddling Miss Pink Shoe.

***

Mrs. Peake was not the only visitor. Dr. Blackwell showed up the next afternoon. While Emily was surprised to see her, she knew the good doctor often looked in on people in the area--even sometimes bringing them food when she was aware of a special need.

"Are you and Elizabeth all right?" she asked settling on the edge of the cot where Elizabeth was napping.

"Yes ma'am. Thank you. Could I get you some tea?"

"Some water, please."

Emily poured water from a white pitcher into a small glass. She handed it to the doctor then sat on the edge of her cot near Dr. Blackwell and the sleeping Elizabeth.

"Thanks. It's rather hot walking today, but I wanted to see you and Elizabeth. Then, too, I like to stroll along the river to relax when I can. I've always liked to walk. When I was young, my brother and I used to walk many miles over fields near our home."

Emily looked wistful. "I wish I could walk over the fields in Ireland with Da again. He was so funny. He'd tell me old Irish tales, and sometimes on a hill he'd take his flute from his jacket, play a tune and tell me to dance. I was little and couldn't really dance, but I'd hop around and he'd laugh. I wish Da hadn't died."

"I'm sorry, dear."

"Ma, too. I wish she...."

"I know. She was a good mother--a fine woman." Dr. Blackwell reached out to Pat Emily's hand. "I've come to offer you a job helping keep the Infirmary clean."

"Oh...really? Oh, thank you! Thank you, Dr. Blackwell."

"Not so fast, Emily. It's not easy work, and I do expect it to be done well." She sighed. "If only people could realize how important cleanliness is...but so many don't."

Emily looked troubled.

"Don't worry. I'll show you what needs to be done. Now I want to ask you two girls to come to my home for dinner on March 21st. Does that date sound familiar?" Dr. Blackwell teased. "The dinner party is for my staff, but I wanted, as well, to honor your birthday Emily. There'll also be a few neighborhood children about Elizabeth's age and my Kitty who is a bit older."

"You have a daughter?"

"Yes, I brought her home from the orphanage. She's Irish like you although she's not a red head. She has very black hair."

"But how did you know about my birthday?"

Dr. Blackwell laid a hand on Emily's shoulder. She spoke softly. "Your mother told me. She was always thinking of you girls and talking about you. She asked me to look in on you now and then if I could--if something happened to her. Such a good mother."

Emily swallowed. Tears came to her eyes. When she could speak she said, "I know Ma would thank you."

***

Nurse Mary who came in a carriage for Emily told her the large Blackwell house was often filled with members of the close Blackwell family, but they were not in evidence when Emily arrived. Nurse Mary said this house belonged to the doctor's brother, Henry Browne Blackwell whom they called "Harry." Well, whomever--Emily breathed deeply. She considered the house huge and amazingly beautiful.

Somewhere upstairs soft music played and the sound of laughter occasionally drifted down. Emily thought that must be the family. She remembered hearing Dr. Blackwell speak of the joy she experienced when she could arrange to be surrounded by her large family.

This evening's dinner was for the staff of the Infirmary. That Dr. Blackwell had included her seemed a miracle. Upon entering the parlor Emily caught her breath. The beauty of the room before her bathed in candlelight from scones on red wallpaper seemed magical; carved chairs, gleaming, polished wood, bright, clear mirrors and blue velvet draperies--beauty she'd never seen before. She walked lightly on the rugs of mingled red, gold and green. And the scent of cedar smelled clean--nothing like her usual surroundings, but far more like Da's America.

Nurse Charlene, a rosy-faced young woman with smiling brown eyes, greeted her and led her into the dining room where staff members stood around, talking, laughing and holding crystal glasses of drink in their hands. On the great table covered in white linen, delicate china and silver shone under the gaslight chandelier.

Nurse Mary smiled. "Would you like some cider perhaps?"

Emily swallowed. She wasn't sure what cider was, but she nodded and said, "Yes, I think so."

Moments later she sipped the sweet liquid and grinned. By this time she had also become aware of the aroma of turkey and yeast bread. How wonderful it must be to live like this!

Soon they were seated at the table bearing delicious smelling food. Never had Emily seen so much on one table before. Rosy ham in addition to turkey and dressing, green peas and so much more including the hot yeast rolls made up the feast.

Dr. Blackwell asked that they bow their heads while she asked God to bless them and the food. "Gracious Lord," she said, "I thank thee for these and all servants who do Thy bidding. Bless us and lead us daily. And bless this food to the nourishment of our bodies. Amen."

Soon after Emily began to enjoy her dinner, her stomach felt tight. The problem was Jerry McCord who sat across from her. All through dinner, she could hardly keep from gazing at him. His face was amazing--as perfect as a marble carving she'd seen in an art shop, but he was no carving. His coloring was rich like he'd spent much time in the sun. Oh, yes, he was very much alive, laughing, talking and sometimes pushing back the thick brown hair that fell across his forehead.

He sat beside the beautiful red-haired nurse, Yvonne, and he only looked once in Emily's direction. She smiled and he returned her smile, but it was like an older man acknowledging a friendly child.

Emily wanted to cry out that she was not a child! Hadn't Dr. Blackwell seated her in the fine dining room with the adults while Elizabeth and the three other little girls had been placed at a small table in the large kitchen with a maid? Certainly the good doctor was not treating her as a child.

Jerry McCord was the only other outsider at the dinner; the rest being a part of the Infirmary staff. Yvonne kept referring to him as "Captain."

Finally. Emily had the courage to speak. "What kind of captain are you, sir?" she asked.

"Militia, little girl."

"I'm not a little girl, Captain McCord. I'm going on fifteen and I make a living for myself and my five-year-old sister."

Yvonne smiled brightly. "Going on fifteen Emily? You're fourteen today. Aren't we celebrating your birthday tonight."

"Actually," Emily said, "Ma told me I was born about three o'clock in the morning and this is nighttime--so I've been going on fifteen for hours."

Nurse Charlene joined the others in laughter, but she said, "I think that qualifies you, Emily." Emily had liked the nurse with the smiling brown eyes from the first sip of the cider. She felt love for her in this moment.

"Emily, is it?" Captain McCord asked, and Emily was happy to hear his voice say her name, and to see his glance was different now. He was actually looking directly at her. "And what do you do for a living, Emily?"

"I sew, but...."

"She's coming to work for me," Dr. Blackwell said. "She'll be helping out in the Infirmary."

"Cleaning," Yvonne said. "Doctor insists on strict cleaning and scrubbing of everything. As nurses we have more important work to do."

"Not more important, Yvonne," Dr. Blackwell said. "I know some others consider my insistence on hygiene is extreme, even silly, but I believe one day I'll be proven right."

Yvonne flushed. "I didn't mean..."

Dr. Blackwell stood up from the table. "If we have all finished, I think we might move to the parlor. I have a gift for Emily." She glanced toward the end of the table where another of her nurses sat. "Georgette would you play the spinet? We'll sing a song of celebration for Emily."

As the group sang to her Emily looked at each one trying to remember their names. Five clinic workers would be only a beginning. Dr. Blackwell, once a lone woman doctor, now had a large staff of nurses, doctors and medical students.

Emily knew Ma had greatly admired Dr. Blackwell. "She's a lady with fancy friends in high places, but she's our friend, too. Remember she personally carries food and clothes to the poorest among us. Never shows any disrespect either."

As the birthday song ended, Dr. Blackwell placed a small box in Emily's hand--a shimmering gold-colored package tied with red cord. Emily was dazzled. She held the package gingerly. She looked at the others as though she wondered if she should disturb the beauty of the paper, but she saw that they waited. Carefully, making every effort to preserve the wrapping, she glanced up smiling from time to time until she finished.

She lifted the top of the small box and gasped. A watch on a silver chain! How beautiful! How special! She'd thought only doctors and rich ladies had such wonderful things. Her eyes glistened with tears.

"Here. Let me," the captain said, slipping the cord over Emily's head.

He knows! Emily thought. He knows! She lifted her cheek for his kiss but he had moved aside to allow others to hug her.

The long evening seemed too short to Emily. She hated to leave the great house and return to their tiny apartment, but the time had come. She thought of the events of the evening over and over again as she and Elizabeth were driven home in Dr. Blackwell's carriage.

While she had never had a boy friend, Emily wondered how it would feel to be kissed by a lover. She closed her eyes and tried to imagine it by lifting her chin slightly and touching her lips softly with her fingertips. Would her lips seem sweet to him? As the carriage rounded a curve and jolted her she thought of a more realistic problem. Would she ever see him again?

***

Getting ready for the first day at the Infirmary was hectic for Emily. To begin with, she had to get Elizabeth up and ready to go with her. Elizabeth could stay in the nursery with other children during the day, but she resisted getting dressed, jumped back on her cot and pulled the covers over her head.

"You can't stay here all day by yourself, Elizabeth. I know you sometimes stay while I run an errand, but you can't stay all day by yourself. Now get up and get dressed."

"Not by myself. Miss Pink Shoe--."

"Miss Pink Shoe is not somebody, she's just a doll."

"She is too, somebody!"

"Finish putting your clothes on this minute! We're going."

"No!"

"Elizabeth!"

Sighing deeply Emily jerked a dress over Elizabeth's head, brushed her hair, and buckled her shoes.

"No!" Elizabeth cried kicking at Emily while clutching Miss Pink Shoe to her chest.

"Now!" Emily said, "We're going right now." She picked Elizabeth up, threw the doll back on the cot and left. She negotiated the four flights of steps holding her noisy, squirming little sister around the middle as she might lug a sack of flour. As she adjusted her load, Emily felt thankful she had inherited the bigger, sturdier frame of the Sullivans, and that Elizabeth had taken from their father's side the doll-like petiteness of the McKelvy women.

Chapter Fifteen

Emily's frustration did not end when they reached the Infirmary. So many people coming and going! The whole place was alive with movement, loud talking, babies crying-- a man and a woman yelling at each other, his fist only inches from her face. In a glance, Emily also recognized two teen girls on the far side of the room as ragged, filthy orphans she'd often seen on the street, giggling, pulling at men's coattails, making crude remarks. Ma had said sadly, "It's the way they manage to live. 'Tis a shame. Poor things."

"How?" Emily had asked.

Ma had shaken her head. "Well, it's not easy to talk about, but you need to know. I've sheltered you too much, Emily, and ignorance is not a good thing." It was the first Emily knew of prostitution although she had wondered about the way some coarse women talked in the streets.

At the infirmary another girl was assigned to clean with Emily--a seventeen-year-old of unusual beauty. Her green eyes were slightly Oriental and her smooth complexion the color of pale sand.

Emily said, "You have such pretty light brown hair."

Sue Ling smiled. "I understand what you mean, I think. That my hair should be dark? Well, my father was British, my mother Chinese, my great-grandmother was Norwegian, so I inherited from three sources at least--those I know about anyway. My last name is Clark."

"I'm pure Irish through and through," Emily said, "as you might guess with a name like McKelvy."

"Well, Irish looks good on you," Sue Ling said.

"Thanks. You must have been told many times that you're unique and beautiful."

Sue Ling smiled, "A few times." She looked at Emily. "I'm glad to have you working with me. Some of the old women are grouchy."

"Really?" Emily smiled.

Both girls laughed.

"Did you come here from China?"

"No, my father was a handsome British Naval officer and in his travels he met Mother in Hong Kong. She was a very beautiful Norwegian-Chinese girl of seventeen, and they fell in love."

"I couldn't actually be certain you of your Chinese heritage," Emily said.

"Oh, I think it shows and being Chinese can be hard."

"Being Irish can be, too," Emily said. "We had to do sewing at home because places Ma might have worked had up signs 'No Irish Need Apply.' "

"It's not just in work places. Dad married Mother against a lot of protest."

"Why?"

"Oh, families, you know and silly laws. But Dad never gave up and eventually they were married on an Hawaiian Island. Then when I was nine Mother fell from a runaway horse and died." Tears brightened her eyes for a moment. "I came to America with my father and my grandmother after that. I'm not sure of his reason except he was terribly upset after Mother died and he felt a need to try to escape the pain. Actually, my grandmother might never have been able to come here without my father's influence, as a respected high-ranking officer. He worked it out somehow despite the American rejection of Chinese women."

"Dr. Blackwell doesn't reject people for being Irish, Chinese, Negro or anything," Emily said.

"That's why we're here," Sue Ling said. "I don't understand why anyone blames people for being born whatever they are. We can't help that. We should only be blamed if we do wrong things."

"I know," Emily said, "My mother felt that way."

Sue Ling continued, "My father once thought we should move to California, but then he heard how the Chinese were being treated there and changed his mind out of concern for The Old One and me."

"The Old One?"

"That's what my grandmother is called. I was named for her so, of course, her name is also 'Su Ling,' though spelled without the 'e'. We honor and respect her as the family matriarch."

"Why would they not like you and your grandmother in California?"

"Oh, such terrible disrespect for Chinese women! I'm not sure if it continues to this day, but it may. Such bad things happened there. If a young woman was brought, by a contractor, from China to San Francisco, she was required to work as a prostitute four and a half years--that was for an advance of $524. Even the lower-grade prostitute would earn $850 a year taking on seven a day at thirty-eight cents a customer, but she was not paid any of the extra money and no one did a thing about it! In fact, she suffered all kind of penalties if she was ill or pregnant and had to miss work. Also Chinese wives and children weren't allowed to come so the Chinese population was just men, men, men--thousands, except for a handful of Chinese women besides the prostitutes. Then after the railroad work ran out, the men took to rolling cigars and other such jobs that threatened the poor white workers and caused a fight. Well, you know, like the poor whites here against the free Negroes."

"But you and your grandmother didn't...weren't...."

"I know, but we show our Chinese blood. Just like Negroes have their look. As Irish you don't have some special appearance that marks you."

"But my accent does," Emily said, "and I have to talk don't I?" She laughed. "Well, maybe not. I could pretend to be dumb." She pressed her mouth together and crossed her lips.

Sue Ling smiled, but spoke in a serious tone. "We are blessed that Dr. Blackwell likes us."

"Is your father happy in America? Da loved this country in advance although he died on the ship coming over and never got to see it. By the way, you have a nice voice and I like your accent."

"Thanks. I was born near the same place as Dr. Blackwell--Bristol, England." She smiled and raised her eyebrows a little, as if she felt some pride in the shared birthplace.

"Oh, and your Dad--what about him?"

"He did like America, but he loved England more. He returned there often and finally married a new wife--a pretty British widow. I seldom see him now that he's so involved with his new family."

"I'm sorry."

"He likes having two step-sons to raise. It's all right," she said but Emily heard a catch in her voice.

For a moment they both were silent.

"We came from Donegal, Ireland," Emily said. I was only six years old, but I especially remember the beautiful lakes and the green grass."

"Funny we both think of the water. I remember the storms lashing the harbor and the heavy fog--the "pea soupers" when it was really bad. It put a feeling on you--like ghosts might be nearby." Sue Ling shivered and hugged herself, but she laughed.

"When I was little Ma liked to watch the stormy waves dash against the rocks at Donegal quay, but they kind of scared me," Emily said. "I used to cling to her skirts and just peek out."

"Oh, but there were the good, sunny days, too. Dr. Blackwell likes to talk of her childhood there--the walled garden, the lilacs and wonderful breezes that bring the fresh tang of the sea. Although it's not the same, she likes to walk by the river here."

"I know, "Emily said, "she visited us once on her river walk. Well, better get busy," she said and resumed washing down the hospital bed on the ward they were cleaning.

"Do you want to be a nurse, too?" Sue Ling asked.

"No. I want to marry a captain, live in a big house and have lots of babies."

Sue Ling stopped cleaning the chair she was working on and looked directly at Emily. "You have no ambition? Well, you've just arrived. It's hard to imagine anyone around Dr. Blackwell without the wish to be educated and useful to others."

"I'll be useful to my husband and children," Emily said. She imagined how wonderful it would be to be the wife of Captain Jerry McCord. People would say, *There goes the Captain McCord, his lovely, young wife, Emily, and their first child.*

What would their first child be? A boy or a girl? Maybe a girl named Sally or a boy named Jerry Frank.

Sue Ling looked thoughtful. She said, "Well, I suppose that's fine but I want more."

***

Three weeks later Emily woke one morning with a pounding headache and fever.

"Elizabeth," she said, "I need you to walk to the Infirmary to tell Dr. Blackwell I can't come in today, that I'm sick. Can you do that?"

"I can do it. I could've done it before now. Ma said I was good at noticing."

"But it's quite a long way for you."

"I know all about it. We've been walking it every day."

"You must be careful."

"Why?"

"Because there are thieves on the street and you'll be alone. You'll need to watch all around you. Also, I need you to go by the grocery and buy a can of salmon, and I don't want someone to take it away from you. Oh, I'm afraid this is too much for you. Maybe...."

"No. I'd run."

"Elizabeth, pay attention. Don't walk close to alleyways--no closer than you can help, and keep a sharp eye out. Wait to buy the salmon on the way home--you know, at that little store on the riverfront."

"I will. I know how to do it."

"Here's a coin for the salmon. Push it down in your pocket and stuff this little scarf over it."

Elizabeth did as she was told, smiling, looking very

proud. "I like being big," she said. Just as she reached the door, she turned back, picked up Miss Pink Shoe and set her in the chair by Emily's cot. Sticking a finger close to the doll's face, she gave instructions. "Now you be good. Stay with Emily while I'm gone, and don't open the door to anybody."

"Elizabeth! Go on. And remember if you see Mrs. Peake, keep away from her. Do run away if necessary."

***

Elizabeth descended the steps and walked onto the street of decaying buildings. On a corner nearest the riverfront a building of gray boards had collapsed. From the tip of what had been the roof, a giant rat sniffed the morning air. An elderly, white-bearded street peddler threw a rock and the rat scampered underneath to the basement.

"You nearly got him this time." A wiry-haired hag laughed. She pushed by with her own cart of hot breads. The scent of yeast gave a slight reprieve from the stench of the street.

A man with bundles balanced on a long pole called out, "Potatoes, beans, tomatoes!" Some women in dirty clothes wearing aprons bought from him after haggling over the price.

Along the way many faded structures housed businesses at the ground level. Upstairs tattered curtains suggested families lived there. Elizabeth looked up at one and saw a frowzy red-haired woman in a low-cut blouse part dingy curtains. The woman called down to the busy street where men and women walked to and fro. "Want a good time? Come up and see Syble." Elizabeth stopped. She thought about a good time. She was tempted but Emily had said to hurry. Reluctantly she continued her pace.

The sun was warm on Elizabeth's back as she bounced along the street toward the Infirmany. To her delight a small black and white dog joined her and ran alongside.

Around the bend of the street a crowd had gathered

around a giant man. Elizabeth stopped to gaze. The man had great, fat hands, a long rope of white hair and bulging, milky eyes. A puffy foot was shoeless.

"Somebody help me," he pleaded. "Help me!"

"Help you, you scoundrel? Who did you ever help? You fat-assed thief! Good Irish landed on this shore--nearly penniless and you tricked them! You stole from my own brother. Yeah, I know you! You'll get no help from me now or from the devil in hell!" A woman blurted out the words. The crowd of shabbily dressed men and women echoed her taunts. They booed and spat on him. Elizabeth moved inside the group and listened. She put her fingers to her lips in anxious interest. "Is he a bad man?" she asked, but no one answered. In her distraction she did not see a street boy who grabbed her from behind while another snatched the scarf from her pocket and took her coin.

Yelling in delight the scruffy boys quickly disappeared down an alleyway and into the underground of a rotting tenement. Elizabeth chased them calling out, "Stop! Stop!" but quickly realized she couldn't catch them. She blinked back tears. She had failed and Emily would be mad. Slowly she walked down the street near the giant old man. He was still weeping but now he was alone. Elizabeth ventured close to him. "Why're you crying, sir?"

The old man rubbed across his eyes and his dripping nose with his shirt sleeves, wiping with first one arm, then the other. "Help me!" he cried. "I'm sick." He blasted out the words. Spittle spewed from his mouth and he began sobbing again.

"Ohhhh," Elizabeth said, frowning, feeling sorry for him.

Sobbing the old man continued, "My foot...I can't get my shoe off. I can't." He touched his trembling hands together. "Too stiff. My hands won't bend."

"I'll do it," Elizabeth said. She stooped, untied the leather laces and pulled at the heavy shoe, but let go quickly when the old man screamed in pain.

"I stop now," Elizabeth said, holding her hands behind

her back.

"No...please! Months it's been on, months! I couldn't...I tried and tried."

Elizabeth pulled hard and the shoe came off as the old man bit his lip and tears streamed down his face. A sickening odor arose and pieces of blackened flesh fell to the ground.

Elizabeth held her nose and stared.

Gasping in pain, the old man asked between breaths, "Are you a doorway sleeper, boy? Oh, son, please come live with me. I can't do for myself."

Elizabeth bristled. "Don't you see I'm a girl?"

He touched his milky eyes. "These don't see. I'm most near blind," he said and groped about in the air for her. "A girl. That's even better."

"No!" Elizabeth cried and ran. Block after block she ran as fast as she could in the crowded street...dodging drays, peddlers, drunks, clusters of women and dirty, crying children. Near the infirmary she walked again and then was aware the little dog still followed her. She picked him up and held him in her arms as he squirmed and licked her face. Giggling, she said, "I'll take you home, Bossy-Boy. You can live with me and Emily and Miss Pink Shoe."

Elizabeth climbed the steps back up to the apartment. In a tied cloth bundle, she carried medicine for Emily and some food Dr. Blackwell had provided after hearing about the lost salmon money. Under her arm she held the squirming little dog.

"No, Elizabeth," Emily said, "we can't keep that dog."

With tears streaming down her face, Elizabeth yelled, "Why? Why? I've already named him. He's mine!"

"We can barely feed ourselves, much less a dog," Emily said. She got up from her cot and took the bundle.

"I'll work," Elizabeth said. "I'll wind the thread for you."

"I'm not sewing now, Elizabeth and you can't get a job. You're too little."

"Please, Emily," she cried jumping up and down.

"Stop that!"

129

"I won't eat much, Emily, and every morning you won't have to carry me. I'll walk down the steps just as nice as plum pudding."

Emily laughed. "Well, maybe we could get some scraps at the Infirmary. We'll see."

***

Work became routine at the Infirmary for Emily. As the months passed, she and Sue Ling shared more and more of themselves until they found they had many points of agreement. Sometimes, however, Sue Ling surprised Emily in speaking of intimate details regarding her romance with a young Frenchman. Emily had felt that anything beyond kissing was much too private to tell anyone--unless, of course, one was a whore. She knew whores in the streets spoke crudely and in loud voices--they were everywhere in her neighborhood, but someone nice, someone who would one day be a nurse? Well, perhaps she'd understand it later. At least she was learning new and fascinating details that could come in handy when she had a romance of her own.

Sue Ling's handsome boy friend, Paul Le Clearmont, brought linens to the Infirmary. He wanted to be a doctor. And by now, Emily had learned the source of so much ambition truly was Dr. Blackwell. Sue Ling told her Dr. Blackwell had become a doctor against all odds. Emily now knew that Dr. Elizabeth was the first woman in America to achieve that goal, and that her sister, Dr. Emily Blackwell had managed to study medicine later and to join her, and still later, the German woman, Dr. "Zak." There seemed to be no end to Dr. Blackwell's drive to serve in medicine.

"Even after all she's done, some still put her down," Sue Ling said. "She's amazing...she keeps giving regardless of everything. She says God inspired her, and I believe that."

"Are you religious?" Emily asked.

"I believe God inspires and loves us. I'm going to be a nurse, you know. What about you?"

"I don't know. We read the Bible and prayed and made

confession to the priest, but not about things like becoming a nurse."

"Surely now that you know Dr. Blackwell, you want to help others."

"I don't know how I would do that? I don't think I could be anybody special."

"Listen, Emily, if Dr. Blackwell had been like that, do you suppose she'd be a doctor today?" Sue Ling seemed impatient, even perhaps a little angry.

Nurse Mary, who stood nearby joined in. "Certainly not. Do you suppose she said, 'I don't think I could?' We wouldn't be here today if she had."

"Right. Thanks to her," Sue Ling said, "we have our jobs and I do mean to be a nurse right here with her."

Emily said nothing more. She still dreamed of being married to a captain like Jerry McCord, living in a big house and having lots of happy children. Being Jerry McCord's wife and mother to his children, she thought, must be about as close to Heaven on earth as a girl could get.

Nurse Mary said, "It may come to you later--some ambition, Emily. After all, you're only fourteen."

Emily remembered that Sue Ling was seventeen. Would she want to be a nurse when she reached seventeen? She didn't think so.

***

In the weeks that followed, Emily found herself being admired by Colton Higgs, a husky dark-haired boy who drove the wagon to transport patients...sometimes dead patients. Colton knew where she kept her cleaning supplies and he often hid small presents for her there.

At first Emily had no idea who her admirer might be. Had the gifts not had her name on them, she would have assumed they were for someone else.

"Who would do this?" Emily asked Sue Ling.

"Think, Emily. Who is always hanging around talking with you, paying you little compliments? Who else but

Colton Higgs?"

Next day Emily saw Colton in the hallway. "Thank you for the gifts," she said. "I had no idea...."

Colton flushed brick red.

"It was nice of you," Emily said. "I liked them... especially the lavaliere with the tiny pearls and the garnet. The garnet is my birthstone, but you probably didn't know that."

"I gave it to you especially for that reason. Sue Ling told me."

"Oh...well, thank you again. It's really pretty."

"Birthstones go back to the Bible, you know, so I hope its a blessing."

"To the Bible? No. I never heard that," Emily said.

"In Exodus the high priest Aaron had twelve different gems in his breast plate. Some say that is the beginning of a stone for each month. I don't know if Aaron thought it brought good luck, but many folks today think so. Aaron, you know, was the brother of Moses."

"I had no idea. Are you going to become a priest?"

Colton laughed. "Me a priest? No. My father is a minister so I've been on the front row at church many a time. Some of it soaked in."

"Well, you were nice to think of me. Thank you."

Colton grinned. Emily flushed slightly. She was charmed by his bright smile and stunned by his next words. "None of the little gifts are good enough for you, Emily. I don't have that kind of money yet...even if there's that much money in the world."

All she could manage to say was, "Ahhh," before he turned and walked back down the hall. At the doorway, he stood for a moment looking at her once more and then was gone.

***

Colton invited Emily to an All Hallow's party at Garland's Fine Leather Works and Apprenticeship School where he studied part-time. He told Emily he was learning to be a leather worker and hoped to one day have his own shop.

At first Emily told him she couldn't go, but when Sue Ling agreed to care for Elizabeth, she changed her mind. It would be her first date and she was excited. She thought Colton had a beautiful smile and was quite handsome...if one didn't compare him too much to Captain McCord.

When Nurse Mary heard Emily and Sue Ling discussing Emily's date, the nurse playfully widened her eyes and whispered, "Beware of Stingy Jack woooooooo!"

"Oh, I know about him!" Sue Ling said. "Yes, Emily, he may be wandering the black of night on these very streets and all you'll see is that glowing coal the devil tossed him."

"A dead, evil old drunk with a burning coal in a turnip—well, I'm not scared," Emily said.

"How about the ghosts?" Nurse Mary asked. "They'll be out floating all around."

"Remember." Sue Ling said, "A bowl of food outside your door to keep the ghosts happy."

"Elizabeth's dog would eat it," Emily said.

"Phooey, you're no fun to tease," Nurse Mary said. "Well, have a happy time, Emily." She turned to go, but added, "I like Colton. He's a nice boy."

"Thanks," Emily said.

"Yes, do have a good time," Sue Ling said. "I'll take good care of Elizabeth."

***

All Hallow's night was cold and dark. Despite her disbelief Emily found herself looking into the black night to see if such as Stingy Jack walked with a burning coal in a turnip...or maybe now in a pumpkin. Their carriage clattered through the street with only pale lights here and there. She shivered in her thin coat and her teeth chattered making conversation difficult. She was grateful that Colton had little to say as they traveled in the bitter cold. Perhaps he was having the same problem.

133

They wore masks to ward off evil spirits and that helped against the chill wind. After having teased her, Sue Ling and Nurse Mary made her a pretty yellow mask with shiny red beads. Emily thought Colton's black one trimmed in silver made him look mysteriously handsome. She even told him so which made him throw back his head and laugh. He took her hand for a moment, but then released it, perhaps considering it improper to be so familiar at this time.

Emily was grateful when they finally arrived at Garland's Fine Leather Works. Warm air engulfed them at the door of the brick building. Emily smiled. It was cozy inside with two pot-bellied stoves blushing with heat! But a strong smell of tannin chemicals filled the air and made Emily feel slightly light headed. Everywhere the walls were covered with leather coats, pants, hats and belts. Tables against the walls held food and drink.

Just as they entered the door, Colton introduced her to a few people whose faces she couldn't really see because of their All Hallow's disguises, but everyone was friendly and there was much joking and laughter.

Emily saw thin puffs of smoke inching through some cracks and wondered why. She caught her breath. Was there a fire? "Colton," she began, but he was laughing with a friend over some private joke and did not respond immediately. If others noticed, she thought, they perhaps understood the reason for the smoke and were not concerned.

"Colton...," she said now tugging at his sleeve. Before he could answer a loud rumbling sound filled the room, then a great blast of fire and acrid smoke rolled out in black clouds from the walls. Within seconds, amid screams and frantic scrambling, the building exploded and collapsed.

Outside, flames shot to adjoining old frame buildings and leaped into the black night. The darkness was pierced by a fast roaring orange demon blasting intense heat wide into the icy winter night. Smoke choked the sudden onlookers who gathered to watch the spectacle as dark shadows gave way to the racing, overpowering flames.

People in nightclothes ran from their tenement homes,

crying out, calling to family members and friends in hope of drawing them to their sides...to safety even without their poor possessions. Each building extending down from the tannery fell one after another in crashing, crackling sounds and then became hot, glowing embers. Dazed, thinly clad residents walked the streets weeping. Some cried out and wrung their hands. The more alert began seeking shelter for the night.

An elderly man from the neighborhood recognized Emily lying on the ground near what had been the front door. He halted a passing wagon and he and his wife transported her to The Infirmary along with two other seriously burned young women who had also just entered the door to the tannery. The man and his wife looked around the area for other survivors but found none.

***

Staff members of the Infirmary spoke of the All Hallow's tragedy in hushed tones. Some thought the explosion was the work of a competing tannery, but others were certain it was simply a horrible accident...the result of chemicals stored in the basement igniting.

A barely recognizable Emily lay moaning in the clean, white bed of the Infirmary. Dr. Blackwell had been nearby all morning, frequently coming back into the room to see Emily, to speak to her in soft, encouraging tones.

A patient on a nearby bed said, "Poor girl! But it could have been worse. She must have been right by the door or she would have been killed for sure."

Nurse Yvonne stepped away from Emily's bed. "Doctor, why don't you give her more morphine? You know she's not going to make it so why let her suffer?"

"Don't say that!" snapped Dr. Blackwell. "Patients, especially young ones, have made miraculous recoveries."

"Of course, but...."

"I make the decisions here," the doctor said, but in a softer tone this time. She bit her lip and shook her head.

"Perhaps, a bit more. I do hate to see her suffer, but I must think of her recovery as well."

In leaving the room, Dr. Blackwell met Sue Ling. "Where is Elizabeth?" she asked. "I was told she was with you."

"I-I thought I should come to work and I wasn't sure about bringing her here with Emily...I left her with my grandmother."

"But she is very old and doesn't speak English," Dr. Blackwell said impatiently. "It would be better for you to care for Elizabeth temporarily, at least until we can make other arrangements for her."

"I hardly knew what to do," Sue Ling said.

"I'm sorry I was abrupt," Dr. Blackwell said. She rubbed her brow with the back of her hand. "Go now and take care of Elizabeth. I'll come by later in the afternoon and see what we can arrange."

"Is Emily going to make it?"

"I don't know. I pray she'll survive, but it's too soon to know."

"If she doesn't, what will become of Elizabeth?" Sue Ling asked.

"Even if she does live, she will need a long recovery period. Right now I can't be sure. But, like I said, I'll come by to see Elizabeth later today. Has she been told about Emily?"

"No. Not yet. I wasn't sure what to say." Tears sprang to Sue Ling's eyes.

"It's all right. Don't worry. I'll tell her myself," Dr. Blackwell said. "Now you go on and look after her until then."

"I hope Emily will...."

"Yes, we're all hoping."

***

Sue Ling felt Dr. Blackwell's concern was unfounded with regard to her grandmother's care of Elizabeth. So her grandmother didn't speak English...what did it matter? She'd cared for many a young one in her eighty-six years. What could possibly happen that the Old One couldn't handle? Even now she tended a cousin's young son.

Sue Ling walked softly to Emily's bed and gently touched her arm. Emily's eyes remained closed and she made no movement. "Oh, God," Sue Ling said. Tears flooded her eyes and she turned away.

When she left The Infirmary, Sue Ling walked along the street wishing her beau would come by. She'd ride with him on the linen wagon. Maybe they'd go to their secret place at the laundry. How lovely that would be! What a shame if Emily should die and never have what she knew with Paul. Emily seemed so naïve! Maybe things could have changed soon if Colton hadn't been killed...she didn't want to think of it...not someone close to her own age dying like that.

She looked up and down the street. If only Paul would come along! It was time for his first run. If he came now it would all work out so well since she could still be home hours before Dr. Blackwell arrived.

Wait! She was on the wrong street. Two blocks over to the right should be Paul's route. Yes, that would be logical. He'd be driving there about this time if he had his usual schedule.

For more than half an hour she walked slowly, waited and looked but he did not appear. What if she went on by the laundry? How brazen that would seem in her grandmother's eyes! But grandmother would never know and she believed Paul's family understood about young love. She'd heard the French were so wonderfully romantic and it certainly fit Paul. She smiled and breathed more deeply just thinking of him.

Around a corner the linen wagon appeared at last. "What are you doing here?" Paul asked, his dark eyes alert in surprise.

"Waiting for you. I have a little time and I wanted to be with you."

"Great! Here," he extended his hand. "Jump up."

When she was seated beside him, he circled her waist with his arm and she lay her head on his shoulder.

"Shall we go to our secret place?" she whispered.

"Oh, Sue Ling," he said. He lifted her chin and kissed her lips. "How sweet you are."

Chapter Sixteen

The Old One answered the door and politely bowed to the obese white woman.

"I've come to see my great-niece," Mrs. Peake said.

The Old One turned and called to someone behind a dark blue curtain. A young Chinese boy of about eight years appeared.

"Do you speak English?" Mrs. Peake asked. "What is your name, son?"

"Sing Lee, Ma'am."

"Good. You do speak English. Please, bring Elizabeth here. My poor little one's sister is so wounded. I've come to take her to visit. But first," she lifted the cover on a small basket, "we'll have some cookies and soda pop."

Elizabeth, who had been hiding behind a slatted panel at the kitchen doorway, came forward slowly. What was Mrs. Peake saying about Emily?

"Oh, my dear, dear little Elizabeth. Emily wants you to come. She is so badly hurt...burned in that terrible fire last night, but I guess you knew about that."

Elizabeth frowned. What about Emily? Was it a trick? She kept her distance. Was Mrs. Peake lying? She knew about lying. She'd told lies herself and Ma had spanked her for it. But where was Emily? She had not come last night or this morning.

Mrs. Peake reached out, but Elizabeth moved farther away. She would run if the old woman touched her. "Poor baby. I know you are so upset."

"Emily'll be here. She's working," Elizabeth said.

"Oh, no, my dear. Surely, you know she can't."

Elizabeth stared at her She had heard people in the streets exclaiming about the explosion and fire last night... "like the halls of hell," a woman had babbled in the presence of the Old One who simply looked at her frowning not understanding the words but apparently seeing that she was upset. Was it true that Emily was hurt? No. It had nothing to do with Emily. She would come soon.

"It will make our dear Emily feel better to see you, Elizabeth. I'll take you to the Infirmary."

"No!" Elizabeth cried. Was it true? Was Emily hurt? "I'll go. I know the way." Elizabeth started for the door.

"Wait, dear," Mrs. Peake said. "We have time for tea." Her fat hands were already spreading the little feast from her basket out upon a table.

Elizabeth swallowed. Such fine cookies! And she'd never tasted soda pop.

Mrs. Peake bowed and served the Old One first. Then she served the boy and Elizabeth. She took a plain cookie and a slightly scratched bottle of soda pop herself. Seating herself near the Old One, she spoke pleasantly of the improved weather. "Surely this sun will warm things up a bit," she said.

The Old One smiled and nodded, not understanding the spoken words but being pleased with refreshments and a friendly visitor.

Within a short time Mrs. Peake looked about her with satisfaction. Everyone was quite groggy. Soon they grew limp in sleep. Grunting as she stooped, Mrs. Peake lifted Elizabeth into her arms, and as quickly as her weight would allow, shuffled down the steps and into the waiting carriage where the sharp-faced, wiry man waited.

***

Late in the afternoon Dr. Blackwell arrived at Sue Ling's home and was pleasantly greeted by her. "Do come in. Do have a seat. Would you like some tea?"

"No, thanks. I came to see Elizabeth. Has she been told about Emily?"

"You came to see Elizabeth. I thought...."

"You thought what? Where is she?"

"Oh, I don't know. The Old One said she left while she was napping. She thought the woman who came by may

140

have taken her. We assumed this was someone you had sent who could speak English."

"I sent no one," Dr. Blackwell said. "This is frightening, Sue Ling. I thought you were here."

"She was gone when I arrived," Sue Ling said and hoped she would not be asked the time that she had returned home.

"The woman came so early? Before you had time to return home this morning? That seems odd. What time did your grandmother say it was? Did she describe the woman?"

"She seemed not to know details. She tends to be forgetful, and I don't know exactly what time she came." Sue Ling pressed her hand against her chest. "Oh, I'm so sorry! I hope nothing bad has happened to Elizabeth!"

"This is very troubling. She didn't come to the Infirmary so where is she?" Dr. Blackwell's eyes lingered on Sue Ling. She sighed heavily, and left without another word.

Although, Dr. Blackwell had not accused her, Sue Ling was certain by the doctor's behavior that she was being seen as irresponsible. She felt miserable and hoped with all her heart that Elizabeth would soon be found to be safe perhaps with some kindly neighbor woman.

She was too ashamed to return to the Infirmary. She would send a note by Paul.

***

Elizabeth slept for hours in the lap of an older orphan on The Orphans Train West. At first she didn't realize she was on a train because it was night and dark and the train had stopped. When she knew she began to cry and call for Emily.

A tall gray-haired woman dressed in black whispered, "We mustn't alarm everyone, little girl. Just be quiet. It will be all right. You'll see."

"No! I want Emily," she cried fighting her way out of the older girl's arms. She flew into the woman banging on her knees. "Take me back to Emily. Take me back to Emily!"

The woman restrained her, holding her arms tightly, painfully, while speaking softly, "My dear, your sister is dead. Do be quiet. You will have a nice home out west. You'll see."

"No! No! No!" Elizabeth screamed trying to jerk her arms away. The woman released her and reached into her heavy, black bag and brought out to a small box and a cup. "Here," she said, "have a bite to eat and some tea." Elizabeth knocked them from her hands.

"Well, I see we must take a dose of medicine," the woman said. "Hold her," she ordered the older girl who had held her earlier.

***

Town of Kansas, (<u>Kansas</u> City) Missouri

Elizabeth awoke and rubbed her eyes with her fists. She looked about her at the strange room, and sat up. Where was she? Frightened, she called, "Emily! Emily!"

A slim, middle-aged black woman rushed into the room. "Hush, chile, you'll wake her."

"Where's Emily?"

"I don't know, Sugar. Mrs. Dalk's got you for her little servant."

Elizabeth climbed from the big bed and stood facing the soft-spoken woman. "I want Emily. Now!"

A harsh voice called impatiently from the adjoining room. "Alice!"

"Yes, ma'am. I right here, ma'am."

The guttural voice continued in a demanding tone. "Have that young'un come here and rub my feet."

"Yes, ma'am." Alice knelt in front of Elizabeth. "Chile," she whispered, "you got to be quiet and do as she say do."

"Why? I want Emily!" Tears filled Elizabeth's eyes and slid down her cheeks.

"I tell you later."

"Alice!"

142

"Yes, ma'am, we coming." Alice took Elizabeth's hand. "Shhhhh! Now remember, Chile," she said softly.

The large adjoining bedroom was dimly lit and reeked of stale alcohol. Elizabeth saw a giant poster bed. A figure moved under the quilts.

As Alice drew her near the bed, Elizabeth saw a frowzy-haired old woman with thin lips and a sharp nose. Puffy slits barely revealed shadowy dark eyes. Elizabeth stood, trembling, staring at her.

"What are you looking at?" the old woman demanded, rising up on one elbow.

Elizabeth backed away and ran toward the door. "Emily! Emily!" she cried.

"Get my ruler, Alice. I see I have to make things plain to this young'un right now."

"Oh, Miz Dalk, she's..."Alice protested softly.

"Do as I say, Alice, and be quick about it."

The old woman slid from the bed and stood waiting until Alice produced the slender, wooden ruler. "Bring her here and hold her."

Elizabeth could feel trembling in the black woman's hands as she drew her near the bedside. "She don't know, Ma'am. She's just too little," Alice said.

"The sooner she learns the better," Mrs. Dalk said. To Elizabeth's horror the old woman began to beat her.

"No!" Elizabeth screamed. She tried to pull away, but Mrs. Dalk held a tight grip on her wrist and repeatedly hit her head, back and shoulders. The pain was more than Elizabeth had ever known, and she became wild with it, hitting and kicking at the old woman although unable to reach her.

"A mean one," Mrs. Dalk said, "well, we'll make a believer of her."

"Ma'am," Alice cried as the blows increased, "you're gonna kill her!"

Mrs. Dalk stopped suddenly. "That'll do for now."

Alice put a weeping Elizabeth back on her bed. She lifted the pitcher and poured water in the bowl to sponge

143

Elizabeth's welts, but from the other room Mrs. Dalk demanded, "Alice, you get back in here!"

Quickly, before she left the room, Alice whispered, "Do this, Baby." She gently sponged the seeping wound across Elizabeth's cheek and ear with the cool cloth. Do all over where you been hit." Alice pressed the damp cloth in her small hand and rushed from the room, but Elizabeth lay motionless, crying softly. Where was she and who were these strangers? Was this a bad dream? She touched her arm where a bruise was forming. Ouch! It was real! Then vaguely she remembered being on a train and before that...she couldn't remember. "Oh, oh, oh," she cried, but then remembered the old woman and grew silent. She sat up in bed. *I know what, I'll find Bossy Boy and we'll run away.*

Within the hour, to make clear her control, Mrs. Dalk demanded Elizabeth get up from the bed and come with her to the back porch.

"You do see the fence, young'un, don't you? The whole yard is enclosed so don't think you'll be leaving without my permission. Now," she said, handing Elizabeth a broom too big for her to handle adequately, "sweep this porch clean."

Elizabeth made awkward swipes with the broom and kept sobbing until she was again threatened with the ruler. "I see you are going to be worth little to me, and I thought I was paying for a special girl. Special, indeed! I'd like to get my hands on that Peake woman. I bargained for a big girl and look what I got...a little spoiled brat."

Elizabeth stopped trying to work with the big broom, and opened her mouth to speak.

"Keep sweeping and shut up," Mrs. Dalk said. She went inside and slammed the door behind her.

Later, Mrs. Dalk put on a brown felt hat and gave Alice instructions for dinner. "I'm going to look at some cattle," she said.

"Yes, ma'am. Toby says the stock yard's be going big here."

Mrs. Dalk set her thin lips in disapproval. "What would Toby know?" She reached for her purse opened it and looked inside before snapping in shut with a twist of notty gold-colored metal. "I manage the buying and selling here and I manage well. A good business woman you must admit."

"Yes, ma'am," Alice said. I only meant...."

"Do your work. Your opinion is of no consequence. Lord only knows what we're coming to with talk of setting you Negroes free. Never mind who bought and paid for you." She gripped her purse tighter under her arm and walked away. Then she turned and shouted back at Alice. "You know if Union soldiers should ask you...you are not really a slave since I pay you for your services."

Alice nodded her head.

"Answer me!"

"Yes, Ma'am." Under her breath, Alice said, "Pitiful, pitiful pay. We barely scrapes by."

When the old woman was gone, Alice said, "Come with me, baby." Elizabeth followed her into a spacious kitchen where she became aware of the faint smell of wood smoke and the sound of crackling flames. Nearby a long wooden table held a row of brown crockery containing potatoes, apples and onions. Beside the eartenware jars of canned foods gleamed in the light. Cast iron pots hung from a brick sidewall, which contained a fireplace. A milk churn stood nearby. In front of the hearth, flames from the low fire flickered off a rocking chair.

"Now I tell you," Alice said, taking a seat in the rocking chair. "Come here." She held out her arms to Elizabeth.

Elizabeth hesitated. She saw Alice's soft brown eyes and heard her gentle voice. Slowly, cautiously she approached the outstretched brown arms.

"Don't be afraid of me, Chile. I knows you hurt."

When Elizabeth was within her grasp, Alice picked her up and placed her on her lap. "Just rest a bit," she whispered and began to hum as she rocked gently.

Elizabeth cried softly against Alice's shoulder. "I want Emily," she said.

"Who's Emily, Sugar?"

"My sister. My sister," she said impatiently.

"And where's she?"

"Five Points."

"Five Points? Where that be?"

"Five Points!" Elizabeth sat up abruptly. "You don't know where Five Points is?"

"No, but I 'speck it be a long way from here. We right up by the Town of Kansas on a plantation."

"What's a plantation?" Elizabeth frowned.

"A big farm. We...Toby, my man and me, come up this way from Mississippi being as we the Dalk family slaves. We stays in a little cabin down the way...Toby, his ma and me. Little Mama she worked in the Town of Kansas before she get too old. She be a freed slave."

"Slave? What's a 'slave'?"

"Like you now, baby 'cept she told them she take you to be her child."

"I hate her! I want to go home."

"I know that, Chile. She say she gonna 'dopted you, but that don't be true."

"Can I go in the morning?" Elizabeth asked, hopefully.

"Not tomorrow...can't say when. I see what I can do, but you mustn't say a word." Alice held a finger to her lips. "Shhhhhh! Not a word," she whispered, "and it may take a while. Maybe a long time."

"No!"

"I do my best. Just be quiet and be good." She set Elizabeth on her feet and rose from the rocker. "Right now we gotta fix up supper."

Elizabeth ran to the kitchen window. "I hear Bossy Boy!"

"Oh, that old starvin' hound. I'll throw him a bone." Alice's face brightened. "Or maybe we let him dig under the fence for it."

Alice picked up a large bowl from a corner table. The faded floral pattern was furrowed with tiny, dirty cracks and spattered with dumped food. "Old hound, he love this."

"Bossy-Boy will gobble it all up!" Elizabeth said clapping her hands in her excitement.

146

"Bossy-Boy? Who that?"

"My dog. You know, Bossy-Boy," Elizabeth said.

"No, honey. This not be him. This jest an old hound I took up a fancy to."

"Where's Bossy-Boy?" Tears started to fill Elizabeth's eyes.

Alice set the bowl down and stooped to Elizabeth's level. "Come here, Sugar. We got to talk serious. You understand that?"

"What?"

"It gotta be a secret. You understand secret?"

Elizabeth bristled. "I know about secrets. I'm five years old."

Alice persisted. "Listen. This be a secret for keeping just in that little head. No talking about. No telling." She stood and sighed deeply. "Maybe it be too soon to try but it hurts me deep to see a little tyke like you caught here." Although she didn't say it, Alice thought of old Master Dalk's steel traps capturing little animals. She'd shed no tears for him when he died.

"What, Alice? I won't tell. Honest! Cross my heart." Elizabeth ran a finger across her chest making a quick cross.

Again Alice stooped to Elizabeth's level. "You don't want to stay here do you, baby?"

"No, I want Emily."

"Well, Miz. Dalk she want you to stay."

"I hate her! She's mean."

"I know how you feels, baby. I'm afraid for you, but I'm afraid for me too if you be too little to keep a secret."

"I'm not too little. I won't tell! She can hit me and I won't tell. I may cry, but I won't tell."

"Come with me then." Alice picked up the bowl and this time she stuck a large knife into her apron pocket.

"What you gonna cut?" Elizabeth asked.

"Shuuuuu. I'll show you."

Elizabeth followed her to the yard and around to a windowless side of the big house. Setting the bowl on the ground, Alice used the knife to cut a space under the wooden

147

slab fence. She dumped the contents of the bowl near the hole and whistled. Moments later the hound whined outside the boarded yard.

"Old hungry hound'll dig right through," Alice said. She smiled with a look of satisfaction. "Now nobody can say it was us if he makes a big hole. We didn't open no gates. Old hound'll do it all. Miz Dalk, she won't let me open the gate lest she say so."

Elizabeth frowned.

"Don't worry, Sugar, when he gets through that hole it'll be big enough for you to ease under. See how he's going at it digging like a paddle machine." Alice laughed. "He love to eat."

"Can I play with him?"

"No. Just listen." She stooped and placed her hands on Elizabeth's shoulders. "Most every night Miz. Dalk she drinks and drinks 'fore she fall asleep and snore loud on into the night."

"Snore?"

"Never mind that. When you get under the fence in the night, you scoot fast as you can to that next house. You understand?"

"What house?"

"Just like I say, the next house. Nice folk live there." She hesitated then asked, "You understand right and left?"

"This way," Elizabeth said extending first her right arm, then her left.

"Good! You face the fence. Go under then turn left and go down the hill. Miz. Seldeni stays there. Tell her. Tell her everything."

"Are you going, too, Alice?"

"No. Don't say about me. Don't ever say about me at all, chile! Just show her what Miz. Dalk do to you."

"Why?"

"Maybe she know where Five Points be."

"Five Points!"

Alice lifted Elizabeth's chin so their eyes met. "You not afraid of the dark are you? Anyway the moonlight be out then."

"Do I have to ask Mrs. Dalk?"

"Oh, no, Baby! That be the secret. Don't ever, ever tell her." Alice swallowed. She pressed her fingertips together and bowed her head. "Lord, why you give me this tender heart? At least, please shut that little mouth or we be doomed. Thank you, Jesus. Amen." Sighing deeply, Alice walked back toward the house with Elizabeth trailing behind carrying the empty bowl.

"Tomorrow, Alice?"

"Tonight if you be very, very quiet and say no words about it. If you say...well, I reckon we won't know about Five Points no more."

"I won't, Alice. I won't say."

Near dark Elizabeth was looking out the kitchen window when she saw Mrs. Dalk opening the back gate.

"She's coming," Elizabeth whispered.

"I know. I hear the latch falling into place." Alice touched Elizabeth's head. "Now, Baby, remember."

Elizabeth giggled. "Old hound jumping all over her."

"Oh, Lord!" Alice said, "Oh, Lord. I thought he'd leave when he fill his belly. Baby, go to yo room. Don't say nothin' 'bout that ole hound."

"I won't. I won't."

"Remember you're five and knows about secrets."

Moments later, Mrs. Dalk burst through the door. "Alice! How did that nasty, stinking dog get in the yard?"

"Dog, ma'am? What dog?"

"That one!" Mrs. Dalk shoved Alice toward the window. "Did you open the gate?"

"Oh, no ma'am."

"Well, we'll just go out and see. Those fence boards are sturdy. I can't imagine how he could get in unless somebody knocked one out."

Elizabeth eased quietly out the door and ran to the hole under the fence. She lay down and tried to slip through, but the hole was too small. Briefly she was caught under the boards, but she wiggled free.

"What are you doing?" Mrs. Dalk asked. "Get up off that ground!" she demanded. "Look at your dress. Am I going to have to get my ruler again?"

Elizabeth jumped to her feet. With trembling hands she tried to brush the dirt from her clothes. In her eagerness to leave she'd not waited for night as Alice had directed.

"Why, look," Alice said, "the chile found where Old Hound work his way in. I declare."

Mrs. Dalk squinted in the fading light and stooped a bit to see the hole. "Well," the old woman said, "don't just stand there! Get that filthy beast out of my yard."

"Yes, ma'am."

"And go right now to get Toby. Tell him to fill that place in and set heavy stones all around the outside of the fence. I won't have old, filthy dogs in my yard again."

"Yes, ma'am," Alice said, then hesitated. "Should I take the young'un with me or no?"

"Take her, but make sure she stays right with you. If anything happens, I'll hold you responsible." Mrs. Dalk said. "Remember I could move your mother-in-law out. She's taking up space I could use for someone else...someone useful."

Alice made no response. She thought of all the years of service she and Toby had given to the Dalk family and anger rose in her like a heat wave. That woman never appreciated anything they did! She knew Appolo had killed Master Dalk. That was years ago and Appolo was of another tribe, but they all understood Appolo's fury knowing the ways of old Trenton Dalk. Secretly they had been relieved until they found Mistress Dalk on her own would continue to take out her anger on all of them.

"Did you hear me, Alice? You know I mean what I say. If you lose that young'un you'll be most sorry. I see how you treat her like yours. Well, she's not yours. She's mine and don't you forget it. You know I mean what I say."

"Yes, ma'am. I knows."

The slave quarters where Alice, Toby and Little Mama lived reminded Elizabeth of the gray wooden shacks behind the tenements, making it seem a little like home. She liked the cozy, small room where Alice bent to shift the wood in the fireplace making crackling sounds as the sparks flew.

A black man of average size with a white beard covering most of his dark brown face appeared in the doorway. "So," he said, smiling revealing even teeth, "This be Elizabeth. I say, you a pretty little one."

Elizabeth looked up into his pleasant face. "Do you know where Five Points is?"

"No. Old Toby never heard of it."

"Are you sure? This looks sorta like the place behind our rooms?"

"Places can look alike sometimes but not be the same. Old Toby a half a hundred and he seen places 'tween here and Mississippi, but never no Five Points. Maybe we take a search. Maybe we find it," he said hopefully.

Elizabeth said, "I need Emily."

"I know," Toby said, "I know."

She liked the steady, serious look in his face and the sound of his deep musical voice.

Chapter Seventeen

A pale sun spread its winter rays across the foot of Emily's bed. It had been over a week since the black night had exploded in flames killing members of the All Hallow's party.

Emily slipped in and out of consciousness, but on the ninth day she stirred slightly and opened her eyes. She felt confused. Where was she? Oh the pain! She called Elizabeth and nurse Yvonne answered, "I'm here, Emily. Don't struggle, dear."

Emily's eyes widened. "What? Ohhh."

"You've been hurt, but you're going to make it." Yvonne's tone was soft, comforting.

"What happened?"

"The explosion at the Leather Works. You don't remember?"

Emily struggled to sit up but fell back against the pain.

"I'll get you some morphine," Yvonne said. "Just be still. I'll be right back."

Emily groaned softly. The explosion? What did that mean? But in a moment she thought of Elizabeth and again struggled in vain to sit up. Where was Elizabeth?

Moments later Yvonne returned with the morphine. "Here," she said, "this will help, although we're giving you much less now that you're better."

"Where is Elizabeth?"

Yvonne swallowed. A moment passed, but she replied in a calm voice. "She's all right. You mustn't worry about her. Now let the medicine work and get some rest."

Emily asked, "Where?"

"With Sue Ling," Yvonne lied.

"Oh, well, then...." She relaxed and felt drowsy again.

Yvonne walked through the Infirmary and met Dr. Blackwell. "Emily's been awake and asking for Elizabeth."

"You didn't tell her...."

"Oh, no. I lied. I said she is all right. I hope to God she is."

"We're getting nowhere finding her. That woman she feared...that Mrs. Peake probably is the woman who took her, but she has also disappeared. It's maddening. Nobody seems to know a thing."

"If only we can find Elizabeth before we have to tell Emily." Yvonne shook her head. "I don't think she could take it."

"I've hired an investigator. Just maybe...." Dr. Blackwell shrugged as if she felt a chill. "Just maybe...."

In the background, the sound of someone calling for help, footsteps and the rattling of equipment brought the two back to consider their duties. Without further conversation they moved off in different directions.

***

Two days later the investigator, a stocky, mustached man named Henry Smythe, appeared at the Infirmary. He headed immediately to Dr. Blackwell's office where he found her shuffling through some papers. Behind her, the fireplace held a bed of orange coals. Blue flames licked and crackled.

"I have news," Smythe said abruptly. "The Peake woman is dead. She was found in a muddy ditch behind a tenement not four blocks from here."

"Dead?" Dr. Blackwell's eyes widened.

"Yes, and had been for a while. Face near black and looked like the rats had been at her." Smythe grunted. "A bad scene for a bad woman, I reckon.' "

Dr. Blackwell shook her head. "She was a possible lead and now she's gone. Do you know what happened? Who did this?"

"Don't know. Nobody seems willing to talk," Smythe said.

"I suppose that means you have no word on Elizabeth."

Smythe laid a thick hand on the edge of the desk. "Nobody has seen the little one. Least ways that's what they say."

"Well, keep working on it. Her sister is slowly recovering, but the word that Elizabeth is missing could be very hard on her at this point."

"Yes, ma'am, I understand. I'll do my best. Maybe somebody, somewhere, somehow will give me a tiny lead of some kind." He rose abruptly, turned on his heel and was gone.

***

Emily awoke in the night and heard a loud voice, a woman crying, hysterically demanding, "Get them colored out of here! They is putting us all in danger."

Then she heard the calm voice of Dr. Blackwell. "We will put no one out. Not you. Not any of them."

"But," the woman cried, "They hates the Colored! I seen 'em string 'em up. And that little girl...that one left behind when they tore into the Colored Orphan Asylum. Lord, Lord, they even beat that poor little child to death. That's how much they hates 'em all."

Again she heard Dr. Blackwell's soothing voice. "Now, now calm down. You are perfectly safe. The doors are barred. We are all safe."

"Not if them gangs...them mobs...I still hear the roar of 'em as they beat and plunder in the streets. They knifed and hanged the colored, poured oil into their wounds, and then...Lord, Lord! They set fire to the oil and danced under the screaming Negro torches Yes, and they sang loud filthy songs."

"I know," Dr. Blackwell said, "It's terrible, painful to think about, Kathleen. But they aren't here. They aren't breaking down our hospital doors. You know their fury is over jobs they think the freed people are taking from them."

"But, Doctor, they killed even that child because she was colored. Now they know you have the colored here having babies and such."

"We are prepared in the unlikely event they come here. Now go to sleep. You need your rest."

But Kathleen would not be quieted. "Such an ungodly, terrible time has come upon us," she cried, "The riots and the war all because of the fightin' over the coloreds. North and South they fights over the coloreds."

"But we must do what we can to protect them," Dr. Blackwell said. "They are innocent people. Must I give you something to let you rest?"

"Oh, no. I don't want to be asleep. Don't want to be unable to hide if the doors get crashed in."

"I'll get you something to sleep."

"No. No. I'll be quiet."

"Good." Dr. Blackwell pulled the covers up and tucked them around Kathleen who opened her mouth to speak again, apparently thought better of it and settled down.

Emily moaned. She was in pain, and fear had risen in her as well. She had heard Kathleen. She called out to Dr. Blackwell, at the same time she heard loud banging on the front door.

Dr. Blackwell's small figure in pale gray appeared at Emily's bedside. "Yvonne will bring your medicine for the pain right away," she said softly. "She's coming now."

The incessant banging on the door continued. Voices cried out, "Please! For God's sake, please open the door!"

Emily pushed herself up on her elbows. "Who is that? What is happening? Oh, oh."

The sound of mobs roaring in the distance added to the disturbance. Clearly another outbreak was in progress.

"Lie back down, Emily. I'll tend to the door."

Dr. Blackwell peered through the window and saw a small gathering of black people at the door. Across the way, she saw flames consuming buildings, and heard glass breaking intermingled with cries and shouts. Shadowy figures ran, stooped and threw objects. She knew it was the angry, rioting Irish now out of control of the blue-uniformed Irish cops. Irish battling Irish.

Quietly, she opened the door to the small desperate

family...a woman and three children including a boy of about eighteen. "Come in quickly," Dr. Blackwell said.

"Oh, Praise God," the small colored woman cried. "Oh, bless you. Bless you! They tore up our home and burned it. We barely made it out. Only by the back alley."

"We would have been killed," the boy said. He was trembling, but holding his two small sisters to his side.

"You'll be safe here," Dr. Blackwell said. "Come. I'll find some space for you. Have you eaten?"

"Yes, earlier," the woman said. She spoke quietly as they passed Emily's bed.

Emily relaxed and fell asleep even as she heard the clanging of the fire bells in the distance. She was unaware of the heavy rainstorm that broke and drenched the hoards of rushing, crying people only blocks away.

Chapter Eighteen

Elizabeth tried to keep back tears when Mrs. Dalk sent her with Alice and Toby to gather corn on an unseasonably cold day. Would her feet freeze? She remembered hearing about the little orphan boy made to gather corn in freezing weather. His feet froze, didn't they? Would it happen to her? Would they cut off her feet, too? At the moment she forgot the boy was made to work without shoes in freezing temperatures, but it would not have comforted her much as her own shoes were cracked and a sole was loose.

"Stop that blubbering!" Mrs. Dalk demanded.

"Come, Chile," Alice said, taking her by the hand.

Toby joined them and they continued to work even after a fine mist of sleet began to fall.

"Chile," Alice said, "you too little to get to the top corn and you freezin'. Your little nose be red as a cherry and you fingers, too. Go warm by that ole drum Toby fire up just outside the barn there."

"Oh, Alice," Elizabeth cried, hugging Alice's waist, "I love you!"

***

On a snowy day in November when they went into the kitchen, Alice pulled a small round pan from the oven. "I done baked you a birthday cake."

Elizabeth clapped her hands. "Oh, Alice! A birthday cake for me! Thank you."

"We don't know what the real day be, but we celebratin' now." She smiled. "It jest a little plain cake."

"I love plain cake! I know my birthday. July 19th. Ma told me."

"Well, you be such a smart chile!" Alice said. "Well it not be August, but we celebrate jest the same. Set your little self right here." Alice pulled back a chair from the kitchen table. She cut a slice of the warm cake and placed it on a small plate in front of Elizabeth.

"You best have a bit of milk, too," Alice said pouring a small mug full to the brim.

"I reckon' it be cool. I just pulled it up out of the well water. That well, though, ain't as deep as it need be to keep stuff real cool."

Elizabeth quickly ate the slice of cake. "This is the most wonderfulest cake in the world, Alice."

Mrs. Dalk appeared in the kitchen doorway. She rubbed her baggy eyes with the hem of her dressing gown and yawned.

"Ma'am, you want yo breakfast?"

"No, it's nearly noon. I'll have that cake. It smells good."

"Ma'am, we celebratin' the young' uns birthday."

"Her birthday? Now how would you know that?"

"Just a little celebration."

"I don't care about that," she said. "Give me the cake and some coffee. I'm in charge here. I guess with talk about war, you colored are getting too uppity, thinking you're going to be in charge. Well, you're not in charge. And remember I do pay you and keep Toby's useless old mama on here, too."

"Yes, ma'am."

"And how dare you to waste my sugar and eggs on that young 'un?"

"I just thought...."

"You'd best think better, and just to fix it in your stupid head for the future, take this." The old woman kicked Alice hard on the shin, which left her gasping in pain.

Elizabeth screamed. She jumped from her chair and ran hard into Mrs. Dalk, hitting and kicking her with all her might. The bony old woman grabbed a wooden spoon and beat Elizabeth until she ran from the room.

"Alice," Mrs. Dalk shouted, "lock that brat in the closet, and don't you let her out until I say."

Alice found Elizabeth in the next room rubbing her

head, tears streaming down her face.

"l'm sorry, Chile. I'm sorry. We gotta do something. I dunno what, but we gotta do something." Alice mumbled to herself, "Don't know what to do with peoples that be like her."

When Alice shut the closet door, the small space became totally dark. Elizabeth squirmed about hoping she would scare away any mice or spiders. When she settled down, she realized her head and shoulder burned with hurt from the blows. A close musty smell filled her nostrils in the heat of the airless closet.

"Emily," she sobbed, softly, "Emily." But knew by now that Emily must be far away.

***

Elizabeth awoke and saw a small streak of light around the closet door. Daylight. She stirred and looked about her at the lumpy piles of clothes and boxes. Her head and shoulder felt sore and she was both hungry and thirsty. She tried to open the door but it held against the lock. Finally, she drifted off to sleep again.

Later, she awoke with the sound of a tapping on the door.

"Young'un! Are you awake, young'un?" It was the old woman and her voice was soft.

Elizabeth drew her knees up to her chest and waited.

The old woman rattled the door. "Young'un, wake up! I'm going to let you out now, if you promise to behave yourself."

Elizabeth was puzzled. Was the old woman afraid she'd fight her again?

"Young'un! Alice is sick with the grippe. You must take care of me today. You hear me?"

"Yes."

"Yes, ma'am! Young'un, you mind your manners when you speak to me." The whispered voice had changed. It was now once more angry, sharp, demanding.

"You hear me, young'un?"

Elizabeth defiantly wrapped her arms about herself and remained silent. She heard the key turn in the lock and a flash of bright daylight flooded the closet as the old woman swung the doors aside.

"Now, get yourself up from there and wash yourself. Be quick about it. I need my breakfast cooked."

In her haste, Elizabeth stumbled over a flat iron on the closet floor that pitched her toward Mrs. Dalk. For a brief moment Elizabeth saw fear in the old woman's eyes. She saw, too, that Mrs. Dalk moved unsteadily, limping slightly. Had her kicking really hurt the skinny old legs?

"Cook me eggs and bacon," Mrs. Dalk said, "and don't you burn them."

Elizabeth remained silent as she poured water in the bowl and began to wash her face. Could she cook? She'd watched Alice, but she'd never done any cooking herself.

Still, like Ma had said, she was good at noticing.

Mrs. Dalk stood nearby. "Did you hear me? Answer when I talk to you."

"Yes, ma'am," Elizabeth said.

"Well, be quick about it. I'm ready to eat now."

***

Elizabeth found the fire in the stove had died down to only a few orange coals smothered in gray cinders. Like Alice, she turned the crank to shake down the ashes, then she laid a few thin strips of cedar across the coals. When it flamed, she added chunks of wood. Feeling a sense of accomplishment, she pulled up a chair and stood on it to reach a frying plan hooked on the wall.

Mrs. Dalk appeared in the doorway. "Is it ready yet?"

"No, ma'am. I had to build the fire first. I did it just like Alice."

"Oh, I'm so put out with that Alice, leaving me here like this. And that Peake woman! Sure, she was sending me a big girl. Sure! She's never showed her lying face even once

160

since she took my money. She knew I wouldn't settle for you if she did."

"Mrs. Peake? Where is Mrs. Peake?" Elizabeth asked.

"Where she's always been, of course."

"Five Points? Do you know...."

"Wherever. Now get on with it. Slice me some of that bread and be sure to warm and butter it."

"The butter is in the let-down bucket in the well," Elizabeth said. "Do you know where Five Points is?"

"Five what? No, of course not. Stop asking foolish questions and pull the butter up. Lord, I thought that woman said you were smart."

"It's too heavy. It's full of milk and other things. I can't."

"Oh, well, forget it then. It's just one more burden for me to bear." Mrs. Dalk edged her chair a little back from the heat of the stove. "You might not imagine it, young'un, but once I was a carefree child like you. Oh yes, and the darling of my papa's eye. 'My Little Darling One,' he called me."

Elizabeth remained silent for a moment, then she ventured, "Emily said Da died on the ship." She placed strips of bacon in a pan, unaware that Mrs. Dalk had abruptly left the room.

Moments later the old woman re-appeared with an amber bottle of whiskey. "Get me a glass, young'un," she said, gesturing toward an open cabinet of cut-wear blinking in the firelight from the stove.

Elizabeth did as she was told, then returned to the sizzling bacon. It was cooking too fast! She was frightened. What would Mrs. Dalk do if she ruined it? Then she remembered Alice, at times, muttering to herself, "It be cookin' too fast, better scoot it to the back." Elizabeth moved the pan to the back of the stove. Still, the bacon needed something. It looked crinkled around the edges. Forgetting exactly what Alice did, Elizabeth nevertheless remembered there was some action. She decided to stir the bacon all around the pan like scrambling eggs.

Mrs. Dalk poured a full glass of whiskey and drank it

161

quickly, and then half-filled another with shaking hands. "Life can be very cruel, you know. No, you probably wouldn't...you've never had anything to lose, but I've lost so much!" Tears filled the old woman's eyes. She lifted the half-glass of the amber liquid to her lips, gulped it and wiped her mouth with the back of her hand.

Elizabeth placed the fragrant, smoked bacon onto brown paper to drain. She glanced at Mrs. Dalk and when she saw the old woman sitting with her head down, she broke a piece of bacon and slipped it into her mouth. It tasted so good!

"No, you wouldn't know," Mrs. Dalk continued, now in a slurred voice. "but I loved and lost not once, not twice, but thrice. Oh yes, my papa, my dear husband, then my son left to seek his fortune out in the world somewhere. I don't know. And I'm alone with a few stupid darkies and you. I bought them back in Mississippi before we moved here, and then I paid that lying Mrs. Peake for you. 'A special girl thirteen years old,' she said. Liar! I might as well have picked some free girl from the Orphan Train."

Elizabeth stopped breaking eggs in the skillet. "What is 'a free girl on the Orphan Train?"

"Oh, riffraff. Mobs of young-uns living on the streets of New York City sent out here, and that's what I should have picked from...though the devil only knows what diseased, filthy tramp I might have gotten hold of. So, I let that Peake woman make me believe she could find me a quality girl. She lied about sending me a thirteen-year-old. Thirteen year old! I get a spoiled little brat too dumb to be anywhere near worth the ten-dollar fee I paid. Well, she better enjoy her fees. Somebody not as nice as I am may kill that uppity bitch."

The egg whites curled up at the edges and turned brown in the sizzling hot grease and were browned on the bottom even as Elizabeth moved them to the back of the stove. They cooked so fast! How did Alice fry them smooth and thick with no burned edges? Maybe she was not so good at noticing after all.

Elizabeth's hands trembled slightly as she placed the serving of bacon, bread and the ill-cooked eggs in front of Mrs. Dalk, but the old woman ignored the food. She poured herself another glass of whiskey and sat now staring out the window.

Standing by the sink board, Elizabeth quickly devoured her own breakfast. Then, as Alice always did, she dipped hot water from the stove tank to wash the dishes.

"Your breakfast is there, Ma'am," Elizabeth said.

"I see it. I'm not blind," Mrs. Dalk said. "If only my son would come home. God only knows where he is or where his poor body lies."

"My sister...," Elizabeth began.

Mrs. Dalk interrupted her. "But even the love of a child...well, there's nothing to compare to the thrill of a passionate romance. My beloved! Oh, my beloved," the old woman sobbed, "to never know his embrace again! To know no man's embrace ever again. I might as well be dead. God! I wish I had personally laid my hands on the sharpest knife and killed that damn Appolo. And yet, thank God, his running did no good. He was captured, tortured and buried dead or alive. I hope he was alive when the clods of dirt was thrown in his face."

"Your breakfast is getting cold," Elizabeth said.

"Damn it! I told you I'm not blind. Leave me alone! Just leave me alone like everybody else has." The old woman laid her head on her arms and sobbed.

Elizabeth quietly washed the dishes and started to leave the kitchen when Mrs. Dalk raised her head.

"Help me back to bed, and then shine my shoes. I may go out later. Of course, I have to shop too now that Alice has got herself sick."

Elizabeth took Mrs. Dalk's bony hand and guided her back to her rumpled bed. The old woman held her wrinkled, smelly feet up one at a time for Elizabeth to remove her slippers, then she breathed out a whisky-soured breath, rolled over into her bed and soon was snoring in short gasping sounds.

Elizabeth pulled the shoeshine box from beneath the bed. She took the high-top black shoes with many rows of shiny brown buttons from beneath the bedside table and began to polish them.

Just as she set the shoes back in place she heard the back gate open and ran to see who might be coming. It was Toby! Soon he was unlocking the door and standing before her.

"I guess the missus be restin'."

"Yes. She's snoring."

"Good." he said. "We worried 'bout you. Alice said, 'go see if that baby be all right.' "

"I cooked breakfast," Elizabeth bragged. Then her face sobered. "Alice is not going to die, is she?"

"Oh, no. She be fine in a day or so, and ole Toby help you if you need him. I be comin' by ever' day."

A tumbling sound, and a crash followed by a piercing scream filled the air. Elizabeth's eyes widened.

"That be her!" Toby said, rushing past Elizabeth to the old woman's bedroom.

***

A doctor carrying a little black case came. In time, Mrs. Dalk's screams subsided, and drifted into low moans. Finally, she lay braced in bed on her back, snoring loudly with open mouth.

"Will the devil get me, Toby?" Elizabeth asked biting her lip.

"Now why would he?"

"Oh, you know! I left that shine box out. I forgot."

"But you didn't know she'd fall over it."

"Will she die?"

"I doubts it. Some ole folks die with a busted hip, but that ole lady be tough. Anyways, you didn't mean it. It just happen. Besides, she be drinking'. She not be drinkin', she not fall," he said with conviction, nodding his head in affirmation.

"You think so, Toby?"

"I do. It be her fault. Now that settle that. Only trouble now come wif all that nursin' on her. Whoooo weeee! That one demandin' ole lady." He raised his eyebrows. "But now how she gonna hurt folks? I got shed of everythin' except the beddin'. No sticks, no nothin' round that ole lady for to hit with, and none gonna be give her." He chuckled in his deep, comforting voice and lay a light hand on Elizabeth's head. "Now that all be settle. Don't worry yo pretty little self no more."

Chapter Nineteen

Dr. Blackwell said a small prayer before dressing for the day. She opened her Bible and saw a note scribbled in the margin by her mother. "Mother," she whispered softly. She felt grateful for her parents. Would she have asked God to help her that night years ago when she gazed out on the dark North Carolina mountains except for their influence? Surely the belief that God approved her mission had influenced her greatly. Without that warm assurance she likely would have given in to her fears. Modestly she considered her role small in the education of women as doctors, but others in America and England reminded her that she was the pioneer. Although, there continued to be problems of one kind or another, much seemed to go in her favor now and she was encouraged.

She was grateful for funds from the Countess de Noailles who made another dream of hers come true...her 'sanitary visitor' program. She appointed Dr. Rebecca Cole, a slender black woman who was first in her race to become a full-fledged physician, to fill this important arm of the infirmary. She was not disappointed. Dr. Cole proved to be an intelligent and caring leader.

***

On a late afternoon, a crowd of people yelling in the streets approached the infirmary. From a window, Dr. Blackwell saw figures with raised fists, brandish hoes and shovels. She was reminded of her early life back in Bristol when normally good working people turned into an ugly mob. She had seen the anger on the faces of poor Irish-Americans, bitter over losing jobs to the free Negroes, a frightened group of people themselves who also struggled to survive. It seemed an endless battle. She knew there were those who resented her for treating the colored. But believing as she did in the rights of all people, she was not willing to change even in view of threats.

Just this morning she and her sister, Emily, whom she called "Milly," delivered yet another baby...a mulatto this time. Milly had also heard the commotion outside and rushed to push the front door closed. She even used the second lock to bolt it.

A window glass shattered! A burly Irish workman whose wife had been treated by Dr. Blackwell at the Old Tompkins Square dispensary, pushed through the crowd to the steps of the hospital. He challenged the crowd, "What the divil's going on?" His booming voice rather than the crowbar in his calloused hands seemed to halt the mob. Soon, however, the clamor rose again. Once more in his strong voice he said, "We know these doctors. Ye know them. Dr. Elizabeth and Dr. Milly and the one they calls Dr. Zac. the German. Good women. They've come when other doctors done nothing for ye. Now ye think on that! Who ye callin' next time ye needs the medicine?" He lectured them, with pointed finger. "They ain't gods. So they makes mistakes with some colored. For the saints in heaven, jest leave 'em alone. Go on home now with ye all."

The crowd slowly dispersed. Only a few with angry faces still hung back, continuing to talk among themselves. Soon, however, they also went on their way. Police arrived, but only after the incident. Still there were other threatening scenes which led the doctors to quietly plan an escape from the back of the hospital should it become necessary. But even such an escape plan could fail as they well knew. Nevertheless, they were unwilling to abandon their patients or their work in spite of the threats aimed at them, not only for treating the colored, but also for being female doctors.

A blessing, however, included some liberal male doctors who supported Dr. Blackwell and her staff. Of special help was a male physician, Dr. Kissam, who came to the infirmary to quiet other mobs threatening to do damage to the Infirmary when a woman patient died.

"Them women ain't doctors! They is killers! Divils!"

The patient's relatives cried insults as they threatened to destroy the whole place with knives and axes, but Dr. Kissam was able to calm them. He declared in a strong voice that the patient would have died no matter who treated her.

With the increase in violence, Dr. Blackwell had the recovering Emily moved to the back of the Infirmary where she would be further removed from the sounds of the mobs. Emily, more alert now, asked for Elizabeth. The nurses reminded her she was too ill to be up and about, but could give her no satisfactory answer as to why Elizabeth could not be brought to her. Finally, Dr. Blackwell sat on the side of Emily's bed and told her the truth.

Emily threw back the sheet and attempted to leave the bed. "I have to find her!" she cried. "Ma left me in charge. I have to find her!"

Dr. Blackwell laid a hand on Emily's shoulder."You can't, dear. Besides, I have a detective looking for her. He will be coming back today. Maybe he'll have some word."

Emily broke into sobs. "I have to find her! I have to!" Once again she struggled to leave the bed and would have fallen except Dr. Blackwell held her back.

"Not yet, Emily. Let's see what the detective has to tell us."

"That Mrs. Peake...."

"She's been found dead," Dr. Blackwell said.

"What?"

"Yes, apparently murdered. By whom we don't know."

"Help me, Doctor. Help me get strong enough to find her. I have to. Ma left me in charge."

Dr. Blackwell smoothed Emily's hair gently. "Your Ma would understand that you can't go now. She would care about you, dear. You're improving every day. Now don't struggle and make things worse so it takes longer. Promise?"

Emily sighed and wiped her tears. "Oh, God! Oh, God! I can't...I can't wait and yet I have to."

"Try to be quiet and trust things will work out. I'll let you know when the detective gets here if he has any word."

"I want to talk with him. I want to know what he says."

Later, Emily sat up in bed and listened avidly to the conversation between Dr. Blackwell and Henry Smythe. The investigator said he had been told that some ruffians, some abandoned boys who sleep in doorways, had killed Mrs. Peake.

"One of the boys told me about it for a nickel," Smythe said, "though he claimed he'd only seen them beating and stabbing her."

"Just saw it?" Emily asked.

Smythe said he asked him, " 'So me lad, why was the act committed?' Well, the dirty face of that urchin broke into a smile. He told me, 'It was good. She deserved it. The old bag, she put a boy's little brother on that train out West and he came back with no feet. They cut 'em off from a freezin'.' "

"Oh," Emily said, "I know that boy! That was Sammy Dougan!"

"Do ye know the brother?"

"I used to see him about, but I don't know now. Anyway that woman was evil. She got what she deserved!" Emily cried.

"But do ye know Dougan's brother?"

"Like I said, I used to see him about, but he may have left. I don't know," Emily said.

"Did these boys know anything about Elizabeth?" Dr. Blackwell asked.

"They claimed they didn't," Smythe said.

Emily's face lit up. "Oh, but they might! They just might. If only I could talk to them!"

"I have me doubts," Smythe said, "I already asked real closely if they knew anything about Elizabeth. They said they didn't, but maybe they know something they ain't telling."

"Bring them here," Dr. Blackwell said.

"Yes, ma'am, I will if they'll come. Maybe a few cents will convince them to come."

***

Two ragged, dirty boys with unkempt dark hair appeared with Detective Smythe. The skinnier one reached out his hand to Dr. Blackwell. "The money, ma'am."

"Wait, lad," Smythe said. "First ye tell what ye know about Mrs. Peake.

"The old bitch is dead."

"Not that," Emily spoke up from her bed. "What about Elizabeth? My little sister? Have you seen her?"

"No," one boy said.

The second lad spoke up, "We was promised the two coins to come here."

Dr. Blackwell took the money from her pocket and gave one to each boy.

"What can you tell us about..." the doctor began.

"Don't know nothin'," both boys said in unison.

"But you knew Elizabeth, didn't you?" Emily persisted.

"Don't know nothin'!" the skinny boy said. He took the other boy by the hand and started to run away. Detective Smythe grabbed both boys and taking each by an ear towed them close to Dr. Blackwell. The younger boy started to cry. He whispered. "We never saw nothin'. We just wanted the money."

"Let them go," Dr. Blackwell said, but added, "Boys if you do learn something will you come back to tell us?"

The detective still held their ears until the skinny one said, "Yes ma'am. If'n we hears anything, we will. Would there be more coins?"

"Only if you have something about Elizabeth that we can prove," Emily said.

The detective released his hold on the boys' ears and they ran from the room, down the hall and out the front door.

***

Months passed without another word from the urchins. Smythe said "I never close an unsolved case," but he had not reappeared.

Emily now was able to be up and around. She soon

170

resumed her work cleaning the Infirmary, but she worked alone. She knew that Sue Ling had left in shame after the disappearance of Elizabeth.

Emily no longer had her apartment, but slept in a small room at the Infirmary and took her meals with the staff. While others seemed accustomed to her changed appearance, Emily sometimes looked in a mirror and touched the scars on her face praying they would somehow disappear. She often let her shoulder-length copper hair fall across her left cheek in an effort to partially hide her disfigurement. Her still-lovely dark eyes pleased her, but what man could overlook the scars on her face and body? She felt her wish for a husband and children was only a dream now, never to become a reality.

Chapter Twenty

The August sun burned through Elizabeth's bonnet and scorched her back as she gathered beans. Each time she filled a sack, she dragged her burden to the shade, dumped the beans into a large basket, and dipped a cool sip of water from a bucket Toby had placed on a bench under a giant oak tree.

Elizabeth missed Alice's company, but ever since Mrs. Dalk broke her hip, Alice was bound day and night to the big house. To comfort herself Elizabeth tried to sing the songs Alice sang. Toby heard her and joined in singing in his rich baritone voice, "Gonna' to lay down my burden, down by the river side, down by the river side, Gonna' meet my King Jesus--."

"Toby, you left out 'Goin' to talk with the Prince of Peace'," Elizabeth protested.

"Well, 'pend on you to 'member every word. We git it right this time," he said laughing.

Elizabeth loved singing with him. For the length of the spiritual they forgot the bean picking and raised their voices in song. Then, pleased with their performance, they laughed and shouted gleefully before resuming their task.

Later, Toby lugged the bean baskets to the back porch. He wiped the moisture from his brow with a sweat-damp rag and called to Alice who directed them to Mrs. Dalk's bedroom.

"You know she want me there every minute," Alice said.

Elizabeth knew that. Once when Mrs. Dalk awoke and no one was in the room, she screamed as loud as she could until Alice reappeared. At that time, Alice had been in the yard building a fire under the old black pot to boil the sheets and white clothes so she didn't hear her right away.

"I had to listen to her cursin' at me the longest time," Alice said. "It made my head hurt and she wouldn't stop. You know it was no use to tell her about my pain."

172

"I gotta get you away from her," Toby said and he tried to think how he could do it. Nothing safe came to mind. What with Little Mama old and some people chasing and killing run away slaves it seemed impossible for them to escape.

"Lordy," Alice said, "what we gonna do? I needs to be with you, Toby, but I can't leave her alone."

"We bound up, Honey. They keep talkin' up the war. If that come maybe we be free," Toby said.

"How long that take and what if it don't work?"

Toby sighed. "Even if it go our way, they's gonna be trouble. Some won't let us go free no way."

Their conversation on the back porch ended with the screeching voice of Mrs. Dalk.

All three of them went to her room to work. For a change the old woman hushed. Elizabeth thought it was because she saw the beans had been gathered, but she wasn't sure if that was the reason. It was unusual but whatever the reason, Elizabeth was glad to see her old eyes flutter and close. Even the loud snoring was better than the yelling and Elizabeth laughed at the snorting sounds.

She helped snap the beans for canning, and when Alice left for the kitchen, Elizabeth stayed by the old woman's bedside. She disliked being in Mrs. Dalk's company and listening to her barrage of complaints, but she was proud she could help Alice. Maybe this time, Mrs. Dalk would stay asleep.

***

Crop gathering continued to be a daily chore in late summer, then, in early September, Elizabeth helped Toby plant winter vegetables...collard greens and turnips.

"You works hard for a little one," Toby said, as they gathered the last of the tomato crop. "I figured you might slip away when the ole missus take to bed, but I reckon you 'fraid of the lady down the hill."

Elizabeth stopped work and looked at Toby. With a

tremor in her voice she asked, "Don't you want me here, Toby?"

"Oh, 'course I do. I was just thinkin' of you, Chile. They say that Miz Seldeni down the hill be a real nice old lady."

"I don't want to be with a real nice old lady. I want to be with you and Alice."

He chuckled. "I be glad for me. You a big help to ole Toby, but we gotta think of you, Baby."

"Does Alice want me to leave?"

"Now what would Alice do with you gone? She'd have to make some tall make-do. Still, if we kin ever find Five Points, we work it out some which way be best for you."

Toby pulled up the last of the tomato plants. He would hang them in the basement so that the bigger tomatoes could continue to ripen. Elizabeth gathered the small green ones and put them in a basket for Alice to make pickles.

"I just love Alice's green tomato pickles," Elizabeth said, "she makes them so good."

"She be a good cook, all right," Toby said.

"She's good at everything," Elizabeth said.

Toby laughed. "Ole Alice's ears be burning."

"Why?"

"Well, when folks talk good about you like that, it makes your ears burn, even if you don't hear it."

"Once my ears burned, but Ma said I had a fever."

Not the same thing," Toby said shaking his head. "You may been so busy doin' somethin' you didn't rightly notice it, but your little ears been burning a bunch from talk down at the cabin."

Elizabeth smiled broadly. "I like my ears to burn if it's you and Alice talking."

After the tomatoes were gathered Toby said, "I gotta check on Little Mama. You want to go or no?"

"Will she be awake so I can talk to her?"

"Probably she be sleepin'. Restin' her eyes she say. Old folks nod off a lot. Still, they be ashamed if you think they sleeping. Yeah, just restin' her eyes she say." He chuckled.

"Guess ole Toby be restin' his eyes one of these days."

"No, Toby. I don't want you to get old. I can't do all this by myself while you rest your eyes."

"Well, not for a while anyways. Let's go see Little Mama. If she be sleepin', I make a heap of noise so she wakes up natural like. Now when she really awake she be wide awake and smart as a ole fox, too."

"I want to see her. Maybe she'll tell me about being like a fox."

Toby laughed. "No, Chile, let that go. Just let her see you. She'll talk."

***

The fall weather brought balmy days. Elizabeth loved the feel of it and she bounced along with Toby into the woods, stopping to gather choice red and gold leaves.

"Here," Toby said, stopping at a persimmon tree. He plucked two orange blobs of the fruit.

Elizabeth took a bite, then spat it out. "It's rotten!"

"No, it just draw the mouth a bit. You get use to it, and it be good."

With his encouragement, she bit into the fruit again, but she twisted her mouth as she ate, exaggerating when she saw it made Toby laugh.

"A wild grape vine here somewheres about," Toby said, pushing through some vines into a shallow ditch covered in red, brown and gold leaves.

"Ah, here they is. You gonna like these, Child. We sit on that big log and eats all we wants."

***

The years of learning and discovery found Elizabeth at age nine knowing many things about farming and housekeeping...and even the proper bathing and feeding of a complaining bed-fast old woman. She felt self-confident and able to ignore the old woman's criticism and insults thanks to showers of compliments from Alice and Toby. And no punishing stick was available. Toby had made sure of that. Still she thought of Emily. Would she ever see her again? Sometimes tears slid down her cheeks when she thought of never, ever seeing her again.

Early December arrived and Elizabeth felt a sense of excitement with Christmas approaching. She tagged along when Toby trudged through the woods looking for the right tree. She helped Alice shake the popcorn pan over the coals on the hearth. "That corn sure puts on a big show jumping all around the pan," Alice said. "Just listen to all that fuss it's making snapping and popping."

Elizabeth laughed for the joy of it all. While they later worked stringing the popcorn and pasting chains of colored paper, Alice said, "We scrounge up a few presents for Christmas, too. I be making the missus a extra plump feather pillow, and I knittin' Little Mama socks." Alice held a finger to her lips. "Now you mustn't tell. You know Christmas presents be secret 'till the mornin' of Jesus' birthday."

"I know, Alice. I remember, but I don't have anything to give!"

"Yes you do, Sugar. You big enough now Toby gonna take you in town with him. He gonna give you some coins. You help us and this be your pay."

"I didn't know I had a job!"

"What you call all you been doin' if that ain't a job?" Alice teased.

***

Elizabeth rode with Toby in the buggy for miles on the narrow roads through the barren winter fields and woods into Town of Kansas. When they came upon the bluff Elizabeth saw the wide river and exclaimed, "Oh, Toby, we're at Five Points!"

"No, chile. This be Town of Kansas. I don't know what river you was at, but this river it be the Missouri. And some river! Yeah, that down there be the most meanest water a'tall, just a tumblin' rollin', grabbin', alive as the devil at a camp meetin' tryin' to steal the Lord's souls."

Elizabeth caught her breath. She moved close to Toby and clung to his arm. "Will it get us?"

Toby laughed. "Oh, no, Sugar. Least ways not if you just look at it, and it be good for lookin' at. 'course, steamboats can go on it. Maybe a keelboat now and then."

"Keelboat?" she asked, but before he could answer, she sat forward exclaiming, "Oh, Toby! Hear the bells! See all the people! We're in town. Look, they're going in and out of the stores with lots and lots of packages!"

***

Toby pulled the reins and the horse stopped at a hitching post in front of a gray unpainted store. Fine ankle-length dresses in black velvet were displayed in the window. Pearls and silver necklaces decorated the necklines. The opposite window presented men's formal wear with long tails, cummerbunds and brilliant white shirts. Black boots and fancy slippers were set in front of the clothing.

Elizabeth's attention was drawn to a red brick store with top and ground floor porches enclosed in pegged wooden railings. The top porch held three rich green cedar Christmas trees bright in silvery decorations. She gazed into the lower porch front window at a gleaming white vase holding stems of holly covered with red berries, a collie dog door stop, a porcelain doll dressed in a plaid dress with red coat and bonnet and wearing shiny black button-up high-top shoes.

"I wonder where Miss Pink Shoe is," Elizabeth said, wistfully.

"Miz Pink Shoe?"

"My doll at Five Points," her voice quavered. "I guess I'm too old for dolls now, but I think they are so--so pretty."

"You not too old. You still be a little girl. It's just life has growed you up too fast." He looked sad. "That one in the window, she cost more than ole Toby got."

"I'm not asking, Toby. I'll just look at her awhile, and then go in the store. Will that be all right?"

"Maybe somehow, some way later we can find a way. I hates I can't git it."

Elizabeth smiled up at him. "I've looked enough for now."

Inside the store a pale gray cat with black stripes lay dozing on the counter near an elderly woman clerk perched upon a tall, wooden stool. She looked at Elizabeth with small honey colored brown eyes peering over black-rimmed glasses pushed down on her nose. "Such a pretty little girl you are my dear," she said, "Where is your mother?" she asked, looking at Elizabeth's rough hands, then up and down at her poor clothing.

"Dead. I'm with Toby," Elizabeth said, taking his hand in hers.

"Oh, my, how sad."

"I love Toby and Alice and Little Mama. I came to buy Christmas presents for them." She looked up at Toby. "You can't watch me."

Toby chuckled. "I knows. I'll go over on the other side of the store."

"Mr. Clement is over there or at the back of the store," the lady said.

"No peeping," Elizabeth said and smiled at Toby. To the lady she said, "I don't know what to buy, would you help me?"

"I will. Come with me. I'm Mrs. Clemet, what is your name?"

"Elizabeth."

"And you last name?"

"McKelvy."

When they were far on the other side of the store, Mrs. Clemet whispered, "Are you all right, dear? Surely, you have some family other than darkies."

"I did in Five Points, but I was brought to Mrs. Dalk."

"Oh, so you do live with a white woman." Mrs. Clemet said sighing, smiling, appearing relieved.

Elizabeth made no response. She looked at candy displayed in a glass case. "I think I'll buy Mrs. Dalk candy to sweeten her."

"She's not sweet, but you'll buy her candy. Well, she must not be too bad then."

"Alice says Jesus wants us to love everybody."

Mrs. Clemet frowned. "You don't really like her?"

"No. I love Alice. She's good."

"Oh," Mrs. Clemet said. "That must be her daughter. Well, it's probably natural to like the younger lady."

"I'm going to buy this for Alice," Elizabeth said pointing to two small red combs. She chose a pair of socks for Toby and two large yellow apples for Little Mama. Then she reached in her pocket and laid her small coins on the counter, not knowing how much the items cost. Mrs. Clemet looked surprised, raised her brows a little, and took the coins.

Elizabeth asked, "Is that enough? It's all I have."

"For you, Elizabeth it's enough. I wish you a merry Christmas, dear. Come back to see me when you can."

Elizabeth smiled. "Thank you. Could I pet your cat a little?"

"Of course," Mrs. Clemet said, "Tiger Smoke is old and very gentle."

Elizabeth gently touched the gray cat who looked up at her with green eyes and began to purr. "I never had a cat," Elizabeth said, "but in Five Points I had bossy boy."

"Bossy Boy?"

"My dog," Elizabeth said and then looked up at Mrs. Clemet. "Do you know where Five Points is?"

Mrs. Clemet frowned. "Five Points? No, I can't say I do, but then Missouri is a pretty big place and I don't know every town."

Toby returned with packages stuffed under his arm. "We best go now," he said.

On the way back home Elizabeth said, "I've never bought four Christmas presents before in my whole life. I wish Christmas was every month."

Toby laughed. "Well, now, Sugar, it make it more

special coming like it do. Still I be glad you love it. You know it be Jesus' birthday."

"Well, I guess he couldn't be born every month."

Before they could enter the buggy five soldiers in gray uniforms rode up on horses. One called out. "Hold back there, Darkie."

Toby froze.

"Where do you think you're going with that white child?" the soldier asked.

Toby pulled a paper from his vest pocket. "I be tending this chile for my mistress." He handed the paper to the soldier who read silently then said, "Toby Hughes. Plantation of Mrs. Marina Dalk."

"Toby, is it?"

"Yes, Sir."

The soldier turned to look over his shoulder. "Harris and Johnson. Escort him home and see that the little girl is taken to Mrs. Dalk."

Two soldiers saluted and spoke in unison, "Yes Sir, Captain."

"Leave us alone," Elizabeth said.

"When you're safely home, little miss," the captain said.

Toby loaded the packages in the buggy, then helped Elizabeth aboard. "Why are they doing this?" she asked.

On the way Toby explained to her. It was the first time she knew Toby, Alice and Little Mama were not safe to travel. She clung to Toby's arm and whispered, "I hate them!"

"Don't know what to do with peoples fightin' going more bloody and more bloody. The Feds, the Rebs, then them wild ones. Toby risk the very life in him going on the road anywheres now with that Quantrill bunch killing, killing, killing." Then he saw the fear in Elizabeth's face. "Oh, but old Toby got the paper right here in his pocket. They won't bother long as I got the paper and you wif me."

***

On Christmas Day the prune-dried little woman with white braided twigs about her head came on Toby's arm to the big house. Slowly she mounted the back steps and came into Elizabeth's waiting presence.

"Little Mama," Elizabeth cried. "You're not sleeping!"

"Sleeping? Why you say that? I hardly sleeps a'tall."

"Oh," Elizabeth said, realizing she had not pleased her.

"Little missy see you restin' yo' eyes," Toby said.

"Oh, well," Little Mama said, "I do that some."

"I got you a present," Elizabeth said, taking Little Mama's hand. "I hope you like it."

"Me like it? It bound to be. It bound to be, Chile. I love a present." She laughed and gave Elizabeth a playful little poke in her tummy that made Elizabeth giggle.

Elizabeth saw Mrs. Dalk now awake and looking toward the large Christmas tree. For the first time since her accident she was not drinking. She was propped up in bed.

"You ready we start, ma'am?" Alice asked.

"Go ahead, but I hope you don't have anything for me. Christmas is just for children and darkies."

"I bought you a present," Elizabeth said. She looked at Alice. "Could I give it to her now?"

Alice smiled and nodded.

Elizabeth handed the sack of candy to Mrs. Dalk.

"Well, what is it?" the old woman asked.

"Candy. It's good," Elizabeth said.

"Well, here. You can have it back. I don't eat silly food like that."

Tears filled Elizabeth's eyes.

"You might taste it, ma'am," Alice said. "Just one."

"Oh, well, if you insist. Mrs. Dalk selected a red ball. "Cherry, I suppose," she said.

Elizabeth watched for some sign of approval from the old woman. Finally, Mrs. Dalk said, "It's better than some, but I'd rather had some ribbon for my hair. I used to have the prettiest hair in the whole state, delicate hair that required me to visit the finest salons."

Elizabeth caught Alice's smile and responded. The joy

of the occasion filled her heart as Alice, Toby and Little Mama received their gifts with happy shouts.

"Apples!" Little Mama cried with delight. "I loves apples. I always celebrates with apples."

Toby laughed and hugged his mother.

Little Mama said, "Why, when my last mean old husband died off, I jumped up and shouted in the grave yard. Then I went home and eat me two the biggest yellow apples I could git."

"Ridiculous!" Mrs. Dalk said, but her speech was drowned in the laughter of the others.

Finally, Alice handed Elizabeth a bulky package that she eagerly tore open. A pair of soft black leather shoes fell to the floor. "Oh, I love them!" Elizabeth said, gathering them up pressing them to her heart.

"For nice. For church goin' " Alice said, beaming.

"Church!" Mrs. Dalk snorted. "She has work to do."

"Oh, I need these," Toby said opening the package holding the socks Elizabeth had bought.

"And these combs," Alice said, "I never had combs for my hair before, and I do love red!"

Elizabeth smiled happily and went around the room embracing Alice, Toby and Little Mama. Remembering Alice said Jesus wants us to love everybody, she attempted to embrace Mrs. Dalk but was shoved away. "I've had enough of all this carrying on," the old woman said.

***

That Christmas of 1859 was a happy time for Elizabeth. Sometimes she longed hard for Emily, but her days were filled with the strangers who had become her family-- especially her beloved Alice and Toby.

In November of Elizabeth's ninth year, Alice had knitted her a new dress, and let the hem out of two others.

"You growing like a little weed though you still be little for nine," Alice said. Now when they turned Mrs. Dalk in the bed, Alice often remarked on Elizabeth's quick learning and her strength for "such a little one."

Elizabeth smiled happily. She no longer was disturbed by Mrs. Dalk's behavior. The old woman screamed and complained but Alice and Elizabeth did their best to care for her. "It be our Christian duty," Alice said.

"Someone listening would think we were mean to her," Elizabeth said as Mrs. Dalk screamed, "Ohhhhhhh! You're killing me. You blamed nigger! You idiot young'un! If I could get my hands on that Peake woman, I'd strangle her with my bare...Ohhhhh stop that!"

Alice was firm. "Ma'am, the doctor say we gotta make these turns and you knows we gotta change the sheets. You could sit up a while."

"No! Stop telling me what to do. Remember your place, or you'll be gone from here. Remember I do pay you though you're a worthless darkie."

Alice bit her lip. Later, she told Elizabeth. "Some day, some day I may jest have to tell her. If only we could leave this place." Alice shook her head. "Some day, Lord. Maybe some day."

***

It seemed to Elizabeth taking care of Mrs. Dalk was a constant job. She could easily spoon the medicine, and although she disliked doing it, she often bathed the old woman when Alice was busy.

"Did you wash her feet and her legs up as far as possible?" Alice asked.

"Yes, and above possible, too. Alice, I'm not a baby," Elizabeth stood with arms akimbo. "I did everything. Just like you. See, she's already back asleep."

"You be a smart little thing. I wish I had me a little girl jest like you."

"Why you wishing, Alice? Ain't I yours now?"

Alice stood looking at her for a long moment before stooping and putting her arms around her. "Well, for now you be my baby. Least ways I claimin' you."

183

"Alice, I'm not a baby. I'm nearly grown."

"Grown? No, you small for your age and you got years to go before you be grown. For now you still my little girl."

Elizabeth hugged her tightly. "I love you," she said.

"I loves you, too, sugar, but one day we may find that Five Points place and you'll go to Emily."

Elizabeth looked into Alice's face and brushed back a gray curl from her brown cheek. "I'll still always love you, Alice. Forever! You could live with me, Emily and Bossy Boy. And Toby and Little Mama, they could live with us, too."

Alice laughed. "We'll see. We'll see."

The back door opened and Toby brought in an armload of wood for the box by the stove.

"A blizzard's blowin' up," he said.

"You looks worried, Toby. What be troublin' you?"

"Little Mama. She lookin' bad. It seem like she takin' the grippe. I wish you'd come fix up the chest plaster."

"I will. You knows I loves her." Alice sighed deeply. "Lord, I hates stayin' here day and night while my family be alone and even sick."

"Come here, darlin'," Toby said stretching out his arms. He hugged her close and kissed her on the lips. "We gonna make it through, honey. I loves you and this ain't gonna always be."

"Oh, Toby, I wish it be changed. I misses you so on cold, dark nights."

Elizabeth watched with spellbound interest. It was the first time she'd seen a man speak of love and kiss his wife in a tender embrace.

Chapter Twenty-One

Elizabeth gazed out the kitchen window at the snow falling, covering familiar shapes in the yard and beyond. Only the silver sky, a few black undersides of tree limbs and a shed marred the white perfection. Ice hung in twisted daggers from the roof of the house, and there was no movement anywhere except for the softly falling flakes.

Alice worked in the kitchen back of Elizabeth singing, "Yes, we'll gather at the river, the beautiful, the beautiful river. Yes, we'll gather at the river that flows by the throne of God." Elizabeth remembered the song from the Sunday she went to church with Toby. She hummed the tune as Alice sang. Although Alice protested that she couldn't sing 'good,' Elizabeth was warmed by her voice.

In the background Mrs. Dalk snored lightly and occasionally made small grunting sounds. It seemed she was seldom awake anymore. Alice had told the old woman every day, "Ma'am, this mixin' medicine and drink. It ain't good."

"Hush! Get me a bigger glass. You're not the boss here, Alice."

Alice told Elizabeth, "I think she be just puttin' her life out to roost."

The big hall clock made a grinding sound and then slowly began bonging out the hour.

"Gittin' on toward noon," Alice said. She was stirring a pot of beef soup on the stove. The mingled odors of tomatoes, beans, beef and potatoes made Elizabeth hungry.

"Ummmm Um, Alice. You're the best cook," Elizabeth said, turning momentarily from looking at the falling snow. "I bet a king would pay you to cook for him."

Alice chuckled. "Anybody would like to cook up for you, baby."

"Alice, I'm not a baby. I'm nine years old!"

"I knows, baby," Alice said teasingly.

"Alice!" Elizabeth exclaimed, but she was now distracted by a view outside the widow. In the distance she saw two men walking against the snow, faces down and hands in pockets. Both carried saddlebags strapped on their shoulders.

"Somebody's coming," Elizabeth said.

Alice wiped her hands on her apron and came to peer out the window. She stood gazing as the men drew nearer, and saw that they looked toward the house. "Oh, Lord," Alice cried, "that be Miz Dalk's boy comin' back."

"What boy?"

"Well, he be a boy when he left. Don't rightly know who that older fellow be, though."

When the two men appeared on the back stoop, Elizabeth watched as Alice opened the door. She saw a thick-bellied young man and a bony, white-bearded older man with green, almost colorless eyes. Both men wore shabby brown woolen clothes.

The older man's long brown coat was belted. He sported a white shirt with a neatly placed green tie. The younger man was far more carelessly dressed in a dirty tan shirt and torn black coat with buttons missing.

Now that she could see him clearly, Elizabeth could identify Mrs. Dalk's son. He had the same dark, heavy-lidded eyes and thin-lipped mouth. His narrow face was covered with a dark beard, and he spoke harshly, abruptly.

"Well, Alice, don't just stand there like a fool. Take our coats."

"Yes, sir, Mr. Clayton," she said, taking both coats. "Ma'am gonna be happy to see you."

Ignoring her, Clayton Dalk asked, "Who's this pretty little piece?"

"Elizabeth. She be your mama's little servant girl."

"Come here, Elizabeth, and let me feel of you."

"No!"

Clayton Dalk laughed. "Spunky kid, huh?"

"That lassie is destined to be a real beauty," the older man said.

"Destined? Hell, she already is," Clayton, and reached again for Elizabeth who avoided his touch.

" 'She walks in beauty like the night--'."

"Shut up! I hate that fancy talk," Clayton growled.

"But look at her! She's beautiful!" The older man clasped his hands together as if in prayer. "Like a rosy-cheeked cherub with violet-blue eyes she is! Like a dark-haired angel she is. I must capture her on canvas this very hour."

"You crazy old fool! Cut it out!"

"I'll give you these gold coins for her," the old artist said, removing a purse from his pocket.

"You'll do no such thing. She's mine to keep." Clayton Dalk turned abruptly toward Alice. "Where's Mama?"

"Mr. Clayton," Alice said, "I got bad news. She...."

"She ain't dead is she?" he asked frowning slightly. "Well, I guess it's time I ran the place anyway."

"No, sir, no she ain't dead, but she be in bed with a busted hip," Alice gestured toward Mrs. Dalk's bedroom. "In there."

Clayton shook his head. "Laid up, huh? Guess she's still nursin' the bottle."

"Should I rouse her up, sir?"

"Naw. I'll do it." He walked quickly toward the room, hoisting his gun belt as he went. The older man followed him and Elizabeth saw that he also wore a gun on his hip.

Alice pulled Elizabeth to her side and they waited outside the room.

"Wake up, old mama! Clayton boy is home."

"Oh! Ohhhhh! Alice! Come here!"

Alice and Elizabeth entered the room and stood waiting, but Clayton waved them aside.

"This ain't no dream, Mama. It's me for real."

"Clayton? I thought I might never see you again."

"That I was dead? Naw. Just been bummin' around doing this and that. Picked up a few bills here and there. Some old women gifted me." He pulled a leather wallet on a strap from inside his shirt and withdrew a thick wad of bills. Holding them up, he ruffled some bills like a deck of cards. "Well, I'm home now, Mama. They talkin' war so I reckon'

I'm needed here away from all that fuss, at least, 'til it blows over."

Tears filled Mrs. Dalk's eyes. "I wish I could walk, but I can't even get up on my feet again, ever!"

"Oh, maybe you could. Come on. Get up and let's see." Against her screaming protests, he lifted her from the bed. He held her to his chest and stood her on her feet.

"I can't! I can't!" she cried. "I'm too weak. I'll fall!"

Clayton laid her back down and felt of her hip. "You're mended. Jointed together jay-whomper, but I'd say you're mended."

"Leave me alone, Clayton. Don't pick me up again. You nearly scared me to death!"

"All right for now, but you gettin' up. I yard-worked some for an old doc once when I got down on my luck. Saw some of his old wobbly-walkers."

"No, Clayton. I'll never walk again, but now that you're home...," she raised up slightly. "Who's that man?"

"Oh, that's Lieutenant Isaiah Linktome, an old school master and portrait painter who has been in the militia. Lives on up the way a piece. We just happened on each other on our way back to Missouri."

"Ma'am," Linktome said, tipping his cap.

"Would you want some dinner, Mr. Clayton?" Alice asked.

"Of course, we want dinner. Get it on the table." He waved his arm dismissing her.

Mrs. Dalk laid the back of her hand against her forehead and whined, "My dear boy, you have no idea what I've had to put up with here alone! It's such a relief to have you home."

***

As instructed, Elizabeth sat by lantern-light for the old artist to paint her portrait. She grew tired and wanted to get up, but he insisted she sit still. His voice was quiet, but firm and he gazed at her with his pale green eyes from time to

188

time, between working on his canvas and reciting poetry.

"That's going to be my picture," Clayton said. "You're making her look older, more beautiful than she is."

"I have an eye for the future, sir. No, this portrait is mine, but I'll make you a copy."

As they argued, Elizabeth slipped out of the chair and ran to Alice.

"She be fresher in the mornin'," Alice said. "You see the chile be tired."

"Yes, I see she's tired. Very well, in the morning, though I hate to waste the moment." Linktome said, sighing. He closed up his paints.

Clayton re-opened the box of oils and ordered Elizabeth back on the chair.

"But Mr. Clayton...." Alice protested.

"Look me in the eye. I'm the captain here." He pointed a rigid finger at her.

"Don't you ever forget it again. The old leather strap can still be brought out."

***

When Elizabeth was allowed to go to bed, it was quite late and she was sent directly to her room. She wished she could have undressed by the warm stove in the kitchen as she usually did with Alice nearby. Mrs. Dalk's son was changing everything.

Elizabeth shivered as she undressed and slipped into her gown. Streams of pale moonlight lay over the floor and outside she could see the brilliant snow between deep shadows. In the near distance too, she could see the slave quarters and wished for Alice, but she knew both she and Alice were at Clayton Dalk's mercy.

Alice was sent home, rather than being allowed to recline on the day bed in the old woman's room. Elizabeth felt a sense of foreboding and trembled.

She lay awake playing back the conversation in her thoughts.

"Don't Mama sleep all night?" Clayton had asked Alice.

"Yes, sir, mostly she does, but she like somebody be with her in case...."

"I'll be here," he said, "but before you go, furnish the lieutenant with a bottle and turn down his bed.

"Yes, sir."

Elizabeth remembered that Alice looked worried and was confused. Now that she could be with Toby and Little Mama for the first night in months, why did her face look anxious?

Elizabeth heard the footsteps on the floor above and finally the dropping of boots one at a time. Although she was very tired, she was too cold to fall asleep. She pulled the quilts up over her head and brought her knees up to her chest. Just as she was feeling warmer, she heard someone approaching her room. Peeking out from the cover she saw the outline of Clayton Dalk in the doorway.

He came toward her taking off his gun and holster. He laid them on a chair by her bed and in the pale light she could see his grinning face. "You see this revolver, girl? It's cocked and ready for anybody gets in my way. I'll blow you to hell if you start screeching. You hear me?"

He ripped back the covers. Moments later he pushed her legs apart as she struggled against him crying. "No! No! Leave me alone!"

A searing pain shot through her small body. She could barely breathe with his hand held over her mouth to muffle her screams. She fell limp into darkness.

When she regained consciousness she became aware of the lingering pain and the wet warmth between her legs. Momentarily she felt confused, then she remembered.

She heard his deep breathing, and smelled his dirty woolens. Moving quickly, but carefully, she slipped from the bed. With shaking legs, in clumsy haste, she stumbled over the chair. The gun and holster thudded to the floor.

She swallowed and held her breath. In the semi-darkness she saw him reach around the bed, fumbling for her.

"Get back here!" he commanded, propped up on one elbow. Instinctively, she stooped, grabbed up the gun from the holster and pointed it at him with trembling hands.

"Damn little bitch! You give me that gun!" he cried, leaping from the bed.

In a desperate effort to hold on, she grasped the gun tight with both hands. A shattering blast knocked her against the chair and onto the floor, but in the brief instant even as she fell, she saw Clayton Dalk's face spatter into a bloody mass.

She scrambled to her feet, her eyes wide, her mouth open, gasping. Terrified of discovery, she dropped the gun and ran from the room. Blood trickled from her thighs and dripped onto her bare feet. She stumbled and fell, skinning her arm and knee in her bumbling haste. Finding the back door latched, she slipped out the small kitchen window, and down to the quarters to find Alice. Her bare, bloody footprints marred the new-fallen snow.

Chapter Twenty-Two

The freezing cold engulfed her as she ran, stumbling, falling, running again. Icy stubs of weeds and rocks tore at her bare feet. Burning pain filled her groin area. "Alice! Alice!" she cried as she ran. The distance to the quarters had never seemed so far away.

Before she reached the cabin, she heard the old artist calling her name, and saw that he held a lantern high as he stood on the veranda of the big house.

She gasped for more breath. "Ohhhh!" she cried as the frozen air seared her lungs, but she was in the yard now. Near the wood pile. The cabin stood in semi-darkness. She slipped on the steps falling, scraping the palms of her hands. Sobbing she called, "Alice! Alice!"

***

A faint light from within outlined the porch window. The door opened and Alice, in white flowing gown, came to her. "Chile, chile, what in the world?" She scooped Elizabeth up into her arms and rushed back inside.

Through near-frozen lips Elizabeth cried, "He hurt me! He hurt me!"

"You wet and froze', chile. Blood! Ohhhhh what....?" She grabbed a quilt and wrapped it around Elizabeth's shivering, wet body, tucking it in under her feet. Holding her close, Alice slipped into an old rocker by the stove.

"He hurt me!" Elizabeth cried. "He hurt me here." She pointed to the place.

"Oh, Lord. I be afraid when I hear how he talk."

"Alice," Elizabeth struggled to sit up. "I killed him."

"Killed him? What you be saying, chile?"

Toby now fully awake came forward. "You kill him?"

Her voice trembling, Elizabeth said, "His pistol. I grabbed it up when it fell...."

Alice held her close, and stopped rocking. Elizabeth could feel the tension in Alice's body. "What we gonna do, Toby?" Lord, what we gonna do? We all be killed over this!"

"First. Out go the light," he said. He held his hand over the globe and blew out the flame.

"They bound to come here," Alice said.

"Oh, Alice, I'm hurting, I'm hurting," Elizabeth cried.

"I know, baby. Shhhhhhhh, we gotta figure what to do."

Toby peered out the window and stood alert. "Somebody swinging a lantern in the dark out back of the big house. Searchin' all about."

"We next! We gotta hide her!" Alice said. To the sobbing Elizabeth she said, "Chile, you gotta be quiet. You gotta be quiet no matter what."

"Maybe I run her off down to de barn," Toby said.

"No! No time. Oh, we most forget, Toby. Her footprints on de porch."

"Here, I fetch de broom and swipe it quick!"

"Good! Make your own prints to de wood pile coverin' over. Do it still be snowin'?"

"It be comin' down right good."

Elizabeth moaned softly, but the warmth and Alice's arms about her comforted her.

Toby slipped out the door. Soon he returned with the broom and a few sticks of snow-covered wood. "We gotta do somethin' now!" he said. "The lantern getting close."

"Under de bed? No, dat won't do."

"Ole hound lean-to shed out back! Dat do it!" Toby gathered Elizabeth, quilt and all, and stepped out the back door. As quickly, he retreated. "Too late," he whispered. "Light shinin' cross de yard."

A sleepy-eyed Little Mama stood in her doorway. "Bring de baby here," she said. "Slip her 'neath my feather bed on de wall side. If anybody open the door, all they see if a snorin' ole widow woman."

"Little Mama I afraid you do this," Toby said.

"Why? I be ole anyway. De baby ain't live her life."

193

A pounding on the door set Toby in action. He rushed out the back door, quickly placed Elizabeth in the little lean-to shed with the tail-wagging old hound and returned.

"Why you disobeys me?" Little Mama asked.

"Because I loves you. Suppose you git hurt. I just prays de good Lord save us all." He waved his hand. "Both you sugars jump in bed and be all sleepy. Toby handle this." He selected a splinter from the wood box, ignited it in the stove and lit the lamp.

The pounding on the door grew louder. "Open up in there!" The old artist demanded.

Toby unlatched the door and cracked it. He rubbed the sleep from his eyes, "Yes, suh?"

"Is she here?" Linktome asked, pushing his way inside.

"Who, sir? Alice?"

"Yes," Linktome said, "yes, Alice and I think you know who else...that little servant girl. She shot and killed Mr. Dalk. His mother is hysterical and, yes, she wants Alice immediately and the girl, too."

"What is it Toby?" Alice asked, raising up in bed, yawning.

"Miz Dalk be wantin' you and Elizabeth. He think the chile be here."

"Elizabeth!" Alice slid quickly from her bed. "What about Elizabeth? Is she all right? Why would she be here 'stead of there?"

"I think you'd know that better than I," Linktome said.

"What do you mean?" Alice asked.

"I'll give you this sack of gold coins for her."

"Me? She be Mrs. Dalk's."

"Mrs. Dalk need never know. I'll figure something to tell her. Besides, what's the old lady going to do? She's bedfast." He held up the sack of coins and shook them. "You could move off to some new place, and don't tell me you wouldn't want to. I've seen enough." He paused and rubbed his chin. "You could maybe wait a little while so you don't look suspicious, but this is your big chance to leave here."

Linktome shook the coins again. "Not a pittance here.

We can count them if you wish."

Total silence filled the room except for the crackling of the fire in the stove. "Think about it," he said as he pushed aside the door leading to Little Mama's room.

"What you want?" Little Mama asked, sitting up in bed, pulling the covers up to her chin.

"Never mind," Linktome said. He opened a closet door and looked under the bed. Returning to Toby and Alice, he continued, "You could buy yourself another life. Now how about it?"

"How can we...?" Alice began.

"I'm confident you can, that you know, or will know where she is. If you care about such matters, I have no wish to harm her. All I want is to drink in her beauty as she grows, as she flowers into womanhood. Capturing her beauty on canvas will make me famous."

"Maybe if you look in de barn," Toby suggested. "Sometimes she like to be there, snugglin' in de hay."

"All right. Where else?"

"If she be there, do we git the coins?" Toby asked.

"Some, but if I have to do all the looking, you wouldn't deserve full pay. Bring her to me and you get the full purse."

"Yes, sir. I see," Toby said. "Well, best we look at de barn. " 'Course she could be froze up some place."

"I doubt that. At least not yet. Come help me look."

"Yes, sir. Jes' let me put somethin' on."

When they were gone Alice slipped out the back door to the attached shed. She pulled the battered piece of carpet aside and found Elizabeth sitting up, her head against the wall of the lean-to. "I heard," Elizabeth said. "Is Toby going to sell me? Alice, please, don't."

"Oh, chile, no. Why you think he lead that man off to de barn if he gonna sell you. Come on now. We go inside."

Elizabeth crawled from the shed, shivering. "I'm hurting bad, Alice," she sobbed, "Am I going to die?"

No. Quiet, Sugar. We see what Toby say do, but then I gotta go to de big house."

195

***

After midnight, when all the lights had been out for more than an hour, Toby hitched the horse to his buggy and helped Little Mama and Elizabeth inside. Toby said, "I really hopes this be de right thing to do. Little Mama you too old to be out in de cold night like this. What 'bout de lady down de hill? Miz Seldeni. She be a nice lady."

"Toby, she too close. The city be better. I knows Miz Hannah."

"But a sportin' house. That don't seem right for the chile."

"I knows it will. Hush, Toby. Let her sleep." Little Mama said, then speaking to Elizabeth she said, "Shhhhh, it gonna be all right, sugar. Just you snuggle close and let that spoon medicine rest you."

Less than a mile down the narrow road, Elizabeth's pain eased and she drifted into sleep.

"Now we talk," Little Mama said. "Toby, why you actin' like you is? You knows I did housekeepin' for Miz Hannah. All the years 'fore the Dalk's moved you and Alice up from Mississippi, I see how she be. I told you how she bought me from old man Cooley. She free me right off, and pay me for my work. I try to tell you 'bout her but you stop your ears when I mention sportin' house, but Alice know."

"I don't like the chile be in a sportin' house."

"Miz Hannah love children. Maybe 'specially since she lost her own in a terrible storm. A tornado kill off her husband and five-year-old chile. She talk about her little Caroline off and on. Say Caroline call her 'Marme' 'stead of 'mamma,' " Miz Hannah, she thought that was sweet so she say she never try to change it."

Toby said, "I think this be wrong. We ought to take her back and ask Miz Seldeni keep her, Little Mama. She wouldn't give the chile back to Miz Dalk and we could slip down the road and see her."

"Toby, for now she gotta have doctorin'. And a doctor be there about for Miz Hannah's girls. Like I told you, she

196

don't run no low-class sportin' house. She be a teacher 'fore all her tribulations whip up on her."

"Little Mama, folks lose their babies and even whole family, still they stays straight with the Lord."

The old woman laid a hand on her son's knee. "I knows you don't mean be judgin' so hard. You just loves the chile. She be the little'un you never bless' with. I see that, but Miz Hannah no common white trash. She the best 'cause she hold herself up--don't allow no riff raff and she teach her girls be lady-like. The mens who get in de door be gentlemen. Riff raff be turned away. Like I say, she got a guard at the door."

"I wants the chile be raised a Christian. How that gonna happen in a sportin' house?"

Little Mama sighed. "Later, son. Later. Now we got to hide her in a place she be safe and treated good."

***

Hannah's two-story bordello on Third Street stood in darkness except for small flickering lamps in the window of the parlor area. Although it could not be clearly seen at night the red brick Italian palazzo was one of the finest houses in the entire city.

"There be twenty-four rooms," Little Mama said, "but I knows 'em all. Drive 'round this side," she said indicating the right side of the house, "till I say stop."

Toby drove past the imposing front of the palazzo to a large, one-story attachment to the main building.

"How she come by this fine place?"

"First she have a little white cottage for her business, but a merchant with heaps of money fall deep in love with her and she the same with him."

"She marry again?" Toby asked.

"Well, no. They be lovers. His wife refuse de divorce papers. One day the wife stab him and then her own self. She die on the spot, but he live days. They be a boy at a university who got the heaps of money and the business, but Mr. Sloan he give this place to Miz Hannah and the court

197

uphold it--she have friends in high places. After dat she took on his name. Sloan. I forget her name 'fore that."

"Little Mama she be a loose woman."

"Toby, she didn't kill nobody. She be in love. I give up esplainin' to you. Oh, stop here this be her door," Little Mama said. "Been a while since I be here, but this be it--her own 'partment. And fine it be, too. 'Course I 'member it all--Miz Hannah and her girls. The polished, beauteous carved furniture, de grand ballroom all lined up with gold-framed mirrors. I can just see it now. All dem mirrors reflectin' the fine dressed ladies and gentlemens dancin', swirlin' 'bout, smilin', laughin'. No drinkin' but fine wine. Miz Hannah just have fine wine and good food, and the party go on and on all night long."

"Little Mama, I surprised at you. You love it and it be wrong. You know that."

"I not judge," Little Mama said. "Now go on. Get up them steps and knock on that wood door."

Toby gathered up the sleeping Elizabeth and laid her against his shoulder. She stirred slightly and moaned but said nothing.

At the door, Toby knocked softly. When he got no response, he knocked louder. Finally, a tall, handsome auburn-haired woman in a black velvet robe opened the door. The soft light behind her outlined her well-proportioned body.

By now Little Mama had climbed the steps. "It be me, Miz Hannah. I brung you this chile."

Hannah Sloan frowned and her tone was abrupt. "Why on earth would you do that?

"She's been hurt Miz Hannah. In de private parts."

Elizabeth trembled and now awake, she clung to Toby crying.

Little Mama stroked Elizabeth's hair. "It be all right, chile. Miz Hannah just be surprised."

Hannah's voice softened. "Bring her in," she said, holding the door ajar.

Elizabeth, wiping tears, looked at Hannah's face and

saw that she wore a kindly expression, and that she was beautiful with dark eyes and a mass of auburn hair sweeping her shoulders.

***

Hannah sent her housekeeper for the doctor, and in the meantime, speaking softly, she undressed Elizabeth and instructed her to step into a large tub of warm water. At first the water stung Elizabeth's wounds and she cried out.

Toby waited in an adjoining room, pacing the floor.

"It'll get better soon," Hannah promised soothingly while gently bathing Elizabeth. Little Mama stood by holding a soft yellow towel, talking all the while, telling Hannah all she knew of Elizabeth's coming to the Dalk's and what had happened the last few hours.

Elizabeth continued to sob. She looked up at the serious faces of the adults and felt her heart pounding against her chest.

Hannah shook her head and mumbled something about the cruelties of life before speaking to Little Mama. "We can't let anyone know she's here. I'll keep her in my quarters." Hannah touched Little Mama's arm. "You know you are in danger bringing her here. They could put her in an asylum, but it could be worse for you and Toby. You could be beaten or even killed."

"Oh, it's dangerous for you, too, Miz Hannah!" Little Mama cried. "I forgot--I just didn't think--.I was so...."

"Don't fault yourself. Just be very, very careful. I'll see what I can do."

On a nearby chair lay a white cotton shirtwaist, which Hannah scissored down to serve as a child-size gown. She took the towel from Little Mama and patted Elizabeth dry before slipping the makeshift garment over her head. "Come, little one," Hannah said. She took Elizabeth's hand and led her to a nearby bed.

***

Elizabeth cried, kicked and twisted as the pudgy, gray-haired doctor began to examine her. Both Hannah and Little Mama worked to calm her and finally the doctor was able to complete a brief examination. To Hannah he said, "Clearly, the man was of small endowment or this little girl could have suffered a much greater injury." He patted Elizabeth on her head. "You're going to be all right," he said.

Even though both the madam and the doctor were kind, Elizabeth felt deeply afraid. They did not speak in the soft dialect she'd come to trust, but in sharply defined words. With serious faces they discussed her secret. Was she going to be found and sent to some bad place or even killed? She slipped from the bed and ran to Toby who had just entered the room. "Toby! Toby! Don't leave me!" she cried, pulling at his arm.

"Sugar, we gotta go," Toby said, "It be gittin' most daylight before we can git back. Now you be mindin' Miz Hannah and we be back in a few days. Comin' soon it be so's we can."

"Elizabeth," Hannah said, "Toby and Little Mama could be hurt if we keep them here too long. You wouldn't want that, would you?"

"No," Elizabeth said as tears streamed down her cheeks. But assured by Toby's advice to mind Miz Hanna' she allowed Hannah to hold her hand. Moments later, Hannah guided her to a window where they stood and watched as Toby and Little Mama rode away in the pale light of early morning.

"Will the gray soldiers get them?" Elizabeth asked between snuffles.

"I don't know," Hannah said truthfully.

"It's my fault," Elizabeth cried.

"No. It's not your fault," Hannah said, then wishing to comfort Elizabeth she said, "I think they'll make it. The soldiers probably are still asleep. I'll send someone to check on them tomorrow."

***

At noon the tall sheriff and a chunky deputy rode on horses past the cabin and onto the big house.

"That deputy Leonard have a huffy way 'bout him," Toby said. "I worries 'bout how he talk at Alice."

"Why Sheriff Dobbs not hold him back?" Little Mama asked.

"Dey say he courtin' de deputy's sister."

Toby paced the floor and sighed.

"Sit down, Son," Little Mama said, "Alice know what to say and what not to say."

"But I don't like her bein' bad-talked and I can't help her."

After what seemed an hour, Toby saw the men leaving the big house and headed in their direction. "I know they be stopping here, too," Toby said. He closed the curtain and waited.

A few minutes later one of the horses neighed in front of the cabin. Toby looked out the window and saw the men dismounting, "They be here," Toby said, "You want to stay in the room or no?" Toby asked.

"Stay. 'Course I want to stay by you," Little Mama said, "You reckon Sheriff Dobbs be rememberin' how you caught his runaway horse and buggy?"

"Oh, Little Mama that be twenty years ago." He walked to the door and invited the sheriff and the deputy inside. "I see you come looking for de missing chile," Toby said right up front.

"Yes, Toby. Mr. Linktome believes you know where she is."

"Now why he say that? He know he offer me a sack o' gold coins for her. You know what we could do with a sack of gold coins?"

"You didn't say you don't know where she is," Deputy Leonard said, hitching up his pants and leaning forward, fixing Toby with a steady gaze.

"No, sir, I didn't say, but I figure you know we could buy our freedom with them coins, so I thought...."

"You could," Sheriff Dobbs said. He spoke in a softer

tone than his deputy. "But the thing is, Mrs. Dalk said you were mighty fond of the child."

"Well, we—yes, Sir, she be a sweet chile and you know she be raped."

"Raped?" Dobbs asked. "Who said so?"

"Mr. Dalk be killed in the chile's bed so we...." Toby looked at Little Mama. Had he said too much?

"It be lookin' that way," Little Mama said, "though we not be there so we can't...."

Sheriff Dobbs frowned. "That was the child's bed?"

Toby swallowed. He was afraid of the next question.

But instead of a question, the sheriff mused, "Linktome wouldn't know that. Mrs. Dalk was so upset Alice had her hands full so we didn't get much from them this time around."

"Alice know the chile's bed, but Mr. Dalk he sent her home" Toby said. "She not be there when he be shot, but she know the chile's bed and how it be lookin' with de blood."

Little Mama spoke up, "Mr. Linktome who say he give us gold coins for her, say he not gonna hurt de chile. He jest wanta paint her picture."

"Don't take that long to paint a picture," Deputy Leonard said.

"No, sir," Toby said, "it don't 'cept he wanted to keep painting 'em—thought he'd paint some that would make him a famous art man one time or 'nother."

"Toby," Dobbs spoke softly. "Tell me right off, do you know where the child is?"

"S'cuse me, Sheriff, but do you reckon Mr. Linktome kill Mr. Dalk? Mr. Linktome, he wantin' that child pretty bad, but Alice say that child not want be 'round him. Him makin' her sit for his paintin' when the child wore plumb out."

Dobbs shook his head. "Linktome would kill Dalk in the child's bed? Toby, that's not logical. Now tell me, do you know where the girl is?"

Toby said. "I don't know just where she be. She coulda

202

run back over in the hills and woods. Maybe hid someplace. Could have froze if she...."

Little Mama cried, "Oh, no! Poor chile. Poor chile!" She dabbed at her eyes with the hem of her apron.

Deputy Leonard set his feet in a firm stance. "Sheriff, these darkies are beating around the bush. They know where that girl is." Leonard closed in on Toby. "Now, Boy, you better tell if you care about hanging parties."

The sheriff walked past the deputy and stood beside Toby. "Don't threaten him, Leonard. Toby's never been in trouble. Even old man Dalk before he died said 'Toby's a good Nigger as you bound to find anywhere.' "

Leonard bristled. "He knows and you letting him get away with it."

"Remember the truth, Toby," the sheriff said. "I'm counting on you for it. Don't let me down."

"No, suh. Thank you, suh."

Leonard snorted, "I can't believe you, John Dobbs." He slammed out the door, untied his horse, mounted and rode away at a clip.

"If you hear anything...."

"Yes, sir. I most hope for the best. That be a nice chile," Toby said.

The sheriff hesitated, looked at both Toby and Little Mama before he left. He seemed to be about to speak again, but changed his mind and left.

When he was gone, Little Mama said, "Toby I 'spect he think you know somethin' but he know now about the hurt chile, too. Sheriff Dobbs he be a heap better man than that deputy. Yeah, and though he didn't say I kinda think he'membered about you catching his runaway horse."

Toby clasped his hands over his face and shook his head. "I hates this lyin', but I gotta do it."

"You didn't lie, son. You didn't know the exact spot she be standin' on that minute." Little Mama laughed.

"No, I lied," he said.

"I don't think it be a real lie, son. As man of the house, you gotta save yo family and that chile. The Lord, he understand that."

Toby patted his mother on the shoulder and walked outside. He wondered how Alice was faring in the big house.

Chapter Twenty-Three

Hannah heard cries and gunfire. She rushed to a window worrying that Toby and Little Mama might have been captured. She looked down at the grounds near the entrance to her bordello, but saw no one. The commotion must be on the street beyond her mansion. Normally, her doorman would be visible, but he was nowhere in sight. That was suspicious and troubling.

Minutes later a knocking at the door alerted her. Just outside on the back stoop the doorman stood waiting. She gave a brief sigh of relief. At least, the big man appeared all right.

"Yes?" Hannah asked. "What's wrong, Jason?"

"It's the guerrillas, Ma'am. They rode their horses up to the gate, but spotted some blue coats on the roadway and took chase after them. I know you have set your house to attract gentlemen but them ruffians...I didn't think you'd want them allowed."

"Oh, this war! No, I don't want them, but I don't want you killed either Jason."

"Well, Ma'am, I could have been. A troupe of dirty guerrillas it was. That Quantrill bunch...seen him clear. Blond hair trailing on his shoulders, skin bronzed like a Indian and him wearing that bright red shirt. It was him for sure. Saw them strange gray-blue eyes with drooping eyelids and them down-curled lips and knowed he could easy kill a man."

"I believe you, Jason. Don't take chances if they return. Your size and strength won't deter gunshots. If he does return you'll have to admit him and his gang. They kill men, but not women." Hannah sighed. "The girls will know how to handle the filthy bunch. It's hard to run a high class place these days, and you know I've always tried to do that."

"Yes, Ma'am. I know."

"This miserable war!" Hannah said, flipping back her

mass of red hair. She stood for a moment then turned to go. "Hopefully," she said, "the ruffians will get their thrill from battle and not return, but Jason don't take chances."

Hannah closed the door and returned inside her quarters still hearing gunfire and shouts of fury and pain in the distance. Throughout the night she hadn't slept well. She tried to think of what to do with the child. Perhaps the best thing might be to send her to a woman she knew on a farm in Kansas, but nowhere really seemed safe. Somehow, too, the small girl kept reminding her of her own lost child. Just before dawn she had decided on a plan that seemed far-fletched, but would allow her to keep the child with her.

***

When Elizabeth awoke, Hannah and another woman were speaking in low tones. The slim black-haired woman had striking dark eyes and a high smooth brow. She spoke with a soft, musical accent.

Hannah was saying, "We must disguise her, Monette, and I want you to teach her French. When she finally goes out of this building, she'll appear to be a young boy and she will speak only French. It's more than this thing that happened last night."

"Yes, I know. She's beautiful and the streets are filled with men of all types. Too few gentlemen and family men, I fear. She could be in danger if she went out alone as a girl."

Hannah sighed. "Toby and his family have treated her like a younger child so she seems immature. Hopefully, she's not dull. In any event, we must keep her in and always be with her when she does go out."

Monette nodded.

Hannah studied her hands a moment before she spoke again, "Eventually, she'll understand. In the meantime she must be disguised and learn to speak French. I am convinced that she simply must appear to be a boy...not only for this Dalk problem but for the other reasons you've stated as well."

206

"I wonder if she can read."

"I don't know." Hannah laughed. "We talk of teaching her French as if she were a scholar."

Monette remained humorless. She answered seriously. "I can teach her to speak it even if she can't read."

"And I will teach her other lessons," Hannah said. "Oh, of course, the piano, but I can teach her regular classes as well."

"It's a wonder you left teaching school, Madam. You still teach even here."

"Teaching school in a one room building was dull and paid poorly. Teaching my girls gives them class which quality men appreciate."

"I think you've made a fast attachment to this child," Monette said. "She is appealing even lying there asleep in her innocence, but we have task ahead of us, and a risk as well."

"I think we're up to it. I missed mothering more than I realized." Hannah looked at her hands and swallowed, fighting tears. "She reminds me of my little Caroline."

"Although I've never been a mother," Monette said, "I suppose losing a child keeps hurting."

"Always," Hannah said. "I keep calling up memories of her angelic face, and the way she looked at me with such trust. I feel her small arms about me and hear that sweet voice. She was only five when she brought me a bouquet of three blue wildflowers from the field where we had a picnic." Hannah closed her eyes and shook her head. "It's impossible to forget."

"I'm sorry," Monette said, touching Hannah's arm.

Hannah dried her cheeks with her fingers and looked up. "Elizabeth is a mixed blessing," she said. "It's true she reminds me of Caroline which makes me sad, but she is a child to love which I appreciate now that I'll never be a mother again."

Monette said, "Shall I teach her five days a week? She should be constantly learning the language."

"Yes. It's important that she learn it as quickly as possible."

"She'll absorb it like a sponge. Children are much better than adults at learning a new language. I was blessed to have learned both French and English as a child."

"It sounds promising then. And Monette, you only need carry out your other duties on weekends unless, of course, there is a request for your services by one of our more outstanding gentleman. You were quite a hit with a visiting governor last month, I hear."

"He seemed pleased." Monette smiled.

"Well, he should be. You have quality beyond the decorum I require on everyone's part."

Elizabeth rubbed her sleepy eyes and sat up. "What's decorum? Do I have it?"

Monette's sober mood disappeared, and she joined Hannah in laughter.

Hannah said, "You are a very nice girl. Now tell me, Elizabeth, can you read?"

"No, ma'am."

"Well, breakfast first and then we start school. Oh, and Monette, go buy Elizabeth some clothes. You know, a beret and whatever else she'll need. Boy's clothes, of course, in the proper style for a young French lad."

"No! I'm a girl."

"For a while we have to pretend, Elizabeth. It's safer for you, for all of us that way."

"Am I going to be killed?"

"Not if I can help it, and I feel sure I can if you do as I tell you."

"Toby said...." Elizabeth tried to speak.

"Toby said for you to mind me. He wants you to be safe. Elizabeth, he and Little Mama took a big risk in bringing you here," Hannah said. "Fortunately, they were not discovered. We must never let what they did be known or they could be killed. And you could be sent to a bad place if you...."

"A bad place?"

"An asylum or house of corrections where you

wouldn't be treated well. Now try to behave yourself."

Elizabeth looked at Hannah with wide eyes, but said nothing. She folded her arms over her chest.

"You may call me 'Marme', but you must call Monette 'Mama' pronounced with a French accent. She'll teach you how to say it just right. If at any time, someone asks, you are Monette's son."

"No! I'm not!"

"I know, but we must pretend for a while. I told you Elizabeth, it could be a matter of life or death for people you love."

"What if I forget?"

"You must not forget. Think of Toby and his family if not of yourself. Just do as you're told and don't worry."

But she did worry. She worried about lying. Toby had said lying was a sin. It meant she could go to hell.

***

Elizabeth was fascinated with the books placed before her. She had a slate, but she also had paper. She had never seen so much paper, pencils and paints! It made her catch her breath in wonder. Each morning Hannah had to insist that breakfast came first. Left to her own desire Elizabeth would leave the food half-eaten to learn.

"Such a good little scholar," Hannah said. "My best student ever." Elizabeth warmed to the praise and tried hard to please her. Hannah's face often softened with a smile.

But Monette...Elizabeth knew Monette was less pleased. "She hasn't the ear I'd hoped for, though she learns the words very readily."

"Perhaps she only needs more time. Or," Hannah brightened, "perhaps music would help her ear. I'd planned to delay her piano lessons, but maybe that's a mistake. We'll start tomorrow."

"We should start calling her the new name," Monette said. "How do you like Pierre?"

"You should know better than I."

"Very well. Let's see...ah, I think Pierre...Pierre Garreau. She must learn the name and pronounce it correctly."

"Yes. Yes, that's good. But should we worry so much about her perfect pronunciation? Most people wouldn't know."

"But some could. Besides, it offends my ear. I'll keep trying to help her get it exactly right."

Elizabeth, sitting at a table trying to draw a picture of Alice from memory, heard the conversation and frowned.

Hannah came and stood beside her. "Elizabeth," she said, "from now on we must practice calling you 'Pierre.' "

"I don't want to be a boy," Elizabeth cried, putting her head down on her arms, covering her drawing.

"It won't make you a boy, but we must pretend for a while. Elizabeth, you're a smart girl. Why must I keep reminding you what could happen if we're all found out?"

"I don't like that," Elizabeth said with tears flooding her eyes. "I want to be with Alice."

Hannah drew a chair up beside her. "I know this is hard, but we must do it. Elizabeth, you must stop behaving like a baby."

"I'm not a baby!"

"Then stop acting like one. If you don't do as I tell you about this, I'll have to send you away and you may never see Alice or Toby or Little Mama again."

Elizabeth cried, "I will see them again. I'll run away. I will!"

"If you can't behave yourself, you may not see them because they'll be dead...killed because they tried to save you and were found out."

Sobbing now, Elizabeth kicked the table, and with a swipe of her arm, knocked the books and papers to the floor.

Hannah stood abruptly. Her tone was sharp. "I won't have that, Elizabeth. I can't sacrifice everyone because you refuse to co-operate. Do you understand me?"

The anger in Hannah's voice sent shivers through her. Elizabeth nodded but tears flooded her cheeks. What could she do? She didn't know how to be a boy or how to speak

French. She missed Alice and Toby. She missed the soft drawl of their words. She missed being their little girl.

***

Elizabeth continued to feel Hannah's anger any time she forgot to answer to 'Pierre.' She also hated being inside walls all day every day. Whispering, she asked Monette, "Will I ever in my whole life get outside again?"

Monette laughed. "Of course. Soon now I think."

But days and weeks passed without the door being opened for her.

"I know you're tired of being inside," Hannah would say, "but you're not ready to be seen by others yet. How is her French, Monette?"

"Good, but not good enough. I do think her music has helped some."

"Elizabeth, your reading is impressive and so is your arithmetic. Work harder on your French. "

For some time now Elizabeth thought that Hannah's affection warmed in direct proportion to her learning. Still she felt rewarded at times with smiles and touches... sometimes hugs. Despite the fact that none of the toys were specifically for girls, she liked them as well.

Often at night Elizabeth heard music and laughter coming from somewhere else in the building. She asked Monette about it. Monette appeared surprised, but then said, "A party for adults. Pay it no attention. It does not concern you."

Hannah often left her quarters and was gone for periods of time especially in the evenings. Elizabeth asked her about the 'party for adults,' which for some reason caused her to frown. Like Monette, however, she said, "It does not concern you, Elizabeth. Forget about it." But Elizabeth did not forget it. She determined that when she had a chance, she would follow the music and see the party. It seemed like so much fun with all the laughter.

211

Sometimes Hannah observed Elizabeth's French lessons and learned a little of it herself as Monette taught.

"Pierre, how do you say 'Here it is'?"

"Le voici."

"Good. Now tell me 'good morning.' "

"Bonjour."

"Goodnight?"

"Bonne Nuit."

"Very well, but watch the sound. Try 'nuit' again."

"Nuit."

"Good. Now, Pierre, tell me the name of each item on the table in both French and English."

"Lait, milk. Sucre, sugar...."

A single knock followed by two rapid ones interrupted the lesson. Hannah stepped outside. After a hushed conversation, she returned.

"Good news," she said. "Little Mama and family continue to be safe. I sent someone to investigate again. Toby was pleased to learn that all is well here, but he was feeling very worried about being unable to return for a visit. It seems he and Little Mama were stoutly questioned when they were discovered returning home that early morning. Little Mama dabbing at her eyes, tried to convince the man... the old artist, that they had been searching all over the area for Elizabeth, but he was unconvinced. And then later the sheriff and deputy questioned him and Little Mama. For that reason, Toby dared not venture into town except on orders. And on those occasions, he has scrupulously carried out the trip in detail, feeling he might very well be watched."

Tears came to Elizabeth's eyes, but she remained silent. Ever since Hannah's lecture she'd been careful to avoid any emotion that might be called babyish.

"We've made it so far," Monette said.

"Yes, and our girl is learning fast," Hannah said, embracing Elizabeth. "I'm proud of you. I wasn't sure you could learn so quickly with no schooling before now."

Although she could not bring herself to speak, Elizabeth yielded to the embrace, burying her face in Hannah's shoulder. She liked being told she was smart after spending years with Mrs. Dalk telling her she was stupid.

"You're growing up now, and that's good," Hannah said. "The world is not an easy place, Elizabeth, as you've learned in your short life, but the more you know the easier it'll be."

Monette smiled a quirky little smile.

"What? Why are you smiling? Don't you agree?"

"I do. I keep thinking how much of the teacher remains in you, Madame Hannah. Even the girls...the crude ones who come here, you train in manners and dress."

"And it works, not only for my business, but for those girls, too. Many marry well, and I'm proud of that," Hannah said, "but my special pride is right here." She said and touched Elizabeth's shoulder. "What do you think, Monette, should we trim her hair, put on her beret and take a drive in the carriage?"

Elizabeth forgot to remain sedate in her excitement. It would be her first time outside and a ride in the carriage! She jumped up and down, clapping her hands. "Oh, could we drive by to see the river and the stores? Could we?"

Hannah laughed. "We could indeed."

In her eagerness to go on the outing, Elizabeth did not protest when she was dressed in brown woolen knickers and a matching sweater. A brown beret was pulled down over her short dark curls.

"Are you ready, Pierre?" Monette asked. "You look very handsome."

Elizabeth frowned, but responded, "Oui. Merci beaucoup."

"De rien," Monette said, smiling. She added, "Comment vous appelez-vous?"

"Je m'appelle Pierre Garreau."

"Oui! Yes, very good," Monette said. "Still I think you should talk very little. There's yet much to learn. If someone asks you a question in French that you can't answer in

213

French, frown, look at me and say "Quel?' which, as you know means...."

"What?"

"Yes, that's right. Otherwise, simply pretend not to hear. I will answer for you. But around English-speaking people you and I will have short conversations in French... words and sentences I'm sure you know."

"This is such a nice day for early spring, only a little chilly, perhaps we could find some ice cream if Pierre can say it in French," Hannah teased.

"Glace! Glace!" Elizabeth cried.

"There's a new ice cream saloon near the stagecoach station," Monette said. "Perhaps, we could shop first, take our drive, and then buy ice cream on our way back."

Elizabeth smiled as they walked out into the sunlight toward Hannah's fine carriage. Soon they were on their way to the river front shops.

***

A month later, Alice came. She brought a cake and a small necklace of yellow glass beads.

"Alice, Alice, Alice," Elizabeth cried, clinging to her, hugging her neck, kissing her cheek.

"I brought you a little plain cake and a present now 'cause I don't know if I be able to come again. Miz Dalk, she be in de hospital and Mr. Linktome, he be in charge. He don't say, but Toby thinks he may make us move out. Then some folks keep talking of de war."

"Make you move out?" Elizabeth asked. "Where would you go? Oh, Alice don't go somewhere far away!"

Hannah asked, "What's wrong with Mrs. Dalk?"

"She lose her senses."

"Perhaps, a stroke," Hannah suggested.

"No, ma'am. I seen 'em with strokes. She see snakes and such, screams all wide-eyed, sweats and trembles. De lieutenant—maybe you didn't know they marry up. He take her to de hospital."

214

"He married her? Mrs. Dalk has money, I understand," Hannah said.

"Yes ma'am. Now she be Miz. Linktome and he hold de money."

"If he cared he should have withheld the liquor," Hannah said, "She has delirium tremens."

"What is that?" Elizabeth asked.

"It's what liquor does to your brain if you drink too much of it," Hannah said. She leaned forward toward Alice, "You don't suppose Linktome followed you today, do you?"

"No, ma'am. He told me come in town and I come, but I come watchin', lookin' all around. I never see him nowheres."

"Is he paying your wages, Alice?" Hannah asked.

"He pay now, but if'n Miz Linktome die...well, I dunno what 'den."

Monette slipped quietly in the door. "Madame," she said, "there's an elderly gentleman here to see you," she said. "He says his name is Linktome."

Chapter Twenty-Four

Hannah ushered the well-dressed, white-haired man into the parlor and met his steady gaze.

"Madam Sloan, I'm Professor Linktome, school master and artist, former lieutenant in the militia. I've learned that you have beautiful girls in your service."

"I do. Would you like to be introduced to one?"

"Perhaps more than one. Oh, not for the usual reason, Madam. I'm seeking a name for myself as an artist. A model of exceptional beauty is what I need."

"Sir, even if I have such a beauty, the cost for her service would be very expensive. Sitting for portraits can be most time-consuming...beyond what her usual duties would call for."

"No matter. I've had the good fortune to come into... shall we say, an inheritance."

"An inheritance?"

"Yes. My wife died. Such a sad matter, but then life must go on, mustn't it?"

"Of course. Perhaps, you'd like to return this evening when we have our usual party. Eight o'clock?"

"Splendid." Linktome bowed and reached for Hannah's hand, which she extended for his gentlemanly kiss. "Tonight, Madam," he said.

***

Hannah watched until Linktome's carriage disappeared from sight. She walked quickly back to her quarters.

"Alice...."

"Did he follow me?" Alice asked breathlessly, eyes wide.

"I don't think so. He came for another reason. I feel certain he had no idea you are here."

"Oh, good, good!" Alice said placing her hand at her

throat.

"Did you know Mrs. Dalk...Mrs. Linktome died?"

"Dead. When she die?"

"He didn't say."

"He not be sendin' for me like usual, but why he not tell me she die? When be her funeral? This not right."

"I don't know," Hannah said. She walked a few paces as if she were considering something, shook her head but again simply said, "I don't know."

Alice moaned softly. "Now what we gonna do if he make us move? How we gonna live wif no work?"

"Don't worry. He'll very likely still want your services, but I'll send someone out to check on you tomorrow."

***

Linktome failed to appear at the bordello that evening or the next. A messenger sent to check on Alice and family reported that they were well, but that the man Linktome, had not returned to the big house.

When Linktome was away for more than a week, Toby worried. Would he be accused in some way? He trembled at the thought knowing full well that some riotous white men liked nothing better than any excuse for a hanging party. Toby decided to take his chances with the sheriff.

Alice and Little Mama wanted to go with him, but he refused. With hat in hand, Toby appeared at the sheriff's office. Sheriff Dobbs, leaning back in his chair, listened with a frown on his face.

"And, so, sir," Toby said, "we didn't know if we could stay on or no with the boss man away."

"You did right to come tell me, Toby. We'll check on Linktome's whereabouts. In the meantime, just stay put where you are."

At first it was assumed Linktome had privately, perhaps suddenly, decided on some journey—probably business-related and would return shortly. The usual routine checking was done with no success and no clues.

***

Finally when he did not show up by spring, telegraph offices sent out missing-person notices far and wide. It was as if Isaiah Linktome had vanished from the earth like a vapor.

"Linktome, he be too old for the militia now, so that not where he be. I guess we just stay on 'les' somebody make us move," Toby said.

Later in the day Alice came home from visiting a slave family two miles away on the Harmond plantation. She appeared breathless and took a few minutes to settle in before she spoke to Toby and Little Mama.

"Jodie and Sam say they gonna try to slip away and go up north. They want to know if we wanna go, too. Go with dem."

Toby stood up abruptly from his chair and took a deep breath. "Leave now? That be mighty risky. If we could do it, we be shed of this place," He put a hand on back of the chair. "But it be mighty risky."

Little Mama shook her head, "The war and all the hate and killing." She said, "Well, but we could try now the chile be safe."

"But hate and killing is real, Little Mama. I be afraid for us, and I be afraid for Jodie and Sam, but I been knowin' they be set to go. Dey got a daughter up yonder in Ohio."

"Sure has and we got cousin Joseph in New York," Toby said.

Alice who had remained quiet spoke up. "It be too dangerous, Toby, and we got to think of Little Mama with all that miserable traveling."

"No, Alice, don't you put off on account of me," Little Mama said. "The Lord done give me my three score and ten. I won't hold back, but Toby, son, you be the one be hurt most if we get caught."

"What plan dey set up?" Toby asked stroking his chin. "How dey....?"

"Sam got him a map, said we'd be travelin' at night

through the woods, takin' no chance bein' seen in the daylight." Alice shook her head. "Be mighty hard trip what with winter still on, and then with spring the snakes, bears and such come out."

"We got two horses we could take. You and Little Mama could ride Pappy, he be old but more steady than Tack," Toby said.

"You really studyin' about it for sure," Alice said.

"How long we wanted to go, darlin'? How long?"

"I know, Toby, but...."

"I think maybe we ought to try," Little Mama said. "We not all that safe here with no white folks speakin' for us."

"Let's sleep on it," Alice said. "Jodie and Sam not plannin' to go 'till Thursday night."

"What about the cows? Should we take one along and let the others out so they don't starve locked up?" Alice glanced first at Toby and then Little Mama.

"Better leave all of them," Little Mama said. We may need to ride fast sometimes."

Alice sighed. "Look like we done decided."

"We'll see. Tomorrow. We'll think on it more," Toby said.

The next morning a weary, sleepless Toby said, "It be too soon. We'll bring in de crops and sell 'nough for our pay."

"But what about Sam and Josie?" Alice asked.

"I'll 'splain to dem and say blessings and prayers for dem. Maybe we get on our way and see dem later."

***

Little Mama, who had been taught basic lessons in arithmetic, writing and reading by Hannah, kept careful records. Toby would bring her information and watch her post it in a worn brown book, though he never questioned what she wrote. He could neither read nor write but he liked to watch his mother draw down the funny looking little things on the page.

"This brown book be our record if we need prove our doings," Little Mama said.

"Good you fix it, Little Mama," he said, "I'll show it to de sheriff. We got nobody else."

"Jest don't let that buzzard deputy get he hands on it," Little Mama said holding up the small book and shaking it to emphasize her message.

Chapter Twenty-Five

The early days of the war brought strangers to town. One sunny day when Elizabeth rode in the carriage with Monette they saw men in unusually colorful uniforms. "Who are they?" Elizabeth asked.

Monette said, "They're like an infantry in the French army called Zouave, said to be extremely strong and able to do more than any ordinary man can do." She smiled. "I think they exaggerate. I read several accounts of what they claim to be able to do, but it's hard to believe any man is that strong."

"Their uniforms are so pretty!" Elizabeth said, "I like the red uniforms and the yellow boots. They look like some pictures in my book of Chinese soldiers."

"Yes, that's right they do resemble the Oriental uniforms, but in this case they're Irishmen. I read in the newspaper that President Lincoln asked a number...over six hundred Irish boatmen and deck hands on the St. Louis river front to join up as Zouave in the 8th Missouri Infantry and fight for the Union."

"Why? What can they do?"

"They claim a Zouave can pull up a hundred and ten pound dumbbell, climb up an eighty foot rope, hand over hand with a barrel of flour hanging on each heel." Monette laughed. "Oh, and climb four flights of stairs holding a heavy man in each hand at arms length. Now you know no man can do that! Still, perhaps they are very hardy, daring men as the original Zouave were said to have been."

"I think it would be too bad to kill them and ruin their pretty clothes."

"Elizabeth! It would be a shame for them to be killed, but that's what happens in war. But I agree they certainly can be seen easier than the men in blue or gray."

"Why do they have to kill each other? Why can't they just sit down and decide things?"

"If only they could! War is a terrible thing, Elizabeth. There's so much pain!"

"I'm glad Toby isn't a soldier," Elizabeth said.

***

Unknown to Elizabeth, that same beautiful sunny day was marred for Toby, Alice and Little Mama when the deputy known to them as Leonard, reappeared. Without so much as a knock or call, the man burst through the cabin door. He said, "You're looking at the new sheriff. Maybe you heard Sheriff Dobbs was killed during a brawl down on the riverfront."

"Yes, sir," Toby said. "Most sorry to hear 'bout it, too."

"Well, he was too soft, but I'm not," he said, standing firm, feet slightly apart. "Now Toby, you've had more than enough time to come up with the truth. Where is that girl?"

"Well, sir, I done told...," Toby began. He looked past the new sheriff and swallowed.

"Sheriff Leonard," Little Mama said. "Maybe you know Toby be a Christian. What if he swear on the good book?"

Leonard said. "You know, Toby, that God hates liars. If you are a Christian then you'll swear on the Bible."

Little Mama left the room briefly. She reappeared with the worn, soft-back brown book. "Maybe you knows Toby can't read but Madam she taught me. Would you like me read a verse or two before he swears?"

"No," Leonard said, "Don't be ridiculous."

"Well, then here it be," Little Mama said.

"Put your hand on it," Leonard said placing the book on a small table by the door.

Toby put his hand on the book.

"Now do you swear that you don't know where that girl is?"

"On dis bible?"

"Don't be silly. Yes, of course, on this Bible," Leonard said.

"On dis bible I swears," Toby said.

Leonard sighed. "I damn well better not find out that you're a lying Christian," he said. "Remember if I find out, a hanging party could still be in your future."

When he was gone Little Mama laughed and slapped her hip. "Well," she said, "we know it be a good book, just not de good book."

Alice, who had remained watchfully silent, put her arms around Toby. "Oh, darlin' I be worried."

Toby hung his head and sighed deeply. "I loves you. I prays the Lord help me keep you darlins' safe."

***

"The war keeps spreading," Hannah said. "I worry the whole country will be destroyed before this thing is over."

"Yes," Monette said holding a newspaper, "People everywhere are alarmed. Still most aren't sure what to make of it. Here it says, "Some say it would free the slaves and that was the purpose. Others think it is just a conflict over two ways of life. Industrial as opposed to the agricultural." She laid the paper on her lap, but picked it up again and continued to read. "A number of people insist states have the right to decide their way of life and the right to separate from the union to form their own government."

"Separate? Break up the union? Whatever the reason," Hannah said, "it's bad. People will be killed and many of them innocent.

Monette resumed reading. "The Confederates seized the US Arsenal on April twentieth in Liberty, Missouri, then in May the Rebels were successful in taking the property in Kansas City. The capture of Camp Jackson on May tenth in St. Louis was disturbing, especially to those who had family living in that vicinity. In June the list began to grow almost daily of new locations Jefferson City, Boonville and others until it seems the entire state is now in distressing riots or battles."

Hannah said, "I see men in uniforms on the streets from

both sides. I understand there're skirmishes sometimes, but interestingly enough, often the men seem to ignore each other as if they considered the battleground a different consideration."

"That is interesting. Like a 'time and place for everything.' I wish they could resolve it without war, but that seems hopeless now."

"Oh, much worse! Read this," Hannah said handing Monette another publication and she read aloud. "Great conflict on the Missouri-Kansas border is now a threat to every citizen. A majority of Kansans favor freeing slaves, but more residents of Missouri stand for maintaining slavery. The battle between the two states has increased to a high level and by the opening of the Civil War, groups of men are taking sides to fight according to their persuasion. Not only are the Federal soldiers fighting with the Confederates, but private groups are fighting according to the direction of independent leaders. One such violent leader is handsome, blond Ohio-born William Clarke Quantrill—a man who had from early in his life revealed a pleasure in the torture and killing of animals, now he has turned his murderous drive to the murder of human beings.

To the surprise of people who know them, a number of young men born in good families have joined Quantrill to fight under a black flag where no prisoners are taken and the wounded allowed no mercy. Only death is their lot. A large majority of Quantrill's followers have suffered cruel losses in their families which is undoubtedly an influence in their mission. Fathers, brothers and sisters have been murdered by Federal troops. Many of their homes have been pillaged and burned, crops destroyed, and grave insults imposed on many innocents, but Quantrill's purpose is not to right wrongs to others. Some members of his group possibly believe in their cause, but Quantrill had no noble persuasions of any kind. He simply seeks personal revenge on any who had insulted him and he has a lust for killing vast numbers of innocent people who happen to live in an area he despised. He desires to be known as great but lacks the ability to achieve that goal. In his paranoid thinking he blames others for his lack of success. Under the black flag, his only success comes by fostering the wrath of angry men.

"Quantrill supports slavery and claims to be fighting for the Confederacy but he was rejected as a member of their cause. He is known as the leader of outlaws while members of the Confederate Army believe they are fighting for a way of life for themselves and their families. The Federals believe they are just in fighting to bring the Union together and free the slaves. Still, both the Feds and the Rebels participate in inhuman behavior in acts of war.

"Quantrill's personality is not pleasing to many, but his appeal to their deepest anger allows them to accept an almost suicidal oath of allegiance to his organization. The long rambling oath reads in brief part, 'In the name of God and Devil...I pledge my heart, my brain, my body and my limbs, and I swear by all the powers of hell and heaven to devote my life to obedience to my superiors....'

"Quantrill's targets are not only the Feds, the Jayhawkers and their abettors, but totally innocent people, as in the town of Lawrence, Kansas, where he felt he had been insulted earlier. At dawn he and his guerrillas pulled from homes every man they could find and shot each one in the presence of his wife and children. Quantrill ordered that no women be killed, but every man was to be shot and stores and houses burned in complete destruction." Hannah sighed deeply. "What on earth can we expect with such men as these moving our way?"

"But what can we do? Where can we go?" Monette asked.

"I know of no safe place in war, although I hear there are places. The Shakers, a neutral religious group...."

"Oh, sure," Monette said laughing, "they would love an influx of prostitutes."

"I wasn't thinking of us, Monette. I was thinking of Elizabeth. Oh, I don't know what I can do about that beautiful child."

"Quantrill is said not to kill women and children,"

Monette said.

"What can we believe about such a man? And there are the other groups of crazies. Well, we have locks on our doors and weapons if any should try to drag us from this mansion."

Chapter Twenty-Six

In New York the evidence of the war was everywhere with the draft protests and riots. Bloody fights in the street became common. News of the wounded and dead on the battlefields added to the misery of families and friends.

Dr. Blackwell took on new responsibilities. She began to recruit and train nurses to serve in the war. Considering the urgent need of the men in service, she reluctantly condensed a thirteen months course into two months. In a series of lectures, she tried to prepare the new nurses emphasizing cleanliness, ventilation, care of helpless patients and observation of symptoms to report to doctors.

In the early morning, Dr. Blackwell sat at her desk and made notes for trimming the lessons. A difficult job, as the nurses would need to know so much. Often they would be in the fields alone. She sighed and rubbed her eyes. So much about the war troubled her. She dreaded each day's news not because of the specifics of battles won or lost, but because of the human suffering involved. Still, there was some comfort in knowing she was doing what she could to relieve the hardships of the soldiers.

But there was so much to do! She asked for help and was both amazed and pleased by the response. Large numbers of deeply caring women showed up at the Cooper Institute to prepare bandages and to scrape wool rags with sharp knives to create mountains of lint used for packing wounds of injured soldiers.

The soldiers' terrible living conditions troubled the women volunteers. They had learned that camps were often set in muddy marshes. Poorly cooked food, piles of garbage and many rats led to illnesses and death...sometimes in greater number than those dying from war wounds.

Dr. Blackwell and her helpers sought better supplies of food, clothing and medicines for the soldiers. Some of the women packed the supplies and personally visited the camps to ensure the men received the necessary items. They also pressured the government to do a better job while tirelessly continuing their own work. Their efforts and dedication brought respect to them all the way from privates to generals.

Although Dr. Blackwell did not personally see the slaughter of war, she knew seriously injured patients suffered greatly. Even under the best care there was often great pain. How much worse it must be with fear and inadequate care! It led her to tirelessly do all she could short of leaving her own treatment facility.

After an especially tiring day, Dr. Blackwell sat at her desk and lightly massaged her temples. Yvonne walked into the office, and placed a cup of hot coffee on the desk for the doctor.

"You worry too much about the war," Yvonne said.

"If only worry itself would help. It takes work, as you well know."

Yvonne said, "At least ours is a noble cause. The slaves must be freed." She stood hand on hips in front of Dr. Blackwell's desk.

"No one wants these poor persons freed more than I," Dr. Blackwell said, "but I'm not convinced that's the main purpose in our section of the country. I believe our army's main purpose is to preserve the union. But I'm distressed that my native country considered joining in the struggle to establish Southern independence. Free trade being their only motive. Oh, the love of money!"

"Do you think the British will do that, Doctor?"

"I hope not although I know they have considered it. It makes me heart sick to think my native country could support slavery for the sake of trade." She pushed the coffee aside and stood. "I must keep busy," she said.

"You work so hard, doctor," Yvonne said. "Do take a moment to at least enjoy your coffee."

In the background they heard a patient call for someone to come. "It's that troublesome old man who always wants his pipe filled." Yvonne said. "I fear he'll set the place on fire so I must watch him smoke until he finishes."

"True, but he's not long for this world, so let's indulge him," Dr. Blackwell said.

After Yvonne left, she stood by her desk and quickly finished drinking her coffee.

Later, she returned to her office and made notes, then she propped her head on her fist in reflection, thinking of slavery. A memory came to her of her time as a teacher in Kentucky years before when a slave in rags approached the lady of the house to plead for a clean shirt on Sunday, only to be insulted and dismissed. Her heart was deeply touched at that moment. She believed even if her father before her had not been against slavery, she would have been.

Besides the war, at the Infirmary there was still the problem of caring for the poor, both colored and white with less help now that Dr. Zac had gone to another practice in New Jersey. Milly, who had joined her staff after receiving her medical degree, was also showing the strain. Meanwhile, the streets continued to be rocked with violence bringing in more patients. Thousands of men, women and children over the year came to her clinic and she was glad to serve them despite the weariness of it all. Many of her patients were slaves who had escaped from the South. She made no difference in their care, but angry, frustrated people whose lives had been made worse by the war and the resulting circumstances were hostile toward the colored for the space they took and for the sharing of jobs.

***

Emily made numerous trips to the headquarters of The Children's Aid Society on East Twenty Second Street in hope of seeing if anyone there could provide her with information about Elizabeth. She asked to see the founder, but Mr. Brace was always unavailable when she visited. And she was told repeatedly that neither he, nor anyone there, had the information she sought. With each visit she hoped neverthe-less that someone—maybe someone absent when she visited before would remember something about Elizabeth.

Asking many questions, Emily learned the children were put on platforms at train stops and local people chose the child or children they wanted. The kindly woman Emily interviewed explained that some children were rejected and returned, but a beautiful little girl certainly would be wanted. The woman sighed, "We do what we can, though we know some not so attractive ones may be taken just as laborers. But your little sister—try not to worry so much, dear, surely she will be treasured."

Upon returning to the clinic Emily complained to Dr. Blackwell. "I think it's terrible," she said, "that nobody knows where the children are left!"

"Some do write back home I understand," Dr. Blackwell said.

"But Elizabeth can't write," Emily said. Tears flooded her eyes.

Dr. Blackwell dropped her head and sighed, "I know, dear. I'm confident Mr. Brace would not have allowed Elizabeth to be taken if he realized she had a home, but unfortunately he can't know everything his workers do."

"Why couldn't he see Mrs. Peake was mean? Why?"

"Sometimes bad people can be very charming when it suits their needs."

"But—but didn't he know that?"

"Emily, you see the abandoned children living on the streets...little ragged ones digging in garbage for food and huddled together against cold in doorways." Dr. Blackwell sighed. "It's too bad when someone like Mr. Brace has concern about a problem and tries to correct it, only to have others mishandle their part in it."

"But being put off a train at stops along the way and having strangers say, 'I'll take that one,' and you have to go with them. That sounds so scary."

They heard soft crying and saw Yvonne entering holding a thin blonde child in dirty rags. A purple bruise marked the area just above the child's right eye.

Yvonne said, "A drunken man threw her out on the street as I was passing. He told her not to come back. Where would she go? She's a mere baby as you can see—probably no more than three and a half years at most. I simply couldn't leave her."

Dr. Blackwell went to the child and knelt down to face her. "What's your name, little one?"

The child studied the doctor without speaking. Tears ran down her dirty cheeks, leaving trails on her pale face.

"Are you hungry?" Dr. Blackwell asked softly.

The child rubbed her eyes and nodded her head.

"Well, come then, we'll get you something to eat." She took the child's grimy hand in hers and walked toward the kitchen.

"What will you do with her, Doctor?" Emily asked. "You won't put her on that train, will you?"

"We'll see what we can do. Yvonne can tell our home visitor where the child lives. She may have a mother or someone there who cares for her."

"But if not?" Emily asked.

"I don't know yet," Dr. Blackwell said, "but we'll take care of her one way or another."

Unexpectedly, the child said, "Nonna. I Nonna."

***

Later, when Dr. Blackwell returned from the kitchen to her office, Emily was still there. "I strongly suspect that horrible Mrs. Peake did something with Elizabeth," Emily said. "I'm afraid we'll never find her, and you know Elizabeth is so feisty she could make matters worse if she lands in the wrong hands."

Dr. Blackwell went to her then and laid a hand on her shoulder. "We'll do all we can to find her. Try not to worry so much," she said. "In the meantime, if you think you have the heart for it, I should start you in nurse's training."

Emily was speechless for a moment. "Oh, would you?" she asked.

"I would indeed," Dr. Blackwell said.

Emily felt immediately grateful. She knew with her

disfigurement she could have a problem in securing other employment. Besides, she had come to feel at home in the Infirmary with the medical staff.

Yvonne came back through the infirmary with Nonna. The child was now clean, her blonde hair still damp and curling against her face.

"She's beautiful, isn't she?" Yvonne commented. "I'll keep her if I can."

***

To Emily's surprise, Sue Ling appeared at the Infirmary early one morning. She immediately said, "I can't tell you how sorry I am that I neglected my duty, and now Elizabeth is gone. I asked my grandmother what happened to Elizabeth, but she doesn't know. Later a man came and asked questions. A Mr. Smythe. Since The Old One doesn't speak English, my little boy cousin, Sing Lee, told him what grandmother had said."

"What did she say?"

"She remembered that some woman brought them cookies and pop. The Old One said she fell asleep as she often does in the afternoons. She thought that Dr. Blackwell had chosen an English-speaking woman to care for Elizabeth—and so did I."

"Then it was that woman for sure! Mrs. Peake kidnapped her!" Emily cried.

"I'm so sorry." Sue Ling bit her lip, then whispered again, "I'm so sorry!"

"This does very likely mean she is somewhere out west. But where?" Emily said.

"I'd give anything if I knew—if I could find her. I'll understand if you never forgive me, Emily."

Emily stood silent with her head down for a long moment before she spoke. "I know you didn't do anything intentionally to harm her, Sue Ling. You had told me how much you wanted to be a nurse and then you left denying yourself the training."

"Truly from my very soul, I had no idea such a terrible thing would happen."

Emily sighed. "We have learned that Mrs. Peake was killed by some of the bigger boys...door sleepers, but I haven't given up on trying to find Elizabeth. I only hope and pray that she is alive and happy wherever she is."

"Is there anything I can do? Anything at all? I have a little money."

"No, I don't think so. I appreciate the offer, but I don't know what else to do at this point." Emily then changed the subject. "How is Paul? Are you still seeing him?"

Sue Ling shook her head. "I wish. No, I haven't seen him for three months now. He joined the French Regiment and is in Virginia fighting the Rebs."

"What does Paul say about it? Does he write?"

"Oh, yes...as often as he can. That's why I'm here, other than wanting to tell you...to apologize to you. I do so want to become a nurse so I can go serve the soldiers. Maybe I can even go to Virginia. Who knows, I might even save my own dear Paul's life."

"Why did Paul decide to join? Many refused and rioted, you know."

"I know, but he didn't see it that way...not all of the young men did. Paul felt it was his duty, and maybe those posters encouraging young men to sign up influenced him. Another thing was the pay. Eleven dollars a month! Oh, he was told of excellent opportunities for seeing beyond New York, for promotion, good companions and great opportunities for glory, even fame. I tried to discourage him, but he had made up his mind. Now I think he may wish he hadn't done it, but it's too late."

"What does he say?"

"He says he's luckier than some thus far. The soldiers elect their leaders and sometimes the elected man proves poor at organization and discipline. Benny Pillore is his platoon leader. Do you remember him? Some kids used to tease him calling him—she whispered, 'Benny the bulbous butt.' "

"Yes," Emily said, "I remember him. I didn't think he was all that bunchy, mostly just too much weight on him. A smart fellow. More serious than most his age. Didn't he join the army earlier, before the war?"

"He did. Anyway, Paul likes him and thinks he's one of the better leaders. Maybe Benny's extra training and experience have made the difference, and, by the way, Paul said Benny has lost the weight and therefore lost his nickname...which probably none of these guys knew about anyway."

"Good," Emily said. "I always thought he deserved better. He was kind. One day I saw him help an old man who had fallen. I think he helped the old fellow get all the way back home." Emily brightened. "Did you hear that Dr. Blackwell has shortened the nurses' training for those going to serve the soldiers?"

"Yes, Yvonne told me. That's what I want to do now. Later, I'll want more training, but for now I want the quickest way possible to get to Paul. Some girls have signed up pretending to be males, but even if they don't get found out, I want to serve as a nurse, not a soldier. Besides, I probably couldn't get away with it."

Emily looked sad. "I'm not lovely like you. I probably could get away with it since I'm taller and have less shape. Even my scars might help me seem to have been in battle."

"No, Emily. You're so feminine in your manner and with that soft voice...no you're definitely a girl."

"I wouldn't go as a boy anyway," Emily said. "Like you, I would rather go as a nurse."

"Yes, Emily! Do! Let's go together."

***

Dr. Blackwell welcomed both girls and they started their studies the next day, but they were unprepared for the difficulty in covering much medical material so quickly.

"Well, I tell you one thing," Emily said, "I won't be sleeping much. I mean to do this!"

"My head hurts already," Sue Ling said, "but yes, me, too. I'll do what it takes."

***

Both Emily and Sue Ling worked hard day and into the nights at their studies. Often Dr. Blackwell stood by them and gave instructions, sometimes making a drawing to emphasize a point, sometimes quizzing them and making fuller explanations of some of the more difficult nursing duties they could face.

Finally, after their two months of intensive training they were ready. When Sue Ling requested they be sent to Virginia, Dr. Blackwell agreed and they prepared to leave. The small doctor embraced them both, but Emily knew Dr. Blackwell's feelings were especially strong toward her. "Do be careful," she said gently touching Emily's arm.

Impulsively, Emily kissed Dr. Blackwell's cheek. "You've been like a mother to me," Emily said. "You're in danger here, too, dear doctor. I would feel guilty if something happened to you in my absence."

"No, you mustn't think of it," Dr. Blackwell said, "The Lord will be with us whatever happens."

Chapter Twenty-Seven

Since Elizabeth was seldom allowed to go out, she continued to be a voracious reader and Hannah kept her well supplied with selected books. While she could read elementary French, she now read English better than many adults. Still, she longed to get out and especially now that it was autumn. She wanted to walk in the woods with Toby and to ride in the coach down to the river to watch the steamboats come and go.

One late afternoon when both Hannah and Monette were away, Elizabeth tried the side door to the grounds and found it unlocked. She'd accepted Hannah's orders to stay away from "the business," and therefore had never been in any part of the bordello except Hannah's quarters. But she continued to be curious about the other section of the mansion. In the evenings when she heard the music from the party, she'd asked to go there, but Hannah always said, "No, Elizabeth. I want you to stay here. That's business out there and it has nothing to do with you."

Business in a fine mansion like this? It wasn't a shop or a grocery. Then what? Still dressed as Pierre, she decided to slip out and explore the mysterious business.

The guard, a broad man in dark uniform wearing a fine gold watch chain stood near the entrance of the front door. He stroked his pointed beard and whistled a little tune completely unaware of Elizabeth's presence. She slipped up the steps onto the grand porch and hid behind a large chair.

Soon she saw a carriage stop and a portly gentleman step out. The guard apparently heard the sounds of the arrival and prepared to greet the gentleman. Elizabeth quickly discovered if she stood on her toes she could see in the window. She blinked at the sight of the huge ballroom lined with mirrors but slid back down behind the chair when she heard the guard and the visitor talking.

"Good afternoon, Major Hawthorne," the guard said.

"Good afternoon, Sam."

"I'll see you to the door, sir."

"Not necessary, Sam. She's expecting me."

Elizabeth waited for the major to mount the steps and enter the ballroom. But before he could open the door, a young woman with sky-blue eyes and curly red hair greeted him in a soft, cultured voice as she took his arm. After a brief conversation at the door, she escorted him to a great table covered with wines and food. They took drinks and left the room.

Another carriage drew up. Quickly, Elizabeth pulled hard on the heavy door and slipped inside.

She hid behind another armchair. Peering from her hiding place, she saw a ruddy-faced man and a blonde woman sitting on a divan, talking softly, gazing into each other's eyes. The woman wore a red silk robe and red satin slippers. The robe parted near her hip, revealing one shapely leg--which seemed to charm the man. He gently stroked her thigh.

Two beautifully dressed brunette women sat on elegant carved chairs, talking and laughing. One said, "You really didn't expect the necklace, Diane?"

"No. In fact, I was afraid...since he was so silent during the whole time, that I was not pleasing him. Have you had an experience like that?" She brushed aside long black curls at her neck to better reveal the ruby necklace.

"No, but I've had a few really big talkers who most wore my ears out!"

"Don't you think those are the lonely ones, Flora?" Diane said.

"Perhaps. I wouldn't know." Flora readjusted the deep neckline of her purple gown. "I wouldn't mind a ruby necklace, you lucky girl."

"Who got a mink cape last year?"

"Oh, but that was last year," Flora said, "and a piss sight cheaper than a ruby necklace."

Diane snickered.

"Why are you laughing?" Flora asked abruptly.

"To quote our elegant Madam 'The girls in the low-class houses use filthy language. You absolutely must not do so in this house! If you would perish if you don't dirty your mouth, then take a walk along the privies of the low class where it will blend in with the atmosphere.'"

"Oh, well, shit! What I said wasn't that much and besides she's nowhere around."

In awe Elizabeth looked at the great room before her—a room with beautiful red and gold sculptured carpet and dark, polished furniture. Grand mirrors in gold leaf frames reflected the beauty of the room including large oil paintings on far walls.

Forgetting caution, Elizabeth stepped from behind the chair considering a closer look at a painting of Indians around a campfire that fascinated her.

"Hey, little fella!" Diane cried. "Don't you think you're a bit too young for this?"

Both women laughed. Elizabeth was puzzled and at once, frightened. Why did they laugh and call her too young? She ran past Flora and Diane, and darted up the staircase as fast as she could. On the second floor she ran down the hall. A door was open to a fine bedroom. She closed the door, saw a closet, and hid in it. Her heart pounded. Now what? She wished she had never tried to find out about the business. And what was it anyway?

Within moments she heard footsteps in the hallway and a woman calling, "Come on little boy, you have to leave. Come on. Nobody's going to hurt you. Come on, now."

Elizabeth kept very still. She would wait until everything was quiet, then she'd carefully slip back down the stairs and return to Hannah's quarters. Maybe Hannah would never know.

She heard voices and footsteps. A man's deep voice, and a woman's soft laughter. The door to the room opened. Elizabeth barely breathed.

Through a crack in the doorway, Elizabeth saw the couple that had been on the divan downstairs.

In a husky voice the man said, "Come here, you beautiful doll." The woman slipped into his arms. "Ah, yes," he breathed, "how wonderful you feel!" He untied the red silk robe and threw it aside, leaving the woman's smooth skin glowing in the soft light. He put his hands on her breasts and she moaned, but it didn't sound like hurting.

The woman smiled, unpinned her silky blonde hair and let it fall across her shoulders. She whispered something in the man's ear that made his breath grow deeper. Then she unbuttoned his shirt and his trousers, kissing him repeatedly on his throat and chest. Slowly, she slipped her hands under his suspenders, lifted them and let his trousers fall to his ankles revealing his aroused state. Elizabeth gasped. She burst from the closet and ran from the room, down the stairs and out the front door.

She almost bumped into Hannah as she ran out the front door and down the steps. Even if she could have slipped back into Hannah's quarters unseen, she would not have been able to hide her feelings.

"Elizabeth!" Hannah cried, "What...?"

"I saw...I saw!"

"Come with me this minute," Hannah said, taking Elizabeth by the arm and near-dragging her across the way and into her quarters.

Tears were streaming down Elizabeth's face. She was sobbing so hard she was unable to speak.

"Now, young lady, you sit right here and tell me what happened," Hannah said, putting two chairs close together.

When Elizabeth continued to sob, Hannah took her on her lap whispering, "Shhhhh. Don't cry. Just tell me...."

Between sobs, Elizabeth told her.

Hannah said, "You're too young to understand this now, but there's a great difference between what you saw and what happened to you. One day you'll be a grown lady like the one you saw and you will like a nice man's gentle affection."

"I won't. I know better!"

Hannah frowned. "Elizabeth do listen! You don't understand what you saw. I know that horrible man hurt you

terribly, but what you were about to see can be very...
pleasant. Believe me you will find it so when you're older."

"No!"

Hannah sighed and shook her head.

"You're mad at me?" Elizabeth asked in a quavering
voice.

"No. I'd have preferred you obey me, but it may be just
as well. You're eleven years old. It's time I explained
something to you. Not today. Tomorrow after breakfast. I
have a book...some pictures. We'll see if that will help.
Besides, although you are small for your age, you could soon
begin your menses."

"What's that?"

"Tomorrow. We'll deal with it then."

"What is the business? I didn't see a business," Elizabeth said.

"My business is entertainment. Men pay to have company with the pretty girls and they enjoy the dances and good
food."

"Oh, but I saw!"

"There're different kinds of entertainment, Elizabeth.
You know you would pay to see a play don't you? People
pay for the kind of entertainment they like. Now, honey,
that's enough for now. Later, you'll understand better."

"I never saw a play, but Ma took us to a musical once."

"Well, then, that was still another kind of entertainment
and, of course, your mother paid for you to see it."

"I wish Ma hadn't died," Elizabeth said.

"I know." Hannah pulled her close in an embrace. She
kissed the top of Elizabeth's head and held her for a long
moment. She found herself thinking this could have been her
own Caroline.

***

That fall, Hannah allowed Elizabeth to visit with Toby,
Alice and Little Mama. She felt the danger of possible
recognition of Elizabeth by anyone of significance had

240

passed. Still, she had Elizabeth dress as a boy and cautioned her to speak only French to strangers.

Despite the boy's clothing and Hannah's warning, Elizabeth was happy. She was again going with Toby into the bright, autumn woods. They would taste the wild fruits and gather a basket of red and gold leaves for the dining room table. The wearing of knickers could not dim her happiness when she walked beside Toby.

Once again they gathered the wild grapes and pulled two golden persimmons to eat. The brisk autumn air under a slightly overcast sky felt cool on their faces. They walked past a falling-down gray shed and a plump gray rabbit jumped out. "Oh," Elizabeth cried, "he's so pretty! I wish I could catch him."

"Mr. Rabbit be too fast for us."

Elizabeth chased after him, but he disappeared in a clump of bushes causing some red berries to shatter to the ground.

"Best he stay hid," Toby said. "Some folks like to eat 'em."

"Oh, no! Well then I'm glad he can hop fast."

They came to a clear pond. "Next time, we'll bring fishin' poles," Toby said. "See dem fishes jumpin' up, breakin' the water."

"Could we have a camp fire and cook the fish right here on the bank?" She was remembering the painting of the Indians cooking over a campfire.

"We could. Sho' we could. We build us up a cookin' fire and fry 'em right here. Just need bring a pan and such.'Course we countin' fish 'fore we catch 'em." He chuckled.

"Oh, Toby, let's come back tomorrow and try!"

"We see if we kin," he said. "Fresh fried fish taste mighty good. 'Specially if you has good company to eat 'em wif."

"You're the best company, Toby! I want us to come back tomorrow."

When Elizabeth and Toby returned from their walk,

they saw a lanky white man sitting on the steps of the cabin. He appeared restless, repeatedly taking his hat off, running thin, pale fingers through his sparse graying black hair and plopping the hat back down on his head.

"That be Mr. Ford," Toby said. "He an old man who likes takin' news to the whole settlement. He like being the first with the messages."

"What news?"

"We soon find out," Toby said, and called out, "Mr. Ford, sir, what be the news?"

Ford stood up and dug his hands in his overall pockets. "I reckon' you ain't heard nothing about that fella what stayed up there with Mrs. Dalk?"

"No, sir. Nothin' 'cept he married up with her and then vanish away."

Forgetting to speak French, Elizabeth asked, "You mean Mr. Linktome?"

"Yep, the one and same fella," Ford said. "So you ain't heard." He smiled slightly, apparently relishing the pleasure of being the first to tell the news to them.

Toby waited knowing that Ford liked to tell things in his way, which was often in a round about manner.

Ford sat back down on the steps. "It was him they found, all right. Papers on the body."

"Body? He be dead?"

"Worse'n dead."

"Worse'n dead?"

"They foun' his skeleton down a deep ravine by the river road. Seem like his horse could've got spooked and went runnin' wild. Spooked mayhaps by a steamboat whistle. At least, that's what folks figure. Anyways, that ravine is most deep as the river, and filled with trash and brush. Folks never saw nothin' until some hunters went through there."

"I do say!" Toby said, shaking his head.

"It was him, all right. That is, what was left of him in his suited-up skeleton, and the skeleton of his horse, well it was right there, too." He looked at Toby and added, "Horse

242

still in saddle."

"Look like somebody hear somethin'," Toby said.

"Might o' hollered, but if he did, I reck'n nobody ever heard, or if'n they did, they jest laid it to somethin' else," Ford said. He lifted his old gray hat and ran his pale fingers through his thin hair again. "Well," he said, "I reckon' I must go now. Other folks will want the news."

Ford hesitated and turned back. "I reckon you heard about that new Sheriff Leonard bein'ambushed at a slave hangin' party. He was kilt dead as a rock right there. Hanging man, though, he not die. Some strangers travelin' through cut that lucky slave boy down."

Toby shook his head. "Sheriff dead as a rock. Who kilt him?"

"Dunno. Nobody say yet." He shook his head. "May never know. Leonard's deputy ran off scared and quit the job. Left town they say. Ain't got a sheriff yet, but some say Leonard's brother takin' the job and he's tough as they come and not scared of the old devil hisself." He removed and replaced his hat. "Well, 'til next time." He turned then and walked quickly down the path toward the road.

Chapter Twenty-Eight

Early one morning Elizabeth awoke and saw that Monette was packing clothing. On a chair nearby she saw a small blue woolen dress with a white collar and cuffs.

"Well," Monette said, "It's time you woke up. We've a surprise for you. Today's the day you go back to being a girl."

Elizabeth sat up in bed. "I've always been a girl!"

"I know, dear, but you no longer have to pretend to be a boy," Hannah said, smiling.

"Really? Don't say it if it's not true!" Elizabeth cried.

"It's true. This is the day."

"Is that blue dress mine?" Elizabeth asked.

"Yes. Monette is packing away the boy clothing."

"Pierre was a nice little boy, but things change," Monette teased.

"I never was that boy, nice or not! I was always me."

"Of course," Monette said, "but you were a good little actor. I liked having you for my 'son' I almost believed it at times."

Elizabeth stared at them with her lips set in a straight line, but said nothing.

"After breakfast we're going to take a drive out to the country," Hannah said.

"The country! We're going to see Alice!"

"We may. We're going to look at the Dalk property."

"Why?"

"I thought you'd ask," Monette said. She stopped packing and sat on the bed beside Elizabeth. "I'm getting married to a nice gentleman and we'll be wanting a home. We may buy the Dalk property if it sells for the delinquent taxes."

Hannah asked, "A nice gentleman?" her voice was bitter. "A stage robber riding with Curly Jack and with that Quantrill and his gang of killers. Surely, that cold-blooded William Quantrill and the crazy, blood-thirsty Bill Anderson can't meet with your approval. Anderson, as you must have heard, loves killing so well, he never takes a prisoner— never!"

Monette stood abruptly facing Hannah. "No, I hate that part. I don't approve of the James brothers either, but Madame, consider what the Union soldiers are doing to innocent people here! Surely you don't believe that they are merciful. They destroy the lives of all they consider as favoring the South. They do their murdering, looting, and burning of barns with innocent farm animals still inside. Did you ever see a horse or a cow taking sides?"

Hannah sighed. "It's a terrible war and evil men use it to their advantage on either side. But my dear Monette, I'm thinking of you. Marrying a man of this character is foolish! You could do so much better for yourself! What about that governor, one of the big cattlemen, a banker or even that steamboat captain? Haven't they all fallen for your charms?"

Monette flushed. "Don't sermonize me, Madame! My mind is made up. He's the only one who makes me feel real love. So what if I married some rich bastard? Money wouldn't make me nearly as happy as one adorable smile from my Terrance."

Hannah shook her head. "Do you hear yourself, Monette? You sound like a foolish child. I agree that the man is extremely handsome, but that will fade." Hannah sighed in frustration. "You won't be the first woman with so much beauty and charm who threw herself away on a man unworthy of her, but I believe you'll deeply regret it later."

"And I'm certain I won't!"

Elizabeth felt afraid. It was the first time she'd heard them argue...and so hotly! She lay back in the bed and pulled the sheet over her head. When Monette felt the tug of the covers, she said, "Elizabeth, never mind us. People disagree, you know. Everything is all right."

Hannah said, "Get up young lady, and we'll have breakfast now. I do disagree with Monette, but it's her choice and I'll do what I can to help her."

"If you move to the Dalk house, what about Toby,

Alice and Little Mama?" Elizabeth asked.

"We'd keep them on, if they want to stay."

"And I could come to see you?" Elizabeth asked.

"Yes, of course."

"Oh, Monette, I love you," Elizabeth said throwing her arms around the French woman for the first time.

A surprised Monette, hesitated momentarily, but then she smiled and returned the hug.

"I'd like a hug," Hannah said.

Elizabeth slipped from the bed and ran to Hannah, hugging her around the waist, "Marme, Marme," she said, "I love you." It was true, but at the same time, she knew Alice was her dearest love.

The wind whipped at the flaps of the carriage as they rode along until Monette fastened them down. The sky was overcast and a dusty smell of a storm permeated the atmosphere.

Elizabeth was hardly aware of the gusty winds or the now mild conversation between Hannah and Monette. She happily smoothed the soft blue dress over her knees. She felt pretty and anticipated Alice and Toby telling her so...maybe Little Mama, too. Beside her on the seat was a small leather purse and inside it some coins, a comb and a mirror. Also, she had a new book about France that Monette had given her. She picked up the book and began to read and study the pictures. Monette had said that one day Elizabeth might go there, even though it was far, far away over the ocean.

Rain began to sprinkle the roof of the carriage, making little tapping sounds. Lightning streaked across the sky, thunder rolled and wind shook the carriage.

"Madame, should we turn back?" Monette asked.

"No. We need to look this over, and make some kind of decision so that you and Terrance can complete the legal work before someone buys it more quickly."

Monette sighed. "Oh, I'd be so disappointed if they did! Buying for tax settlement is all that would allow Terrance and me to have such a big house."

"Accepting so little when you could have so much,"

Hannah said. "All right, I know you've made up your mind, but I'm concerned. Something about him...he makes me uneasy."

"That's just because you've never spent more than a few minutes with him. He's not only exceptionally handsome; he's charming and a wonderful man."

"If you say so."

The pattering rain increased its tempo to a downpour. Hannah pulled the horses to the edge of the road and waited. It was difficult to talk above the noise, so they sat in silence waiting.

Eventually, the rain slackened to a mist, but the road was covered with mud and yellow water. Hannah guided the horses as best she could to keep from getting mired down.

"What will they do with the Dalk money?" Monette asked.

"It may be held indefinitely and grow in value. More than a hundred and fifty thousand dollars in gold and certificates, or so I've heard."

"Well, some distant relative...some heir may appear yet," Monette said.

"Yes or some sharpie claiming to be one," Hannah said.

Monette suddenly sat erect. "Look! I see Terrance. I told him we were coming, and he's decided to surprise me."

The darkly handsome Terrance stood, hat shoved back on his head, waiting at the house. He was not alone. Stocky, red-haired Curly Jack came around the house and stood near him. Curly, ever cautious, glanced about. He stood shoulders squared, hands resting at his waist just above his gun belt.

"I'm surprised to see Curly," Monette said. "I thought he was going home. He's devoted to his wife and daughters, as I've told you."

"But robbing comes first," Hannah said, bitterly. "Time to rob stages, businesses, banks or any place to take other people's money."

"Don't be so self-righteous, Madame," Monette said, angrily.

"Whatever my faults, I'm not a thief."

"I'm not so sure the gentlemen's wives would agree with you," Monette said.

"Perhaps not, but those men would go somewhere. Don't you think wives would prefer us over the crude houses of Grace Jellon or Mary Tompkins?"

"You always come up with the last word, Madame," Monette said.

"Well, don't you agree?"

"As stated, yes," Monette said.

Elizabeth had remained silent, preoccupied, reading her book, but now she looked out the side window of the carriage. She gasped. "Men with guns!" she cried. "Men with guns!"

Monette moaned and covered her face as gunfire filled the air. Terrance and Curly dodged around the house and disappeared from view.

The uniformed men with guns fired from the field and fanned out covering a wide area. They ran in stooped positions toward the house.

Monette sobbed, "They're going to kill them!"

Gunfire disturbed the horses. They became restless, neighing, prancing about. Hannah held the reins firmly and spoke in reassuring tones, "Steady, boys, Steady. Steady. There. There. That's good. That's good."

All the while Monette sobbed and cried over and over again. "Oh, God, don't let him be killed."

Hannah laid a firm hand on Monette's thigh. "Calm down, Monette. Get hold of yourself."

"I'm scared!" Elizabeth said. "I'm scared."

"Now don't you start," Hannah said, "You're all right. They're not shooting at us."

"They're getting away!" Monette cried. The stampede of horses running mingled with the sounds of gunfire. "Oh, I hope he's not hurt. Dear Jesus, don't let him be hurt."

"I never knew you to be so religious," Hannah said. "Now I hope this little scene has taught you a lesson. Is this the way you want to live?"

Monette made no reply. She sat, head down, trembling,

her fingertips pressed together in a prayerful pose.

Four of the men in the field ran toward the horse barn. One man came jogging toward the carriage, holding his revolvers secure at his side. He called out, "Are you ladies all right?"

Hannah, with hand at her throat replied, "I believe so, though you certainly frightened us."

"Sorry, ma'am but we had a tip Curly Jack was out this way."

"I understand," Hannah said.

"He's wanted for murder of a coachman, though I've not known him to harm ladies. Still, I'd advise you to be careful."

"Thank you kindly, sir. We'll be most careful," Hannah said.

The man tipped his hat and trotted down the field road toward four men mounted on horses. One man leading an extra horse waited. The others whipped their horses into full speed as they followed the path taken by Curly and Terrance.

The man leading the horse yelled, "Hurry. We may be able to catch them. I think we made a hit."

Monette whispered, "Oh, God."

"Are they killed?" Elizabeth asked in hushed tones.

"No," Hannah said, "Everything is all right. They rode away on their horses."

"We don't know they're all right," Monette said.

"There's nothing we can do about it anyway," Hannah said, "Besides, they'll take care of each other."

Monette dabbed at her eyes. "He can't keep running with Curly. It was Curly they were after. You heard that. They'll chase him forever."

"All right, see if you can get him to make a living some other way. In the meantime, now that we've made the trip, shall we look at the house? Though I imagine if anyone is here from the tax office, he may be in hiding with all this commotion going on."

***

A bald little man with sallow skin appeared at the door. He stood silently staring at them with piercing dark eyes, sullen and threatening with a set jaw. Elizabeth saw he looked like the Dalks, and ran down the porch steps to the carriage.

"Are you from the tax office?" Hannah asked.

"No," he said.

"We've come to see the property," Monette said.

"The property is not for sale," the man said. His tone was blunt, final.

"But...." Monette began.

"I'm Dorcett Dalk, heir to my mother's property." He stood for a moment seemingly challenging them with his stare, then abruptly closed the door and latched it.

***

When they drove away, Monette said, "Now what are we going to do?"

"Check on this character, that's what. You and Terrance can find something else, but what about Toby's family? Unless Dalk's looks are misleading, they're in trouble."

Chapter Twenty-Nine

The next day a welcome change in the weather brought warm sunshine. Hannah took the carriage into town to check on Dorcett Dalk, and, as had become her recent custom, let Elizabeth accompany her, with a trip by the ice cream saloon a promised capping to the drive.

Hannah drew the carriage to a stop in front of a row of plain, gray buildings unmarked except for a street number and a panel listing various offices.

"Elizabeth, wait here. I don't expect this business to take long." She drew closures to the carriage so that Elizabeth was not visible. She hesitated. "Maybe I should take you with me," she said, but reconsidered. "Well, this won't take long. Just keep quiet and I'll be back soon."

As she waited, Elizabeth was aware of the rustling and bumping sounds of carriages passing on the brick street. From time to time she heard the shrill whistles of the riverboats. Ignoring Hannah's directions, she slipped a curtain back to look at the people riding past.

One open buggy pulled to a stop under a tree on the opposite side of the street. Briefly but eagerly, the man and woman inside embraced and kissed. The man placed a ring on the woman's finger, then lifted her hand to his lips while looking into her radiant face. Moments later they drove on. The incident reminded Elizabeth of what Hannah had told her the next morning after her frightening visit to the 'business' side of the house. She still wondered about it. How could a woman really like a man that way? But then she thought of Toby and Alice. Did they do that? She would ask Hannah. From the books it was true that those who had children did it, but Toby and Alice had no children.

A group of six men gathered on the sidewalk near the carriage. They wore long-tailed frock coats of black broadcloth with velvet collars and black string ties. Most wore neatly trimmed mustaches or beards. Elizabeth liked their pleasant faces...like Toby, though only two were Negro. The men stood tall, thumbs in vest pockets, often politely joking, laughing. Each of them drew on big cigars. A door to the building opened and Hannah stepped out. Elizabeth jerked the closing together.

Hannah stepped up into the carriage. "Well, that settles that. Dorcett Dalk is the legitimate heir. He was Mrs. Dalk's younger son, whom she put away in an asylum years ago."

"In an asylum? Why?"

"Because she was not a good mother, I suspect, but supposedly because of his epileptic 'fits'."

"What's that?"

"An ailment. We can read about it later. Anyway, he managed to get out of the asylum several years ago, and had been working with some so-called 'free people.' Their priest, who was traveling with them at the time, came upon the notice of the search for Dalk heirs when he visited a telegraph office."

"What's 'free people'?"

"Nomads from Canada. Do you remember that day we drove a long distance out of town to the cook's farm house?"

"Yes."

"Those were 'free people' we saw that day in the long single-file caravan. Remember? Before we ever saw them, we heard their two-wheeled oxcarts. Those wood-on-wood carts screaming and whining like caged wild cats! I don't know how they could stand that screeching day after day."

Elizabeth looked pensive. "Will that Dalk man come and get me?"

"No. Forget him. Actually, I think he's just an unhappy man, the product of many years of being rejected and perhaps mistreated. He may have found his only kindness from the free people who apparently accepted him."

Elizabeth smiled. She sat forward. "It's the next street," she said.

"What? Oh, the ice cream saloon. Nothing ever makes you forget that, does it?"

"No," Elizabeth said, still smiling. But it wasn't just the

ice cream. It was being reassured that Dorcett Dalk would not come for her.

***

Now that she was unafraid to visit, Alice came by the bordello from time to time. From what she reported, Hannah gathered Dalk maintained his sullen outlook, but was not unkind to her. In fact, he seemed to like her help and, on occasion, would reward her with a little extra pay. Alice said she never knew what brought the extra pay on, but suspected it had to do with her attention when he had seizures.

Hannah nodded. "Of course, he enjoys gentle care, but it speaks well of him that he can show appreciation. Sometimes people who have been hurt are too full of hatred to do so."

"I reckon we be safe for now," Alice said.

"I'm glad for you," Hannah said, but even as she spoke she thought of the war and wondered if any of them would remain safe.

***

On a chilly, wet day in November, Elizabeth and Monette sat near the kitchen in a little alcove overlooking the street. They were sipping hot cocoa. Below they saw a lone old man, bent against the wind and rain, carrying a huge black umbrella.

"Qelle heure est il?" Monette asked.

"About two o'clock, I think," Elizabeth said.

"You'll forget your French if you don't use it," Monette said.

"Pourquoi?" Elizabeth asked.

"That's just the way it is with a new language and with many other things as well. Madame has told you it's true of your music and it is. You should practice a little every day."

A forceful, rapid knocking on the door startled them, but Monette quickly recovered. "Probably, just one of the girls being playful."

Elizabeth was curious. She had been kept so strictly apart from "the business" that she seldom saw any of the girls, and then only in passing as they chanced to meet at the carriage house. She saw the dumpy, squarely built housekeeper, Maude, and the tall, skinny cook, Mary Sue, but they were older and sometimes so abrupt in their conversations with each other that Elizabeth preferred to avoid them.

As Monette opened the door, Elizabeth heard a man's voice. "I think you've had a letter or two, but I...."

"Oh, Curly! Do come in," Monette said, "How is Terrance? Is he all right?"

"Well, yeah and no. That's what I've come for."

"What do you mean?"

"I'll tell you in a minute. Could I first have some water? I'm thirsty as all git out."

"Of course," Monette said, but before she left the room, she said, "Oh, Mr. Conners this is Elizabeth."

Elizabeth remembered seeing the stocky, red-haired man that day at the Dalk place although he had not seen her.

Curly stooped to take Elizabeth's hand. "Howdy, beautiful. Are you Monette's kid?" he asked.

"I used to be when I was a boy." She said, grinning.

"What?"

Monette returned with a glass of water. "Never mind, she's joking," Monette said. "No, she's not my child. Hannah has kind of adopted her." She motioned for him to be seated, but he continued to stand, gulping the water.

She said, "Elizabeth, please be quiet. I want to talk with Curly now. Tell me about Terrance. In his letters he sounded all right, but I wonder since he hasn't been back to see me."

Curly turned a straight chair around and sat astride it, arms propped on the ladder style back. "It's his leg. He didn't want to tell you, but they got him in the leg that day."

"Oh, no! So how...?"

"He kept trying to think it would get well...kept working, you know. But it got worse. Finally, he landed in a

254

hospital in Kentucky."

"Kentucky?"

"Well, you know we get around. We wound up around Lexington before he had to give in."

"I'm going to him," Monette said, "just as soon as I can pack."

"He thought you'd say that, but he wants you to wait a while. Thinks he'll be well in a month or two, and then you could get married. He has folks in Kentucky so he'd like to settle there."

"Wait? I don't want to wait! What if he gets worse? Maybe I could help him."

Curly stood and set the chair aside. "Terrance's right proud, and strong in his word, Monette...yep, he means what he says. Don't think he'd want you to see him like he is now."

"What kind of pride is that? I love him," she said.

Curly shook his head. "He didn't want me to tell you nothin'. Still, secretly, I think he wanted you to know so you'd understand why he's not coming back to Missouri soon. Truth is, he's afraid you might take up with somebody else with him being away so long."

"I'd never do that! Of course, I have to do my work, but he's the only one I care about."

"You can let him know whatever you decide." He fished in his pocket and brought out a piece of paper. "This is his address at the hospital and he writ a little word or two."

Monette took the note and quickly opened it.

Curly glanced back at Elizabeth. "Does Madam Hannah mean to grow this girl into the profession?"

"No. She replaces Hannah's little daughter killed in a storm years ago."

"Well, just a word to think about then. She's too pretty to live around here much longer. Got a couple of little girls myself."

Monette smiled. "I've heard you were quite the family man. How do you mix that with your work?"

"Not the same thing. It's my own foolish neck out

there, and I get one hell of a kick out of the game...you know, them or me, and I believe in me. I like finding out who's the smartest in a gamble that's not just for peanuts. The game and the money both count with me. 'Course my wife wants me to quit. Maylene, she worries about me killin' that coach driver. That was a accident...didn't mean to. The horses jerked and moved him into my line of fire," he rubbed his red bearded chin. "Anyways, I ain't been able to give up the game."

"And Terrance? Do you think he can give it up?"

Curly sighed and gave the chair a light kick. " 'Tween me and you, Monette, I think he'll never ride in the game again. Think he'll lose that leg."

"Oh, no."

"Could be wrong, but don't think so. Well, he's got family in Kentucky. They'll help him get into somethin' else...maybe working in selling. They got a feed and seed store, but nothing ain't been said yet. Rather you didn't tell him, I mentioned it, but just thought you'd like to be prepared a bit in advance."

"Thanks, Curly. I won't say a word. For his sake, I'd be sorry about his leg, but for the future, I'd like him doing other work."

"I understand, though I ain't ready to give it up myself."

Elizabeth was confused by most of the conversation, but kept quiet as Monette had requested. What did it mean 'grow her into the profession'? And what was 'adopted?' She'd ask Monette as soon as the red haired man left.

***

Elizabeth happily learned what it meant to be adopted, but the "profession" was a mystery somehow related to the "business." What did it mean? Why were they keeping it a secret from her?

Monette said, "The profession? Oh, Elizabeth it's nothing to concern you."

256

"But what is it?" Elizabeth pressed.

Elizabeth thought she seemed annoyed but she replied, "It's knowing how to be entertaining to—to the gentlemen." Elizabeth frowned. Both Monette and Hannah seemed uncomfortable in speaking with her on any subject related to the business. She was still troubled by the memory of the naked man and woman she had seen. How was that entertainment? She was now more curious than ever. She meant to find out one way or another.

One evening after she was in bed, Elizabeth overheard Hannah say, "I'm concerned. I don't think it's safe to keep her here much longer, and yet there's the war going on. I'm afraid for her to travel as well. Concerned for you, too, Monette, but I know you will go to Terrance now."

"Yes, and I'm happy that he's no longer with Curly and the gang, but I know he's grieving over the loss of his leg."

"So now he's a retired robber. It's really a blessing for him and you," Hannah said.

"He works in the family's farm store."

Still thinking of Elizabeth, Hannah said, "This town is full of every kind of man from everywhere and she naturally keeps wanting more freedom to go out. I'm afraid for her to go unaccompanied even for a walk. Her beauty is a blessing and a curse."

Monette said. "Terrance has a sister who lives on a house boat on the Ohio River. Elizabeth should be safe there."

"A house boat? I don't know. What kind of person is his sister?"

"From what he says, she's a good-hearted woman who makes a living for herself and her children selling goods to the other shanty boaters. There're quite a number of families living on house boats of different sizes on the river."

Hannah said, "I imagine they're basically untouched by the war and it sounds like a community of families, but getting there...battles are going on everywhere!"

"I doubt as travelers on train and by coach we'd be bothered by the fighting," Monette said. "Besides, a Missouri train on single track is probably mostly used by travelers rather than by the army. Not like in states east of here where there are many trains. I don't think the war would...."

"Maybe...except by possible accident or by robbers," Hannah said.

"I think there're fewer train and coach robbers now because of the war. You know I would try to choose our route wisely," Monette said. "At least, it's not like the trains in the East and South transporting many soldiers and war materials. I hear they blow up those bridges and derail the trains in an effort to defeat each other."

"What do I do?" Hannah asked. "Neither plan is good. If she stays here or if she goes."

"Nothing is for certain now" Monette said, "but I think the river family will be best for her. Perhaps, if she stays a year, the war will be over by then."

"If she goes, I'll want you to bring her back for a visit, of course. Come during the spring freshet as the river is higher then and that will allow for a pleasant steamboat ride, something of a new experience for her. We'll celebrate her birthday early then." Hannah sighed. "It's hard to believe, but she'll be a young woman in little more than a year from now. The time has gone too fast."

"Then you'll let her go with me?"

"Reluctantly, but I think it could be best. However, in the next couple of years I'll need to make other plans. Perhaps, something like a proper finishing school in New York."

Elizabeth stirred slightly, but pretended to be asleep. Tears filled her eyes. She didn't want to go to Kentucky.

Hannah said, "It appears the best route to take would be by stagecoach from here to St Joseph. There you can get the train to St. Louis. Your trip will be from stagecoach to train and back to stagecoach as no one conveyance will hold for the entire trip--oh, and, of course, there're the rivers to cross by ferry."

"I know it will be exhausting and dirty, but probably the best we can do. At least it seems most of the battles in

258

Missouri are south of our route."

"That's true at this time, but Monette, you can't count on the war not expanding northward. Of course, there could always be accidents, stray gunfire and oh, Lord...I hate to have you and Elizabeth leave."

"Madame, we can't be guaranteed safety anywhere, not even here, but I do believe Elizabeth will be safer with the houseboat families."

"I think so, too, once you get there. I understand these families tend to be gentle people who love freedom and being close to nature—possibly taking no sides in the war."

"It's getting late, Madame. Perhaps, we should retire. I'll begin packing for myself and Elizabeth tomorrow."

By now Elizabeth was crying and Hannah heard her. She said, "Oh, honey, don't worry. I didn't know you were listening, but I think you'll like your new adventure."

"I won't," Elizabeth said. "I want to stay here with you, Marme."

"You'll be coming back. It won't be forever." Hannah swallowed knowing she could lose her if something went wrong. Was she making the right decision? Should she keep her in Kansas City after all?

Chapter Thirty

Shortly before her twelfth birthday in July of 1862, Elizabeth left Kansas City for Maysville, Kentucky. She rode in the carriage to the stagecoach station with a happy, talkative Monette and a solemn Hannah.

Elizabeth was near tears remembering her farewell visit with Toby, Alice and Little Mama. Alice tried to comfort her saying, "The time, it will go fast, sugar. Why 'fore you knows it you'll be right back here telling us 'bout all kinds of things." But Elizabeth had seen their sad faces and knew each of them barely held back tears.

When they reached the station, Elizabeth saw they were not the only travelers. Clusters of people stood chatting with each other. Some had flower-decorated carpetbags or other luggage resting at their heels. A gentleman in a brown waistcoat suit and black top hat escorted a tiny white-haired lady into the station office. Some men paced restlessly as they waited; several wore military uniforms. Two ruggedly dressed cowboys stalked about...one, a dark-eyed man who appeared to be Mexican, and the other, a blue-eyed Nordic type with sun-streaked hair. They joked with each other. The blond one shouted with laughter and slapped his knee. Hannah appeared annoyed by the noise, but the light-hearted Monette smiled and moved slightly toward them hoping to overhear something funny.

Elizabeth observed three empty stagecoaches stood waiting. Likely each would go to a different destination, so it would be important to board the one going to St Joseph. Monette would make sure of the right coach. Elizabeth's concern was she had to go at all.

In one last effort, Elizabeth asked, "Do I really have to go?"

Hannah's voice was firm. "For now, yes, my daughter. It's best." My daughter? It was the first time Hannah had claimed in those words her as her own child. Their tear-filled eyes met, but neither spoke. Hannah drew her near and kissed her forehead.

In too short a time for Elizabeth, she and Monette boarded the stagecoach and rode down a gravel road. Looking back she could see Hannah, her hand shading her eyes against the sun, watching as they drove away. Elizabeth fought tears knowing that all too soon they wouldn't see each other for a long time.

Although, she had been repeatedly reassured of a return visit, the separation from all those she loved in Kansas City filled Elizabeth with pain and dread. She continued to look where Hannah stood and waved until she could see only the edge of the station. There was no turning back. Her throat ached thinking of being sent away for any reason. What if she never saw Alice again? Or Toby and Little Mama? Tears ran down her cheeks and she swallowed hard. Though she said nothing Monette took her hand and lightly squeezed her fingers. It occurred to Elizabeth that cruel people like the Dalks could again enter her life, although she felt less concern about that now that she was older. Besides, she was not really alone. She dried her eyes and glanced at Monette, who smiled at her.

They sat in the stagecoach facing the front with the tiny white-haired lady, now known as Mrs. Rawlings from San Diego, wedged between them. St Joseph would be her final destination. The elderly lady volunteered, "I hated to leave my son back there. Oh, not worrying about him, but dreading this Concord stagecoach ride. I rode the Seeley & Wright stage line to Los Angeles, and it was bad enough. And from Los Angeles to Kansas City, well, I thought I'd never make it. I fear this will be worse, but I'm determined to visit my sister in St. Joseph one last time before we die. You see, I'm eighty years as of last month and she's eighty-seven and unwell."

Monette laid a hand on the old woman's thin arm. "I surely hope you'll make it and have a wonderful visit. Perhaps, there will even be time for another one later."

"You're very kind, but I know this will be the last."

Elizabeth whispered, "Is Little Mama eighty? Do people die when they get eighty?"

"Not necessarily," Monette said, "and Little Mama is probably not more than seventy."

Facing them, riding with backs to the driver were the two cowboys and a boy in ragged clothes about Elizabeth's age. It soon became clear the dark-eyed cowboy was the child's uncle who expected the boy to be quiet while he and his friend continued to carry on an avid conversation about happenings back at the ranch. At least, at this time they spoke in quieter voices with only a word heard now and then, but enough that Monette realized the content of their subject matter. She thought they tried to speak quietly because they talked of sex and knew they were in the presence of ladies. She smiled. Of course, they had no idea that she was a prostitute. No one could tell simply by looking at her as a well dressed and properly behaving young woman.

While they were still riding slowly the stagecoach rode smoothly, but that was soon to change. The driver slapped the horses into a trot and the coach became a bumping, swaying, rolling ride through billowing dust...much of it blowing into the coach.

"Oh, my!" Mrs. Rawlings said, trying to stay put in her seat, "this is worse than the ride up from Los Angeles! I hope it will improve with a better road and perhaps a little less speed."

"There ain't no better road," the blond cowboy volunteered. He ran a hand over his head. "You see we didn't grease down our hair because we knowed better. A real greasy head can collect enough dirt on one of these trips to start a garden patch."

When his friend laughed, he said, "Ladies, this here is Juan, and I'm Leroy. I see the lady has a silk scarf around her neck to cut out the dust from her chest. You and the young girl would do well to do the same before it gets any worse," he said directing his message to Monette.

"Uncle Juan, I'm hungry," the boy said.

"Well, Sammy," Juan said, "it's gonna be a long time before we reach a home station to grab some grub. You shoulda ate before we left."

"Didn't have nothin' to eat. Ma been laid out two days."

"Drunk again? I swear!" He seemed deeply annoyed. "I ain't puttin' up with this no more. Your Pa ain't gonna be no better either. You're going with me and Leroy back to the ranch. I reckon' I could scratch up chores for you to do for your keep."

Sammy teared up. "Really? Honest? I wana, but they won't let me."

"I ain't asking them," Juan said. "What would they know anyhow all boozed up? Forget it, kid, you're with us from now on."

"Do you live near St. Joseph?" Elizabeth asked.

"Nope, I was taking Sammy to see his Pa there, but I just changed my mind. We'll get off at the home station and turn back."

"Really?" Sammy asked. "Really?"

"Yes sir. You ain't going back to living with either my brother or his old lady."

"But will they be all right? I always took care of them best I could." Tears stood in his eyes and then rolled down his cheeks. "Who'll see after them if I'm gone?"

"I'll get 'em checked out once in a while. Not for you to worry about, Sam boy. You ain't putting them bottles to their lips. Not for you to worry about a 'tall."

After a dirty, exhausting four hour ride, they arrived at the home station. They washed up the best they could and then sat down to a meal of boiled beans, salted meat and bitter coffee.

The large-boned woman who served them yawned and scratched her fat behind. "More beans if you want 'em." she said.

True to his word, after the meal, Juan arranged for coach tickets back to Kansas City. He tousled Sammy's hair and said, "Boy, I'm gonna make a cowboy out of you. Roping, riding—you're gonna be a good one."

Sammy smiled. He said a shy " 'Bye," to Elizabeth when he passed her table. She looked surprised, but then waved to him.

Mrs. Rawlings yawned against her hand. She elected to stay overnight at the home station in one tiny room set aside for travelers. There were no more rooms available. Besides Monette had decided they should ride two more hours before stopping at a small hotel for the night. They would continue on the next day with another stagecoach having a new driver and a fresh team of horses. She once again wished Mrs. Rawlings a good trip and hoped that she and her sister would have a happy time together.

Near sunset, the stagecoach drew up to a small, weather-beaten hotel. Monette found it offered only cots for beds and, after seeing the room, she worried that the sheets were less than clean. She sighed and shrugged. She and Elizabeth were tired, so she paid the gruff, bearded owner and they took to their room for such rest as they might get. Monette bolted the door, but since they were on the second floor she opened the window to let cool air into the small, musty room. At least there was a large white pitcher of water and a bowl, but the one dingy towel...wrinkled by obvious use of previous visitors offended Monette.

"Let's take clean handkerchiefs to wash up with," she told Elizabeth. "Then we'll hang them on this ladder back chair by the window to dry overnight."

"They're too little," Elizabeth complained.

"I know, but do the best you can. Then dry off with a petticoat and spread it on the foot of your cot."

Chapter Thirty-One

Next day they arrived in St Joseph and took a hack to the railroad station. Elizabeth smelled the smoke from the wood-burning locomotive and heard the bell clanging even before she saw the train. Small groups of people milled about the boarding platform. Finely dressed ladies with skirts barely topping high buttonshoes, chatted with each other, sometimes nodding their heads, causing the feathers on their hats to bob.

Elizabeth watched the waiting passengers with interest. Three gentlemen in dark suits, wearing white scarves and top hats waited. Each smoked big cigars. One of these men, a heavy-set older man wore a gray vest and coughed frequently; another stroked his dark beard as he spoke in a deep, slow voice. A third member of the small group, frequently interrupted his companions to talk at a rapid pace. He spoke with conviction expressing his opinions with a down gesture of his gloved hand. Elizabeth wondered what had stirred him to this point although it was clearly something about the war and decisions he'd not liked.

Two other gentlemen, although not elderly, walked with elegant gold handle canes, and one of these looked all about in the crowd appearing either bored with the talk or looking for someone. Elizabeth saw with interest and mild fear, that some robust men in rough clothing carried revolvers in holsters but they did not appear threatening. Still other men, wearing work clothes, checked around the train and loaded more wood into the tender. Someone unseen stoked the furnance. Smoke and soot billowed into the air covering the hapless group who made futile attempts to fight it off. Fortunately, a change in the wind soon blew it slightly in another direction, but the air was still filled with the noxious odor and fragments of cinders.

"Now we're dirty again," Elizabeth said.

"Yes, but it won't last forever. We'll just have to endure," Monette said.

"Will the ride on the train be better than the stage-coach?"

"I hope so. We'll soon see," Monette said.

The boarding call went out and people began to move quickly toward the train whose engine chugged in steady rhythm as a dark cloud of smoke poured from the smoke stack into the October sky.

Monette and Elizabeth found a seat near a grimy window and settled in. Soon one of the gentlemen carrying a gold-handled cane tipped his hat to them and decided on a seat nearby, but he made no effort to engage them in conversation...rather, he opened a small, red book and began to read. Soon most of the seats were taken by men and women who chatted among themselves before selecting a location to settle into. Monette thought she and Elizabeth would not have a social exchange such as they'd had on the stagecoach, and it suited her well enough as she liked time to think of Terrance and their upcoming wedding.

A male voice from outside the train shouted, "Allll Aboard!" once more. Soon afterward the train began to move forward. At first it only rocked gently, but as it gathered speed the ride became bumpy and the train swayed in an alarming manner from time to time.

"Oh, no!" Elizabeth cried. "This is not better."

"Sorry, honey. But like I said, it won't last forever."

"Let's hope it does last," the gentleman holding the red book said. "I hope if we have a trestle to cross that we'll make it. You know the Rebels are blowing them up."

"I hope there aren't any on this route," Monette said.

"Are we going to get wrecked?" Elizabeth asked.

"I trust not," Monette said.

"Well, let's hope if there are blown bridges or trestles that Herman Haupt is around to rebuild them before we get there," he said.

"Who is Herman Haupt?" Elizabeth asked.

"A fine engineer, young lady. Last May, he along with some unskilled workers, put up a fine trestle nearly 80 feet in height and 400 feet long. That was over the Potomac Creek in Virginia after the Rebs had knocked the bridge out. Haupt and the men built that trestle in nine days...a finer latticework of sticks you never saw. Now it's true these sticks are conveniently cut to fit every which way and sometimes hauled in advance, but in this case he had to cut most of the timber from local woods. Soon that trestle withstood from ten to twenty heavy railway trains in both directions daily."

"That really is impressive," Monette said.

The gentleman laughed. "Why when President Lincoln saw it, he said, 'That man Haupt has built a bridge across Potomac Creek, and upon my word, gentlemen, there is nothing in it but beanpoles and cornstalks.' Well, it looked that way, but it was much more...stood severe freshets and storms without injury."

"Well," Elizabeth said, "I hope we don't have to wait nine days for him to fix something for us."

"Better still," the gentleman said, "let's hope there's nothing to fix."

"I agree, sir," Monette said.

They fell silent then and tried to watch the passing scenery through the dirty window. Elizabeth wiped it with a handkerchief, but most of the dirt was on the outside so it did little good.

On in the late afternoon, not long before there was to be a stop for dinner, the train came to a shuddering stop.

"Have we come to a blown up trestle?" Elizabeth asked, eyes wide.

"No," the gentleman said. "We're halted due to a herd of buffalo. Look out your window and you'll see them."

Sounds of gunfire and bellowing animals alarmed Elizabeth. "What is that?" she asked.

"Men are shooting the buffalo," the gentleman said.

"Why?" Elizabeth asked.

"Because if the train tries to run through them, it could derail us," he said.

"Why don't they just shoo them away?" Elizabeth asked.

"They're not flies, Elizabeth," Monette said. "Apparently, the men can't get them to move."

"Sometimes something will cause them to stampede... even as little as leaves blown up, but then there are the hunters," the gentleman said. "You perhaps saw them—the men with guns in holsters back at the station. They ride the engine hoping for the kill. You see that can be profitable for them. They can sell the meat. They can also sell the hides for lap robes."

"Poor things!" Elizabeth cried. "I wish they had moved."

The train jerked, stopped and jerked again before it began to move continuously. The gray evening sky revealed little but silhouettes of trees and rock formations now, though the rank odor of gunfire and blood hung still in the atmosphere.

Chapter Thirty -Two

In St. Louis they hustled to change from the train to another stagecoach for some distance before they could again board a train. "Service is not direct from here," Monette said, "it consists of several lesser companies but hopefully we'll have no more buffalo stops. We'll have to take a ferry when we reach the river. I think that will be a new experience for you, won't it?"

"Yes. I hope it won't be shaking and bouncing us around like we've been doing," Elizabeth said. "I like boats. They look pretty steaming along on the water."

Monette smiled. "It's not a steamboat, but the ferry won't bounce and shake us. It'll be big and slow moving. You can look out at the river as we cross over to the opposite bank."

***

After changing from train to stagecoach, to a ferry and back again to land travel, they finally reached Kentucky. In the last part of their trip they traveled by stagecoach. This one, however, provided a smoother ride than before. The roads were dry without being dusty and the coach seemed better made. Elizabeth was pleased that this time she and Monette were the only passengers.

Wide, rolling pastures with rich, green grass seemed refreshingly beautiful to her. Sleek horses grazing and frisky colts playing in gleeful abandon delighted her. Her imagination grew as she viewed great white houses perched on hills...houses with handsome porches and tall columns all enclosed by white-washed fences.

"Will your house be like these?" Elizabeth asked.

Monette laughed. "Hardly. More like those plain little houses we saw earlier unless we live in part of a rugged farm house with his family."

The stagecoach passed through a residential section in a village where Elizabeth saw children waving and playfully jumping...some running, trying to keep pace with the stagecoach.

She had not played with other children since she lived at Five Points.

Watching the squealing, laughing children, Elizabeth felt a sense of excitement, but the feeling quickly changed to a sense of loss. She was too old for that now. Some girls married when they were twelve...not that she ever meant to marry at any age. Maybe she'd be a madam like Hannah and live in a fine house, though she still wasn't clear about the business. Hannah had said she'd understand when she was older. She realized there were secrets about the business, and thought she might never really know so being a madam probably was out. She would ask Hannah what she should do.

They had stopped earlier for breakfast at a small cafe. Now Monette seemed to feel unwell. "The eggs were a bit greasy, I think," she said.

"I liked mine," Elizabeth said. She looked at the passing scenery. "Are we almost there?"

"Soon, I believe, but not soon enough for me," Monette said. "I feel really sick." She called up to the driver and asked him to stop the stagecoach. Within minutes after she stepped down from the coach, she walked a few steps from the coach to relieve herself of her breakfast.

Elizabeth jumped down and ran to her. "What's the matter?" She felt concerned. Monette had been sick the day before as well.

"I don't know...maybe the excitement, maybe it's the rocking of the coach," Monette said. She looked pale, and her eyes were red. She returned to the stagecoach holding a handkerchief to her mouth. "I hope it's not...."

"Not what?"

"Oh, it's terrible, Elizabeth." She began to cry.

Elizabeth hugged her. "Don't cry," she said, "we'll soon be there."

"I'm afraid. I'm pretty sure I'm pregnant," Monette said. She covered her face with her hands and sobbed.

Elizabeth frowned. She remembered the book and pictures Hannah had shown her about pregnancy and how babies are made, but she in no way connected it with the business that continued to be a mystery to her.

In her pain, Monette poured out her fears, and Elizabeth finally heard about the real nature of the bordello. Her mind whirled in disbelief. Though she bombarded the sad-faced Monette with countless questions, she found it hard to comprehend the business.

Monette spoke softly, sadly. "Will Terrance still want me now? Of course, he knew my work. Surely, if I can accept his handicap, he can learn to love an innocent little baby."

Elizabeth had no answer. She was still trying to understand what it all meant. Why would people do that? She could make no association with pleasure despite what she had been told.

***

Terrance was waiting for them when the stagecoach arrived in Maysville. Elizabeth saw that he was extremely handsome with thick dark wavy hair, a full, soft beard and a wide smile. His clothing, however, was rumpled and his fingernails long and dirty. His peg leg was hidden from view, but he limped and scowled when he walked.

Monette was blind to everything except the presence of the man she loved. She threw her arms about him, exclaiming, "Darling! Darling! I'm so happy to see you."

He embraced her momentarily, then held her at arms length looking directly into her face. "If you have any doubts about my leg, speak up now," he said. His voice was blunt, even harsh. "I don't want no woman seein' me as less a man than I am."

"Oh, Terrance, darling man," Monette said, taking both of his hands in hers, "believe me, I have no doubt."

"I see you brought the kid," he said, glancing at Elizabeth.

"Yes. Perhaps, you don't remember her."

"I would remember if I'd ever seen her. She favors you."

"That's a compliment," Monette said. "Elizabeth is so beautiful."

"So are you," he said, "but I don't want no kids. Like I said, my sister'll keep her."

Elizabeth felt a rush of blood to her face. She felt like crying with his rejection, but she had more concern now for Monette in her pregnancy.

"But, of course, you can visit us, Elizabeth," Monette said.

"Maybe," he said. "Don't cross me, Monette. I set the rules, and I speak my mind. Ain't much of a man who don't."

Monette put a hand on Elizabeth's shoulder. "Don't worry, honey. I've heard nice things about his sister."

"I remember," Elizabeth said, still fighting tears.

"We'll work it out," Monette said.

"I want to go back to Alice, please!"

Terrance stood by an old carriage. "You gals cut the chatter and git in," he said.

***

Soon they were standing on the Ohio River bank. Shanty boats gently bobbed on the wide river against a setting sun. The water drifted and swirled in shades of green and chocolate brown.

"La belle riviere," Monette said.

"What?" Terrance asked.

"The beautiful river," Elizabeth translated, feeling proud she knew something he didn't.

"Oh, it's just the Ohio," Terrance said, "You'll get used to it." He spat a stream of tobacco juice.

Elizabeth saw the tobacco spit as one more offensive

272

thing about him. She wondered how Monette could love him. Of course, he was handsome, but Elizabeth sensed him as a worthless gift wrapped in fine packaging. She thought of a day long ago in Five Points when a cruel older girl gave her a glob of mud wrapped in beautiful Christmas foil. She'd been so disappointed she'd cried. She didn't want Monette to cry.

Watching his hard face now, Elizabeth remembered the day Hannah had tried to warn Monette against him, but that was because of his reckless life and uncertain money.

Elizabeth felt his meanness was worse. Why couldn't Monette feel it too?

"Catch me!" Elizabeth cried, tugging at Monette's hand, then breaking free to run ahead. Monette accepted the challenge and they wound up laughing, breathless at the water's edge.

"Monette," Elizabeth whispered, "don't marry him. He's bad."

"What? Oh, honey he didn't mean to hurt you."

"No, Monette! Not me! I mean...."

Terrance appeared. "You mean what?"

"Nothing," Elizabeth said, "I was just...." Her voice trailed off.

"All right, All right, let's go," he said.

Chapter Thirty-Three

At the river where most of the houseboats were gathered, Terrance shouted to Junie. She flashed a big smile, waved and called back to him. She brought her boat to the dock and greeted them with warm hugs. Elizabeth gave silent thanks that Junie Madissom was nothing like her half-brother. She spoke in a gentle voice. While she was not homely, she was not pretty either. Gray-haired and wrinkled, Junie appeared nearer fifty than barely forty. Elizabeth knew Junie lived alone except for her two young sons, her husband having left her for another woman.

Monette had said that in the spring, summer and early fall, Junie and her boys traveled the river selling a variety of small items from their boat to the other house boaters. In the winter they lived in a shack on a hill overlooking the river. The boys, Leon and James, were seven and nine, with James being the older. Both were slim, attractive, brown-eyed blond youngsters.

Junie's boat bore a faded red sign over the doorway reading MADISSOM'S GOODS AND SERVICES. The services, Elizabeth had been told, included washing down boats, taking care of children, running errands on shore... anything and everything Junie and her boys could do to make a little money.

After brief introductions, Terrance sidled up to his sister. "This'un will soon bring you in more money than you'll need. Came from Hannah's, you know."

Junie nodded, but made no reply. "Come on aboard, Elizabeth. We'll work out something."

Elizabeth boarded the small houseboat without difficulty although it rocked against the dock on rolling waves with the passing of another boat.

"Monette...," Elizabeth began, turning to look at her.

"It'll be all right," Monette said. "I'll be back in a few days.

When Terrance and Monette were gone, Junie said, "River life ain't easy, girl, but I ain't makin' no whore out of you, so you can rest easy."

"What's a whore?"

Junie's mouth gaped in amazement. "You come from a sportin' house and you don't know what a whore is?"

"Well, maybe. Is it a prostitute?"

"Oh, fancy. Fan--cee! Sure, well about the same. To most folks they're the same. Whore's likely a husband-stealer, plans it that way...like the one that took my man. A prostitute is more like a dolled-up, perfumed business woman who sells herself, but generally not planning to steal a husband."

Elizabeth frowned. The description Junie made of a prostitute didn't seem right for Monette and she bit her lip not to protest now. Maybe later. Instead she said, "Marme sent money for my keep, but I would like to work, too." Elizabeth fished in her shirt pocket and handed Junie some bills.

"My goodness," Junie said, "she's generous. This will really help."

"Don't tell Terrance about the money. Just let me work like anybody else."

"Don't tell Terrance? Why?"

"The money is just for you," Elizabeth said, "Don't tell anyone, and please, don't mention Madame. People might not understand how she really is."

"I won't. I'll just say that you're an orphan and a young friend of Terrance's bride-to-be. Most folks in the shanties ain't nosey anyway. We all just sorta accept people as we see them unless they act up in some way."

"What kind of work do you want me to do?" Elizabeth asked.

"Mostly watching after children, some washing and ironing, and maybe helping my boys with errands. We'll see. It won't be hard. Come on, I'll show you your spot...not much more than a bunk and a little corner shelf, but you'll find you can do without more things than you ever imagined."

***

The first few days on the river, Elizabeth met other shanty boat families. Junie encouraged her to get acquainted and took her in a flatboat for afternoon visits, usually returning only short of suppertime.

Elizabeth met the red-haired Sullivans from Minnesota. Junie had told her they were really nice people she would like. They invited her aboard their oversized shanty boat. Beyond a "Hello," Mae and Mazie, the nine-year-old twins appeared barely aware of Elizabeth. They were making up a childish story and giggling. Elizabeth was glad they didn't invite her to play. Despite being only three years older, she would not have been comfortable in such a babyish game.

Elizabeth was invited to sit in one of the old rocking chairs on the front deck of the boat beside Mrs. Sullivan who was snapping green beans. She interrupted her work briefly to bring Elizabeth some sugar cookies and a cool bottle of pop. Mr. Sullivan, a portly man, rocked slowly in his chair and listened to the polite conversation between his wife and Elizabeth while he drew on his pipe.

In recounting her travel experiences from Kansas City, Elizabeth told of her sadness about the killing of the buffalo.

Mr. Sullivan responded readily to her story. "Yes," he said, "I know what you mean. It's a shame so many are being slaughtered. Money is what it's all about, of course."

Mrs. Sullivan said, "Those hunters make a hundred dollars a day shooting those poor beasts. They keep shooting until their guns get too hot to fire. Imagine a hundred dollars a day! Such greed."

"Monette told me that even our combs and buttons are made from buffalo horns," Elizabeth said. "Almost makes me not want to comb my hair or button my clothes."

The Sullivans laughed. "Well, what can we do?" Mr. Sullivan asked. "Write Washington? Who listens? Besides, with the war on, the last thing on their minds would be the suffering of a placid herd of buffalo."

"You see, Elizabeth, how strongly he feels about it. His need for a peaceful life is what led us here. Of course, he's too old for the draft and he wouldn't volunteer. Wouldn't go kill anyone, so what good would he be to an army?"

"Monette says the war is a terrible, bloody thing. I think they should just sit down and agree on what to do," Elizabeth said.

"You're right, young lady, but it almost never works out that way. As for me, I choose to be on the river, away from it all. Out here we can feel free. We hurt nobody. Nobody hurts us. I like it that way. If soldiers from either side come by we let them know we're neutral, feed them and send them on their way."

"He and I may not agree on everything," Mrs. Sullivan said, "but we agree on that." She studied Elizabeth for a long moment. "You seem so grown up for your age," Mrs. Sullivan said smiling.

"I'm twelve and I've been only with adults since I was five," Elizabeth said.

"I see," Mrs. Sullivan said, "but I also think you're a very bright girl."

Elizabeth smiled. "Thanks."

Mr. Sullivan stretched his legs. "Soon," he said, "we'll make our way slowly south, enjoying each new scene, gathering special plants and foods along the way. No schedules to meet, no business pressures...beholden to no man. Of course, we have our struggles with nature. Dangerous waters, storms sometimes, but all in all it's a good life."

"We planned this for several years," Mrs. Sullivan said, "Doesn't take much money the way we live, and sometime he makes a little money on stories he writes. People seem to like to read about our little adventures on the river."

"Mae and Mazie seem happy here, too," Elizabeth said. "Do you teach them lessons?"

"I was a teacher," Mrs. Sullivan said, "so I do teach them, but sometimes in the winter they attend class at a school in Maysville. Good for them to have that experience as well I think. We don't isolate ourselves. We deal with businesses in towns and villages as we travel on the river."

Mr. Sullivan spoke up. "New scenes and new people are a pleasure for us. Something to look forward to on every trip, even almost every day. I wouldn't change our lives on the river for a packet of pickled gold."

"Pickled gold?" Elizabeth asked. "What is a packet of pickled gold?"

Mrs. Sullivan laughed. "Who knows? It's just something he says. By the way, I'm going to the post office to check the mail. Would you like to come along Elizabeth?"

Mr. Sullivan turned the boat around and they headed for the dock down stream.

At the post office, Elizabeth was happy to have a letter from Hannah.

In the same envelope was one page for her and two pages for Monette. Elizabeth wondered when Monette would return, but the thought passed quickly. She stuffed the extra pages in her pocket and read her own letter.

Hannah had written to them a week after they left. She expressed her feelings of loneliness, but again stated it was her belief that the river life was best for now. She wanted to know how she liked the families there. "With your charm and beauty," Hannah wrote, "I'm sure you'll easily make new friends." Tears blurred Elizabeth's vision. She wished with all her heart she were back with all those she loved in Kansas City at this very moment. It helped little when Hannah wrote they would have a big celebration upon her return. She was comforted, however, with the postscript that Alice, Toby and Little Mama were well. She dried her tears with a swipe of her sleeve, hoping Mrs. Sullivan didn't notice.

Later, when she was back with Junie and yet alone sitting on the front deck of the boat, she removed the letter Hannah had written to Monette from her pocket. Would it be all right to read it? Since it was in the same envelope and not sealed, it didn't seem private. She unfolded the page and read:

Dear Monette,

I am sure you are aware that you will be greatly missed by the gentlemen who treasure their time with you. I do hope, however, that you will be happy with the man you love.

I think you might be interested to learn that the priest who traveled with the Canadian Free People, visited Dorcett Dalk. Little Mama was in the big house at the time as Alice needed to travel to town for supplies. They seem really comfortable with this Dalk in spite of his illness. He can be kind and patient--very unlike the rapist brother his parents raised. Anyway, Little Mama heard the men praying for healing for Mr.Dalk. Healing she said from the 'falling sickness,' which I gather is what they call his problem.

Since the aged priest was most kind and Little Mama more forward than Alice or Toby, she asked questions of him. It seems years ago the priest felt sorry for the frightened little boy when he saw him at the asylum and learned he had been abandoned. In the passing of a year, the parents never visited the six-year-old, so the crowded Asylum for the Insane and Mentally Unbalanced, released him to the priest when Dorcett was seven. The child had been given medicines which the priest thought were harmful.

Some treatments terrorized him--like spinning him around at a high speed on a machine. The priest begged for him the day he saw Dorcett punished for screaming and crying in an effort to avoid the blood-letting knife. Permission was given for the "unruly" child to leave that day. When the priest began to serve the Free People, the boy was only nine so he was virtually raised by them. Just thought you'd be interested.

Do write soon and tell me you're happy. All the best wishes.

Madame

Elizabeth sighed. Monette would want to know, but where was she?

Chapter Thirty-Four

A most surprising meeting was with the Seldeni family...which turned out to be the son, daughter-in-law and grandson of Mrs. Seldeni in Missouri...the lady down the hill from Mrs. Dalk. They even knew Alice, Toby and Little Mama, which thrilled Elizabeth.

She might not have noticed Mr. Seldeni's blue eyes, except Junie said it was unusual for an Italian to have blue eyes. Elizabeth thought him, with his regular features, handsome for a white-haired older man. Mrs. Seldeni, Italian or not, was sun-browned with large dark eyes and softly curled black hair. On this day, she wore her abundant shoulder-length hair tied back at the nape of her neck with a pale yellow scarf.

"How do you like river life so far, Elizabeth?" Mrs. Seldeni asked.

"I would like it all right, except I miss...." Elizabeth hesitated when she remembered she should not mention Hannah. "I miss being in Kansas City. I came here with Monette to get married." Realizing what she had just said, she laughed. "Not me. Monette."

"Ah, marriage," Mr. Seldeni said. "This bossy Kentucky woman lured me away from Missouri and socked me on this river."

Mrs. Seldeni grinned and shook her head. "Sure! Who romanced who? Hush, you'll have Elizabeth believing you."

"Bossy, like I said. Nature girl wanted to live on the river and here we are."

Mrs. Seldeni gave him a playful shove and they both laughed.

"I like rivers, too," Elizabeth said. "Long time ago when I was little, we lived by a river. And now I've been living near the Missouri River. Do you know where it is?"

"The Big Muddy? Of course. I like Kansas City, but

missy, nobody could manage a shanty boat on the Big Muddy. Even keelboats have a tough time."

"Here he goes again," Mrs. Seldeni said, grinning, casting her eyes upward.

"Yeah, traveling the Big Muddy takes talent. I heard it said, 'most any fella who is strong as an ox, can twang a snappy tune on a mouth harp, is full of ambition and has a double crew of seasoned, amphibious river men, can take a keelboat up the Big Muddy, but if he wants a boat to take him up, he sure better buy passage on a steamer.' " He grinned mischievously at her. "Like they say, the cussedness of an old mule is small pickles compared to the devilishness of the Big Muddy."

Elizabeth grinned but remained speechless.

"You'll learn he's a big kidder," Mrs. Seldeni said.

A sturdy boy who looked to be thirteen or fourteen emerged from the cabin of the boat, dressed only in cut-off pants and sandals.

"Donato," Mrs. Seldeni said, "this is Elizabeth. Donato is going swimming."

Donato flashed a smile. Elizabeth thought him handsome with his thick brown hair and dark blue eyes. Obviously, he inherited his father's good looks.

Donato slipped off his sandals.

"Aren't you afraid to get in this big river?" Elizabeth asked.

Donato laughed. "I can swim. Can't you?"

"No."

"Everybody who lives on the river needs to be able to swim," Mr. Seldeni said. "Women, children, dogs, cats, cows, chickens...."

"Really, Ronald!" Mrs. Seldeni laughed.

"Get on something, and I'll teach you," Donato said.

"Here. I'll get you something," Mrs. Seldeni said taking Elizabeth by the hand.

Minutes later, wearing an outgrown pair of Donato's cut-off pants and a faded shirt, Elizabeth slipped into the water. She gasped at the chill of it and gripped a rod attached to the side of the boat.

"Hold on and kick a while," Mr. Seldeni instructed. "Kick like this," he said, moving his arms to demonstrate.

Elizabeth did as she was told, thus beginning her first swimming lesson. She found it exhilarating! If only Alice could see her.

***

Ten days passed and Monette did not appear. Junie said, "Well, lovers like to be alone. She'll show up any day now. But you're all right, ain't you? Got new friends and we all git along."

"Yes, it's just...."

"Well, don't fret. They'll be around soon."

But they did not appear and three weeks passed without a word. Not even a letter.

Junie said, "Well, I reckon' they just mean to be hermits. Surely, though they'll show up any day now."

***

Elizabeth loved the water. After a faltering start, she worked hard to become an expert swimmer. Mr. Seldeni called her "Little Duckling," and delighted in watching her and the other children play games of chase and hide-and-seek around the boats in the river.

One pleasant fall day, he challenged her to swim the width of the river, promising to follow her in a johnboat. She made the swim with ease, climbed upon the bank and waved to Mr. Seldeni and the two other men and a woman who had joined in the adventure.

On the water's edge, a green snake slithered through the reeds. Elizabeth ran back from the bank only to be met with something infinitely more horrifying.

Chapter Thirty-Five

The nude body lay in disarray, as if it had been flung from a passing boat. The once-lovely face was discolored and bloated, and the swollen abdomen had been stabbed and slashed. Elizabeth covered her face against the stench and the pain of recognition. She cried out in anguished sobs, calling to her murdered teacher and friend. "Monette! Monette! Oh, oh, oh! Oh, God how could he? How could he?" She turned aside and stumbled toward the bank crying, "Help! Come here. Come here."

Mr. Seldeni and the others heard her crying and rushed to the edge of the bank. All but Mr. Seldeni turned quickly away. They coughed, held their noses and backed away from the decaying corpse. He laid a hand on Elizabeth's shoulder.

"I knew her," Elizabeth said, choking on her tears. "Her name was Monette."

"This spot is so wild and unsettled," he said. "Whoever did this thought she'd never be found."

Too distraught to talk, Elizabeth was uncertain of what she should say beyond identifying her friend. Would Terrance know she suspected him...in fact, was virtually certain of his guilt? It occurred to her that possibly only she and Terrance knew of the pregnancy. Did he know that Monette had told her? She trembled. She could only hope he had seen her as an ignorant child who knew nothing about it.

Elizabeth was glad she had never talked about Terrance to Junie, and comforted herself by remembering she'd tried to warn Monette. Still, an element of guilt troubled her. Was there anything else she could have done? Tears filled her eyes.

When she learned of the murder, Junie was also troubled, but for other reasons. Should she tell the officials Monette had come from Hannah's? Junie decided she should be careful in what she said when questioned about the young woman's background and family as that might involve

Elizabeth as well. Besides, she preferred people not know Terrance had been engaged to a prostitute.

"She came from Kansas City, is all I know," Junie said. Elizabeth heard the tremor in her voice. In response to a question, she said, she didn't know where her brother was. Reluctantly, she admitted that he and the woman had been "friends." Only friends? If his sister was that careful Elizabeth knew she'd better watch what she said as well.

Elizabeth knew the sheriff had been told that she had come to Maysville with Monette. Taking a cue from Junie, she planned in advance what she would say when questioned, and prayed it was enough.

"I'm an orphan," she said, "and Miss Monette took care of me for a while, and then we came here." She added truthfully, she knew nothing of Monette's family, but thought she had come to Kansas City from France since she could speak French. Elizabeth kept silent being very afraid of letting any other information slip out. To her great relief the sheriff seemed satisfied.

The local authorities made such notes as they could with the limited information and when there was no money for a funeral, they buried Monette in a pauper's grave.

***

Less than a week after the funeral, Terrance came aboard the shanty boat. At first Elizabeth did not see him. She was alone and preoccupied as she stoked the stove to heat the flat iron for her work.

"Where's Junie?" he demanded.

Elizabeth swallowed. She could barely speak. "Uhhhh," she said.

"Well, what's the matter with you, can't you talk?"

"I didn't see you come aboard," she said.

"Well, where is she?"

"She took the boys into town. I think she'll be back soon."

"Have you seen Monette?" he asked. "The bitch left

284

me."

"She left you?" She did not want to meet his gaze, so she kept her eyes on the flat iron, moving it to a hotter position on the stove.

"Are you deaf? That's what I said."

"Maybe, Junie...."

"I know where you said she went. You didn't answer me about Monette. Have you seen her?"

"She was found...."

"What? Found? Good god!" His eyes widened, but he recovered quickly. "What do you mean? Where is she?"

"She's dead...she's buried," Elizabeth said. When she saw his rigid face and glaring eyes, she gripped the padded handle of the hot iron.

"What did you tell them?" he demanded.

Elizabeth trembled. "What could I say? Just that she cared for me, an orphan."

"You didn't know...."

"Know what?" she asked looking innocently at him.

She heard the chattering voices of the children and breathed a sigh of relief. "Junie's back," she said.

He turned around and was met by his sister's embrace.

"Terrance! Oh, Terrance, something terrible has happened," she cried.

"What?"

Elizabeth was amazed at his display of shock when told the story. "They'll think I did it," he said, "but that bitch left me. Back to her business, I guess. I should've known better."

"Maybe, you shouldn't...." Junie began.

"The damn bitch. Now I've got to leave because of her," he said. He banged his fist on the table, causing a small jar to fall to the floor. Junie quickly grabbed it up and replaced it.

"No, Terrance!" she said, "That'll make you look guilty. You'll stay right here. I'm sure the Seldeni's can make room for Elizabeth while you're here. Their boat is much larger."

Elizabeth felt the tension drain from her shoulders. She

would feel safer with the Seldenis, but could she let him get away with his crime? She would write Hannah. Hannah would know what to do.

* * *

The Seldeni's welcomed her. "Just in time," Mrs. Seldeni said. "We're going down river for a couple of months. It'll be an experience you won't forget."

Most of all Elizabeth wanted to be away from Terrance, so it was to her dismay that she learned Junie planned to join the group of shanty boaters on the river trip.

Mrs. Seldeni said, "It's an unusually mild fall and just cool enough to be pleasant. I think you'll enjoy the trip."

"Will we be the only two boats?" Elizabeth asked.

"Oh, no. There'll be six, maybe eight boats in a loose travel plan...though it's not really a plan at all. It's just that we get stirring wanting to get away about the same time sometimes, and the service boats generally tag along. You know we have practically a village on water, what with the blacksmith, druggist, store-boats, and a few other odd-businesses...the carpenters and drift-wood sellers, you must have seen, too."

So that was why Junie would be going with the group. She had a store-boat and other services to offer. Maybe, she also wanted to hide Terrance, but how could she care about such a mean man even if he was her brother? Elizabeth had seen his convincing performance of innocence and finally a grief-stricken act. She remembered also that Junie didn't know about Monette's pregnancy, so maybe she really believed him.

"Do the service boats always go? What if they didn't?" Elizabeth asked.

"It's not really a problem," Mrs. Seldeni said. "We tie up and walk into towns and villages along the way...do that for various reasons and to pick up our mail at designated places. We'll get ours many days down river at General Delivery in Shawneetown, Illinois, the first time in case you'd like to notify someone."

"Will the other shanty boats be close by?" Elizabeth asked, hoping Junie's boat would not.

"Sometimes a day or two passes before we see another boat; other times we may see several in a day. Then occasionally at night we tie up fairly close to each other...not for any special reason except we can't tie up just any place."

***

The first day out, Elizabeth saw one unfamiliar red-and-yellow shanty boat drift by. A blond-haired boy peeked out a window, and a big, black retriever barked from the deck. The roof of the boat was stacked with a crate of chickens, fish boxes and piles of fishing nets. Smoke swirled from a crooked chimney and filled the air with an odor of wood burning.

Nowhere did Elizabeth see Junie's boat. She breathed a sigh of relief.

A little farther down the river, Mr. Seldeni guided the boat away from a large fallen tree. "The river is a gobbler," he said. "Nothing's safe within its reach; it undermines trees and eventually plunders whatever is left on the banks. You'd be surprised at the valuables we come by. All us shanty boaters watch out to see what's floating by and every morning we scan the shores to see what may have lodged overnight." He laughed. "Yeah, we're really big treasure hunters and it's fun."

"Treasure hunting sounds like fun," Elizabeth said smiling and clasping her hands.

"I like the adventure," Mr. Seldeni said. "Don't think I could stand going back to the world out there with all its rigidness...the tightness of it...the rules, you know. 'Course it's all right for them that like it. It just is not for me."

Toward nightfall a steamboat passed, its wake pounding against the shanty boat. The force of it rattled crates and tipped an empty pan off the stove, sending it clanging to the floor. Elizabeth jumped. Donato laughed. "That's nothing," he said "Wait till we get a storm. When that wind comes up, you'll think you're in a little wooden box about to be smashed to pieces."

"Donato," Mrs. Seldeni said, "Don't be scaring Elizabeth. Your father is as skillful a shanty boater as they come. Haven't we always made it? Sure, and we'll be just fine, whatever."

Mr. Seldeni pulled into a deep cove and tied up for the night. "Plenty of room here for another boat," he said, "so we may get company."

The thought of the wrong company sent fear running through Elizabeth. She was convinced that Terrance could kill again. At bedtime she checked behind Mr. Seldeni to make sure that the door was securely latched.

***

Elizabeth began to relax as the lazy days passed without incident, and Junie's boat was never close to them. She loved the feel of the clean, cool air, and didn't mind two days of rain. The chill of the rain kept them inside close to the stove. Still, even that was pleasant as Mrs. Seldeni popped corn... some of which she salted and some she rolled with syrup and peanuts to make popcorn balls.

A week later, Elizabeth experienced her first shore trip for treasure hunting. She and Donato came upon an abandoned shack and found small discarded items. Elizabeth delighted in a broken necklace of red beads that she could string back together, and Donato found a small hand saw. They also helped Mrs. Seldeni gather remnants of fruit and vegetable crops left by people who had moved away from a rustic farmhouse. Foraging, Elizabeth learned was a common occurrence in the life of the shanty boaters.

"We plant our own gardens at times, too," Mrs. Seldeni said. "It can be hard digging along these riverbanks, but the soil is rich and good, and most times the landowners don't mind."

"Let's go," Donato said, "I want to show Dad this saw.

We have needed just this kind lots of times."

When they were almost back to the boat, Elizabeth drew in a sharp breath. Junie's boat was tied nearby. Junie and Leon were on deck peeling potatoes, but Terrance was not in sight. When they drew near, Mrs. Seldeni called to Junie, "I see you came by some potatoes."

"Yes, and a good thing, too," Junie said, "we're low on food."

"Well, men tend to eat more. Has Terrance gone into town for something?" Mrs. Seldeni asked when they drew near the edge of the boat.

"I'm not sure," Junie said. She appeared hesitant, guarded.

By this time Elizabeth was sure Mrs. Seldeni and Donato must have seen, as she did, the bruise on Junie's temple, but they said nothing. Did they know something about Terrance from his previous stay with Junie? Otherwise, she thought it would have been natural to ask Junie how she came by the bruise.

Elizabeth did dare to ask. "What happened to your head, Junie?"

Seven-year-old Leon looked frightened. He glanced at his mother, waiting.

"Oh, I was careless, not paying attention and bumped myself on the door facing."

Mrs. Seldeni shook her head. "We gathered some greens, Junie. More than we'll need. Could you use some?"

"Thanks. I could. As you said, feeding a man...."

Behind them on the bank they heard raucous laughter. Within moments, they realized it was Terrance. He was holding onto a bottle, swaying, stumbling, finally falling, lying for a moment and then pushing himself up, taking a swig from the bottle and stumbling on down the bank.

"Get inside," Junie said to Leon. "Hurry!"

Mrs. Seldeni handed the greater part of the greens to Junie, turned and went back inside her own boat.

It was too much for Elizabeth. Seeing the fear on Leon's small face reminded her of her own ordeal with Mrs.

Dalk. Let Junie suffer if she wouldn't defend herself, but Elizabeth knew she would have to do what she could to put a stop to Leon's pain. And James? Where was James? He usually helped his mother.

When they were inside their own boat, Elizabeth said, "Terrance must be stopped."

"We don't interfere..." Mrs. Seldeni began.

"But we have to! That man is a murderer!"

"What?" Mr. Seldeni asked, only hearing that part of the conversation as he entered the cabin.

When Elizabeth finished her story, the Seldenis sat quietly looking at each other. Finally, Donato said, "We could beat him up. Maybe that would teach him a lesson."

"No," Mrs. Seldeni said. "We'll do nothing of the kind, and you keep quiet about all this, Donato."

"Your mother is right. It's not the way of river folk. We'll keep quiet until we return to Maysville, then I'll have a talk with the sheriff."

"That might be too late," Elizabeth protested.

"We can't take a chance down river where we're not known," Mrs. Seldeni said. "He'll still be around. He may hurt Junie, but I very much doubt he'd kill her. He needs her now."

Mr. Seldeni said, "Now that he's not agile enough to rob stage coaches, he may try easier marks. Might get caught that way and then the other matter could be brought in."

"It's the best we can do for now," Mrs. Seldeni said, "except we'll try to help Junie with food."

"And we'll keep an eye out," Mr. Seldeni said. "If I must, I will transgress the river code and beat the tar out of him, but Donato, you're not to try it. He wagged a finger at his son. "This is not for you. You do nothing and say nothing."

Donato frowned and stalked out onto the deck. Elizabeth worried that Donato might do something foolish. "Listen to your father," she called after him.

Chapter Thirty-Six

Two days later, shortly before noon, they pulled into a grove of trees above Shawneetown shortly before noon, and tied up to the shore. Mr. Seldeni said, "I'm going in to check the mail."

"Could I go?" Elizabeth asked. "I might have a letter."

"Sure. We'll take the johnboat and row down close as we can get, but we'll still have a levee to climb. Town's bad to flood so they keep building the levee higher. "Though, a tough little critter like you wouldn't mind that, I guess," he teased.

"Nope," Elizabeth said, grinning. "I'll race you up."

"Mercy! Little Duckling, have mercy! You know I'll never see sixteen again."

Mrs. Seldeni laughed. "Sixteen? She may need to shove you up the bank, old fella."

Mr. Seldeni grabbed his wife and wrestled her into an embrace, kissing her. "Take that, sassy wife," he said.

"And you take that," she said, kissing him back.

***

Elizabeth prayed she'd have a letter from Hannah. She knew Hannah wouldn't be willing to let Terrance off when she heard what he'd done to Monette. She'd have a plan. Elizabeth was sure of it.

Once above the levee they walked past a line of steamboat style brick buildings. Finally, as part of a bank building, Elizabeth saw the post office; a large, brown stone structure with broad steps and four columns.

The letter from Hannah was there! Elizabeth was ecstatic. She ripped it open and read:

"My dearest Elizabeth,

I can't tell you how my heart aches. We can only imagine the horrors Monette must have known at that monster's hands. But he will not go unpunished. Immediately, after I received your letter, I notified the marshall where they could find one missing stagecoach robber. Don't be surprised when they drag him off the boat. Of course, I couldn't prove anything about Monette's murder, but his record with Curly Jack Conners and quite possibly William Quantrill and the James brothers, I expect them to lay hands on him any day now.

Take care of yourself, dear. It won't be long until you'll be returning here for a visit. It's been very lonely without you, but until you're a little older, I think you're better off where you are. For one reason, while I worry about your traveling, you seem untouched by the war which seems to be going on endlessly so many places now.

I love you,

Marme

Elizabeth sighed in relief. Of course, she didn't have to prove he was a murderer! He was wanted anyway. She'd forgotten.

***

When they returned to the shanty boat landing Elizabeth and Mr. Seldeni saw Terrance struggling against two men on Junie's boat. "Look!" Elizabeth cried. "She sent them!"

Mr. Seldeni took Elizabeth's hand in a protective gesture although they weren't close to the boat. "Must be the law," he said. "They're strangers. Must be the law, but they haven't gunned him down. Guess they want to question him," Mr. Seldeni said.

Elizabeth said, "Yes, probably 'bout where the other mean men are."

"He sure is wild," Mr. Seldeni said, "and good with that stick."

They heard his shouted curses as he held the men at bay swinging a thick wooden rod.

"Look how fast he moves! I don't know he can handle himself so well with that peg leg." Mr. Seldeni said.

"What if he kills them?" Elizabeth asked. She pressed her fingers to her lips.

"With that blood streaming from his head they got at him, too," Mr. Seldeni said, "probably before we got here."

The larger of the two men waded in and jerked the rod from Terrance. He threw it aside.

Terrance grabbed a broken chair and shoved hard against the big man who lost his balance and fell.

"Oh, no!" Elizabeth cried.

"Woah! Now the shorter guy's got hold of him."

"But he can't hold him," Elizabeth said. "He got away. Look!"

"It's pure rage. Even with that peg leg he comes off like a giant, but they must have gotten in a surprise attack before he grabbed the stick—maybe their gun barrels. That blood on his scalp running down his neck—must have caught a lick there."

"But now—oh, they're trying to hold him, to tie him," Elizabeth cried, "but look how he's fighting, fighting and stumbling...."

Elizabeth caught her breath as she saw Terrance fall overboard. Junie screamed and tried to jump in after him, but the taller man held her back.

Terrance struggled and yelled in the swirling water. His awkward attempts to swim against the current failed. In a matter of moments, the wild-eyed, screaming man disappeared from view.

"Save him! Let me save him!!" Junie screamed trying

to free herself from the grasp of one of the men. "There's no saving him," Mr. Seldeni said to Elizabeth. "That current is twisting him to his grave."

**

After Terrance's death, summer passed and moved into fall and winter but Elizabeth did not return to Kansas City. Hannah thought it best for her to wait until she could travel with the Seldenis who would return to visit Mr. Seldeni's mother at Christmas time. She hoped the war would be over by then.

So it was that more than a year had passed from the date of her arrival in Maysville. Her thirteenth birthday had come and gone, and Elizabeth wanted to go home. She continued to fear something happening to Little Mama and she longed to see Alice and Toby. Still, she had learned to be happy with the river people, which made waiting tolerable.

**

Finally, the day of departure arrived, and an excited Elizabeth went with the Seldenis to the landing.

The great steamboat, The Missouri Queen, was thrilling to see. Its pounding, restless engines were as her own heartbeat. At last, she would once again see all those she loved.

Chapter Thirty-Seven

In New York, the chill of the November day was made worse by freezing rain. Emily and Sue Ling wore ankle-length warm brown coats and gray fur-lined bonnets. A silvery mist veiled the dark buildings where people huddled against the punishing winds or peered around doorways waiting for a break in the weather. But Emily and Sue Ling ran giggling, bouncing their umbrellas and clicking their heels on the cobblestone street to Dr. Blackwell's waiting carriage.

As soon as they were settled, the driver prodded the horse to move forward and they were on their way to the harbor to board a military boat.

Emily said, "When I was a very little girl we came to America from Ireland on a terrible ship. I trust this boat instead will be like the ones I've seen on the river."

"It will not be bad," Sue Ling said and fell silent for a moment before taking a letter from her pocket. "I want to share some of this letter I received from Paul with you." She opened the page quickly and began to read.

"I now realize the seriousness of this war. How could I have missed knowing there would be death all around me?! You, my dear love, I know feared for me and wished me not to go, and now you will endanger yourself in an effort to be near me! I wish with all my heart the whole thing would vanish, or better still, never have started."

Sue Ling wiped a tear from her cheek. "Emily, I'm so afraid he'll be killed. I have even dreamed about it. I try not to, but I think of him lying face down in a pool of blood on a battlefield.

Emily placed her hand on Sue Ling's. "I pray that will not be so," she said.

Returning to Paul's letter Sue Ling read once again:

"Each of us in the infantry carries a knapsack filled with clothing, toilet articles, a sewing kit (can you see me holding a needle and sticking in the right places on the garment? It would be like my two-year-old brother hunting his mouth with a fork!) Well, we have so many things in our knapsacks--stationary, photos (except for yours which I carry in my shirt pocket over my heart.) Some carry extra ammunition but I haven't yet. After we fold our knapsacks, we have two woolen blankets and an oiled ground cloth to strap around it. Our rations and utensils we carry in haversacks we wear slung over a shoulder across our chests. I carry my canteen like the haversack, but some men stuff it inside. Well, you should see me fully fitted! I'm carrying about twenty-five pounds what with my cartridge box, percussion cap pouch, and my bayonet scabbard hanging from a wide leather belt buckled at my waist. Can you see me now? These things pack a pretty big load and some men get tired and ditch part of it in the field. Most of the men dump the change of clothing and one of the blankets. This war makes dirty men and bloody ones."

"Bad as this is," Sue Ling said, "It gets worse. So much worse."

She resumed reading.

"Gunshots, cannon thunder and the smell of blood is with us daily. Worse yet are the wounded moaning, mostly uncared for, and the stench of the dead. Even now from my tent, I see the smoke from cannon fire fading in the distance.

Oh, I wish you would reconsider coming! You will be forever pained by the memories if you will yourself to make the sacrifice. It's too much for you. Stay home and wait for me."

Sue Ling said, "What about too much for him? For all of them! No, I must go and do what I can."

"He wishes to protect you," Emily said.

"I know. He would speak that way. What about his sacrifice? I think of his wonderful dark eyes changing in a moment from crinkling with laughter to staring, dull with pain. A thousand times I want to make him smile and never to see him hurting. Oh, Emily I'm so afraid for him!"

"Don't torture yourself. It may never happen. Besides, what more can you do? You are going to be near him, to do all in your power for him and for others, as well. Try to take heart."

Sue Ling sighed and dried her eyes with a handkerchief. She folded the letter and put it back into her pocket. "I'm really going to be great in this work behaving like a cry baby," she said and laughed.

"You'll do what you must. Don't belittle yourself."

Soon the carriage arrived at the dock and they boarded the boat that would take them to Fredericksburg. Other nurses from farther north were already on board. Men handling cargo called to each other as they made way for new crates. Although the skies were lighter now, everything was wet and icy under foot. They picked their way up the gangplank and gave their documents to a waiting officer who whistled for a cabin boy to show them to their quarters.

***

Emily lay resting on a cot when they reached the last leg of the trip on the Rappahannock River. But Sue Ling, in her excitement over the possibility of seeing Paul, paced about, wondering how much longer before they would arrive. While they waited a skinny, older nurse with a long, bony face approached Sue Ling and studied her.

"You may not be able to serve," the older woman said.

"You're surely too young and more beautiful than Miss Dix will accept."

"Miss Dix?"

"Yes, didn't you know? Dorothea Dix has been given charge of all women nurses working in army hospitals. She denies attractive young women under age thirty. I am fifty-two and as you can see, plain as a weather beaten scarecrow."

Sue Ling gasped, then laughed. "You exaggerate. You are much more attractive than that."

"Hardly," the woman said. "I know my flaws as well as my gifts. My name is Minnie Skyler and I'm willing to help you if I can. From what I hear more nurses are needed and I believe the lady Dix thinks too narrowly about this. All nurses shouldn't have to have gray hair and spectacles," she adjusted her own gold-rims. "A young woman turned down by Miss Dix called her 'Dragon Dix'" Minnie laughed. "I think the name pretty well stuck."

"I would so hate to be turned away," Sue Ling said, "Paul, my fiancé, is in this area and I want to be near him."

"Oops! Better keep quiet on that," Minnie said pressing a finger to her lips.

"But...."

"You'll do as you choose, but you're forewarned." Minnie frowned. "I should say I do see Miss Dix's problem. Loose women have poured in sometimes calling themselves nurses when they're whores."

"We have papers...oh, this is my friend Emily McKelvy."

"Hello, Emily. I see you're young, too."

"Yes," Emily said, "but not pretty."

Minnie smiled. "You have beautiful eyes and the scars failed to destroy your nice smile."

"Thanks," Emily said, "You're very kind."

"Our documents," Emily said, "prove we are nurses. Dr. Blackwell made the effort to declare us as such." She fumbled through her papers. "Perhaps, Miss Dix...oh, let's see, yes, there's a letter to the Miss Dix you mention."

"Really? What does it say?" Minnie asked.

" 'Take into consideration that these are trained, serious nurses who will not bring you problems with silliness. In other words, my friend, make exception for their youth. You will not be sorry'."

Sue Ling looked up from the reading. "I remember now that I read the letter earlier but didn't remember the mention of Miss Dix and I overlooked the part about youth. I suppose all I could think about was getting there."

Emily said, "I remember Dr. Blackwell telling us to dress in modest black or brown skirts and wear no jewelry. She also said for us to keep seriously to our work as long as we were serving...that Miss Dix would demand that. It didn't seem to be a problem."

"Well," Minnie said, "at least, you know what to expect. I do think she will have whoever is in charge of you aware of your exception. You see the military officials had to be convinced to use female nurses in the first place. Miss Dix convinced them and now it's up to her to keep us in line."

"But I've heard volunteers who aren't nurses work on the battlefields. Is that true?" Sue Ling asked.

"Some say so. And the Confederate nurses may have different rules. I don't know about them. Just can tell you about Miss Dix."

"Thank you, Miss Skyler," Sue Ling said.

"Yes, thank you," Emily said. "I hope we'll see you again."

"I'm sure you will," she said.

The boat jolted. They had arrived at the small, beautiful city of Fredericksburg where stately homes were being taken over by the blue-clad military.

***

An elegant white mansion had been emptied of most of its grand furnishings and converted into a hospital. Rows of cots filled the entrance area and the ballroom. When the nurses entered the front door, they were assaulted by the smell of blood and other acrid odors. A number of the wounded moaned, others talked and some slept. Screams came from a far room. Minnie frowned. "It's those waiting the sawing of a limb. Thank God we have morphine for the surgery."

"What about ether?" Emily asked.

"Not safe," Minnie said. "You know it's flammable and if...."

"I understand. It could be set off."

"With battles not so far removed, it could happen."

A young man with slight limp greeted them. "My name is John Henry," he said. "I'm the quartermaster here." He smiled. "That's a high sounding title for what I actually do."

Emily saw that he wore a faded blue uniform. "You're a soldier?" she asked.

"I was wounded in battle and reassigned here." He smiled. "I see you've met an adversary, too, miss."

Emily was surprised but not offended by his direct reference to her scars. The tone of his voice was warm and she found him appealing...especially his uniform-matching blue eyes and the shock of blond hair that fell on his forehead.

"This way," he said as he escorted Emily, Sue Ling and Minnie Skyler up two flights of stairs to their space in the attic where they would share narrow quarters with one other nurse. The fourth nurse, a large breasted woman with narrow hips, arrived panting from her climb up the stairs.

"They tried to stick us up in the damn sky," the new arrival said. "I should have been given private quarters. We are not equals, ladies. You happen to be under my direction. That should have been recognized."

Minnie said, "Well, Symanthie, you could ask if it's all that important to you."

"Oh, it's you again, Minnie," she said, hands on flat hips, "I asked, but the places are all taken. Surely you know I can speak for myself."

Symanthie turned her attention to Emily and Sue Ling. "Who are these children? Surely, they are too young to be here."

"We are nurses from Dr. Blackwell's in New York," Emily said. "Didn't John Henry give you our papers?"

"He did, but I didn't have a girl's face on the papers."

"We won't lean on you," Sue Ling said, "but if we can help you, do let us know."

"Ha!" Symanthie said and turned her back on them.

Minnie smiled and winked at the girls.

Later, after dinner down stairs in the kitchen, Minnie said, "I've known Symanthie for years. She'll try to march you around, but don't let it get to you. She's a good nurse... just a bitch for other nurses to get along with." Minnie grinned. "She actually believes she knows best, and can't bear to stop giving direction."

"What happens when she's wrong?" Emily asks.

"Never admits it," Minnie said. "She'll simply restate her opinion and say, 'This is how it is. It's given up to be.' "

" 'It's given up to be.' What does that mean?" Emily shook her head and frowned.

"It means no further discussion."

"Even with the doctors?" Sue Ling asked.

"Well, no. Anything male gets special treatment. I think she doesn't like other women. Probably something to do with her upbringing. Oh, I don't know. I wish for your sakes she'd been bedded down elsewhere."

"We can handle it," the girls said in unison and laughed at their blended voices.

Minnie smiled, then set her lips in a fine line. "I'll try to help if she makes an effort to get you booted for your youth."

"I never thought of that," Sue Ling said. "Oh, I want to find Paul as soon as I can." She walked to the window and looked out across the expanse of darkness. "I see the camps from here. Log cabins, I think. I see lighted windows." She pushed open the window and a rush of cold air entered the room, but now she could hear music, shouts of laughter and faintly see a figure now and then pass around or next to a small bonfire.

Someone shoved her aside and slammed the window shut. "I knew it." Symanthie Harris said. "No sense at all. I best report you to Superintendent Dix. She clearly said no nurse under thirty and she was right."

Minnie put a finger to her lips and smiled at Sue Ling. "I think," Minnie said, "that Miss Dix is at another hospital this week."

"She won't stay there forever, and I won't forget," Symanthie said, "but for now I'll give you your assignments. You can make it easier or harder on yourselves depending upon how you behave. Young, silly women are guaranteed not to last."

Sue Ling bit her lip and tears blurred her vision. Emily placed her hand on Sue Ling's arm. "Don't believe it," she whispered.

***

Early the next morning, the nurses had a breakfast of eggs, bacon and hard bread. Emily and Sue Ling then were assigned to different sections of the wards to feed and bathe the wounded men. Some soldiers still slept, but others watched with fever-bright eyes. It troubled Emily that many moaned in pain. She went from one to the other doing what she could in both word and care to add comfort. Some reached out to her and begged her to stay beside them longer than she could. One very young boy with dried blood on his pale blond hair sobbed and wiped his tears on his sleeve.

"What can I do for you?" Emily asked.

"Get me home to my Ma," he said. "Get me out of here so I can die beside the fireplace at home with my Ma holding my hand and praying up to God."

Emily glanced at the name on his cot. "Tell me what hurts you Tommy Galbreath."

He drew back the gray sheet revealing a blood-soaked bandage on his side. "A minnie ball struck me. I'm dying for sure and I ain't even had a drink of water."

"Let's see," Emily said. She gently loosened the bandage to reveal an ugly wound. The foul odor made her hold her breath. "Well," she said, "don't send for your angel wings just yet. I'll clean this and put on a fresh bandage, then bring you some water."

"You...you don't think I'm going to die?" he asked studying her with fever-glazed eyes.

"You're a brave boy," she said. "How old are you?"

"Thirteen."

"I'll be back with soap and water and a clean bandage," Emily said and walked to the back of the room to a storage area. Minutes later she returned, handed him a cup of water, then bathed his face, cleaning as well the dried blood from his light hair. Carefully, ever so gently she washed his wound and put on a fresh bandage. Even before she finished he was asleep.

***

At dinner that evening, Emily, Sue Ling and Minnie sat together. They were served a tasteless cabbage soup and hard bread. Sue Ling pushed her food aside. "That surgeon today, especially that big one...that Surgeon Samuel Hallous...Dr. Blackwell would be...well, I just don't know what she would do." She shook her head. "I don't know, but I have to do something."

"What do you mean?" Emily asked.

"You know I was sent to help in surgery. That Dr. Hallous stood there naked to the waist, blood spattered all over his hairy chest, holding a knife in his teeth while he sawed through a leg bone. Then he laid the saw aside, took the knife from his teeth to cut through the remaining flesh before throwing the leg on a pile of other limbs. Men who knew they were to be next were screaming like the ones like we heard yesterday."

"Oh!" Emily said. "Why must those waiting watch?"

"They aren't actually watching. They're in the next room, but they know. They can hear what's happening."

Minnie said, "And imagine how the pool of blood under the table and the blood-splattered surgeon must look to the next patient. So little concern about sanitation, although that may be the least of the poor patient's concern."

"No concern for sanitation!" Sue Ling shook her head. "Dr. Blackwell taught us to be so careful about cleanliness!"

"At least with morphine, the poor fellows are not feeling the pain," Minnie said.

"Oh, but later, will they heal?" Emily asked.

Minnie said. "Many come down with surgical fevers. Most surgeons believe the laudable pus to be the lining of the wound expelling so clean tissues can appear. One must wonder about that, though, as many of these men die."

Sue Ling said, "I'm sure Dr. Blackwell, though she wasn't a surgeon, would prefer healing by first intention rather than covering the wound with a flap."

"Yes, first intention...leaving it open to the air brings better results," Minnie said. She sighed, "These surgeons know, I think, but they just don't act on it."

"Why would they want to be so careless?" Sue Ling asked. "Don't they care? That surgeon never one time washed his hands!"

"Most surprising is the fact the whole medical group ignores knowledge available to them for centuries. We know that notes made on Egyptian papyrus fifteen hundred years before Christ revealed their skill in diagnosis. Just for example, they had defined twenty different ailments for the stomach and prescribed caster oil mixed with beer for constipation."

Symanthie, who had just walked up said, "Could it be doctors don't take it seriously since these learned Egyptians placed skinned mice in the alimentary canals of children as a treatment?"

"But Symanthie," Minnie said, "this was at a much earlier time. Around four thousand B.C. wasn't it? Of course, this does seem terrible. It was said to have been used as a last resort." She lifted her hands in a frustrated gesture then dropped them to her lap. "So many experiments before truth comes out. And just like we're discussing, things aren't right yet either."

"Just do your job and leave matters to the doctors," Symanthie said and passed on by them.

Minnie said, "They do know to wash their hands, but sometimes there's not enough water. Besides, they get so exhausted standing on their feet twelve to fourteen hours. Gets so they can barely stand while more and more wounded are brought in."

"There's plenty of water here!" Sue Ling said raising her voice and I'll get John Henry to keep us well supplied."

"Of course, you'll try, dear," Minnie said, "but the doctors seldom listen to us."

"Well," Sue Ling said, "I'm going to take him soap and water. I'm not going to have that going on here. Just think that could be my Paul in there! Oh, God, I pray not--ever! I'm going to tell that big man what Dr. Blackwell taught us and see that he does it."

Minnie laughed, but then sighed. "Good luck, dear. You know well that men seldom listen to women. Do you imagine a doctor will listen to you, a young nurse?"

"He might," Sue Ling said, "He is attracted to me. I'll use that power if I must. Not another day like today! I'll wash the knives and saws in soap and water, and insist that big man wash his hands."

***

The next day, Sue Ling found she had another problem. As she entered the surgery room, Dr. Hallous drained the last of brandy from a bottle. Brandy that was supposed to be for the patients to help them through the trauma.

"Dr. Hallous was that not for the patients?" she asked.

He appeared startled. "You would question me? Who do you think you are?"

"Sir, I am a nurse who cares deeply for these patients."

"And you think I don't ? Do you imagine I enjoy standing here in a pool of blood sawing off limbs? Would you like

305

to do this for one day...no, for the usual twelve hours?" He glared at her. "Oh, why do I argue with a...a silly woman?" He threw the empty brandy bottle hard against the wall shattering the glass. "Get that damned John Henry in here and tell him to bring me another bottle of brandy. Now!"

"You tell him!" Sue Ling shouted.

"Come here," he said. He grabbed her to himself and placed a hard kiss on her mouth. "I know what you need," he said. "Come to my quarters tonight and I'll give it to you."

"You should be so lucky!"

He stood back momentarily stunned, then laughed. "Damn! What a little tiger you are! I didn't know mixed breeds were so sassy."

"What does it matter if I speak as Chinese, Norwegian, or British I'm speaking up for our soldiers, sir."

"All right, you've made your point," he said, "Tell John Henry to bring in the first patient."

"Yes, doctor," she said, wiping her mouth, "but first you wash your hands. We're cleaning this place up today."

"Mother! Yes, Mother," he said, sarcastically.

"Good. Your mother taught you right. Wash your hands," she repeated, "while I get John Henry to bring in the patient."

"She taught me to wash my feet as well when I came in from plowing our fields."

"Good."

He took her by her arm, gently this time. "On our first free time, I think a buggy ride would do us both good," he said.

"There is no free time," she said, but she spoke softly, having decided a blunt response could lose her ground.

"Later, there will be the time and the opportunity," he said, "Our time will come."

"Perhaps, there will eventually be the time and the opportunity." She hoped he failed to notice she simply restated his suggestion rather than accepted his proposal for the ride. "I'll get John Henry to bring in the patient," she said releasing herself from his touch.

After a week at the hospital Sue Ling was more than eager to try to find Paul. Every night she had looked across the darkness to the camp. "I could go at night," she said to Emily and Minnie.

"No, honey," Minnie said, "Too dangerous."

"Then I know what I'll do. I'll slip out at daybreak and go. I'll go the first light of dawn tomorrow."

"I'll go with you," Emily said. "I'm concerned about your going alone."

"No. You have early duty feeding and caring for the patients and I may stay longer than you could."

"Promise me you'll be careful!" Emily said.

Minnie shook her head. "You'll see dreadful things. Things you won't be able to help resolve," she said.

"I've seen so much here I can't think what would be worse," Sue Ling said.

Minnie touched Sue Ling 's cheek and looked into her face. "Believe me, my dear, it will be worse. You'll smell death and filth. The dead and the dying will lie together where they have fallen. Spinal cord and head injury soldiers will be lined up and some simply left to die as there's no treatment for them. Ah, I even saw them lying there in the hot sun or with rain falling in their faces. Some of us at least gave them morphine...that is, when we had it to spare."

"Surely this could not be!" Emily said, tears springing in her eyes.

"Yes, my dear, it's true. And those who are up and about are dirty. Men without women will not care for clothes, and even the latrines are often not used...just the grounds and the stench is beyond description."

"I will see for myself," Sue Ling said, "and I'll make The Sanitary Commission and The Christian Commission aware."

"They are aware and they do what they can to nurse and nourish the men. Wagons filled with everything from chloroform to chewing tobacco have been taken across the fields to them. What you don't understand, is the enormity of the problem," Minnie said, "And then there are the so-called workers who steal from the wagons, drink the liquor and abandon their work entirely."

Sue Ling said. "Well, I'll just see what is there and what I can do, but first of all I must find Paul."

Emily looked thoughtfully at her friend. She recognized that at one time she'd had such spunk. She had come to realize that her scars had dimmed her courage. Now she no longer felt attractive and like fighting. She felt only like giving help and comfort wherever she could.

Would Ma still feel proud of her? Should she go out onto the battlefields and risk her life to help the wounded and the dying? At once, she felt that was exactly what she should do. If she could not move others to help, at least she could give tirelessly of herself. She would ask to be assigned to the field tomorrow. Another nurse could carry out her present assignment, which now seemed less important to her than serving the more or less abandoned men on the field.

***

Next morning Sue Ling arose before dawn, dressed quickly and slipped out of the mansion. At first she walked carefully in the dark, but soon daylight began on the horizon which allowed her to see where her footsteps fell. The bitter cold chilled her so she walked more quickly in an effort to keep warm. Although she could see the camp, she now realized the distance was greater than she had believed. She began to run across the frozen ground. She fell and scrapped her knee, but quickly got up. Icicles on limbs of trees gleamed in the early light and she saw a frozen pond with blackbirds flying overhead.

As she neared the camp she saw smoke rising and smelled the scent of bacon cooking. She saw the frozen bodies of three soldiers in blue off to her right, and shivered. Still closer to camp she saw men stirring about, the smoky vapor of their breath in the morning chill. She could not

308

make out faces yet, although she tried to see if she could recognize Paul. At least, except for the frozen bodies, no sign of battle reminded her of the war. It was peaceful for now, in this moment, hopefully for this day.

When she came to the edge of the camp she saw men loading their guns and heard commands being barked. Within minutes the whole area was being cleared as the soldiers rushed off toward the Rappahannock River. She thought she caught a glimpse of Paul and ran toward him, but upon closer view she realized her mistake.

"Oh, no!" she cried and slowed her pace.

She knew even if she saw him now, he could be leaving. Inside the campground she came upon a scrawny woman carrying a gray woolen blanket over her arm.

"Ma'am," Sue Ling said, "Would you know where Lt. Paul Pillore is?"

"And who may you be young woman? One of them?"

"Them?"

"Whores, of course," the woman said.

"Oh, no I'm a nurse. Paul is my fiancé."

"Well, then." The old woman studied her for a moment. "I'm going to his tent now."

"Is the blanket for him?"

"It is. He's been scraped up some and I'm a-looking after him."

"Oh, is he badly hurt?"

"Wounded in his laig. Don't know how he kept from gettin' kilt. One on either side of him got it."

"Got it?"

"Wuz kilt."

"Thank God he's safe," Sue Ling said, "but I'm sorry the others were killed."

"They'll be a mess of them done in today," the old woman said. "They plan to attack over them pontoon bridges. Yeah, trying to make it across and up the hill."

"To where?"

"To Marye's Heights. Burnside's sendin' 'em."

"Up a hill? Won't the Rebels just look down on them

and fire?"

"Been doin' that when they laid them pontoons. Burnside ain't much of a general if you ask me," the old woman said. "Oh, we're here. This tent." She pulled aside the curtain door.

Paul raised up on an elbow at the sound. "Thank you, Marvella," he said seeing her with the blanket.

"You got company," Marvella said, stepping aside.

Sue Ling rushed in and knelt beside his cot. "Darling," both she and Paul said in unison and then laughed. She bent down and kissed him.

"Well," Marvella said, "You won't be needing me to spread your blanket so I'll just go."

"I'll do it,"Sue Ling said. She took the blanket and spread it over him tucking it in at his feet.

Paul said, "Thanks, Marvella. What would we do without you?"

"I like to make myself useful to them that needs me."

When the old woman was gone, Sue Ling asked, "Where are you hurt?"

"My left leg. Got something of a tear. Bled like pump water, but I'll be all right now. Dear, sweet Sue Ling," he said, "you shouldn't have come. I'm afraid for you."

She put a finger to his lips. "Quiet. I'll be fine. Let's not waste the time." She slipped into his cot beside him.

"You are so cold!" he said pulling her to him touching her face, stroking her hair and kissing her lips.

She cuddled close to him happy to once more be in his arms.

Chapter Thirty-Eight

The bloody battle raged as the Federal army mounted a series of frontal assaults on Marye's Heights from below. The retaining wall on the eastern boundary of the Heights and the sunken road below gave Lee's Confederates the advantage.

After six heroic efforts to defeat the Southern army, the Federals retreated losing three out of every five men. The smoke of battle and thunder of artillery finally ceased only to be replaced by the cries and moans of the wounded and dying.

***

Sue Ling wrapped her coat around against the chill. She hoped she had not been missed, but worried about that possibility. She needed to be back before the patients' breakfast ended, but she was so reluctant to leave Paul that she had let the time pass. Now she was hungry as well. Perhaps she could find something, at least some bread in the kitchen...anything to calm her complaining stomach.

When she finally approached the hospital she saw the frozen grounds were covered with injured men lying out in the cold...only a few covered with blankets. She knew there was no room inside for them. She had not realized the attack on Marye's Heights had wounded so many! Undoubtedly there were countless others dead at the site.

Bloody soldiers called to her and reached out with trembling arms as she worked her way through them. Their pitiful cries brought tears to her eyes, especially since she could see no way to help them...until, others inside died to make room.

Symanthie Harris met Sue Ling at the front door. "And where have you been, young woman?" Symanthie stood with hands on hips and glared at her as she waited for an answer.

Sue Ling asked, "What are we going to do about those poor men lying on the frozen ground?"

Symanthie said, "You will do nothing. You are discharged, leaving this very day. I knew you were not to be trusted. Most likely just a young whore visiting the camp when you thought no one would know. I've had my eye on you, and now I see I was right to do so. I'm confident Miss Dix will approve of my action."

Sue Ling swallowed. "I'm not a whore! And you must not call me that."

Symanthie said, "Oh, I suppose whores never consider what they really are. They see themselves on some kind of mission worthy of praise and honor. Disgraceful!"

Sue Ling caught a glance of a doctor in the background and considered a way out for herself. Would Dr. Hallous be willing for her to leave? And didn't Minnie say Symanthie catered to men, especially the doctors? Sue Ling smiled. "Miss Harris," she said, "do you have Dr. Hallous's permission to send me away?"

Symanthie's eyes widened, but she recovered. "I have assigned him another nurse. I think he'll be pleased with...."

Sue Ling interrupted, "I will ask him."

She moved past Symanthie and walked quickly to the surgery room.

"Where the hell have you been?" Dr. Hallous asked. "This woman she sent to me wouldn't know how to find her own...."

"Well, you may have to get used to her, doctor. Miss Harris is sending me away."

Hallous shouted, "What? The hell she is!"

Sue Ling said, "She is sending me away. I've been outside and she accused me of being--well, of being a whore."

Dr. Hallous laughed. "You? A whore? That dried up old bitch can forget it. You're going nowhere. We need at least some beauty around this place." He grinned. "Of course, to say nothing of your skills as a nurse. Now get yourself in here and help me with the next patient."

Sue Ling smiled. "In a minute. I'll be right back," she said and dashed to the kitchen for any quick snack she could find...which happened to be a fried piece of coarse bacon and a crust of bread. She crammed it in her mouth and made quick work of her breakfast. On her way back she met Symanthie who frowned at her, "All right, you've been saved this time, but don't try anything again. I have my eye on you and Miss Dix will surely be here within the month. We'll see how she views this thing with you, young woman. I think she'll be even more convinced her original idea of a nurse for the soldiers will be firmly set forth and there'll be no more of the likes of you."

Later, Sue Ling came upon Emily serving a soldier who had been brought into the crowded room of makeshift cots. The soldier had deep, bleeding wounds on his scalp and on his right forearm. Emily applied a thick bandange to his head and a tourniquet on his arm.

"Why Emily!" Sue Ling exclaimed, "isn't that Benny Pillore?"

Benny smiled through his pain. "Old home week," he joked. "I recognized Emily immediately, and now here you are."

Sue Ling said, "You're a good one, Benny, able to joke with your right arm such a mess. He moaned, but then said, "Well if I lose it, I'm a lefty."

Sue Ling said, "Paul told me you were a good platoon leader. The best. I'm...I'm so sorry about this."

"I believe I have the bleeding under control, Benny," Emily said, "Try to get some rest. I'll look in on you later."

Benny took Emily's hand in his. "Thank you so much. I know you chose me from those lying on the ground to be brought in. What about the others? I'm afraid too many of them are not going to survive."

"One of our doctors is having more of the upstairs of the mansion made into a make shift ward," Emily said. "At least, the men will be inside even if they must lie on bare floors."

"Which doctor?" Sue Ling asked.

"Yours...Hallous."

"Oh, well, he isn't mine, but I'm glad to learn he has a heart."

Emily smiled. "There's a good side to him. I hear Miss Dix will visit us sooner than expected. Symanthie says she has total control over all nurses in the service, but Dr. Hallous will stand for you."

"Yes," Sue Ling said, "but will that matter if she has total control?"

Chapter Thirty-Nine

Although Emily and Sue Ling worked eighteen hours a day, Emily always managed a brief time to spend with Benny as his upbeat attitude lifted her spirits and often made her laugh. He also reminded her of home as they spoke of others they knew. He was healing well and would soon be going back into combat. She felt sorry he would be leaving and feared he would be injured again or even killed. She shuddered at the thought, but knew there was nothing she could do. She abaondoned her idea of serving the men in the field instead of the hospital as the field patients near the mansion were few in number now after the battle at Mary's Heights.

Emily also felt concern for her thirteen-year-old patient. Tommy Galbreath had recovered in spite of what could have been a fatal wound. She knew most men died of minie ball wounds, but Tommy made steady progress. He carried a deep wound on his shoulder but it no longer showed infection. Still, like herself, he was deeply scarred for life. But scars were not what troubled her; she worried about his going back into combat as a mere child.

Early one morning to Emily's surprise Tommy whispered to her that he meant to go home to his mother. "I'm not going back to fight," he said. "I'm going to slip out tonight and start walking home."

"Oh, Tommy," Emily said, "you can't do that. You aren't strong enough."

"I'm going anyway. I'd rather die on the way home than be in the war." He spoke with determination. "I'm never, ever going back."

Seeing that he meant to go, Emily said, "Wait a few more days, Tommy. Each day you'll be a little stronger and they won't send you back for at least another week."

"You've been like a mama to me, Nurse Emily. Tell me when if not now." He reached for her hand and held it as he

315

looked into her face.

Emily felt a great tenderness for him seeing him as a lost child. "Let me...let me see what I can come up with, Tommy. Maybe a few days from now."

He relaxed as he always did in her presence. "I'm going to tell my mama about you. I know she'd do anything for you."

"I'm glad you're almost well, Tommy. Now don't worry. Maybe we can work out something. I don't want you to go back into combat. You're too young."

"If I can get home, I'll help my mother with the farm. She needs me. I should never have joined up...fool that I was. I deserve the punishment I got for leaving her."

"You didn't deserve that minie ball, nobody does," she said. "I must go now. I'll be back later." Emily left his bedside. What could she do? She wondered if she had the courage to help him desert. Both excitement and fear flooded her at the prospect.

Emily debated about telling Sue Ling of her plan to help Tommy. She eventually decided against it. What if Sue Ling discouraged her or if they were caught--well, Sue Ling was already on Symanthie's black list. No, this was something she must do alone without telling anyone.

Emily waited until Sue Ling, Minnie and Symanthie were asleep before carefully leaving the room sometime after midnight. She slipped down the stairs and out the back door. She thought there were horses in the barn, but she had to make sure. The moonlight was clear and bright which she considered both a blessing and a curse. It would make her easier to see, but give some more light in the barn. Having lived in the city she realized she had little knowledge about horses, but she would do what she could. She heard some kind of noise when she approached the barn. Her skin prickled with fear and she held her breath.

A horse snorted and another neighed. Good there were horses! For a moment she felt glad, but frustrated. How would she be able to get one out? Somehow she must manage, but she'd never be able to saddle a horse. At least he could ride bare back. She was troubled by the shadowy darkness in the barn, but she could make out three horses at least. She'd need to come to the barn when it was light enough to see and to select one. She placed her hand on the gate and found it was padlocked. Now what? Who had the key? Well, that must be whoever fed the horses. At least there was a little time but she knew she must somehow work out the details. She sighed heavily. One way or another, she was determined to get a horse for Tommy.

Next morning Emily awoke to the sound of thunder and heavy rain. No way to slip around to see who would come to tend the horses. She didn't trust any of the staff well enough to ask leading questions, and believed few would know the answer anyway. No, this was something she must handle alone. Could she slip the lock in her pocket when the man was preoccupied with feeding or watering the horses? She thought the lock would hang loose once undone. Then surely there would be time to take a horse before the lock was replaced.

Very early the next morning a commotion drew Emily's attention when she went downstairs to feed her patients. Someone of importance had arrived. She heard Symanthie say, "Welcome, Miss Dix!"

Symanthie must have expected her as she met her at the door, and now talked eagerly with her. "I'm so happy you've come. I have such respect for all you've done and we certainly want to please you in every way in our operation here. Please, know if what I see as a possible problem is one in your eyes, it will be taken care of immediately."

Emily's forehead prickled with apprehension. Would she because of her youth be immediately dischargedeven before she could help Tommy escape? Then another thought crossed her mind. What about the horse or horses that had brought Miss Dix? With her heart pounding, Emily slipped out the side door and made her way to the front of the house. Yes! A one-horse buggy. In the dim morning light she watched a tall man carry luggage into the house. She knew timing was crucial. What if she were seen? She fought panic.

With trembling hands, she untied the horse and stepped into the buggy. Taking the reins, she urged the horse to a grove of nearby trees. Not daring to be missed, she tied the horse to a sapling and ran back to the mansion. She re-entered the side door and immediately began to collect breakfast for her patients, while trying to still her pounding heart.

She served Tommy first and whispered her news. "Eat your breakfast quickly and then go," she said, "time is important."

Tommy slipped bread into his pocket. "I have to go to the privy," he said aloud "besides I ain't hungry right now."

She nodded, and turned to feed another patient, greeting the new patient pleasantly, trying not to show her anxiety.

Just then the carriage driver burst though the front door exclaiming that the buggy had disappeared.

Emily held her breath. Tommy could very well be caught. What had she done? It would be her fault. Would they send such a child to prison? Would he tell them about her? She must distract the driver in his search. She approached him and said, "Sir, it may be that the one who tends the horses has taken your horses to the barn." She deliberately said 'horses' in an effort to mislead him about her knowledge.

"Oh," the driver said, "without my permission? Where is this barn?"

Emily said, "I'm pretty sure it's out back of the mansion."

Good! The driver went immediately out toward the back. She breathed a sigh of relief. Tommy was a farm boy he'd know how to manage the horse and buggy. What good fortune he'd have the buggy instead of having to ride bare back in his weakened condition.

In a fleeting moment of guilt, Emily realized she had stolen Miss Dix's horse and carriage. Still, she made herself comfortable by considering the lady could easily get another one and Tommy badly needed the help. She resumed feeding breakfast to the patients and thereby failed to see she was being approached.

"Miss Dix," Emily recognized the stern voice of Symanthie Harris, "this young woman is Emily McKelvy." Emily saw the strong bearing of the lady with authority and felt shaken. She bowed slightly and said, "Miss Dix, we're happy to have you here."

In seeing the famous Miss Dix's expression as warm, Emily's guilt pained her deeply. She remembered Minnie telling of Miss Dix's great compassion for the mentally ill and how she worked unceasingly to influence better care for men, women and children in dismal, dungeon-like institutions where they were often chained and beaten. Emily especially remembered one comment a caretaker made that the mentally ill needed no warm clothing or blankets because "they ain't normal like us. They don't feel the cold."

"I'm truly honored to be in your presence," Emily said and meant it. In a fleeting moment, Emily wondered if Miss Dix could forgive her for helping Tommy. Somehow she believed the compassionate woman would understand. Still, she dared not speak of it.

Miss Dix smiled. "You're young, Miss McKelvy, but having come from Dr. Blackwell's, I trust you are a level-headed, educated nurse."

Symanthie said, "She is too young, but we try as best we can to help her."

Anger burned in Emily. How dare Symanthie lie! Never once had she helped her do anything! Emily said, "Miss Harris is afraid you'll be offended by my youth, but I carry out my duties just as Dr. Blackwell instructed." Her voice was firm. A slight smile of recognition crossed Miss Dix's face.

"Well," Symanthie said, "she has not been the problem that the other one has. You met Sue Ling Clark earlier."

"Yes. Dr. Hallous seems to find her exceptionally helpful," Miss Dix said.

"He would say that," Symanthie said. "What man doesn't cater to a pretty young woman?"

"Sue Ling and I were trained together at Dr. Blackwell's," Emily said. "She wanted to be a nurse before I considered it. She's very dedicated."

"I observed her work for a time earlier," Miss Dix said.

"We'll keep an eye on her," Symanthie said. "She disappeared one morning, like I said. Claimed she was tending the wounded out front, but I think she went to the camp."

Miss Dix said, "Proof would be in order, Miss Harris, not just suspicion. You do know, however, I would not allow loose behavior. Immediate dismissal would be in order with proof of such behavior."

Symanthie smiled. "I will watch her and I'm betting my good gloves, she'll run off again any day."

Miss Dix's driver rushed into the room. "Your horse is gone," he said, "but I found the buggy nearby in a clump of trees."

"Oh, how terrible," Symanthie said. Her hand flew to her mouth.

"Do you think the horse could have gotten loose and run away?" Emily asked.

"No, no," the driver said, "absolutely not, he was hitched to the buggy."

Symanthie still frowning in her distress, said, "I'm so sorry about this, but we will furnish you a horse when you get ready to leave."

"Thank you," Miss Dix said, "I'll surely need one."

Emily thought Tommy preferred to ride bareback. The buggy would have offered him more comfort, but as a farm boy he had probably ridden horses without a saddle many times. Besides, now Miss Dix's carriage was back in her possession. Emily sighed. She was torn between guilt and relief. Now if only the child could get home safely to his mother.

***

Sue Ling found herself feeling more compassion for Dr. Hallous. From early morning until late night, he did nothing but saw off arms and legs. The sound of the saw and the

320

gushing of blood became a long, hourly routine leaving him often drenched in blood. and frequently covering her with it as well. The squeaking carts filled with their moaning, ragged and bloody cargo arrived hourly, making her wonder if the chain of horror would never stop.

Nowadays, in spite of his weariness, Dr. Hallous had lost most of his abrupt speech. Often he spoke to her in gentle, polite terms that calmed her earlier annoyance. For the first time, she realized that in spite of his horrible assignment, he was doing what he thought best. She tried harder to assist him and was often rewarded with a nod and a smile.

"Thanks," he said from time to time, "You're a big help. And yes, I washed my hands. Didn't you notice?"

"I noticed," she'd said, and smiled at him.

She saw as her major problem now finding a way to visit Paul again without Symanthie's knowledge.

Chapter Forty

After the first blush of her trip was over, Elizabeth asked to spend a whole day with Alice. She had something on her mind since a swim she'd taken with Donato in August. At first Toby and Little Mama visited with her, but in time Toby left for his chores and Little Mama went to her room for an afternoon nap.

"Alice," Elizabeth said, "if I liked a boy, I'd like Donato, but there's that love stuff. I wondered about it."

"What about it, Sugar?"

"Well, last summer when Donato and I were swimming playing hide-and-seek in the water around the shanty boats, he caught me and kissed me on the mouth."

Alice laughed. "Sho 'nough?"

"But that's not all. He held me up real close and kissed me again, and Alice it was kind of thrilling in a funny sort of way. Do you know what I mean?" Elizabeth asked.

"I knows. It be all right to like a boy," Alice said, "that be like it supposed to be."

"But Alice that love-making stuff. Did you and Toby do that?"

Alice laughed. "Sho."

Elizabeth frowned. "It didn't hurt? I know Marme and Monette said it didn't, but I wanted to know what you think."

"No. It be fine."

"Then maybe I'll do it."

"Not now, Sugar. Wait 'till you be older and gets married up with some good man."

"Older! Alice, what's this older business? Everybody says 'when you're older' you can do this or that...now even you!"

"Well, it be 'cause things come in stages. Firs' you be a baby, then a little girl, then a big girl, then a young woman, then a middle-age woman like me, and then old like Little Mama. The good book say there be a time for everything.

Rushin' up stages don't be good. This time you a big girl, next you be a young woman and that be the time if you find yo man."

"Maybe it's Donato, but he'll be leaving to apprentice with his uncle this spring after we get back...learning to build ships down in Mobile, Alabama. That is, unless he gets himself in the war which I sure hope he doesn't."

"He be 'bout sixteen now?"

"Yes, he's older than I am, but plenty of girls get married at my age."

"I know, but later be better," Alice said, "like when you be eighteen at least."

"Eighteen!"

"Yes. Eighteen be soon enough."

"Well, I'm going back to the river where he is, but Marme said I can come back here for my fifteenth birthday."

"You going back to the river? I thought you be staying this time."

"Not right away. We'll go back when the weather clears up some. That's what Mr. Seldenis says. Probably not before the end of February."

"So you do be going back?"

"Yes, Marme says it's best for me to be with the Seldenis for a while longer, and except for being away from you all, I love life on the river. Oh, Alice if...I wish you could be there! It's so beautiful, and we have lots of fun."

"Maybe I see it some day. Toby nephew up North, he keep wantin' us come up there. Ever since Toby brother die, Julian keep wantin' us come, but we be 'fraid to try it jest yet."

"Where up north?"

"That place dey calls New York," Alice said. "But like I say, we can't go jest now. Besides, I still be taking care of Mr. Dalk. He need me, and if we go I'd have to find help for him. He been mighty good to us...not one speck like his ma was."

"Oh, Alice, maybe we could be going the same time! Marme wants me to go to New York to boarding school when I'm fifteen. Now I was dreading it something awful, and thought I just wouldn't do it, but if you and Toby go I won't feel so bad. In fact, if you go, I'll be happy."

Alice laughed. "Now I feels better, too. Just soon as this ole war be over, we have us 'nother place to go."

"But Alice maybe we could all live on the river instead. If I marry Donato we could just get us a big houseboat. Wouldn't that be fun?"

"I don't know 'bout that. You young yet, Sugar. You might change yo' mind." Alice hugged her. "Where ever we be, though, we still love each other."

***

Leaving Kansas City this time was not upsetting for Elizabeth. She realized she would be returning for her birthday, but also because she looked forward to being back on the river and seeing Donato.

When she arrived she was greeted warmly with embraces and life resumed as usual except for one thing. Once when his parents were gone, Donato kissed her fully on her lips and caressed her breast.

"Don't," she whispered.

"Sweetheart," he said, kissing her cheek, holding her close. She felt that special feeling again, but she remembered what Alice had told her and twisted out of his embrace.

"Not until we're married," Elizabeth said.

"What?"

"Not until we're married," she repeated.

"Oh, come on, Elizabeth!" He tried to embrace her again, but she slipped away and yelled at him. "Donato Seldeni, I'm going to tell your parents if you don't stop this minute."

"For Christ's sake," he said, "I didn't know you were such a baby, and as for marrying you...forget it!" He stalked out, climbed in a johnboat and rowed to the bank, but on the day he left to start his apprenticeship, he whispered in Elizabeth's ear, "Sweetheart, I didn't mean what I said...

I mean about not marrying you."

***

In Donato's first letter he wrote:

March 23, 1865

Dear Mother and Dad,

I have arrived in Mobile and find Uncle and family well, but not feeling safe from the war. We hear the sounds of battle although not at the ship-yard yet. Uncle Mack thinks it could happen any day and he's sorry I left the river because I could get hurt. He doesn't say it, but I think he really means killed.

As for me, well, I think the whole thing will soon be over and the Confederates, though fighting hard will lose. Why do I think this? Well, I had an interesting experience on my way here.

When I was waiting for my Steamer in Selma, I met this girl. She drove up in a wagon with a mammy with her. First thing I know, she sells her horse and wagon and buys passage on the steamer for herself and her mammy. She seemed like she felt drawn to me right away and we talked. Pauline Eberhart is her name. Guess I ought to say she's a beautiful girl with long, blonde hair so I wasn't unhappy about talking or listening to her. Seem like she stole the papers on her mammy from her stepmother so she could travel with her. You know, like if she was stopped. She got away with it and I'm glad because her stepmother was mean to her mammy and to her, too.

So what does that have to do with believing the Union boys will win Pauline's father said so. She said he was sad about it, but he told his fam-ily, "Our boys only have single-shot rifles, shot-

325

gun and carbines. The Union Cavalry has new equipment and seven-shot Spencer repeating carbines, besides there are more of them. It's just a matter of time." Pauline said she hated to leave her father, but that he always sided with her step-mother so she decided to run away to Mobile to be with her mother. Whoever wins has the problem of muddy roads and overflowing streams due to the heavy rain. But don't worry. For now we seem safe, and even if they blow up Uncle Mack's business, I don't think they'll kill us.

Greetings to Elizabeth.

Your loving son,

Donato

Elizabeth could not hide her tears. Only 'Greetings to Elizabeth.' And what about this beautiful Pauline with the long blonde hair? She turned quickly away and made herself busy folding clothes on her cot.

But within days a letter came to her, addressed only to her. She tore it open with trembling hands. He wrote:

Dear Elizabeth,

I've been thinking of you and your kisses. You really are a pretty girl and nice, too. Maybe when I come back we can be together more of the time.

I was thinking of how pretty you look first thing in the morning when you wash your face and just seem to glow. If the war would only be over so I could get into my training! The sooner it's done, the sooner I'll be back looking at your pretty face.

Yours,

Donato

Elizabeth clasped the letter to her heart. Marme could forget that boarding school in New York! She was going to marry Donato and let him kiss her as much as he wanted to... much as she wanted to, also. At last, she would find out what that special feeling would really be like. A thought of Alice crossed her mind and she frowned. She would never give up Alice, but why couldn't Alice and them come visit her on the nice boat she and Donato would surely have. He could even set up his own boat-building business in Maysville and they could raise their children on the river. Mrs. Seldeni called to her twice before Elizabeth finally heard her.

"What did Donato say?" Mrs. Seldeni asked.

"Oh, just nice things, like missing us and he'll be glad when the war is over and he can start his training. Do you think he'll make his own boat-building business here in Maysville?"

"I hope so, but I don't know. After all, he has a way to go and much to learn before he might decide on that."

After two months, Donato sent Elizabeth a tintype photograph of himself. She often gazed with happiness at the dim, gray image of him and longed for his presence. Sometimes she could almost feel his arms around her and the warmth of his kiss.

Once he even wrote of love! She read it over and over again. "You know how I love the river, but I love you an ocean more."

But as the months passed, his letters came less often and were shorter. Elizabeth ached for a renewed sign of his love, but his notes remained short and almost impersonal. After reading one especially brief, unaffectionate note, tears ran down her cheeks.

"Why, Elizabeth," Mrs. Seldeni said, "what did Donato write that could make you cry?"

"It's just that I miss...miss him," she said.

"I know. You've been like brother and sister," Mrs. Seldeni said.

Chapter Forty-One

The ninth of April, 1865, came as a closing date...after much destruction, 600,000 deaths and countless tears shed in broken families. General Robert E. Lee surrendered his Confederate Army to General Ulysses S. Grant. It was the official end of four years of conflict, courage, bloodshed and death for thousands of young soldiers and innocent civilians. But soldiers in far-flung places fought and died still because the word had not reached them that the war had ended. Countless historic buildings and landmarks stood with ragged wounds, while others had been reduced to rubble.

Still, the next day after the signing, there was great celebration in Washington. At last a weary President Lincoln had won the united nation that he wanted. No one knew in that moment of celebration that in five days he would be dead from John Wilkes Booth's gunshot.

***

Now that the war was over, Hannah was prepared to have Elizabeth return to Kansas City months earlier. To Hannah's great surprise, Elizabeth pleaded to put off returning until the next spring. Hannah accepted the postponement, however, when Elizabeth told her that would be when the Seldenis would make their next trip. Unlike the year before, Elizabeth explained, they weren't making the Christmas trip because their son would be coming home to the river in the winter.

Since Elizabeth had told only Alice about Donato, Hannah had no reason to suspect her feelings for him as a reason for Elizabeth's desire to delay her return to Kansas City. Besides, Hannah still was not comfortable with Elizabeth traveling alone so the matter was settled.

Donato had been gone for more than a year when he returned one cold November day. He stood tall in his beaver coat and top hat and looked far more man than boy. Now, at eighteen, he wore a beard and smoked a pipe. Elizabeth thought him even more handsome than before. She put aside her hurt over his brief letters when he took her in his arms and kissed her. She relaxed even more when he gazed into her face and then embraced and kissed her again. "Sweet Elizabeth," he said, "my sweet Elizabeth."

Now when he kissed her, Elizabeth knew it would be harder to resist his advances. At almost sixteen and eighteen, they were old enough to marry, and he had almost finished his apprenticeship. Surely he would propose before he left.

The freezing temperatures and heavy snow of late January made extra work for all of them. Mr. Seldeni and Donato worked to keep the water running free between the shanty boat and the icy bank, knowing well the danger of a solid freeze. They worked with probes, dealt with frozen lines, and kept the fire going with ash as the best-heating wood.

Finally, the weather warmed and then the break-up sent scattered floes of ice scraping and crunching against the boat making it difficult for Elizabeth to sleep. As she looked at the ceiling in the dim light she wondered how Donato was feeling about her. He had been so exhausted in dealing with the ice they'd spent little time together. She lay awake a long time on her cot recalling their experiences and wondering how he felt about her. On the other side of the thin wall, she heard him snoring lightly so he was not thinking of her now. Surely, sometime before he left, he'd say the words she hoped to hear. But the day came for his departure and he had not mentioned taking her as his bride. His parents were present so he only kissed her on her cheek, and said, "Keep the chin up, little girl."

Little girl? What did that mean?

Only after he was gone, Mrs. Seldeni who was making dough for bread, commented, "Well, next visit I suppose we'll see our daughter-in-law. I think from what he says, Pauline Eberhart must be a very clever girl...brave, too, taking herself and her mammy on that trip during the war.

Beautiful, he says, with her long, blonde hair."

Elizabeth's throat ached and sudden tears blinded her. Why had he not told her? After a long, silent moment Mrs. Seldeni glanced her way questioningly. Elizabeth ducked her head to hide her tears and managed to say, "I suppose so."

A towboat passed, clanging and panting pouring forth clouds of steam and smoke. Elizabeth grabbed a coat and went on deck to watch, glad for the distraction. The steam and smoke smelled of rust, but the icy air felt fresh on her flushed face. So that was it, Donato wanted a blonde. She felt ugly for the first time in her life.

When Elizabeth returned inside, Mrs. Seldeni said, "It won't be long now until time to plant our riverbank gardens. They'll flourish after the frost and snow melts. Maybe you've noticed the riverbanks and roads are bare when higher roads are still covered in ice. We'll plant lettuce, spinach, peas, beets and carrots just as soon as the weather permits."

"I remember the green peas...."

"Yes, the ones some call English peas do well in the cool weather of springtime. Well, of course, we like the poke sallet. Some say that anything that bleeds milk when you break its stalk is good to eat, but I think there are exceptions."

Elizabeth could contain her tears no longer. A surprised Mrs. Seldeni put an arm around her. "Why, what's wrong, honey?"

"I'm...I'm homesick for Kansas City," she said. "I want to leave as soon as Marme can send me money for the trip."

"Oh, have I offended you in some way? I wouldn't do that for the world! Why you're like a daughter to me."

"No, it's not you. You've been wonderful. I love all of you, but I want to go home."

Chapter Forty-Two

Elizabeth reassured Hannah that she could safely take the steamboat alone as she remembered the details of the trip from her Christmas visit home. Hannah agreed that now at fifteen and a half, she was old enough to be aware of strangers and the usual problems that might occur with a beautiful young girl traveling alone. Beautiful? She no longer felt beautiful.

It seemed the day for Hannah's letter and the money for the trip would never arrive now that she was so ready to leave. Still, she realized she owed much of her happiness on the river to the shanty boat families and took time to visit each of them before the day of her departure arrived. She was surprised when Junie clung to her and wept.

"I'll miss you," Elizabeth said, returning her embrace. "You were so good to me."

"It was easy to be good to you," Junie said. "I am sorry to see you go."

When Leon and James hugged her, Elizabeth could not hold back her tears. Such sweet little boys and who knew how much they'd endured when Terrance was with them? It always reminded her of her painful time with Mrs. Dalk. But her tears seemed near the surface anyway now that Donato had rejected her.

"Come back anytime," Junie said, embracing her again, then releasing her but reaching for Elizabeth's fingers and clinging to them as she spoke. "I'll never forget you."

"I won't forget you either, Junie. Take good care of yourself and my favorite little boys."

***

The first week in April Hannah's letter with the funds for the trip arrived. She also sent three beautiful dresses for her to wear on the steamship home.

Inside the box was a note reading, "These are to welcome you home, my dear, dear Elizabeth. Love, Marme."

Mrs. Seldeni looked on in awe. "I've seen beautiful dresses before, but these are the most gorgeous ones I've ever seen. It's the wonderful material, but the colors as well. You will outshine any other beauty on the ship."

Elizabeth smiled. She held the muted gold dress against her body and admired the fitted bodice with tiny brown buttons. Then she displayed the deep rose-red dress trimmed in black lace. Finally, she held up the royal blue one that seemed to match her eyes. "What do you think?" she asked, "which one should I wear on the steamer?"

"It's impossible to say, Elizabeth. You look so beautiful in each."

For a moment she wondered if Donato would have thought so, but she knew she had to forget him...or at least try to do so. Once Marme, in her effort to get Monette to give up Terrance, confessed "I had to give up the deepest love of my life...admittedly for a different reason, but you need to give up Terrance, then stop the weeping and get on with your future." Elizabeth was grateful for the memory as she was tired of feeling miserable. She decided to force herself to give up dwelling on thoughts of Donato. Each time a thought of him tried to creep into her mind she'd make herself think of something pleasant instead. And in having decided to do so, at least at the moment, she felt hot anger replace the humiliation and sadness. No more silly tears from now on! She'd go to boarding school as Marme wished and maybe teach French as Monette had taught her. She would make herself useful to children and then maybe some day, if she were fortunate, some man more wonderful than Donato would love her. That would be her dream. She sighed and caressed the beautiful dresses before putting them aside until time to get ready for her trip.

***

The clear blue sky and warm sun on the day of her

departure from Kentucky pleased Elizabeth. She decided to wear the gold dress. "Like the sunshine," she said.

"I'll miss you," Mrs. Seldeni said, "but I'm pleased to see you happy once again. I suppose being homesick made you feel sad, and now I can admit that it made me feel down as well...seeing that pretty face looking so gloomy."

"Oh, I'm sorry I made you sad," Elizabeth said, "You've been wonderful to me, I'll always remember you with...with love."

Mrs. Seldeni reached to embraced her, but not before Elizabeth saw her tears. "Promise," she said, "that you'll visit us again."

Elizabeth knew she would not want to come back to the river until Donato was no longer around if indeed that time ever came. She said, "Well, surely I'll be seeing you when we're both back in Kansas City on a Christmas visit."

On the morning of her departure, Elizabeth packed her belongings in the rich, brown leather suitcase Hannah had given her before her first leaving Kansas City.

"She provides you with such lovely things," Mrs. Seldeni said.

"Yes, but I'm thinking now one of the most valuable things she has provided is the love of books," Elizabeth said taking her copies of Walt Whitman's poetry, a thin volume containing Mark Twain's "The Celebrated Jumping Frog of Calaveras County," and a book of French poetry Monette had given her.

"These," Elizabeth said, "will give me good company while I travel." It will, she thought, also push Donato Seldeni out of my thoughts.

***

The lilting music of the calliope thrilled Elizabeth as she prepared to board The Sterling Expedition. People waved from the decks of the great white ship and the roll of the waves and hustle-bustle on the docks all reminded her of a wider world waiting for her. Forget Donato in his other world!

Once on board she waved to Mr. and Mrs. Seldeni and soon the steamer moved from the shore out into the Ohio River. She knew there would be days of travel from the Ohio to the Mississippi and finally to the Missouri River. This would be a good time to read and reflect on her future. Perhaps Marme was right to help her prepare for a teaching career.

Although, Elizabeth would not have been able to express it as such, the pain and subsequent resolution of the matter she had felt with Donato's rejection, seemed to awaken her to a new level of maturity. She took pride in being able to get over what she now labeled 'childish foolishness.' Never again would she allow herself to be taken in by some kissing pretender! She knew the signs now. The change in his letters alone should have awakened her, but no, she was a silly child taken in by love. Anger flooded her each time she thought of it. Best not to think of it, she decided and walked out to the deck to watch the river scenes.

She traveled without incident on the Ohio, but on the Mississippi River when she was on deck with her books, two young men flirted with her before their girl friends (or wives) drew them away. She simply smiled and returned to her reading.

Her first day on the Missouri River at dusk, Elizabeth sat alone at a table in the steamer's dining room waiting for her dinner. The blended scents of roast pork and apples made her hungry. While she waited, she took Hannah's letter from her purse and read it again. The warmth and love of the message lifted her spirits. It was good to be going home again.

When her dinner arrived, she laid Hannah's letter aside, eager to enjoy her food. She was pleased with the generous slice of light roast pork, the baked apples, lima beans and a lightly browned slice of bread. Her tea was steaming hot so she added cream and a little sugar.

A male voice startled her. "I see I'm in luck," the man said. "What is your price for the night?"

"Price for the night? What do you mean?" Elizabeth asked.

"I know Hannah Sloan. I see you have a letter from her."

For the first time Elizabeth looked at him. He was smiling down at her with his hand on the back of her chair...a mildly handsome middle-aged man with reddish beard and mustache, gold chains lying across his vest.

"You don't understand, sir. I am not what you think. Please, go away."

He stooped to whisper in her ear. "No one will know and with one so beautiful, I will be most generous...money all your own to keep."

Across the way Elizabeth saw a gentle appearing older couple at a nearby table. "Go away," she said "I must speak to my family." She rose at once almost toppling the chair. When she approached the older couple, she pleaded softly, "Please, pretend to be my parents!"

The distinguished appearing gray-haired woman took Elizabeth's hand. "Anything wrong, darling?" she asked.

"It's that man," Elizabeth said, but in turning she saw that he had gone.

"You seem to be alone, dear," the lady said. "May we be of help?"

"Thank you," Elizabeth said, "you already have."

"Would you care to join us at our table, young lady?" the gentleman asked.

"I don't want to be a bother," Elizabeth said.

"Here, let me transfer your dinner for you." He made the move quickly but carefully. Elizabeth saw by his manner and his clothing that he was not ordinary, but likely a professional or an important businessman of some kind.

"Thank you, sir." Elizabeth took a chair near the lady. "I'm Elizabeth McKelvy," she said.

"We're George and Mary Markham," Mrs. Markham said. "We're on vacation from our home in New York City. Where do you live?"

"Kansas City," Elizabeth said. "I'm going home."

After transferring her food to their table, the gentleman handed Elizabeth Hannah's letter but she felt a bit uncomfortable seeing his friendly expression change to a decidedly serious one. Did he know Hannah, or more exactly her business?

"A letter from your mother?" Mrs. Markham asked. Elizabeth noticed the kindly expression of her eyes.

"No. I'm an orphan, but this wonderful woman raised me."

"I see," Mrs. Markham said in a soft voice and asked no further questions.

Soon to Elizabeth's surprise a handsome young man slid into a chair at their table. "Sorry I'm late," he said. He smiled and nodded. Except for one minor overlap of two front teeth his smile was perfect. Elizabeth thought his gray-blue eyes with thick dark eyelashes were remarkably good looking.

"Miss McKelvy, this is our son, Will." Mrs. Markham said. "Elizabeth is on her way to Kansas City."

"Elizabeth," Will said. "What a nice surprise. Glad to meet you."

"And I, you," Elizabeth said, smiling.

Elizabeth saw that Will had inherited the color of his father's now fading chestnut hair, and the color of his mother's eyes. A good-looking family.

"Some man on deck was troubling Elizabeth so she came to us." Mrs. Markham explained. She laid a comforting hand over Elizabeth's.

"Your parents were kind enough to let me join them."

When dinner was over, they continued to talk. Will asked, "Have you been to New York, Elizabeth?"

"No, but it must be an interesting place."

"Oh, you would enjoy the musicals and stage perform-ances," Will said. "I was in London a few months ago and caught Joseph Jefferson in Rip Van Winkle. You would have loved it! Now I understand it will be in New York."

Mrs. Markham interjected, "Will travels as a buyer for our fabric and manufacturing business."

Elizabeth smiled. "Oh, I'm sure I would enjoy the performance. I've read the story."

"They say it took Jefferson a while to perfect his act, but that he is now great in it," Mrs. Markham said. "Well, delightful as that may be, nothing could charm us more than seeing Jenny Lynn, but that was in 1850 when Will was only seven years old so I doubt he remembers much about it."

"I remember some of it," Will said.

Elizabeth was acutely aware of Mr. Markham's silence and the rather stern expression on his face. He must have known Hannah or at least to have heard of her. Was he concerned now that his son seemed interested in her? She felt accused unjustly and decided to speak about her life in a way she had not planned to do.

"I think," Elizabeth said, "I should make something clear. I was rescued from a bad family when I was a little girl by Hannah Sloan, a famous madam in Kansas City. Mrs. Sloan never actually adopted me but she brought me up as her daughter. Contrary to what that man thought who approached me earlier, I am not a prostitute. Apparently, he saw my letter from her and assumed I was what I am not and never shall be."

"Oh, my dear," Mrs. Markham said, "I had no idea! I simply thought since you were a beautiful young girl alone."

"Do you live with Mrs. Sloan?" Mr. Markham asked.

"In her private quarters, yes, but she is sending me away to boarding school soon. I believe that will be in New York so perhaps I can see the Rip Van Winkle performance after all." Elizabeth gathered her purse and said, "Now if you will please excuse me, I'll go to my quarters."

"Don't leave," Will said. "Tell me...us more about yourself."

Elizabeth glanced at all of them and said, "Well, perhaps you'd like to hear about my life on the river." She smiled seeing Mrs. Markham's and Will's curious, eager faces. Mr. Markham's facial expression changed from stern to serious. Clearly he was not totally convinced of her innocence.

For now she would tell them only the pleasant things.

***

The next day Will joined Elizabeth on deck. She was wearing her red dress. Her smooth skin had a glow and the fresh breeze lifted tendrils of her dark hair. She smiled when he joined her as she had hoped he would.

"Good morning," he said. "May I have your company?"

"You may. How are you?"

"Fine," he said. "I didn't see you at breakfast. I suppose you were up earlier."

"I was."

"Look at this muddy, swirling water." He frowned. "Too thick to drink and too thin to plow, but much traveled. I suppose we could have chosen some overland way, but we risk our necks for the pleasure of the steamer."

"Is it really that dangerous?" Elizabeth asked.

"Well, many a mile has been navigated safely, but unseen fallen trees in this dark river water can snag and fatally pierce a steamboat's hull."

"I knew steamboats sank, but I didn't know quite why. Of course, I've been living on the Ohio River and all of our boats stayed afloat while I was there."

He smiled at her. "You seem very mature for a girl of your obvious youth," he said.

"Do I? I have spent most of my life with adults and Mrs. Sloan did provide several years of education for me. Perhaps that's why."

Elizabeth heard footsteps and turned to see Mrs. Markham. "Do you suppose I could have your company for a little while?"

"Of course." Elizabeth said. "How are you?"

"Very well, thank you. I can tell by looking at you that you are in excellent health," Mrs. Markham said.

Elizabeth said, "Will was telling me about steamboats on this river. I didn't really know the danger. I had traveled on a steamer home before but the people who were with me at the time didn't mention it."

"Well, dear, your friends probably felt reasonably safe and didn't want to frighten you. Some say it's a wonder I travel by steamer as I was on the Arabia that day in August of '56 when it sank. August thirteenth the date. The oak hull was snagged by a large walnut trunk lying in the mud unseen. We all escaped by boat to the shore, but a poor mule who was tied was forgotten in the panic that ensued."

"How sad," Elizabeth said, "I mean for the mule."

"Yes, I felt badly about that, too," Mrs. Markham said.

"You must be an animal lover," Will said.

"I simply don't like to see anything or anybody suffer."

Mr. Markham appeared and asked his wife and son to join him. He nodded a greeting to Elizabeth but did not include her.

While she stood alone still looking out over the waters of the Missouri, Mr. Markham returned. She had not seen him coming and was startled when he spoke to her.

"What would it cost me for you to be my companion?" He asked. "I can pay you handsomely, buy you a lovely home...."

Tears flooded Elizabeth's eyes. "I see you don't believe me! Sir, there are not enough riches in the world to make me be anyone's 'companion' or mistress which is what I think you really mean. Please, leave me alone," she said and turned to leave when he caught her arm.

"Elizabeth," he said, "please, forgive me. I confess this was a trick to see how honest you really were. My wife and son seem so taken with you, I felt I needed to protect them if you weren't as you claimed to be."

"Who and what I claimed to be?" Elizabeth snapped."How dare you judge me after I told you my background."

"I'm sorry. I hope you can understand." He released her arm. "I hope you won't mention this to my family."

"Don't ever accuse me again," she said.

"Well, now that I've made a fool of myself I'll leave, but I hope you'll join us later for dinner."

Elizabeth said nothing. She turned from him and resumed her view of the river water and the forest scenes along the bank. She realized that this mistaken view of her could happen again. People, she thought, not only misjudged her but overlooked the good in Hannah as well. Even Toby had a problem with Hannah because he thought she couldn't be a Christian and at the same time run a 'sportin' house, as he called it.

Elizabeth did not join the Markhams for dinner, but waited until a later time when she thought they would no longer be in the dining room. She had, however, barely begun her dinner when Will appeared. In the background she also saw the middle-aged man who had propositioned her. To her surprise, Will and the man carried on a brief, but friendly conversation. The man slapped Will on his back and made his way to a table where a flamboyantly dressed woman sat primping in front of a hand mirror.

Will came to Elizabeth's table. "Where were you? I'd hoped you would be with us at dinner."

"I thought your family might prefer to be alone."

"No, not at all. I suppose it's none of my business but I was disappointed. Are you all right?"

"Will, who is that man you were talking with just now?"

"Oh, that was my uncle Jerome. He's not only my uncle, he's my boss at the company."

Elizabeth replaced her coffee cup in the saucer. Should she tell him her experience with that man? What would he think?

"You seem suddenly quiet. What's wrong?" Will asked.

Hardly thinking at that point, Elizabeth blurted out what happened.

Will shook his head. "I'm sorry,' he said. "Clearly he misunderstood."

"I don't want him near me ever again," Elizabeth said.

"I'm sure he won't bother you now that he knows," Will said, but Elizabeth saw he flushed slightly. What did that mean?

"What? What are you thinking?" she asked.

"Oh, it's just that he puts people in categories, but don't concern yourself about it."

"Like he finds me unacceptable because of my upbringing," Elizabeth said.

"He's mistaken about you," Will said. He gently touched her sleeve. You have such great taste in clothing. I should know. I'm in the business, remember."

"Thank you, but it's not my good taste. Marme...Mrs. Sloan sent them to me. She's a mother to me and I love her."

"Yes, but how do you feel about what she does?" Will asked.

So, Elizabeth thought, he also wonders! She spoke firmly, "I'd prefer she had another business, but she didn't ask me for my opinion. What I know is I was a child needing help and she took me in and gave me wonderful care." Elizabeth flushed. She pushed back her chair to leave.

"Please, don't go. I'm sorry if I offended you. I'm glad she rescued you," he said. "Maybe some day you can tell me about it," Will said.

It occurred to her he was speaking of keeping in touch with her. She said, "Maybe. Someday."

In the background she saw his Uncle Jerome look in their direction, frown, and set his lips in a tight line. What was he thinking? That she was a prostitute who had rejected him for Will?

***

The night before she was to arrive in Kansas City, Will took her hand. "Would you let me write to you?" he asked.

"Yes," she said. She felt the gentleness of his touch and while knowing it was improper and too soon, she would have liked for him to kiss her.

"I like you very much," he said. "I'll write soon."

"Good," she said. "I'll look forward to your letter."

Early in the morning the day The Sterling Expedition was to arrive, Elizabeth sat at her breakfast table reading

341

from the French poetry book Monette had given her.

She saw Will approaching and smiled. When he reached her table, she said, "I thought you liked to sleep later."

"Not when I can have breakfast with you," he said. "May I?"

"Yes, of course." She started to close the small volume of poetry, but he caught her hand and held the book open.

"I see you're reading Stéphane Mallarmé. Je connais bien cette poésie. Etes-vous allée en France?" he asked.

"Non, j' aimerais beaucoup y aller un jour. Une belle fançaise m' a appris." she said and cast her eyes downward.

"Pourquoi paraisses-vou si triste?"

"Elle a été assassinee." Elizabeth said.

"She was murdered? Your French instructor was murdered. Pourquoi?"

"It's...perhaps it is something I may be able to tell you later."

"Why not now?"

"Because it makes me too sad, and it's a rather long story."

"Very well. Some later time." he said taking up the small volume of poetry. "I see you were reading Le Guignon."

"No, I had read that long poem earlier. I was reading 'Apparition'. I especially like the last two lines, 'Opening her hands to scatter through the years, Snowy bouquets of richly scented stars.' "

"I like best the line that reads 'It was the blessed day of your first kiss.'" Elizabeth smiled. Will's parents who were approaching took her smile as a greeting for them, though it was not for them. So he was thinking of a kiss, too! Would he kiss her before they heard the three bells signaling their arrival in Kansas City? Since the steamer moved at only about six miles an hour it would be afternoon before she would be leaving the boat.

"May we join you?" his mother asked.

Will pulled back a chair. "For you, Mother," he said.

342

Mr. Markham sat across from Elizabeth. "Good morning," he said, "you look fresh as the morning itself."

"Thank you," Elizabeth said smiling. She had mixed feelings. Apparently now he had accepted her, but the expression reminded her of Donato's remark about how fresh and lovely she appeared in the morning. Forget Donato Seldeni! Thank heaven there was no connection.

"Elizabeth reads and speaks French," Will said.

"Really?" Mr. Markham said. "Have you traveled in France?"

"No, as I told Will earlier a beautiful French woman instructed me. Actually, I was taught a great deal by Mrs. Sloan as well. You may not know that she was a teacher before she became a madam."

Mrs. Markham smiled. "It proves that what is being said about us ladies is wrong. I was also educated, but many still say our female brains are simply too weak to take in much learning."

"Mrs. Sloan...I call her 'Marme', said it was a lie and she meant for me to learn everything she and my French tutor could teach me. Marme said having much information," Elizabeth smiled, " 'in my little head,' would keep me from being handicapped by those who might wish to harm or cheat me." Elizabeth looked directly at Mr. Markham. "She didn't teach me about prostitution, in fact she hid the nature of her business from me for years. She did, however, teach me from a book how my body functions."

Both Mr. and Mrs. Markham breathed deeply as if in shock at this frank statement, but Will laughed. "You are in a class by yourself, Elizabeth," he said. "I can see your intelligence is not inferior, and neither is yours, dear Mother," he said giving his mother a wink.

Within moments the conversation turned to the lovely weather and all appeared to be normal once more.

Later, when the three bells sounded, signaling arrival at port, there had been no private moment for Elizabeth and Will, but he took her hand and said, "These days have been special thanks to you. Look for my letter soon."

Mrs. Markham said, "It has been a pleasure, Elizabeth. I wish you the best."

"It's getting late afternoon," Mr. Markham said, "I trust someone will be meeting you."

"Yes," Elizabeth said, "but thank you for your concern." She was pleased to once again be in his good graces. Was it possible he might one day become her father-in-law? Or would the fact she was attached to Hannah cause the family to see her as unsuitable? Clearly the uncle would think so.

Chapter Forty-Three

Elizabeth was surprised to be met by Maude, the chubby housekeeper, rather than by Hannah. The normally grouchy woman appeared subdued. She was neatly dressed in a black dress and her gray hair was smooth in a bun on top of her head. "Miz Hannah is ill," she said. "It's her heart they say, and she needs to rest."

Tears sprang to Elizabeth's eyes. "Why didn't she tell me?"

"She didn't want to worry you, I think. She's been seen by her doctor and there's this minister whose been coming, too. A Reverend Stuart Bell. Well, a lot has changed, Elizabeth. The girls are all gone now."

"The girls are gone?"

"Yes, Miz Hannah shut down the house except for Mary, a new cook, and me."

"But why? How?"

"She gave each girl bonus money and told them to find some other way to earn their living. She didn't want them working for any of the low-down houses."

Elizabeth fought her tears but more ran down her cheeks. *Marme must be terribly ill!* What a silly fool she'd been staying on the river waiting for Donato Seldeni! If only someone had let her know.

It was dusk at the mansion when they drove up in the carriage. No other carriages, no gas lights, no lilting music, no sudden peals of laughter from the ballroom...only silence with the dark of night falling. A soft light from Hannah's quarters the only sign of life.

"She's most likely in bed," Maude said. "Seems too weak to be up for long."

Elizabeth ran up the steps, opened the door, and rushed to Hannah's bedroom. In seeing Hannah she gasped and swallowed. Hannah's lovely red hair was unpinned and spread over the pillow. Her fine cheek bones were now pronounced and her skin without color. Even her normally rich voice was thin. "Oh, Elizabeth," she said opening her arms, "I'm so happy to see you."

Elizabeth knelt by her bed and was folded in her embrace. "Oh, Marme," she cried, "Why didn't you let me know you were ill? I would have come as fast as I could get here."

"I know, my darling, but there really was nothing for you to do. Besides, the war was still on and and moving this way when I first learned I was not well. It was not a safe time to travel."

Elizabeth pulled a chair beside the bed. "But surely there was something I could have done if I'd been here. Oh, I'm so sorry I lingered."

"No, there was nothing you could do. Don't be sorry, honey. It was for the best."

"Can I do something...anything for you," Elizabeth pleaded taking Hannah's frail hand.

"Well, yes. You can read to me a little while."

"What would you like?"

"Some poetry, I think. Maybe something from the English poets."

Elizabeth selected a book from a nearby shelf and read from Lord Byron, but more quickly than she'd expected Hannah fell asleep.

***

After dinner, as Elizabeth and Maude lingered at the table, Maude said, "Miz Hannah wrote a paper she wanted you to have. Well, she said if she passed on before you got here. Maybe she wanted to tell you, but if she couldn't, she wanted you to know some things."

"She seems so weak. Maybe I should read it anyway and save her the energy," Elizabeth said.

"I'll fetch it," Maude said leaving her chair and going into another room. She returned with an envelope and handed it to Elizabeth who opened it quickly and read:

My dearest Elizabeth,

I will soon be leaving this world and there are matters to be settled. You will inherit a rather large sum of money in trust. A minister, the Reverend Stuart Bell, will handle it for you until you are of age. You may be surprised I am now trying to get into Heaven. Not a good joke. I have been listening when Reverend Bell reads from the book of John in the Bible. It seems too good to be true that there really is a God who loves us and who has a wonderful place waiting for us when we die. Still, seeing how his beliefs have made him into such a sensitive and caring man, though one of poor means, I'm almost a believer. You should see--and you shall see, the light in his eyes! So much has he convinced me of his character and desire to do good, that I am leaving this mansion to him and his wife, Martha Ann. I suggested they use it as a hotel to make money, and my quarters as their home. My only request of them is that they serve poor women who come seeking help. I know how desperate some thrown-away girls can be, and I don't want them to work in the low down houses. Some of them surely can earn a living working in the hotel, which the minister will open not long after my passing. I have made arrangements for you to enter Madame Lucille Lemont's French boarding school in New York City. We taught at an academy some years ago and I knew she established a boarding school in New York. She understands you are not a beginner in French and will set your classes accordingly. Unlike many schools, her school provides for a wider range of learning for girls than most allow. This should prepare you for your future as a teacher or for some related employment you may discover. The Reverend Bell will assist you in whatever you may need, but I have arranged for Madame Lemont to personally meet you when you arrive in New York. You will find details about the school in a packet in the top drawer of your Bureau. You know I love you as if you were truly my own child. I hope I have prepared you to live a good life.

Marme

Elizabeth put her head down on her arms and wept bitterly. Maude awkwardly patted her shoulders. "There, there. I know you love her. 'Tis a bad time."

Elizabeth sat up and dried her tears while still making soft sobbing sounds. "I can't stand for her to die. I just can't!"

"Maybe she'll live a while yet," Maude said. "Some days she seems stronger than others."

***

The next morning, a bright clear April day, Elizabeth found Maude helping Hannah to dress. "Oh, you look so much better today," Elizabeth said smiling.

"I feel better than I have in some time," Hannah said. "Maybe it's seeing you again. I'm so happy to have you near."

Elizabeth knew Hannah in no way meant to make her feel guilty for not being with her, but she wished with all her heart she'd come home sooner.

"We're going out in the carriage," Hannah said. "I don't want to put a damper on this lovely day, but I want to show you the cemetery. It's not very far from here. I've made all the arrangements to be buried beside my little Caroline, my husband and my mother."

"I didn't know...."

"I never mentioned it to you, but I went there from time to time to put flowers on their graves. Actually, my husband

and I weren't happily married, but he was my husband and the father of Caroline so I had him buried near her. My mother lived with me the last two years of her life. She'd had a hard life, poor darling. My father left her and went to California during the gold rush. He never returned and maybe it was just as well. Sadly, he was not a good man."

They drove slowly out to the edge of town to the cemetery. Maude hitched the horse to a tree and both she and Elizabeth helped Hannah down from the carriage. They walked as Hannah directed until they reached the gravesite marked for Hannah...between her mother and her child. It was on the slight rise of a hill. In the background Elizabeth saw a lake and a small, weather-beaten church with a cross on a steeple.

"Is that Reverend Bell's church?" Elizabeth asked.

"Yes." Hannah said. "My mother's funeral was conducted there years ago when the building was new. I never thought she was religious, but she asked for a minister to 'say words' over her. I don't remember that minister's name. He didn't know my mother so mostly he just read some comforting verses from the Bible."

"Shouldn't we go now, Miz Hannah?" Maude said. "You must be getting tired."

"I'm all right, but our mission has been accomplished, so yes we'll go now."

When they returned to the mansion, Hannah appeared exhausted and walked toward her bedroom, sometimes steadying herself by reaching out to the wall.

"Should I bring your lunch in?" Maude asked.

"Not yet. I want to rest some now," Hannah said.

Mary, the new young cook, stood in the doorway to the kitchen. She was a tall, thin girl with an eager face and nice brown eyes. "I made your favorite fish plate, Ma'am," she said.

"Thank you, Mary. I appreciate it. You cook so well, but for now...."

"I'll take you back to bed, Marme," Elizabeth said placing her arm around Hannah's waist to steady her.

When they reached the bedroom, Hannah undressed and slipped on a soft pink gown with Elizabeth's help. Before she lay back in the bed, she embraced Elizabeth. "Do take care of yourself, darling," she said. "I want you to know you've been a wonderful blessing to me. Because you're beautiful you'll have more chances with men than most, but take your time, choose wisely. A word of advice, don't throw yourself away on some worthless...." She became breathless, smiled and said, "Later."

"Marme," Elizabeth said, "when you wake from your nap, I want to tell you about my trip home and the people I met on The Sterling Expedition. I want to tell you about Will."

Less than an hour later Elizabeth found Hannah ashen, silent and very still. "Marme," she whispered, "Marme!"she called. She touched Hannah's cold arm. "No, no, no!" Elizabeth cried. She choked back tears hardly able to breathe. Impossible now, she felt such a need to be mothered...for connection and talk which could never happen again. She felt abandoned and hopelessly alone until she remembered Alice. Alice would understand.

Chapter Forty-Four

Will stood before a gilt-framed mirror near the front door and straightend his black bow tie. "I don't want to go," he said.

"I know, son," his mother said, "but Jerome is your boss and the party might even be enjoyable. I understand the Colberts entertain lavishly."

Will donned his hat and turned aside from the mirror now being totally ready. "I'm thankful Father recovered, but I wish he hadn't retired."

"Yes, it was a mistake, but at the time it seemed to be the thing to do."

Moments later the doorknocker fell heavily twice. Will said, "I'll go now. See you later."

"Try to enjoy yourself. It might not be so boring after all."

***

The prestigious red brick houses in Greek revival style known as "The Row" on Greenwich Village's North side housed the wealthy in the area. Entrances to the residences were flanked by Ionic and Doric columns and each boasted marble balustrades. Although it was not yet dark, gaslights glowed at the doorways.

"We have arrived," Jerome said. He was in great spirits from a glass of fine wine, but also because he believed his plan was unfolding.

Will remained silent while Jerome dismissed the driver of his brougham.

They walked the short distance toward the row. "It can make a great difference," Jerome said. "If you marry Delica Colbert, old Marlton Colbert will surely add to our company."

"You are assuming too much, Uncle Jerome. The young

lady and I have not met. She may not care for me. I may not care for her."

"Don't be foolish. You're quite eligible and so is she. What would prevent it?"

"Maybe not liking each other...love maybe."

"Will, my boy. You don't have to love her. You just have to marry her."

"Like you, perhaps?" Will asked.

"Well, I didn't do badly did I? Nelda is a good woman and a proper one with all the assets." He elbowed Will. "And, of course, there're always dolls for the taking. Like, say that pretty little gal you met on the Sterling."

Will made no reply and Jerome said nothing more until he'd rapped the doorknocker twice.

While they waited, Jerome said, "Soon you'll see Delica Colbert and realize that she could make you pretty happy. Yes, I'd say she has much to offer you as Nelda offered me. Colbert's textile mills are growing and shall we say 'mated' with ours...."

A formally dressed butler opened the door. "Good evening," he said, "do come in, gentlemen. May I take your hats?"

"Thanks, Ruthorford. This is my nephew Mr. Will Markham."

"Mr. Markham," Ruthorford said bowing slightly.

"I trust the festivities have not yet begun," Jerome said.

"No, Sir. Please, come this way."

Down the corridor past a lighted but empty parlor a doorway opened into a ballroom filled with esquisitiely dressed people of all ages. A young woman at a Chickering console played "Jeanie With the Light Brown Hair." Although the room was lined with chairs filled with the elegantly attired guests, only the softest murmurs could be heard.

Jerome and Will chose chairs near the entry and nodded to others who acknowledged their presence.

"That's your future bride," Jerome whispered, "that beauty is Delica Colbert. See how well she plays the piano."

"I see," Will said.

"The song fits her don't you think?" Jerome asked.

"She does have light brown hair if that's what you mean."

"Yes, pretty curls bound with black satin ribbon, and see how beautifully she's dressed in pale blue. The lace alone on that gown...well, her father is wealthy, you know."

"I think we should listen to her music," Will said.

Jerome nodded. "We perhaps are talking too much."

Will smiled. *We?* He kept the thought to himself.

When Delica finished playing she stood and bowed to the applause before taking a seat near a Patrician older dark-haired woman dressed in a pale yellow silk dress.

Nodding in Mrs. Colber's direction, Jerome whispered, "Her mother. See what a striking, aristocratic woman she is? And there is her distinguished father...."

Marlton Colbert stood near the piano. He raised his voice. "Welcome, ladies and gentlemen," he said. "Now Mr. Springfeld will play a polka for us. Shall we dance?" he asked. A broad smile covered his face.

Jerome said, "He's older and may want to consider retirement if...."

"He's coming this way," Will said.

"Yes. He's seen us. I mentioned you to him."

The room was filled with the joyful polka music. Couples danced, talked and laughed.

Before Marlton Colbert reached them, Jerome whispered once again, "Although older now, see he's tall and once quite handsome. You've seen his wife and, of course, Delica. Think what beautiful children you would have."

Will laughed.

"Don't laugh. I'm serious."

"I know you are. Well, Uncle, your salesmanship has worked at the mills."

"And it shall here, too," Jerome said.

Marlton Colbert extended his hand as he approached. "Wecome, Jerome Markham. I'm glad you could make the party. This young man is, I trust, your nephew...the buyer

353

and traveler to foreign ports."

"Yes. May I present Will, my brilliant up-and-coming partner in the company?"

Will extended his hand with the suprising statement *Up and coming partner* still ringing in his ears. "Mr. Colbert," he said bowing slightly to the older gentleman. *Up and coming partner? What did it mean?* Probably only a way to lead Colbert to think of him as desirable for his daughter.

"We must prepare the young to replace us in time," Jerome said.

"You're fortunate to have one who can," Colbert said.

Colbert hesitated then said, "I don't think you've been introduced to my family. Come, I'll introduce you."

"Yes, we'd be happy to meet them." Jerome smiled. Will thought this turn must delight him beyond description.

The polka ended but people remained on the dance floor laughing, catching their breath and waiting for the next dance that turned out to be a waltz.

Colbert led them down the side of the ballroom where his wife and daughter sat. Mrs. Colbert warmly greeted them. "So glad you could come," she said.

When introduced to Will, Delica extended her small, white hand. Will felt its warmth and softness. He knew she was showing acceptance of him beyond a nod or a smile. While her gesture surprised him, he thought from her blush that she was a very proper young woman.

The soft strains of a violin now brought forth the Blue Danube waltz. Will glanced at her. "May I have this dance?" he asked.

"Yes, with pleasure, sir." A flush of pink covered her face. She stood and placed her hand on his shoulder. She had seemed so child-like he had not realized how tall and willowy she was with curves that emphasized a shapely bustline and small waist.

When they began dancing he found her exceptionally light and agile. "You dance so well," he said.

"The music moves me," she said. Again pink tinged her cheeks.

"I enjoyed your piano playing," Will said.

"Thank you." She smiled at him and he saw her eyes were really lovely...like the color of wild violets.

"Do you speak French?" he asked.

"Only a very little. Of course, I must study it, but language is not easy for me. I'm better at my sewing."

"Sewing is important, too," Will said although he was disappointed she did not speak French.

"I suppose so," she said. "You know we have so many lessons to learn about so many things."

"Yes, a great many," he said, knowing that she meant all the proper ways one must live and behave in polite upper class society.

It seemed natural to stay with her during dinner. She spoke of social happenings in the city and of those on the calendar for an upcoming charity event. Then she smiled behind her napkin mentioning one unnamed socialite "who forgot to wear any jewelry at all to a theatre opening and was so embarrassed. Poor lady, I saw her that morning and know she knew not to wear pearls or diamonds early in the day. Perhaps, she simply forgot to add them later," Delica said as if to excuse the lady for the later omission.

Will thought of the far more stimulating conversations he'd had with Elizabeth. How different they were! Delica was a model young lady in New York society totally ingrained in proper conduct whose life experiences had prepared her for her expected role. He, as well, had been taught the social lessons. Certainly he knew never to smoke in the presence of a lady and to use his napkin not his sleeve to wipe his mouth. He smiled. Ah, yes, all the rules of conduct for upper class society!

He glanced at Delica's pretty face and momentarily felt sad for her. She was lovely and perhaps more intelligent than her conversation indicated. Will smiled remembering Elizabeth's spunk and the day she revealed Hannah educated her about her body. He wondered what she might be doing this very evening.

Delica was speaking of the button string of a friend.

"She is waiting for her Prince Charming to arrive to string the thousandth button."

Will knew buttons were of great importance, but he knew only vaguely of the button string. He understood a girl started stringing buttons on her special string with a large button and then friends and family added one button at a time until the string was completed but what then?

When he made no response, Delica said, "You know each button must be different and very pretty...small glass or jewel buttons with a loop shank...no sew-through buttons."

"And your friend has a completed string?"

"Yes, so she's ready for her groom-to-be to appear. My button string is also almost completed."

Was she suggesting something? Had she been prepared to see him as her "groom-to-be?" He thought now that Jerome and Marlton Colbert may have conspired to bring their wedding about.

When the dinner ended, Will joined the other gentlemen in a separate parlor from the ladies. Some men smoked. Will examined some books lying on a table and tried to calm himself. He would not be set up for marriage. That much he knew, but how to handle it with Jerome was another matter.

When the party was over and they had gone outside, Jerome asked Will if he had invited Delica to dinner and a show.

"No," Will said.

"I was afraid you'd fail to ask her so I invited her and her parents to join us for dinner next Tuesday evening. Of course, you and your parents will be there. You'll get to know Delica better then. She is beautiful, isn't she?"

"Yes, in a child-like sort of way," Will said.

"You do want a proper, innocent wife, don't you?"

"I'm not ready to marry," Will said.

"You will be. We'll work this out in a matter of months," Jerome said.

The driver appeared with the Brougham and they entered in silence. As they drove away, Will said, "You mentioned me as a partner."

"Yes, yes I did. After you and Delica are married you will need a more prominent position in the company." He paused to light a cigar. "Your cousin, Reginald, has been working hard, trying for a promotion, and I have to admit he's a very able young man, but I prefer you. I believe, given time, you'll find Delica is exactly the wife you need."

Chapter Forty-Five

The morning of Hannah's funeral the clouds came and then a downpour, but by afternoon the sun was out again. Elizabeth thought it was as if the sky lit up for Marme's sake. Soon a number of carriages arrived and many women who had worked for her...some with their husbands and young children came forward. The small church was filled with the fragrance of spring flowers and baskets of roses.

Beautifully dressed young women, who were strangers to her, spoke words of sympathy to Elizabeth as she stood near Hannah's coffin, and older women wrapped their arms about her as she sobbed.

The Reverend Bell came to her, a small man in a worn black suit. She saw the light in his eyes and felt the warmth in his touch as he took her hand. "You made a great difference in her life Elizabeth," he said. "She told me that before you came to her, she often felt life was boring. With you she felt the wells of her motherhood spring up and found a new reason to devote herself to something and someone of promise."

"Thank you," Elizabeth said, drying her tears. His words eased the pain in her heart more than he could know. She'd seen herself totally on the receiving end of Hannah's compassion and generosity, never considering she had made Hannah's life better. She breathed more deeply and relaxed.

"My wife and I will visit you this evening and we'll talk about the plans Mrs. Sloan made for you."

"I know something about it," Elizabeth said, "but do come."

Moments later the Reverend Bell stood at the pulpit. "We are gathered here to pay our last respects to a woman who loved and was loved by many of you. I did not known her long, but I soon realized despite her business, that this was a woman of worth. She told me to speak briefly, but to play the song she'd requested and to read her favorite scripture." He opened the Bible before him and read from the first chapter of Isaiah, verse eighteen. "Though your sins be as scarlet, they shall be made white as snow." He turned then to the choir before taking a seat in a chair near the podium.

The solemn words of "Amazing Grace," filled the church. Elizabeth was surprised to hear several especially beautiful voices rise above the others. The service ended with only the sounds of the small organ continuing the music while those present filed by Hannah's coffin. Some of them touched her still, white face colored now only by a little rouge. Her red hair was loose and lay on her shoulders against the pale blue dress draped on her thin frame.

When they walked out to the graveyard, Toby said, "It be just what she wanted. I think if she look down, she be happy as any angel up there."

In the evening the Reverend and Mrs. Bell arrived at Hannah's quarters. At first Elizabeth thought Mrs. Bell had not attended the funeral, but in seeing her now she knew that she was mistaken. The middle-aged lady stood out in the group because of her ivory skin, black hair and eyes so dark they appeared to be as black as her hair. She reminded Elizabeth of a matronly doll she'd seen in a Kansas City store window one Christmas.

"Elizabeth," Mrs. Bell said extending a warm hand to her. "You must always consider this your home. I will keep your room ready for you anytime you wish to return to stay with us. Mrs. Sloan had requested that we do so, and we are more than happy to comply. We want you to know that this is your home any time you wish to return."

"I'm grateful for all you've done to comfort Marme," Elizabeth said.

The Reverend Bell said, "We'll not actually move in until you leave for boarding school. I think you may be more comfortable here with just Maude and Mary at this time."

***

In the days following the funeral, Elizabeth walked

from room to room, hoping somehow that Hannah would be there, though knowing she would not. She opened the closet that held Hannah's dresses and clung to empty sleeves, trying to feel some warmth, some comfort but being left as empty as the cool sleeves.

Maude looked at her with sad eyes and Mary tried to prepare food she would like. For their sakes, Elizabeth tried not to cry in their presence. She thanked Mary for the good food, but ate little of it. She took Hannah's carriage and drove around to places they had been, but she could only weep on reaching the ice cream saloon. She passed on by the saloon and the stagecoach station where she and Monette had waved goodbye to Hannah on that first trip to the river. Later, back at home, she took the books Hannah had used to teach her as a child and read Hannah's notes in the margins.

She found a small portrait of Hannah and pressed it to her heart. Her books and the portrait, she would take with her to New York.

***

Reverend Bell had purchased the steamboat ticket in advance with the date of her planned departure on September 5, 1866.

Later as she dressed for bed she felt afraid considering she would be alone in New York. What if Madam Lemont did not meet her? But the moment passed. She was no longer a child, she was sixteen and would manage whatever happened.

More troubling to her was the fact she'd not heard from Will. Each day she looked for a letter, but none came. He had seemed so sincere. Had his Uncle Jerome set him against any serious relationship? Or had he simply forgotten her?

Chapter Forty-Six

A week after General Lee surrendered at the McLean Home in Appomattox, Emily and Sue Ling prepared to return to New York.

They were, however, unable to leave immediately. Wounded soldiers in their hospital still needed care.

Dr. Hallous, Minnie and the stiff-necked Symanthie were packing up, preparing to leave as well. All of them had somehow managed to build a bond as they struggled to save the lives of the men in blue. Death and dying had become a daily reality, but they were thankful for those who survived and healed.

During the last days after the war ended, a few wounded were brought in but the numbers dwindled to one every now and then. Some spoke sadly of comrades who had died needlessly, not having heard the news of the war being over. For the hospital staff, the larger part of the work at this time consisted in preparing transfers of all the patients to the permanent hospitals as soon as they could be moved.

In taking a rest from their work, Emily and Sue Ling sat outside on the wide porch steps. "A beautiful day," Sue Ling said.

"In more ways than one." Emily sighed. She pinned back a stray curl. "Thank God, the flow of blood has stopped. I can never forget the suffering we've seen, and I suppose it was as bad on the other side."

"Worse, some say. The South lacked many things needed for war. I wish all this had never happened, but it's over. It's over!" She stood, stretched up her arms, and shouted, "It's Ooooover!"

Emily laughed at her friend's dramatic outburst, though she well understood the release it brought her.

"I keep hoping Paul will show up, and I imagine you wouldn't mind seeing Benny. I really thought he was taken with you, Emily."

"Oh, he liked me well enough. I laughed at his jokes and I tried to take good care of him when he was here."

"I think you'll find out it was more than that."

"Be serious, Sue Ling. Why would he want me? I'm ugly."

"You are not ugly! Besides, inside you're beautiful and I think he realizes that."

"I hear someone calling for us. I suppose we must get back inside now." Emily rose from the steps. "You really think Benny could care for me?"

"Of course. And if not him, some other man with good sense."

***

The day before the hospital staff was to leave, Sue Ling stood on the veranda and looked all around the area hoping to see Paul approaching, but he was nowhere to be seen. In a kind of strange quietness, not one soul was seen anywhere near in the fields or coming down the narrow gravel road. Times before, the sick and wounded had been brought, in great numbers, down this road. Others, dirty, weary and stained with blood managed to walk across the fields. Even before the war ended, however, fewer had come to this hospital. More were being served in makeshift tents closer to the battle areas.

Later Emily sat alone on the steps and thought about what Sue Ling had said. She would like to see Benny. Spending time in his company was so pleasant. If only...no, she must not set herself up for a disappointment. She would return to Dr. Blackwell's Infirmary and resume nursing the poor people there.

At dusk a lone figure walked along the road and toward the hospital mansion. Emily was still sitting alone on the steps, but she waited watching the man as he approached. The walk looked familiar. Could it be—no, just someone who moved like Benny. Still, as he drew nearer she could see it was indeed a whiskered Benny! She wanted to run to greet him, but restrained herself.

Within minutes he walked into her presence. "Just the one I wanted to see," Benny said.

"Oh, me?"

"Yes. I would say could we take a little walk together, but I have walked too much the last day and a half."

"Then, do sit down. Could I get you something? Some food, or water?"

"Not now." He sighed and sat on the steps near her. "I wanted to see you, Emily. I've been thinking of you ever since I left here. You were so good to me and—well, being with you felt so right, so comfortable."

"I'm glad," she said. "You were fun to be with despite your suffering."

"I didn't notice the suffering as much when you were around," he said.

"I'm glad."

"Emily, do you think it's too soon for us to consider seeing each other?"

"Seeing each other?"

"Well, seeing each other back in New York. You do plan to go back there, don't you?"

"I do."

"Soon as you'd be comfortable with it, there's something I'd like you to say."

"What?" Her heart was pounding. Tears crept into her eyes. She looked down at her hands to prevent his seeing them.

" 'I do' " He reached for her hand. "At our wedding, I mean. That's if you'll have me. You know I'm in the militia so I won't always be home."

"Are you sure you'll have me?" she asked. "You know how I look."

"I love how you look, but I wouldn't be marrying you for how you look. I'd be marrying you for you. I can't think of anyone I'd rather be near day in and day out."

"But you just said you'd be gone at times, so maybe you could stand me some days," she teased, feeling breathlessly happy.

"Emily, may I hold you for just a moment? It would mean so much to this tired, dirty soldier."

She stood and stretched out her arms. They did not hear Sue Ling calling from the doorway. Seeing their embrace, Sue Ling quietly closed the door and went back inside.

***

On the day the hospital staff was to leave Sue Ling received a letter from Paul. She opened it with eager hands only to soon press the pages to her chest and break into sobs. Emily went to her and asked softly, "What? What's wrong?"

"Read it. Read it!" Sue Ling cried. "How could he? I don't understand."

Emily took the pages and read:

Dear Sue Ling,

How can I begin to tell you this? I didn't mean for it to happen, and never thought it would, but I have fallen in love with someone else...a beautiful Southern girl. I would tell you the circumstances but I doubt you would care to know.

I feel badly about hurting you, but dear Sue Ling, I would hurt you more if I pretended what I no longer feel. You are a beautiful, wonderful girl and some fortunate man will win your heart and love you, as you deserve to be loved.

Forgive me if you can.

Paul

Sue Ling ran blindly from the room and bumped into first Symanthie and then Dr. Hallous. Symanthie yelled at her, "Where do you think you're going?"

Dr. Hallous held her at arms length. "What's wrong, Sue Ling? Has someone hurt you? I'll tear the brute limb from limb." His voice was teasing, but then he gathered her to himself."Little firecracker, we'll get them."

She allowed him to hold her for a long moment before breaking free and running through the house and up the stairs to her bedroom.

When Sue Ling was gone, Emily said, "She's been very badly hurt. You should not tease or yell at her. The man she loves is in love with someone else. Please, be kind."

"I'm sorry," Dr. Hallous said.

"So am I," Symanthie said in a voice softer than she usually spoke. Emily looked at her twice. Could this mean old nurse really have a heart after all? Maybe some man had failed her in the past.

***

In the early afternoon the hospital staff said goodbye to the stately, white mansion and departed their separate ways in carriages. The now dry-eyed, but sad Sue Ling and the happy but quiet Emily were headed back to New York. Minnie was going to Chicago and the complaining Symanthie to Chicago as well. Dr. Hallous, in a separate carriage, was returning to Boston.

Before he left, Dr. Hallous walked over to Sue Ling's carriage and reached for her hand. "You were the finest nurse I've ever had to work beside me. When I get to New York, as I do from time to time, I'll come by The Infirmary to see you."

Sue Ling smiled. "I think we worked well to-gether...once I got you to wash your hands."

They both laughed. "I'll see you," he said and walked over to his carriage. Once inside he waited for the other carriages to leave before departing himself.

A light rain began falling as Emily looked back at the old mansion. She thought the raindrops were like the many tears the house had weathered inside those stately walls over the past four years. She sighed deeply. "Dear God," she prayed, "let there never, ever, be another war."

Chapter Forty-Seven

On the day of her departure from Kansas City, the Reverend Bell drove Elizabeth to the wharf. He placed a gentle hand on her arm as she prepared to leave. "Do take care. I'll be in touch and I'll pray for you."

"Thank you," Elizabeth said.

Earlier she had said her farewells to Alice, Toby and Little Mama.

"I'll be back to visit at Christmas," Elizabeth said. "We'll put up a tree in your cabin and have our presents. Toby, will you wait until I return to get the tree? Like always, I want to go with you into the woods to select our tree."

"I sho will," he said, "we likes our walks in the woods anytime and 'specially to get our Christmas tree...that be great."

Alice smiled and clasped her hands together. "We be looking forward to then, won't we Little Mama?"

"Don't ya'll forget my Christmas apples," Little Mama said. "I can almost taste them right now."

On her drive back into town, Elizabeth decided she would bring not just one or two apples to Little Mama, but a lovely basket full of them that she'd personally select at the market.

***

Her first day on the steamer, Elizabeth wore a bronze-colored dress with ruffles at the neck and the cuffs. She also wore a gold locket Hannah had often worn. She liked to think of it as Hannah's arms about her neck.

Before she left, Elizabeth told the minister, "I am expecting a letter to arrive one of these days." She realized that letter might never come as almost four months had passed since she'd met Will and his family.

"Don't worry," Reverend Bell said. "I'll send your mail. And do let me know of anything you might need that we may not have considered."

When the steamer was under way, Elizabeth stood on the deck and looked out at the rippling water. She thought of Will. Vaguely, she remembered he was going to Europe. Perhaps, that had delayed him. She still dared to hope.

On this trip Elizabeth no longer felt ugly. She received many admiring glances and polite offers to escort her to dinner, or help her in a number of ways simply for her attention. She smiled, but declined each offer. At this time she preferred to be alone to think and to read rather than to socialize.

***

On September 25, after having changed from steamboat to trains Elizabeth arrived in New York at last. She felt a sense of recognition when she saw the great New York City skyline, and wondered why she should feel that way. Perhaps, she thought, it was only that she had seen photographs of the place. She had a moment of panic in the midst of the crowd and all the noise of business. What if for some reason Madame Lemont failed to arrive? She chided herself. She would find a way, if not to the school, back into the arms of those she loved in Kansas City. She was not without funds. She would only need to keep her wits about her.

In standing on the platform of the station, she thought surely her imagination was playing tricks because even the odors of the city seemed vaguely familiar. She stood beside a bench and waited to be met by Madame Lemont. As prearranged, she wore a royal blue outfit, including hat and gloves. She was shaking her head in an effort to clear her mind at the odd sense of recognition of the city, when a most proper-appearing thin lady dressed in a fine wine-colored dress with hat to match, called her name and spoke to her in French saying that she must be Miss McKelvy.

Elizabeth smiled broadly, relieved, and responded in French, but then spoke in English. "Thank you so much for meeting me, Madame Lemont."

"My driver is here," Madame Lemont said. She turned to the stocky, gray-haired man who stood near her. "Horace," she said, "Take care of locating the young lady's luggage."

"Isn't this a glorious day, Miss McKelvy? It's such a wonderful time for the American Jockey Club to hold its first meet. We shall see some aspects of it as we travel to the school." She lifted her slightly pointed nose and pursed her thin lips, "The cream of society will participate," she said. "Of course, I was invited by the Belmont family to join them, but I declined." She took a lacy handkerchief from her fine leather purse and touched her cheeks under each eye as if dabbing tears. "Sadly, since my dear husband passed away, I haven't the inclination to attend such affairs."

"I'm sorry," Elizabeth said vaguely, softly. Part of her attention was drawn to the hustle and bustle in the station with more people mingling than she had ever seen before in one place. In the background she heard shouting voices as men unloaded cargo.

Immediately outside the train station, peddlers competed in trying to sell their wares to incoming passengers, Their high-pitched voices mingled with the pandemonium of cries from a group of young men quarreling over some unseen object.

"We're ready," Madame Lemont said. "Horace has found your trunk and loaded it into the carriage."

Soon they rode away from the dock with Madame Lemont still speaking of the races.

"This morning every house lining Fifth Avenue from Washington Square to Madison Square will have carriages leaving their residences. A sight to see with the burnished harnesses buckled on the sleek horses and the liveried grooms driving in grand style. Thousands will go. Picnic baskets will be filled with marvelous foods. Even the poor will go in shabby vehicles. We, however, shall not go. We must be about our work."

She again took her fine, lacy handkerchief and dabbed at her cheeks under her eyes, though again Elizabeth saw no tears.

Seemingly about an hour and some distance from the noise of the city, they came to rows of large houses set back from fenced-in lawns. Some houses in gray stone seemed to fit no particular style of architecture, but Elizabeth recognized two red brick houses sitting side by side as Queen Anne structures. The chateau at the far end of the street bore a sign reading "Madame Lemont's School For Young Ladies." So they had arrived at last.

Elizabeth thought the grand house with pointed arches and stone vaults, seemed at once impressive and somewhat gloomy. "What are the carved lizards near the door...that is, why are they there?"

Madame Lemont stiffened."Well, my dear, I would have thought you would have known from reading French history. I had understood you were an excellent student."

Elizabeth frowned. Was she supposed to know every-thing from French history? She said, "Apparently, that's something I missed."

"Well, this time I shall tell you, but in the future you must look up information. One must take responsibility for one's own learning."

Anger flooded Elizabeth. "Show me the book and I will find out for myself."

"Since you are new, I'll tell you this time. Do you see what appears to be flames around the salamander? Back in the sixteenth century people believed salamanders enjoyed being put into a fire; the hotter the better. Francis I took the salamander as his trademark and had crowns put on the ones lining his staircase and in other parts of his chateau at Blois in the Chateau Country. You may travel there some day. Oh, perhaps I should say that some believe salamanders are mythical rather than real animals. Since in reality we can't go back to the sixteenth century, we may never know for sure."

Horace brought Elizabeth's trunk on a wheeled cart to a side door. She saw him flush-faced lift the heavy trunk in through a door.

Since Elizabeth had made no response Madame asked, "Now do you understand?"

"I shall never forget salamanders as long as I live," Elizabeth said.

Madame Lemont seemed momentarily stunned. Was this young woman being insolent? She let it pass. Time would tell the character of this one as it did with all the young ladies who came under her roof.

Once they were inside the grand entry hall, Elizabeth met with other young women. Madame Lemont introduced her to Katherine Smith, Joyce Mae Williams and Cornelia Jones. Cornelia, who appeared to be the younger of the three, stood out from the other two because of her freckles and flaming, kinky hair. She stood with her head cocked to one side and twisted a curl over her forehead. Elizabeth thought she looked sad.

"Stop that, Cornelia!" Madame Lemont said. "It isn't ladylike. A Lemont girl is a lady. All of my girls are ladies, not nervous children who twist their hair."

Katherine giggled softly behind long, slender fingers. She was tall, dark-eyed and feminine in her graceful movements despite being overly broad in her shoulders.

"Katherine is quite knowledgeable about French history," Madame Lemont said.

"Thank you Madame. It is due to your fine teaching," Katherine said.

Joyce Mae whom Elizabeth thought most plain with limp brown hair and pale blue eyes, said, "I'll show you where we study and sleep."

"Joyce Mae is the practical one around here," Madame said.

So it was that Elizabeth met her classmates. She had expected a larger number and now wondered how Madame Lemont could live in such grand style.

Later, Elizabeth wondered even more about the small

number of students. In the large room, probably once a ballroom, there were spaces and furniture for twelve residents. Each section could be made private by the drawing of heavy brown curtains. The far side of the room was given up to wash basins and dressing tables.

If Madame Lemont had a need to reduce expenses it was not evident at dinner. A delicious meal of roast duckling and vegetables along with prepared fresh fruit in a sauce graced the long table. Celine, an ordinary appearing servant girl in uniform, quietly served them.

Each student sitting at the table told Elizabeth something of herself. Katherine and Joyce Mae had come from Philadelphia, Pennsylvania, where they as neighbors had lived at home with their apparently prosperous parents. Cornelia said, "My parents gave me into adoption. My foster mother died and my foster father sent me here after her death." She reached to twist her hair, but apparently thought better of it quickly putting her hand in her lap.

Elizabeth wanted to touch her, to comfort her, but she sat across the table from her. "Like you, Cornelia," Elizabeth said, "I have no natural family. I did have a sister, but we were separated and I have no knowledge of where she might be."

"Well," Madame said, "if one has friends one does not require a family. No family at all is to be greatly preferred over a bad one. Forget feeling sorry for yourselves. How you live your life is completely up to you."

Elizabeth realized in that moment she was considered an adult. She had always depended on others for guidance but now she must think and plan for herself. It both frightened and excited her.

Chapter Forty-Eight

The first day of class Madame Lemont appeared quite regal seated in a great chair on a platform in front of the class. Once again she was dressed in fine clothing. A cream colored silk dress clung to her thin figure and long crystal beads swung below her small breasts. She took a lacy handkerchief from her pocket and laid it across her lap.

Madame cleared her voice and looked across the room waiting for total silence that came quickly. "Today," she said, "we shall cover some material on history. In this case, on the Middle Ages. Cornelia, how was the world governed by the barbarians different from the one ruled by Rome or Constantinople?"

"I don't remember. I couldn't keep it in my mind."

"I thought so," snapped Madame. Katherine can you tell us?"

"Yes, ma'am. The barbarians ruled by force without the consent of the people under their rule. A barbarian chief was limited only by the customs and traditions of his tribal code. He could do anything to anyone as he wished."

Madame smiled. "Thank you, Katherine. I knew you would get it right. Now Elizabeth, I trust you read the lesson."

"I did, ma'am."

"How did we come by the term 'vandals'?"

"Vandals, a barbaric tribe, went into Gaul where they stole, smashed and burned destroying everything in their way."

"Yes, yes and so?"

"That's where we came by the word 'vandals'"

"Very well."

The class continued into the hour. Then with a break, a gloomy appearing gentleman came to teach rhetoric. Elizabeth was surprised to hear his speech which was clear and pleasant to the ear. He asked no questions, but simply lectured for a half hour.

"Now, young ladies," he said, "open your Botany books and look at the sketches on page 17." Again, he asked no questions but lectured for another half hour, arose from the chair and left giving no assignment.

When he was gone, Elizabeth asked. "Are we to continue to study from page seventeen?"

"Yes," Joyce Mae said. "He told us in the beginning to read ten pages for every lesson."

Elizabeth found she hardly needed the French lessons, but attended class dutifully as expected. In fact, she enjoyed hearing and speaking the language as well as reading French literature. She also enjoyed the classes in music and dancing. She found, however, German difficult to pronounce, and was corrected more than once in a fit of temper by Madame. She was bothered little by the screaming woman's attack, but she had become increasingly disturbed by Madame's treatment of Cornelia.

After one particularly brutal attack on the shy Cornelia, Elizabeth took her aside after class and offered to tutor her.

"I'm stupid, Elizabeth," Cornelia said. "It would be too boring for you."

"We'll see about that." Elizabeth said. "We'll start tonight after dinner."

"It will be all right if you give up on me. I'll understand."

"I will not give up on you," Elizabeth said. "I know you can learn."

"I try, but somehow I can't remember."

After dinner, Elizabeth took Cornelia to a far corner of the room where they studied. Elizabeth soon realized that Cornelia's mind wandered from the lesson although she seemed to try to stay on the subject.

"Maybe," Elizabeth said, "we should just talk awhile first. Tell me what is bothering you. Can you do that?"

Cornelia broke into tears. "I feel...I know nobody cares about me since my mother died. I don't know what is to become of me. Everything I do seems hateful to my father and now to Madame."

"Cornelia, I barely know you and I like you. Let me help you learn your lessons and then you...maybe you won't have to go back home. Perhaps, you can find work as a teacher somewhere."

"I can't learn, so how can I do that?" she sobbed. "I would kill myself except I'm afraid I would go to hell."

"You're not going to kill yourself. You're going to learn tomorrow's lesson and surprise that witch Lemont when she asks you a question."

Cornelia laughed. "You're funny," she said.

"Enough laughter for now. Open your book."

Elizabeth soon realized Cornelia needed everything broken down into small sections or she would forget details. They spent two hours on seven pages of the Middle ages, but Elizabeth was satisfied when they finished that Cornelia could answer any question Madame might ask her.

***

The following day Madame Lemont came to class in a soft pink dress, took out her usual lacy handkerchief, laid it across her lap and looked across the room at her students. Satisfied that all were present, she fastened her glance on Cornelia.

"Now," Madame said, "let's find out how England first came by her navy. Cornelia, you begin."

"The Saxon King, Alfred the Great...."

"Yes, yes what did he do and why?"

"He saw that he was losing a battle to pirates called Northmen or Danes...."

"So, so get to the point if you can."

"He decided fighting them on water would be best."

"And, and?"

"He built boats, larger boats than the Danes had and that was the beginning of the English navy."

"Well, well, I was finally able to pull the information from you. Now let's see if you can tell us how knights who went into battle were able to distinguish their own men. Remember they were covered in suits of armor."

Elizabeth saw Cornelia frown, but before the girl could speak, Elizabeth said, "Madame, I believe that's in the next lesson, but I can tell you. They designed a figure like a lion or a rose and called it their coat of arms." Elizabeth smiled. "I became interested so I read ahead last night."

Madame sat rigidly and dabbed at first one cheek then the other with her lacy handkerchief, then she said abruptly. "Very good."

Katherine said, "Madame, I think we all should be pleased that Cornelia, for a change, learned her lesson. Of course, Elizabeth helped her."

Madame glared at Elizabeth. "Who gave you permission?"

"I didn't know I needed permission. I think what we have seen very clearly is that Cornelia knew the lesson."

"Each young lady is to learn on her own," Madame said. "You are no teacher, Elizabeth."

"What difference does it make how one learns a lesson? The point is to learn, isn't it?"

"Of course, of course, but you are here to develop your own learning, and fussing over Cornelia is not part of the plan. Cornelia must learn the lesson on her own. Do you understand?"

"I do understand," Elizabeth said.

Later, back in the living quarters, Elizabeth said. "Listen, I suggest that we can all help each other. Let's study together. Each one can read a section and share that with the rest of us. That way we'll finish our lessons sooner."

"Madame will not approve of that," Katherine said. "She made it clear she wants independent study."

"What about you Joyce Mae, would you like to study together?"

"I would like it, but I'm afraid Madame...."

"All right," Elizabeth said, "I thought you might think that way. I'm going to study with Cornelia whether Madame Lemont likes it or not."

"You could be expelled," Katherine said.

"There are other schools," Elizabeth said. "I doubt she will expel us, but if she should, I'll at least know I've done the right thing. Cornelia and I are going to be teachers and we both will learn the lessons here or elsewhere."

"I...." Cornelia began, but Elizabeth took her arm and squeezed it as a signal to be quiet.

Later, when they were alone Cornelia said, "My father might not pay for another school."

"We'll convince him if we must. Besides, I doubt Madame will want to lose the money we pay. She seems quite short on students now."

"Oh," Cornelia said, "she doesn't rely entirely on us for her money. She has a man friend that Joyce Mae says gives her money."

"How would she know that?"

"She was passing in the hallway when Madame and the man stepped out from Madame's room. She saw him kiss her and hand her a package of money. You know, money with a band around it."

"Wasn't Madame angry that Joyce Mae saw her?"

"She didn't see her. But we have seen the man before. He comes to take Madame to church on Sundays and to prayer meetings at times. She has even introduced us to him."

"Really? And what is his name?"

"Harry Hill. Joyce Mae read in the newspaper about a very unsavory Harry Hill who has a dance hall, but probably some other man having the same name.

***

Elizabeth continued to tutor Cornelia, and to her surprise Madame said no more about it. Did Madame, in thinking it over, decide she might look better to Cornelia's father if the girl left with good marks? Or did she not want another upstaging in the classroom by Elizabeth? Whatever it was, Elizabeth was pleased.

376

On one snowy day in early December, Elizabeth decided to take a walk. She dressed warmly and walked out the door when she, with head down, bumped into someone. "Oh," she said, "I'm sorry...oh, Will! Will! What a surprise. I thought you had forgotten me."

"I tried," he confessed, "but you were unforgettable. I know I never wrote to you, but I went to Kansas City looking for you." He took her arm. "Shall we take a walk or were you going somewhere in particular?"

"I...I," she said, breathlessly. She had not remembered how pleasant his deep voice was. In seeing now how handsome he looked in his fine coat and leather cap she could hardly breathe. So he had found her unforgettable! How amazingly wonderful!

"You were going somewhere special and I interrupted your plan. I'm sorry."

"No, I merely meant to take a walk. I think the falling snow is so beautiful I wanted to be in it. Then I meant to stop at a little place down the way and have a cup of hot chocolate."

He smiled. "Great! We can do that. I want to talk with you."

He stooped to make a snowball and toss it hitting her arm. She laughed, made a snowball and hit his leather cap knocking it at an angle. He straightened it, laughed and chased her. They ran and played until they gasped for breath in the frigid air. Then they walked the rest of the way to the small café.

Inside, the building was warm. They shed their coats and hung them on hooks near the door. No one else except the owner, a bearded young man, was present.

"Too cold for some to be out today," the owner said, "but I'm glad you made it. Getting too quiet in here." Elizabeth hoped he would not expect them to talk with him. She wanted to hear what Will had to say.

"It is cold indeed," Will said. "We'd like two mugs of hot chocolate."

When the man was gone, Will looked into Elizabeth's

face searchingly. "How do you keep getting more beautiful?" he asked.

"By the same means you get more handsome," she said, and they laughed. He reached across the table and squeezed her hand.

The man returned and set two mugs of steaming hot chocolate in front of them. "Here," he said, "this should warm you up." When they only smiled at him, he returned to the back of his business where they heard him whistle softly. Then they heard the clang of a fallen pan followed by the man's colorful exclamations in French. Will and Elizabeth laughed.

"Elizabeth," Will said reaching for her hand, "I went to Hannah's place and learned what had happened and where you were. The Reverend Bell said I might want to visit with the former slaves you loved if I planned to see you. He was certain you would want news of them first hand. I did just that."

Elizabeth sat forward, eyes wide "Really? You saw Alice and Toby and Little Mama!?"

"I did. I found them warm and charming. I stayed more than an hour in their cabin. Alice told me how you had been brought out there at age five and how the old woman mistreated you."

"Oh." Elizabeth swallowed. She didn't think Alice would have told him about her rape and the murder, but she wondered. "What else did she tell you?"

"What a fine little girl you were. She said you were the smartest child a person could know. I got the distinct impression that she likes you." He teased.

Relief flooded Elizabeth. Alice had not told him! When she could regain her composure, she said, "Without Alice and her family I could be dead. I love all three of them dearly. They are my family."

"I told my parents I had found you. They want to see you. Perhaps, we could all attend the theatre. The famous Madame Ristori is playing Medea."

"Yes, yes," Elizabeth cried, "I would love it."

"We should have dinner at the Clarendon Hotel before time for the theatre. Would leaving the school early and returning late be a problem for you?"

"I won't allow it to be," Elizabeth said.

He laughed. "Now I remember what a determined young lady you can be."

"I think Madame Lemont may not present me with a problem in any event since I will be being, in her mind, chaperoned."

"If this coming Saturday night will please you, we'll come for you at six."

Elizabeth smiled. "I'll look forward to it. Do tell your parents I'll be happy to see them again."

Chapter Forty-Nine

Elizabeth had lived in elegance at Hannah's but she still found herself charmed by the soft gaslights, crystal vases of fresh flowers, and dark, carved furniture in the grand hotel. She thought that the black and gold oriental carpet in the lobby was especially beautiful.

In the dining room the tables were covered in white linen and candles flickered with soft flames in silver holders. Elizabeth smelled the scent of good food—possibly roast pork, beef and yeast breads, and there was definitely the sweet scent of chocolate.

She was so thrilled to be in the company of Will and his parents that she had not thought that she was hungry until the delicious aromas awakened her appetite.

When they were seated for dinner, Mr. Markham asked their preferences, but when none of a specific nature were named, he ordered dinner which included beef, pork and fresh salmon, as well as, a host of vegetables and fruit side dishes.

While they waited for the food to arrive, Mrs. Markham asked Elizabeth how her studies were progressing at school and whether she liked living in New York.

"Fine," Elizabeth said, "but at school there are only a few of us. Just four so perhaps we get more attention than if all twelve spaces were filled."

"Only four students?" Mr. Markham asked.

"That's right. I wondered how Madame Lemont could manage financially, but one of the girls told me her friend...some man named Harry Hill provides for her financially, at least to some extent. He comes in his excellent carriage for her on Sunday and they go to church. Other times they go to prayer meetings, so it would seem."

"Harry Hill?" Will asked. "There is a well-known Harry Hill who is said to be a God-fearing man, but who is in reality, an unsavory character. Would that be the big man who just entered the dining room?"

"Why, yes it is!" Elizabeth said.

"The round, short man with him is Boss Tweed," Will said.

"Boss Tweed? I've never seen him before."

"Boss Tweed operates a corrupt political machine," Mr. Markham interjected, "but let me tell you Harry Hill is no saint. I wonder if Madame Lemont really knows this man."

"I understand that she met him in church and they often attend church together. Still, if he is not a nice man...." Elizabeth frowned.

"Well, present company excepted," Mrs. Markham said, "some men lie about their business and their source of income, if it suits their needs. Perhaps, he would fear she wouldn't accept his company if she knew the dirty side of his life."

"My dear," Mr. Markham said, "the newspapers have written of him. I know you seldom read such articles, preferring the society pages."

"So could Madame Lemont." Mrs. Markham said.

"In any event, articles have been written about him and his notorious dance hall. Perhaps, the sad thing is that men considered respectable, frequent the place mingling with a host of fighters, gamblers and thieves such as 'Big Nose Bunker,' and prostitutes like 'Sadie the Goat.' "

"Sadie the Goat?" Elizabeth laughed. "What a strange name."

"She's called that because she lowers her head and butts like a goat when fighting."

"Really!"

"Well, she's not alone in that crowd of female fighters," Mr. Markham said, warming to his story. "Take 'Gallus Mag,' six feet tall, supports her skirt with suspenders and is mean as the devil himself. She arms herself with a pistol and a club, works as a bouncer. Then there's 'Hell-Cat Maggie.' She had her teeth filed to points which served her well in a fight with 'Sadie-the-Goat'. She bit off one of Sadie's ears." He leaned back in his chair and laughed.

"Oh, stop, stop!" Mrs. Markham said. "This is really too much for Elizabeth, and I don't care for it myself."

"I know, my dear. You prefer the beautiful and sweet things in life, but the dark side is quite real."

"I prefer not to think on it," Mrs. Markham said.

"Do you plan to continue to stay at the school with Madame Lemont after hearing all of this?" Will asked, laughing.

"Yes...well, as long as Madame Lemont goes to church and doesn't bring any of her beau's crazies to the school. I will graduate in the spring and I have a friend there I want to help until we both are prepared to become teachers."

The steaming dishes of food arrived. The feast of roast beef, roast pork, fresh salmon and yeasty rolls gave off savory odors. Peaches, dark, silky plums and golden bananas were presented in a shimmering crystal bowl, making the green and white vegetables pale by comparison.

"Perhaps, now," Mrs. Markham said, "we can enjoy some of the more lovely things in life."

Following dinner, they returned to the carriage and drove to the theatre to see Madame Ristori's performance in Medea. The spectacular performance charmed but horrified Elizabeth.

Later, she said, "How could that mother do that? How could any mother murder her children?"

"She was driven mad by the rejection of her lover," Will said.

"If one man rejected her, it doesn't mean every man would," Elizabeth said. "She was really insane to think that way."

"Yes, she was, but she was madly in love," Will said.

"If someone doesn't love you, it won't work. No use being silly about it," Elizabeth said.

"Oh, then you don't believe in passionate, undying love?" Will asked, teasingly.

"Sure," Elizabeth said, "if both people are in love, but that one-way thing is not any good, and sure is no reason for killing children."

"I think you would make a good mother," Mrs. Markham said.

"If I should ever marry, perhaps."

"You are more likely to win a husband than any young woman I can imagine," Will said.

Elizabeth smiled. "Well...we'll see."

***

The next day Elizabeth set to wondering how Hannah could have liked a person like Madame Lemont. She decided to ask Madame how they came to be friends.

"Oh," Madame Lemont said, "we weren't really friends. We were two young women in the same school. She knew my dream was to have my own boarding school for young women. I can't think why she turned away from teaching and became—a—well, immoral person."

Elizabeth flushed. "She was a very kind and loving woman. I see you didn't know her well. An individual can be a bad person in more ways than one," Elizabeth said. She wanted to accuse Madame regarding her relationship with Harry Hill, but she denied herself that confrontation. She knew Madame held the key to whether or not she and Cornelia graduated and that was more important than saying what could have caused her to be expelled. Besides, she had the answer she sought. Clearly, Hannah and Lemont only knew each other in a surface relationship.

Will visited Elizabeth almost every day for a month. Then he told her he had to go on another business trip and would miss her very much until he could return.

"I'll miss you, too," Elizabeth said. "I like talking with you about my lessons and so many other things—like what we read in the newspapers."

"You're very intelligent, Elizabeth. Many girls your age have no interest in deep subjects. Even some of my male friends lose interest pretty quickly in matters that require contemplation. I do feel fortunate when I can spend time with you."

"Oh, Will, you make me think I'm smarter than I am," she said, smiling up at him.

Although, they read some very romantic French poetry together, Will never attempted to embrace her. She thought he wanted to hold her, but if so, he restrained himself.

"I'll be gone until just before Christmas," he said taking her hand and looking into her eyes. "Don't go away."

"But I am going away, Will. That is, I'm going to Kansas City to be with Alice, Toby and Little Mama."

"But you'll will be back?"

"Yes, until we graduate it May."

"Elizabeth," he said, "I want you to know I care very much for you. I hope you'll still want to see me when I return."

"Will, I think you're shy," she said.

"You're so wonderful I—well, I don't think you realize how special you are."

"You've stood apart too long, Will Markham. Come here," she said, reaching out to him pulling him into her arms and kissing him full on his lips.

"Elizabeth, Elizabeth," he said, breathlessly. "I adore you."

She kissed him again. "Don't forget me," she said.

He laughed then. "Forget you? Impossible. In fact, I tried that earlier and found I couldn't."

"Have a safe trip, dear Will. Take care of yourself and come back to me."

"I'll be back for sure," he said.

"I'll be waiting."

"I don't think I'm good enough for you, but you make me very happy," he said.

"Must I kiss you again, Will, to make you know how I feel?"

He smiled and held her in a long embrace, kissing her with more passion than she had imagined. She was so warmed with that special feeling, she was reluctant to draw apart from him. For so many reasons now, she knew that she would find it much harder to lose him, if that should happen, than it had been in losing Donato Seldeni. She thought they seemed to be so right for each other. Was this then undying love? One that she would hold in her heart in a special place no matter what? She felt there was no way she would ever completely get over wanting Will Markham. But why think that way? He said he would be back, even though he still had not said he loved her. Or maybe he did, but just without the words. Didn't 'adore' mean 'love'? She wanted him to return soon, although she knew it would be weeks to months before she could see him again.

***

Will had not returned from Europe when Elizabeth left New York for Kansas City. She wished he could be with her as she celebrated Christmas with Alice, Toby and Little Mama. He said in his letters that he would probably be delayed until the first of the year in returning to New York. Christmas without the family would be his first, he wrote, and, "of course, time away from you when I want so much to be with you."

Elizabeth arrived back in Kansas City on a snowy day, and paid a hack to take her to what she still considered Hannah's quarters although the Bells now lived there according to plan. She had notified them she would be coming, but was uncertain of the date so they should not plan to meet her.

When she arrived at the mansion, she saw lights and activity now as a hotel in what had been Hannah's brothel. Mixed feelings assailed her. She liked seeing the lights and people moving about in what had been closed and dark during her last visit, but there was no music and no Hannah.

Mrs. Bell greeted her at the door with a big smile, a quick embrace and a hearty "Welcome!"

"How was your trip?" Reverend Bell asked.

"Good. I'm just a bit tired," Elizabeth said.

"Would you like to rest first, Elizabeth?" Mrs. Bell asked. "We'll have dinner in a little more than an hour."

385

"That would be fine, thank you," she said, removing her brown knit hat and matching scarf.

She had conflicting feelings in seeing that the Reverend and Mrs. Bell had not changed the appearance of Hannah's quarters except for some books and other personal items of their own. The familiar furnishings made her sad since they were empty reminders of Hannah, but at the same time she thought she would have felt disappointed had everything appeared totally different.

In her bedroom, when she took off her coat and hung it in the closet, she saw the small royal blue dress with white collar Hannah had bought for her years ago. Her throat ached with the pain of her loss. She wept silently as she closed the closet door.

***

On December 23, Elizabeth drove Hannah's carriage out to visit with Alice, Toby and Little Mama. The snow was still on the ground and a mist of sleet was falling. Still, she was determined not to let it cancel her plans.

When she arrived, she was greeted with hugs and laughter and once again called 'chile.' She knew she was no longer a child, but somehow in their arms she felt like one again.

"Oh," Elizabeth said, "I'm so happy to see you. I wouldn't have wanted to be anywhere else at Christmas."

Toby said, "I almost went and got our tree, but I didn't. We gonna go pick it out together."

"It's really cold outside," Alice said. "Do you suppose tomorrow might be any better?"

"I can go if you can," Elizabeth said, touching Toby's arm.

"We'll do it then. Right now." He put on his ragged coat. Little Mama handed him the red woolen cap she had made for him. He pulled the cap down over his graying hair and over his ears. "I be ready," he said.

Seeing his ragged coat and his worn boots, Elizabeth

was glad she had put money in Christmas cards adequate for each of them to buy new, warm clothes. She was, however, holding back on presenting them until Christmas Day. Knowing that she had been able to buy a number of smaller presents for each of them as well, and the basket of apples for Little Mama made her happy. It seemed hard to wait for Christmas Day.

"Let's go find our tree," Elizabeth said.

They left the cabin and faced the chill of the blowing sleet. "Let's run," Elizabeth said, "that'll help keep us warm."

"I wish I could, Chile, but ole rheumatism done got in me."

"Oh, Toby, I'm sorry. Maybe we shouldn't try to find our tree after all."

"We gonna find it," Toby said. "I sorta know where there's a drove of good'uns not too far up yonder hill."

Elizabeth ran a short distance ahead, but returned to walk beside Toby. "Are you all right?" she asked.

"Now that you be home, how could I be anything but all right?"

"Oh, Toby. You know I love you same as if you were my father."

"I knows that. You been our chile since you first came here."

The sleet let up and a pale sun slipped through the clouds as they continued their trek across the icy stubble toward the patch of forest on the hill.

When they arrived at a grove of cedars, Elizabeth ran to a lovely full tree. "Would this one be right?" she asked.

"It be a pretty one, but we need a littler one to fit in the cabin. See what else you can find us."

Elizabeth passed a number of trees before she came to a small, full tree. "This one?"

"That one be just right," Toby said. He swung his ax off his shoulder and chopped at the tree. The sound echoed across the way until the tree fell in the snow. He hoisted it to his shoulder.

They walked back toward the cabin, noses red from the cold and foggy breath like smoke in the air. "It sho be cold," Toby said, "but we got a good'un and that's just what we wuz after."

"Getting our tree has always been fun. I love it," Elizabeth said.

Later, when Toby set the tree up in the cabin, each of them decorated it with popped corn and loops of colored paper Alice and Little Mama had pasted together with homemade glue of flour and water. Little Mama put three packages under the tree. Alice smiled. "I still gotta wrap mine," she said.

Elizabeth gave each of them a hug. "See you Christmas morning. I can hardly wait!" She ran through the snow to her carriage, feeling grateful now that it was snow instead of sleet. Still it was cold enough. Blossom shook her head and snorted sending a silvery mist into the air.

On her way back into town, she thought of the love she felt in that little cabin. She thought, too, of how different her life would have been had not Alice been there for her from that first day in the Dalk house. It seemed incredible that Alice, Toby and Little Mama loved her enough to risk their lives for her that terrible night Clayton Dalk raped her. Their risk impressed her even more considering the gold coins Linktome offered them that could have bought them a better life had they been willing to offer her up. Oh, she owed them so much—more than she could ever repay, but she meant to provide a way for them to move whenever they were ready. Perhaps, they would soon want to go to New York to be near Toby's nephew. On the other hand, knowing Alice's giving spirit she might hesitate to leave Dorcett Dalk as long as he needed her. And would they be happy living in New York? Well, the decision would be theirs, but she would make it possible when and if they wanted another place to live.

Chapter Fifty

Elizabeth awoke to the scent of bacon cooking. She wrapped herself in a white woolen robe and went to the kitchen where she saw Mrs. Bell putting a pan of biscuits in the oven.

"Good Christmas morning," Elizabeth said.

"Good Christmas morning to you, dear." Mrs. Bell smiled. "How would you like your eggs?"

"One killed," Elizabeth said.

"Killed?"

"Scrambled dry."

Mrs. Bell laughed. "You'll have it—one killed."

Reverend Bell appeared, sleepy-eyed but smiling.

They gathered around the kitchen table and waited for the biscuits to brown before the meal was ready. Reverend Bell looked toward the window. "I see a few flakes falling," he said, "but it doesn't appear to be as cold today."

The aroma of steaming coffee added to the scent of bacon and eggs. When the coffee was placed on the table, Reverend Bell bowed his head, "Thank you Father God for your Son. Thank you for all our blessings and this food for the nourishment of our bodies. Amen."

Elizabeth was not accustomed to prayer at the table and almost forgot to bow her head. All of her life she'd heard in one way or another about God, but she never understood much about Him. She wondered why someone would give their lives trying to please Him. She knew Toby was a Christian. She'd ask him.

Later, Elizabeth drove in the carriage through a light falling snow. Blossom, Hannah's gentle white horse, was near the shade of the falling snow, but clearly visible by the brown leather straps on her body. She moved along the now familiar route with little need for direction.

When Elizabeth arrived the little cabin was filled with the buttery aroma of chicken and dressing, and the sweet smell of chocolate cupcakes. The warmth from the stove and the warmth of the love filled Elizabeth with joy. "Merry Christmas!" she called out.

"Merry Christmas to you," greeted her in a unison of voices with Toby's male voice dominating.

"You wanta have the tree first or dinner?" Alice asked.

"Oh, the tree!" Elizabeth said.

"I be Santa," Toby said even as he began to distribute the presents.

Elizabeth waited with anxious eyes to see if she had pleased them with her gifts and was rewarded with shouts of pleasure and thanks. "My, my lookey at my apples," Little Mama said placing her hands on her cheeks.

The monetary gifts were greeted with tears of happiness. "Oh, chile, now we can get us coats and dress up shoes for church," Toby said.

"Toby," Elizabeth asked, "why are you—why is anyone a Christian?"

"Here, Chile," he said, "is my present for you. It be telling you why."

She opened the package and found a small, brown Bible. "But, Toby," she said, "you've never read it."

"I knows that, but the preacher be able, and you be able."

"Thank you," Elizabeth said and hugged him.

Alice gave her a lacy, white blouse with tiny tucks down the front that she'd made by hand, and Little Mama had knitted her a warm cap and mittens in a soft shade of pink.

When dinner was over, Little Mama said, "I think I be taking myself a nap."

Elizabeth helped Alice with the dishes while Toby brought in more wood for the stove.

"Snow still falling," he said, "but slacked up some now."

Before they were quite finished with their chores, a carriage drove up and a handsome copper-haired man stepped out. Elizabeth saw him from the window. "Will!"

she cried. "It's Will!" She ran from the room, across the porch and down the steps into his embrace.

"Darling," he said, "I couldn't wait to see you."

"I thought you couldn't get back from Europe in time for Christmas."

"I managed. The important thing is we're together again," he said.

"Oh, Will, I couldn't be happier! You know Alice...."

"Yes. Remember I met them before."

"Come in and see them," she said taking his hand and leading him.

Alice and Toby greeted Will warmly, commenting on how they'd enjoyed his brief visit before. After a few minutes of pleasantries, Alice excused herself to take a dinner plate up to Mr. Dalk. She tucked in her coat pocket a gift package for him as well. "He be alone on Christmas," she said. "I asked him to come here with us, but he be a rather quiet, shy person."

"What gift are you taking him?" Elizabeth asked.

"A block of fudge candy I made special for him. He love chocolate."

Toby said, "I reckon you young folk might like to be alone for a spell, and I gotta go feed the horses and cows anyways." He put on his ragged brown coat and pulled his red knit cap on down over his ears. "I be back," he said, raising his hand in a farewell gesture.

"Where...?" Will began.

"Little Mama? Taking a nap."

"Fine. Elizabeth," he said, "I hope it's not too soon to ask you to marry me."

"It is too soon, Will. I have something to tell you that Alice left out when she told you about me and...you see..." Elizabeth sighed. Tears rushed to her eyes.

"Yes. What, darling? What is it?"

"Oh, Will, I killed a man." She sobbed as she told him about the night when she was raped.

"You killed him by accident?" Will asked. "If you'd killed him on purpose, he would have deserved it." Will took her in his arms, and taking a handkerchief from his pocket, dried her tears and kissed her cheek. "Don't cry, my darling. It's all over."

She told him then how she came to know French and about Monette. She wept anew in telling him of how Monette had died.

"My God, Elizabeth!" he said, "Life has brought you tragedies that could have warped or killed you."

"I would not have survived except for Alice and...."

"Darling," he whispered, holding her close and kissing the top of her head, and lifting her chin, kissed her cheeks and finally her lips.

He reached in his pocket and brought out a box with a diamond ring in it.

"Do marry me, Elizabeth," he said, "I love you and I want to take care of you as long as we live."

"Oh, Will. Are you sure?" she asked. "Are you really sure?"

"I've never been more sure of anything in my life."

"Then—yes, I'll marry you. I love you. I love you!" She said, throwing her arms around him, burying her head against his chest. For a long moment he held her in a close embrace before he slipped the ring on her finger. Tears came again, but this time for joy.

"Oh, Will," she said. "It's so beautiful I could cry, only I already am!" She laughed then. She turned her hand from side to side looking at her ring. The light from the flames in the stove made the diamond sparkle in blue and white lights delighting her.

"Let's sit down right now and plan," he said. "My parents will want us to have a grand wedding in the church. There'll be parties before and many people will come to wish us happiness."

Elizabeth smiled, but then looked thoughtful. "Will," she said, "I want to be married here so Alice, Toby and Little Mama can be with us. We could marry at the little church down by the lake where Reverend Bell preaches."

"But, what about my parents?"

"They should come. Yes, I'd want them to come." Elizabeth said.

"That would take away Mother's joy in the big wedding surrounded by her friends and family."

Elizabeth said, "Oh, I didn't mean to be thoughtless, but...."

"Why don't we get married twice?" Will said. "Here and there?"

"Oh, yes! That would work. Will, would you want to marry while we're here now. Tomorrow or the next day?"

He appeared momentarily surprised, but quickly recovered. "Would I? Yes, for sure. Let's do it."

"I'd have to keep it a secret at school until I graduate," Elizabeth said.

"But, darling you won't need to go back to school."

"I do, Will. I must see Cornelia through. You and I can find ways to be together until May. Besides, if your mother wants us to have a big wedding, that will take time."

"You're right. She will love all the planning, and you can be sure I'll find ways and times for us to be together."

"Oh, Will, I'm so happy."

"So am I. So am I," he said, taking her in his arms.

Elizabeth drew back from him and frowned. "What about your uncle Jerome?"

"No problem. Now that the sewing machine has been invented ready-made clothing has come into fashion. My store...Markhams Department Store has become profitable. I still travel part time for his benefit as well as for mine, but I'm not letting him run my life."

"Ready-made clothing? I think that's great. I never liked standing while the seamstress pinned and measured although I only had to do that a few times once she knew my size."

"Actually, I offer ready-made clothes, fine fabrics and taylor-made suits. We should do quite well."

"You're so smart Will!"

"Smart enough to win you anyway," he said, grinning.

393

Chapter Fifty-One

On December 27, 1867, Elizabeth and Will drove to the small church in the valley by the lake. They wore no formal attire. "The fancy clothes can come later," They said in unison and laughed.

"People who've been married a long time often think alike," Will said. "We're already doing it." He took her hand and kissed it.

They entered the small church where Reverend Bell and Mrs. Bell waited for them and their guests. Elizabeth was surprised to see some of Hannah's "girls" in attendance and to find wedding gifts stacked on the last pew of the church.

Alice, Toby and Little Mama sat in the back on the left side of the aisle. Elizabeth rushed to them and embraced each one saying, "I love you," and hearing the same in return.

"Come with me, family is supposed to sit up front," she said leading them to the front row.

A fire in a pot-bellied stove crackled gently, lapping flames over small logs, filling the tiny church with warmth. Elizabeth and Will removed their coats, gloves and hats in preparation for the simple wedding.

Soon Mrs. Bell began playing a medley of love and devotional songs. She continued to play as Elizabeth and Will walked hand in hand down the aisle.

Elizabeth looked at Will and thought he'd never looked more handsome. He smiled at her and squeezed her hand gently. Reverend Bell stood by the altar looking solemn, with Bible in hand waiting for them.

Throughout the ceremony, Elizabeth thought of the soft words as lovely poetry...poetry promises that would change the rest of her life. "Do you," "I do" "Forsaking all others." "Until death do us part."

When the ceremony ended, Will held her close and kissed her. "My wife," he whispered, "my darling, beautiful wife."

They left the church with a light snow falling and entered the carriage. Will said, "Are you sure you wouldn't prefer that we spend our wedding night at the hotel?"

"No, I want to be in my room that Marme prepared for me. It's a big room and private. Actually, it's really two rooms with a study for my books." She couldn't bring herself to say it but she wanted to feel somehow that Hannah's presence would be there. Besides, back in the far reaches of her mind, she had some concern about the wedding night. If something went wrong, she would be only doors away from Reverend and Mrs. Bell. She had thought the rape was totally out of her mind, but in spite of everything she'd been told, she knew some fear lingered to haunt her.

Will smiled at her. "Very well, we'll stay in your room at the mansion. We'll be leaving tomorrow anyway."

In her room, dressed in a soft white gown, Elizabeth allowed Will to hold her close. She could feel the excitement in his breath and in his body. Responding to his embrace, she trembled. Her heart was pounding.

"Don't be afraid," he whispered. "I wouldn't hurt you for the world." He kissed her gently, then more passionately.

Soon, that special feeling arose in her and she responded to his kiss. She knew she wanted his closeness and his love, but she worried that her fear would cause her to disappoint him.

"Will, I love you," she whispered. "I do love you."

"My darling," he said softly. "I love you so much, so very much." He caressed her face, her shoulders and her back with a soft touch. Soon she relaxed feeling pleasure in his caresses even as they became more intimate.

Afterward she sighed and kissed Will's cheek. It was as Marme and Alice had told her, only it was so much more than nice. She felt very happy.

***

On the journey back to New York, they shared more of

their early life. Will spoke of his private school and an instructor who cracked a ruler on his desk to make points. Students not well prepared might have a swat on their backs rather than the desk.

"Did you ever get swatted?" Elizabeth asked.

"Once when I'd not read the lesson and gave a stupid answer." He laughed. "It didn't hurt that much, but I always read the lesson after that."

He spoke of his days at college and of his work. "When we get to New York I'll take you to our fine, new store then we'll drive down to the mills and manufacturing company," he said. "Markham Mills and Manufacturing Company will be more meaningful to you now that you're officially Mrs. Will Markham." He smiled. "I'll be happy to escort you around and let everyone see how beautiful you are."

"Will, remember our wedding must be kept a secret for a while."

"I know. I'll call you my fiancé," he said.

In speaking of her very early life, Elizabeth told him as much as she could remember of her mother and Emily. She said, however, "I could never find out where I was kidnapped from. No one ever seemed to know where Five Points is, so I...."

"Five Points!" he exclaimed. "Five Points is a slum district in New York City!"

"Really? Are you sure? I remember we lived in a poor place, but I thought it was a town."

"No, honey, it's not a town, but a section of the city known for housing immigrants from various countries. Its called Five Points because its located at the intersection of Park, Worth, and Baxter streets. The Old Brewery and the The New Mission House are establishments long known in that area."

"Really? That's Five Points? Oh, Will, I must go there as soon as we get back. I must try to find Emily if she...if she didn't die."

"As soon as we get back, we'll go, but Elizabeth this is a bad slum. A dangerous place to go so we'll have to be

396

careful."

"I must go Will. If I must, I'll go alone."

"No! I won't hear of it. We'll take an old carriage, dress down which will probably make it safer for us."

Elizabeth could hardly wait for the trip to end. She wanted to go to Five Points the day they arrived back in New York, but it was late evening so it was necessary to wait until the next morning.

***

Madame Lemont and the students were excited to learn of Elizabeth's forthcoming big wedding. They were greatly impressed with her large diamond engagement ring. Cornelia seemed especially happy for her. The others seemed delighted as well which left Elizabeth feeling that she was surrounded by friends.

***

Will came to the school for Elizabeth at eight o'clock in the morning, which was just after breakfast for her. She asked permission of Madame Lemont to make the trip of a few hours for her search. The request was granted most graciously, but Elizabeth knew she would have gone regardless. Still, she was grateful that there would be no punishment as a result, especially that no reprisals would occur that could affect Cornelia.

Will greeted her with a kiss. "Oh, I missed you," he said.

"I missed you, too. I'll be so glad when May comes," Elizabeth said.

"I respect your loyalty to your friend, but I can't help wishing we could be together now."

"I know, Will, but I can't let her down. It could mean a hard life for her instead of one of possible happiness."

"All right," he said, "I'll just suffer."

She hit him playfully and they both laughed.

The day was sunny but cold. Most of the snow lay in dirty piles along the roads, at the sides of buildings and in the vacant lots. The old carriage bumped along the way and Elizabeth smiled seeing Will in rough clothes.

"Oh, honey," he said, "better slip your ring off and let me put it in my pocket."

"I forgot," she said. "Be sure you give it back to me."

"No, I'll find some other lovely woman and...."

"Don't joke, Will. I don't want to even make fun over that."

"You know I wouldn't," he said.

"I know, but I don't want to even think of it." In spite of herself she thought of Donato and the blonde he chose over her. And yet, she was truly, truly happy she had Will instead of him.

The ride to Five Points seemed long, but there was no mistaking it—with the streets that divided into five sections, but more clearly the stench of open sewers and the crumbling tenements. Little children dressed in rags raced around in the streets playing tag. Elizabeth felt sad seeing their grimy faces and matted, uncombed hair. Old men and women peddlers called out their wares and both young and older women prostitutes paraded about or fought among themselves. Elizabeth shook her head as she saw a mother with a child in her arms and one clinging to her skirts, make her way to a peddler. Had she really lived in all this squalor? She must have, though her memories were dim and few in detail. In seeing an elderly woman, scarf tied on her head, ambling along with a little dog beside her, Elizabeth said, "Stop. I want to ask this lady."

Elizabeth stepped from the carriage and approached the old woman. "Excuse me, ma'am. May I ask you a question?"

The old woman smiled, crinkling her wrinkled face, revealing decaying teeth. "Ask if you wish, but I don't know much, don't know much a'tall, young lady."

"Did you ever know a McKelvy woman who had two little girls. That would have been more than ten years ago... about twelve years, actually."

"Never knew nobody by that name," the old woman said. "You could ask down yonder," she pointed down the street. "The store man down there, now he might know. He's been there a spell."

Elizabeth returned to the carriage and they drove to the store. The storeowner was not able to help, and neither were countless other people Elizabeth asked. Finally, as it was the end of the day and growing dark, she gave up her search. She wept quietly as they drove back to the school. Several times Will tried to comfort her without success.

When he left her at the school, Will said, "Honey, I can't go back tomorrow, but we can try again the next day after that."

Elizabeth nodded. She accepted his hug and responded to his kiss, but she felt sadder than she had since Hannah died, even as he slipped her beautiful ring back on her finger. One thing she knew was that she would not wait until the day after tomorrow. She would get Horace, the school coach driver, to take her after breakfast tomorrow.

Madame Lemont seemed less pleased to allow Elizabeth another day absent from classes, but she agreed when Elizabeth promised to make up every class with the assigned homework.

Horace agreed to drive her only after she offered him a sizeable bill for his trouble. She had forgotten to remove her ring, but she slipped it in her pocket and pinned the top of the pocket with a simple broach she had been wearing.

Five Points again was as foul smelling as the day before, but a gentle rain had washed down much of the dirty snow. Elizabeth began her search anew asking every likely man or woman she saw, but without any information about Emily.

One elderly white-haired woman did remember Elizabeth's mother, but she said, "I never knew what become of her or the young'uns. All I can tell you was, that lady was a cut above. A lady for sure and clean, not fitted to this nasty place, but I reckon she had no choice."

To the old woman's surprise, Elizabeth hugged her.

"Thank you," she said. How good it was to at least hear of her mother, and know that she was seen as a lady.

When noon came Elizabeth saw a nurse climbing stairs to a tenement building. She called to her and the young woman stopped. "Please," Elizabeth said, "Do me a favor. Will you ask the people you see if they knew a McKelvy family? I will pay you for it."

"No need to pay me. I'll find it no problem to ask."

"I'm looking for Emily McKelvy, but I want to know anything you can find out about the McKelvy family."

The young nurse smiled. "Emily McKelvy...well, Emily Pillore now, is a nurse at the New York Infirmary For Women and Children."

Elizabeth gasped and tears rushed to her eyes. "Oh, have I really found her? Have I?" Her hand trembled as she placed it over her heart.

The young nurse frowned, "Yes," she said, "but she's not in New York just now. She's with her friend Sue Ling in Boston."

"Sue Ling. Yes, I remember her." Elizabeth said.

"Then you might like to know Sue Ling and her husband, Dr. Hallous, have a new baby boy. Are you related to Emily?"

"Just her sister," Elizabeth said laughing and crying at the same time.

"A happy reunion then," the young nurse said.

"I probably won't sleep a wink tonight waiting for tomorrow," Elizabeth said. She slipped from the carriage and ran to hug the young nurse.

The End